Wquote"hat else do I have to fear from the berserker?"

Tallis tightened his fingers around Kavya's until she winced. He pulled her fists to his chest. "I was able to evade your brother's psychic attacks because there isn't anything logical left when I go that deep. Just . . ."

He swallowed. He'd never been ashamed of his gift before.

"I work by instinct and take on an animal's compulsion to survive at all costs," he said. "And . . . to reproduce at all costs."

Confusion marred Kavya's soft brow. "We're a dying race. We can't reproduce."

He pulled her closer. Their mouths could touch if he wanted that connection. Or if she did. "That doesn't stop the animal from trying. A primal part of me wants you any way I can get you."

→ • ←

ALSO BY LINDSEY PIPER

LINDSEY PIPER

BLOOD WARRIOR

The Dragon Kings
Book Two

POCKET BOOKS

New York   London   Toronto   Sydney   New Delhi

Pocket Books
A Division of Simon & Schuster, Inc.
1230 Avenue of the Americas
New York, NY 10020

Copyright © 2013 by Lindsey Piper

All rights reserved, including the right to reproduce this book or portions thereof in any form whatsoever. For information, address Pocket Books Subsidiary Rights Department, 1230 Avenue of the Americas, New York, NY 10020.

First Pocket Books paperback edition August 2013

POCKET and colophon are registered trademarks of Simon & Schuster, Inc.

For information about special discounts for bulk purchases, please contact Simon & Schuster Special Sales at 1-866-506-1949 or business@simonandschuster.com.

The Simon & Schuster Speakers Bureau can bring authors to your live event. For more information or to book an event, contact the Simon & Schuster Speakers Bureau at 1-866-248-3049 or visit our website at www.simonspeakers.com.

Manufactured in the United States of America

10 9 8 7 6 5 4 3 2 1

ISBN 978-1-4516-9592-2
ISBN 978-1-4516-9595-3 (ebook)

To JD and EC.
Because confidence is sexy.

ACKNOWLEDGMENTS

I can't imagine writing a word, let alone a novel, without the support of my family, friends, and amazing colleagues. My eternal gratitude to my tireless agent, and once again to Lauren and Kate for pushing, pulling, and sometimes shoving me to the next level. Thank you all.

⊹ PROLOGUE ⊹

TWENTY YEARS AGO

I need your help. Tallis, please, I need you."

The Sun. She was back.

Tallis of Pendray wanted to jerk free of his dream. He wouldn't listen to her exotic, lilting seductions. He would wake up this time. He *would*.

"You try my patience and break my heart," she whispered. "You're fighting me when there's no need to fight. Don't wake. Stay with me. Stay . . ."

Her steely words were coated with sweet honey. This was the sixth time she'd slipped into his nighttime mind. Five times previous, he'd refused to obey unthinkable entreaties spoken by a wide, smiling mouth. Five times previous, he'd awoken to the dawn sunlight streaming through the windows of Castle Clannarah, convinced he was losing his mind.

By the Dragon or the Chasm, he wasn't going to look himself in the mirror come morning and ask the same questions.

Is she real? Is she right?

Am I going mad?

"Always the same worries in that fevered mind of yours."

"*You're* in my mind," he replied, although his voice sounded metallic and distant. "It will always be fevered."

"I'm afraid that's true. You deserve better than all this confusion."

Tallis wanted to wake, but there was a reason he'd endured her nightmare appearances. Again. And again. And again. Colors glistened on her skin, as if she were a woman made of light rather than flesh. The swirl of her silken gown created yet another shimmer that haloed her entire body. Dark hair with caramel highlights swished back to reveal ethereally perfect features. Eve, Helen of Troy, Lady Godiva—none of them would compare. How could they? They were human.

The Sun was a Dragon King.

Tallis was, too, but she made him feel like a commoner crawling in the dirt just to bow at her feet. She had chosen *him*. Who was he to deny the wishes of a goddess when she offered the warmth of her golden attention?

"I've asked you before." She hovered just out of reach, but her breath brushed his cheek. "Are you ready?"

"I can't," he rasped. "What you ask . . . It's obscene. It's criminal. I will not kill for you."

"The true crime is what has become of your people. The Pendray are ready to rip one another to pieces. You are so few in numbers compared to the other Five Clans. Soon you'll be as lost as the Garnis, reduced to a few frail remnants who'd rather spit at one another than claim kinship."

"Murder will stop more murder?"

"Shhh."

She placed a hand to his brow. Tallis hissed through his teeth. It was the first time she'd touched him. His body went rigid so quickly that he feared he'd wake. He didn't want to, not now, not when she was finally skin to skin. He closed his eyes and absorbed the soft warmth of her fingers threading into his hair. He sank deeper into the realm of sleep.

"Tallis." She said his name with a slice of warning.

As with the hours after sunset when cool shadows reign, the Sun's withdrawal was just as chilling. Tallis reached out to grab her hand, but she slipped away. A frustrated growl reminded him of his capacity to do harm. A beast waited in his blood—the Pendray gift from the Dragon—and that beast was rousing from its sleep.

"You want me in your arms," the Sun said, her voice bold with confidence.

"Yes."

"And what else?"

"I want you beneath me."

"And?"

"I want to be inside you."

She smiled as if she'd already given permission and was only waiting for him to grab her and lay her down. "I want that, too. Shall I show you how much?"

He nodded, or he thought he did. The dream world had become as real as the North Sea, with its icy aqua waters. He loved the view from the top of the crest, just north of his family's ancient castle. Although the sea's waves were a roiling tempest, they had the opposite effect on his thoughts. He was always calm when looking out across that imposing scene, knowing his people had mastered its waters for millennia.

This was real. As real as the sea.

"Show me," he said. "Please."

The Sun began to disrobe. She wore a sari worthy of an Indian princess. That she slid into his dreams meant she was likely Indranan, those of the Five Clans blessed by the Dragon with telepathy. Whether real or telepathic didn't matter when she unwrapped gossamer layer after layer to reveal the pristine, luminous skin of a naked woman. She was breathtaking. Breasts tipped with pale gold. Waist and hips a perfectly symmetrical set of curves. Legs long and elegant, all the way to her pointed toes. She tossed back her hair and spread her arms skyward, as if she were the one worshiping an ancient pagan god, rather than a goddess presenting herself to Tallis.

If he was mad, he didn't care.

"Whatever you want," he said. "I can't . . . I can't resist anymore."

"You make this sound so terrible, Tallis, my handsome one."

"Beheading a priest? Of course it's terrible." Lust hummed through his body, burning with the strength of an angered animal caged by iron bars and prodded from all sides. He was aroused, hard, aching. He craved sanity, but he was willing to forgo it for what he really craved. Violence. Sex. The freeing release of both.

She shifted so that her mouth was merely inches from his. "Right now, you *want* to kill. You'd kill me if you could."

"I would."

"You won't. You want to make me happy."

She was nude, beautiful, and so very close. But that

could've described any woman. The Sun, however, was hypnotic. Every time Tallis thought he could peer through the soft rays of light that surrounded her and blurred her features, she shifted. He saw only what she wanted him to see. She was the ultimate mystery, even when she presented herself as a vulnerable, stripped goddess.

"I'll make you happy, too, Tallis. Let me show you."

She kissed him.

Lip to lip.

Then *deeper*.

Without words she gave Tallis permission to unleash his gathering violence. They kissed like Pendray in the midst of a berserker rage, where pleasure and pain merged into a ferocious dance of push, pull, scratch, claw.

He had her in his arms. *Yes*.

He had her stretched beneath him. *Yes*.

But as Tallis gripped his ready cock and positioned the head between her wet folds, she was gone. He thrust into nothing. He bucked and fought, howling his frustration, spitting with anger at her and at himself. She'd taken him so far. She'd given him so much.

She'd snatched it all away.

He couldn't see himself from that dream perspective, but he felt the embarrassment of kneeling and being unable to hide his erection. Shame burned his cheeks as he looked up. The Sun was hovering again, clothed again, smiling as if she hadn't just teased him within an inch of insanity.

"Get back here," he growled.

"You're not giving orders, Tallis. We have so much

to do. And I have more to do than show you my bare skin."

He blinked and looked at her again—and froze. She was no longer hovering but riding a dragon as real as anything he'd ever beheld while conscious. The creature was even more real than the Sun, who continued to shift though myriad colors and forms.

"Do you see? You and I are bound. I will tease you, cajole you, even pity you. You will hate me and worship me. And in the end, you will do as I bid because we have both been chosen by the Great Dragon."

The magnificent creature turned its face toward Tallis. Strong ridges outlined its brow and hid small, dark eyes. It wasn't scaly but layered with what appeared to be endless varieties of fabric, in shades of black, orange, blue, purple, a fiery red—anything a waking eye could behold. The effect was radiant. Every movement rippled across its long torso and forked tail. It bared its teeth in a wide grimace. A lolling tongue appeared just before a burst of flame and a snort of smoke escaped.

Elegant and eternal, the Dragon was so humbling that Tallis hugged the ground in a deep bow. He shuddered. He could no longer look upon the creature that had birthed their race, knowing his eyes would burn to cinders and madness would follow.

The Sun rode the Dragon. A true goddess.

"You know what I say is true and just. Our people are dying."

He didn't lift his head. The dream had become the most astonishing nightmare. "We can reverse that?"

"Yes, we can. The Chasm isn't fixed."

Chilly air rippled across his back, accompanied by

the swish of flapping wings. The Sun traced two fingers beneath his chin, lifting, so that they looked each other in the eye. The Great Dragon was near yet far in that way dreams could warp perspective, yet she still rode upon its back like Boudicca into battle. No mist or light or golden silk swirled between them. He clearly saw the color of her eyes. Amber. The swirling amber of a consuming fire—the fire breathed by the Dragon as it began to fly away.

"I will let you touch me every time we meet," she said, her voice receding. "One day, I will let you unleash that monstrous temper and take what you want from my body. Take from *me*. I will be yours completely."

"Fix the Chasm. How?"

"You kill for me. Whenever I ask. No matter who it is. You'll behead one Dragon King after another. We will rid our people of those who sow discord and hatred. Only when we achieve unity will we be able to heal what has been bleeding for thousands of years. Our people. I command you just as the Dragon commands me."

She'd won. Even without the miracle of witnessing their Creator, the tingle up his spine whispered that she would've won anyway. She *always* would.

"I'll be hated. I'll have to flee. Leave my family. I'll never have a home after tonight."

The Sun blew him a kiss before fading into darkness. "Yes, dear one, but you will always have me."

⊰ CHAPTER ⊱
ONE

Kavya's thoughts were weighted by responsibility, and the ever-pressing knowledge that the Dragon Kings were a people on the edge of extinction. That meant the collection of faithful gathered in a craggy notch in the Pir Panjal foothills of the Himalayas was exceptional. From her secluded place behind an altar made of burnished orange granite, Kavya extended her awareness into the vast crowd.

She was especially heartened to feel so many assembled from the Indranan, one of the Dragon's sacred Five Clans. *Her* clan. The telepathic Indranan had been divided for three thousand years of civil war. Northern versus Southern factions. And for reasons every Dragon King knew too well, they were collectively known as the Heartless.

Although physically sluggish from bearing the mantle of her duties, Kavya cleared her consciousness of outside thoughts. She would need the full extent of her limited telepathy for the task awaiting her. Today was special. Intimidatingly so. She would make her first appearance before these hundreds who'd traveled the globe to see her in person.

To see the woman they'd dubbed the Sun.

Kavya waited until exactly noon to ascend the altar's few makeshift granite steps. This moment was her burden and her joy.

Standing tall, she sucked in a shallow breath. "So many."

Before her extended a valley, like a deep bowl being held by rocky, jutting fingers. Evergreens were scattered throughout, but few dared set their roots in the valley's steep walls. Worn canvas tents of varying sizes were packed side by side—countless grains of rice in that mountain bowl, seasoned by smoke from small cooking fires. Despite having grown up in some of India's most populous cities, Kavya had never witnessed an assembly to rival this, with so many minds and senses working in concert, focused as one.

On her.

A gust of cold air rushed down from the slopes. Whispers—those given voice and those passed from mind to mind—faded to nothing. That late autumn wind blowing through crevices became the only sound.

"So many of you," she said, with volume enough to be heard. "Welcome. Oh, thank the Dragon. *Welcome*."

She worked to steady the pitch and cadence of her voice. *She* hadn't dubbed herself the Sun, but that's what most had come to expect—radiance and incandescent light. Kavya had fostered that image for years, for her own anonymous safety and to promote the growing influence of her cause. People responded to symbols even more readily than to earnest people. People could have agendas; symbols had the power to transcend suspicions born of rational thought.

She needed to become everything to everyone. No sudden movements. No reason for anyone to turn around and walk up the valley pass.

Especially the Indranan.

Her head already throbbed from the effort. After all, she had been born as one of three triplets. She possessed only a third of the Dragon's gift.

"I'm humbled by the distances you've traveled and the seas, mountains, and plains you've crossed to join me here. You are the first of a new age. Northern and Southern Indranan together, sharing the same air and the same hopes for a future forged of trust, not continued spite. Some of you come to us from the other four clans. I welcome you and ask for your aid as we of the Indranan work to heal old hurts."

Even members of Clan Garnis were present. They were known as the Lost, but they weren't extinct. She could pick out those rare minds as if finding diamonds among dust. They were skittish among the press of so many bodies.

"Our people are dying," she said bluntly.

Many gasped. Some cried out in quiet despair.

Kavya extended her hands before clasping them together—a woman giving a gift, a woman begging for help. She was both. "Please help me. We must not be the ones to bring about our own extinction. Previous generations turned away from the truth. We will be the last if we follow their example."

Looking out, she couldn't identify any particular face. Instead she saw black—the ceremonial robes and saris of the Dragon Kings, each accented with their clan's color. The Indranan were the exception in that they did not wear a uniform shade of blue. Those from the north of the Indian subcontinent wore the pale turquoise of a high mountain sky. Those from the south wore the deep ultramarine of the ocean coastlines they called home. A trio of Indranan women, roughly eighty years old in middle age, stood nearest to the altar with upturned faces. Two Northern and one Southern.

Holding hands.

Astonishing.

"Each of our Leaderships know that conception has become nearly impossible. Not even the Dragon King Council can deny that we are a dying race—we, who have shaped the civilizations of this world from their infancies. What would each culture, each continent, be without our influence? This has led many, dare I say *most* of our kind, to believe us better than humans."

She paused, breathed, recentered. An Indranan could only touch one mind at a time. To mentally project the image of an appealing yet unassuming woman—one who radiated the indescribable shine her followers longed to worship—she individually brushed that impression over every mind in the valley. Over and over again. She used her gift at a speed beyond conscious thought, a skill she'd honed through the years as the number of faithful increased. If she became too impassioned, she lost her trancelike concentration. Yet passion was exactly what she needed to impart.

Those few followers she knew personally were out there somewhere, among the rapt throng. She wished she could find one of them, to derive a measure of comfort, like a familiar blanket to hold during long, frigid nights. Knowing she was in the right would have to shore up her courage.

"What's the use of thinking ourselves better if we can't hold children of our own? The time has come for reconciliation, and through reconciliation will come solutions—and the future we long for."

Her words must've touched her followers because the murmurs that had threaded through her soliloquy strengthened into applause and even shouts of approval.

"At dusk this evening, I will make an announcement to reward your faith. Some call us a cult. The Sun Cult. But we are not a religion. We all have our means of worshiping the Dragon. This, our gathering, is a meeting of forward-thinking individuals. And finally, with hope, I can say that two such individuals are here among us, joined in a vow of cooperation."

With a swell of pride behind her breastbone, she once again lifted her hands—this time in triumph. "Northern and Southern, at last you will have better than bellowed accusations of past crimes and threats of retribution. You will use peaceful voices in thoughtful discussion. As the woman you call the Sun, I swear it."

The applause was breathtaking. Slack, stunned faces transformed. Kavya saw relief and curiosity, but mostly joy. Some embraced or turned to clap each other on the back. None gave any sign of typical clan suspicions, either physically or with what she could sense of the crowd's mood. Neither Indranan faction seemed to remember that they'd warred for countless years, or that fresh blood spilled a generation before—at the massacre known as the Juvine—had renewed three millennia of hatred.

Kavya lowered her head and interlaced her fingers. Her mother had taught her, *You can hold our homeland in your hands. The rise and fall of your fingers become our mountains and valleys.*

That was Kavya's earliest memory. Her last memories of her mother were colored by madness and an indescribable sense of loss.

She needed order. Although beautiful, the ridges of rock that marked the far western edge of the Himalayas had no order. Random peaks. Irregular riverbeds. High glaciers that changed with the seasons and the passing of time, and trees that bent beneath fierce wind and heavy snow. Kavya aligned her knuckles. None stood higher than the others. Only then did she feel calmer, which was more important than happiness. Those who'd gathered in the Pir Panjal could be happy. She still had work to do.

When she lifted her face to the crowd, she unclasped her hands and lowered them straight to her sides. The silk of her sari was more luxurious than any she'd ever owned. She gently toyed with the flowing fabric. "Now," she said, "our day must continue as it has. With purpose. Join me in the noon benediction."

She was no cult leader, but she understood the importance of ritual. The rituals she'd fashioned were an amalgam of practices from all Five Clans. Words from each language. Praise to each version of the Dragon. Affirmation of each special gift. Although the origin of her work had focused on peace among the Indranan, she'd since expanded her purpose to include all of the Dragon Kings. They needed each other. She was convinced.

Thus the words she spoke in daily blessing were meant to appeal to as many as possible, just as her appearance was. Once again, Kavya's brain—her entire body—ached from the effort. And once again, she persevered.

"Eat, my friends. Peace be with you."

She turned to the rear of the altar and descended. She was alone. No one followed her. Even her bodyguards maintained a respectful distance on the other side of a natural archway. She basked in the privilege of lowering her mental shields and releasing the crowd from the spell of her mind. There was no need for anonymous luminosity when she was alone.

Yet she was so very alone.

How could she be otherwise?

Pashkah would find her someday. Her triplet would kill her or she would kill him. Relying on even the most devoted follower was a risk she rarely took. That meant hiding her real self. She had long since abandoned the innocent child named Kavya of the Northern Indranan. The little girl she'd been was a photograph faded to gray.

"Very pretty words."

Her head jerked up by reflex. An Indranan so lost in thought was a telepath stripped naked of defenses. For a slip of a moment, she couldn't remember how to hide. The danger of her mistake shot flame through her bones.

Had he been Pashkah . . .

Instead the man was a stranger. Not exactly slim, but not overly brawny, he straddled the solid middle ground where muscle and skill hid beneath an unassuming exterior. He was paler than members of her clan, although he retained the golden shimmer of the Dragon Kings. And as a Dragon King, that meant exceptional male beauty. Dark hair was tipped with glinting silver—not the gray of an old man, but a gleam like the shine of mica flecks. His hair didn't reach his collar, but it was long at his crown and stood in disarray.

He wore lightweight layered sweaters, cargo pants, heavy black boots, and an open leather coat lined with wool. No ceremonial robes. Just the clothes of a human. The straight, narrow swords that crossed in an X at his back, however, were the weapons of a Pendray. He radiated wildness, from that mass of careless hair to the way his relaxed, almost negligent stance proclaimed him a killer.

Her gift would confirm what made her senses prickle and cringe. In self-defense, she reached out to learn his identity and his intentions.

And to her profound shock, she couldn't read his mind. Not a single thought.

"Who are you?"

He walked toward her with swagger, leading with his shoulders. His scabbards moved with a hiss of leather over leather. Bright blue eyes narrowed. "You'll find out before I'm through with you."

The Sun was a fraud.

Worse, she was a vile manipulator.

As an upward surge of violence scribbled red across his vision, Tallis of Pendray could've been staring at the interior of a slaughterhouse. Droning pulses of cruelty beat a counterpoint to the rhythm of his heart. He wanted to loose his fury.

He *needed* to stay in control.

Otherwise he would never be able to discredit the Sun and thwart the commands she had thrust into his mind for two decades.

Always dripping in gold. Always riding away on the back of the Dragon.

A berserker rage would ruin months of preparation—sensible, *rational* preparation. Finding her hadn't been easy. Everyone knew of the Sun Cult, but its ever-changing location had taken him almost a year to pinpoint. It was bad enough that the gift of Tallis's clan, the Pendray, was the mindless fury of a berserker. Because the Sun had deluded him for so long, he'd come to prize rationality. He would not be a pawn to his blood-born impulses or a puppet to a charismatic charlatan.

Yet . . . she was *real*.

Some part of him had always feared he was well and truly mad. What if he'd been acting on a delusion so clear and all-consuming that he needed a scapegoat? How convenient to blame bloodied hands on a woman conjured by a guilty, disturbed conscience, then top off his mental self-defense with delusions of the Dragon. He put away his doubts and laid the gory blame where it belonged—there on an altar of stacked rocks the color of bronze.

His only regret was that, truth be told, the Sun's professed ambition was noble and worth his sacrifices. Her appearances were rare enough to be treasured, but constant enough to reinforce her design for the future of the Dragon Kings. And Tallis's role in it.

However, the violence he'd guided to the home of his niece, Nynn, had sapped his optimism. Whether the

Sun's plan to unify the clans would protect the Dragon Kings from extinction was no longer his concern. After what he'd endured, what he'd done, what he'd become *for her*—he deserved to embrace a personal grudge.

"You cannot threaten me," she said, head tilted at an assessing angle. "And you cannot harm me."

"I did, and I can."

Tallis leapt forward—the fluid, trustworthy movement of a body honed for fighting. One of his seaxes was easy to retrieve. He grabbed the woman's hair, twisted fistfuls in his free hand, and held a razor's edge of steel to her throat.

Her eyes bulged. She froze.

"That's right," Tallis said. "Very still."

"It's not Dragon-forged." Her voice was a near-silent rasp.

"Correct." A Dragon King could only be killed by rare swords forged in the Chasm where the Great Dragon had lived and died, high in the Himalayas. "But killing you would make you a martyr. Not my intention."

Her appearance as she'd addressed the crowd had struck Tallis like a blow to the jaw. A faint, otherworldly shimmer had surrounded her as would the wavy heat of a mirage. Hair that should've been deep brown, flowing in animated waves down her back, had been a bland, neutral shade in a style that sat primly on her shoulders. Her mud-colored eyes had been wrong, too. Nothing distinctive except for that inviting shimmer, urging people to believe the false front she presented.

Now he was near enough to see each lash. Wide irises as rich as amber. Lush hair as luscious as chocolate. Realizing the full extent of how well she could deceive others, including Tallis, was overwhelming.

At least her figure matched his visions. He held her resilient, athletic body close to his. A gold silk sari wrapped around womanly curves he'd seen in the nude.

He restrained a frustrated growl.

The Sun still hadn't moved, but her lips tilted into a ghostly smile. Nothing about her seemed false, yet he could feel the potential for deception like a slick of oil on his fingertips. His only chance was to keep her distracted. With the ability to focus on only one mind at a time, his threat of violence might keep her from assuming too many of the false impressions she gleaned from other individuals.

"This way," he said, yanking her hair. The blade nicked a line of red across her delicate neck.

Delicate? No. It was just a neck.

She deserved no adjectives. He could trust no adjectives.

"I don't know what I've done to anger you," she said with surprising calm. Only her near-frantic respiration gave away her fear. "But we can discuss it. We can make amends."

"No, we can't. Now, this blade is going back in its scabbard. You're going to walk with me."

She actually laughed, although the action pressed her neck more firmly against his seax. Her laughter was truncated by a gasp as another streak of red appeared. "How do you expect to accomplish that?"

"You have an announcement this evening."

"I do." She still breathed without rhythm. "It's important. More important than you can imagine."

"You have done my imagining for too long."

"I've never seen you before!"

"Save it. You want to make that announcement, right? Can't have these people disappointed."

A gleam of moisture coated brown eyes that matched the rocky landscape of her homeland. "That's right."

"Then we're walking. Calmly. I hold no grudge against anyone else, but I will do harm if you cause them to interfere."

"They would demolish you in a second. We're the Indranan. Telepathy can be a nasty weapon. You'd live the rest of your life with your body intact and your mind flipped inside out."

Tallis pulled her hair and brought their faces together, close enough to share the same chilly air. "How much chaos could I cause before that happened? The precious Sun in danger. A hundred Dragon Kings running scared. Your cult destroyed."

The woman grasped his forearm with both hands. Her nails dug into his flesh. "You have no right. Why would you plan violence, here of all places? These people live in peace and they *believe in me*."

"And in time they'll learn the truth." Tallis held her neck in his palm as he sheathed his blade. "Just like I did."

❖ CHAPTER ❖
TWO

What's to stop me from screaming with my mouth and shouting with my mind?"

Grinning tightly, Tallis shook his head. "You would've done both already. And even on your lying face, I can see it—you can't read my thoughts. Frustrating, goddess?"

"I'm not a goddess. My name is Kavya."

He raised his brows. "Very pretty."

Her jaw tightened. "No. I can't read your mind. Who *are* you?"

"Tallis. Search that piecemeal soul of yours. You'll know me."

"They warned me," she said, almost to herself. "I didn't listen. How long have you been tracking me?"

He was pleased his gamble had paid off. Everyone had heard of the Sun Cult, but its leader was elusive. Cult bodyguards had felt his presence as he'd neared his objective. They'd reached out with tap-tap touches into his mind. Curious, then angered. Repeatedly they'd warned her of a coming danger. She'd reached out with her own gift—and sensed nothing. He'd been reluctant to depend on her telepathic blind spot, but recognizing it had been the genesis of his plan.

There behind the altar, he slowly released her neck. There was no explanation for why he trailed the soft, fine strands of her hair down over one shoulder.

She shivered.

No, there *was* an explanation. He'd been seduced by this woman for twenty years. That he'd want to admire her, to touch her—

He cut off his thought as surely as he would've cut her out of his mind, had he been able.

While he'd waited for her to finish her infuriating speech about peace and hope, Tallis had witnessed a living lie—a slippery eel pretending to be Everywoman. Now he had her attention. The disguise she drew from the impressions of a hundred minds began to slip.

Or simply . . . *change*. He couldn't tell.

A man who lived rough in the world learned to trust his instincts, yet his had been corrupted by the Sun's voice in his sleeping mind. She bled into every aspect of his life, like placing a magnet next to a compass. His true north was long gone.

For a Pendray that was especially infuriating. As creatures of the elements, his clan had inspired a pantheon of deities among hearty Celts, Picts, Norse, and Saxons. To remain so uncertain of the natural world would be even worse than losing his berserker rage.

This woman deceived everyone who looked upon her face. Who could trust her words if she presented whatever facade a person wanted to see?

"I'll go with you," she said at last. "Peacefully."

"Good."

He slid his fingers down her golden sari and clasped

her hand, then mocked her with a smile. "We're just taking a walk."

"Where?"

"My tent."

She jerked her arm, but Tallis wouldn't let go. "You're sick. No one . . . No one—"

"Takes you to his tent? I'm not surprised. You play in dreamscapes instead." He adjusted his hold so that their bodies pressed side to side. "Come."

Tallis dragged her through the stone archway that led away from the rear of the altar. They emerged into plain sight. Several dozen followers stood nearby.

"They may wonder why you're walking so close to a Pendray," he said near her ear. "But they trust you. Everyone you've touched with that witch's mind has come to trust you. So keep walking."

He tightened his hold on the low curve of her hip. She flinched and tried to draw away. "Let me go. I've come willingly this far."

Tallis ignored her entreaty. Too much bitterness needed to be purged from his blood. "I wonder how many wish they could hold you this closely. Do you lie awake counting the minds you've warped? Enjoy becoming their fantasy?"

"I've never done anything of the kind," she hissed. "I am a peaceful woman. I keep my thoughts to myself."

"Being one of the Heartless must be useful when you use people the way you do."

"Clan-based hatred is revolting. Don't tell me you subscribe to those old prejudices."

"I subscribe to bare facts. A deceiving witch leading gullible worshipers is a threat to every Dragon King."

The sun—the *real* sun—was arcing westward. The valley would be dark long before nightfall. The steep angles of the Pir Panjal determined when the rays no longer reached the earth. Tallis strained every sense, trustworthy or not, and steadily guided his captive to his tent.

Then he shoved her between parted canvas folds. She fell to her knees as he pushed in behind her. "Much better, goddess."

"Kavya."

"Fine. Hold still, *Kavya*."

She gasped as he searched for weapons concealed within layers of gold silk. Wiggling away from each touch, she was wide-eyed and edgy. She jerked as if his hands were hot irons. Tallis grabbed a rope from his knapsack and bound her wrists and ankles. She struggled against the hemp, but every movement tightened the sharp grip.

He rolled her onto her side. "Being helpless at the will of a more powerful force is a scary thing. I never liked it. You?"

Kavya looked away and blinked a sheen of moisture from her eyes. "You could at least tell me what you want! I can help you. Obviously you don't want to be here."

"We're staying put," he said. "Days will come and go. Your followers will know what I've learned—that you've deceived them. Wasted their hopes." He traced a finger along her cheek, down to where blood had dried on her neck. "You'll witness one disappointed face at a time, until no one will ever again worship a woman named the Sun."

He retreated a few feet and crossed his legs. Kavya

had stopped moving after her initial struggle. Self-preservation? Scheming? Probably both. A woman didn't rise up from dirt-strewn slums to command an army without possessing canny skills.

The Sun was no idiot.

She wasn't the goddess of his dreams. Neither was she the plain, almost anonymous orator.

Instead she was able to gather ready-made inspiration straight from her followers' minds. *En masse*. How did she do that? What if she had the power to affect other Dragon Kings the way she'd manipulated him? Her influence could be catastrophic. Not even the Honorable Giva, the leader of the Five Clans, could compete with such a rival.

No Indranan should have that much power. *No one* should.

So he stared. And she did. As the hours passed, they played poker with their gazes.

"You might as well sleep." His voice was rough, especially since his last words to her had been filled with such bile. He was going to hate her for a very long time. "You would have rested before your announcement."

Light blazed in her brown eyes, as if mountains could glow. "No, I would've been walking among my people, making sure the agreement I've helped broker remains secure. You have no idea what's at stake today."

"You're probably right," he said flippantly.

She pushed her feet against the hard ground, found purchase, and struggled to sit up. The hemp rope creaked. The effort to appear strong for pride's sake must have cost her body. Kneeling on her heels, with her hair a mess around her heart-shaped face, she raised her chin. Tallis was perturbed by his unconscious re-action, because that subtle movement chastened him without a word.

Why did he keep underestimating her? Maybe he remained susceptible to her ways—not to her telepathy, but to her natural charisma. He couldn't find a strong line between the two, which was disturbing as hell.

"You are a bigot and a troublemaker," she said with a voice made of bells and iron. "Some petty slight has brought this injustice on me. You're going to ruin every-thing."

Her expression hardened. Nothing overt. Eyes that had been passive took on a cold distance. Her mouth was shaped by voluptuous lips that pressed into a fixed line. Her hair was noticeably longer now—dark, with caramel streaks that highlighted its thick richness. Even her cheekbones seemed higher and more exotic. The anonymous image she'd presented on the altar was com-pletely gone. Tallis's memory of it lingered like having looked at the sun before closing his eyes, still seeing the image behind his eyelids.

"Your slights have not been petty," he grated out.

"How do you know I haven't been contacting my people for the last few hours, telling them to lie in wait for you?"

"I'll take that chance. I've *been* taking it." He grinned, which actually made her flinch. The Pendray weren't very guarded with their expressions, and he'd lived in the human world for years. He liked the freedom of making his feelings known without language. That also meant being able to surprise Dragon Kings, who never expected such animation from their own kind. "You've been too distracted. At best, you've been successful and I'll find out soon enough. But I think you suffer from the illusion you've created. How many would know your genuine call of distress?"

He shifted onto his knees before leaning down to kiss her cheek. Softly. Innocently. The touch was nothing more impassioned than a man might bestow on a sister.

The telltale hitch of her unsteady breath gave her away, despite how quickly she reclaimed her composure. He smiled. How often were Indranan surprised?

She smelled of the thin, cold Himalayan wind. She was warm beneath his lips when he kissed her again—an impression he could trust. Her shiver was honest, too. The Sun would've concealed that weakness had she been able.

"My seaxes didn't intimidate you as much as when I held your waist," he whispered against her temple. "Violence won't keep your mind occupied. But I can."

He traced his tongue along the line of her jaw. His stir of reaction was not surprising. His people had always been base and earthy, and she'd been tempting him for years. Now . . .

Now he knew how she tasted.

"I intend to use every method I can to make sure your thoughts remain right here, in this tent. With me."

This man, Tallis, was as intimidating as he was impossible to understand. He spoke in riddles. Being unable to skim his thoughts was pure frustration, like attempting to see through granite or hear a pin drop halfway around the world. She'd tried to find her bodyguards among a multitude of Indranan thoughts, but so many wore Masks—mental distortion blocks to protect them from being detected by prowling siblings.

Even if she had found them, Kavya couldn't jeopardize the tranquility of the assembly. To do so now would bring about Tallis's dreadful scenario: the failure of all she'd worked toward for decades.

Her mind raced. Her wrists and ankles ached. And her lips burned with the touch of this stranger's kiss.

Tallis was different. Frighteningly different.

A mind I can't read.

She shouted into his brain until her gift retaliated with a walloping headache. She'd have been better served by smacking her forehead against the ground. Trying to compensate with her senses was nearly useless. Who of her clan needed them?

All they really needed was a Dragon-forged sword to kill . . . or a Mask to hide.

Every Indranan was born as a twin or, in Kavya's case, as a triplet. Siblings grew up knowing that the Dragon had divvied up their true potential in the womb. *Learn to share.* So few did. By committing fratricide, the Indranan could unite fractured pieces into a whole. Some called them twice-blessed, although twice-cursed was more accurate. Murderous twins carried with them the screams of the departed.

The ability to read another's mind was the most intoxicating, terrifying gift among the Five Clans. To keep from wanting more was the ultimate responsibility.

The Heartless.

Kavya had never protested the derogatory nickname. She'd simply fought to rise above that hideous legacy.

Her fight at the moment centered on Tallis. With his face tilted down and decorated with a maddening smile, he was as solid in body as he was opaque of mind. She'd suspected that he hid strength under unassuming clothing and a lean fighter's frame. She hadn't known how that strength would feel, pressed intimately along her silk-clad hip as they'd walked through the valley.

Now he knelt before her. Body to body. Heat against heat.

He was *holding* her.

He'd slipped his hands beneath the long sleeves of her sari and cupped her restrained arms. His fingers were warm, blunt, strong. When was the last time she'd been graced by anything more than reverent touches? This was prolonged contact. This was calluses against smooth skin. Because she couldn't read his mind, she compensated with a desperate scramble for information.

He smelled of dust and juniper.

He was a foot taller.

He had eyes the color of the sea at its darkest depths, but not the Indian Ocean—some frigid, azure wasteland.

Kavya's attention kept slipping back to him. She couldn't even find Chandrani, her best friend and closest ally since childhood. Chandrani was the only person who knew Kavya's mind without its Mask—the only person except for Pashkah. Without the Masks she'd worn since the age of twelve, Kavya would've been at her brother's mercy. If he succeeded in killing her, Pashkah would become something unholy.

This stranger knew how he was affecting her and

had piercingly guessed that violence was a fact of life for Kavya, as it was for every Indranan. She'd spent her adolescence in the rough cubbies and alleys of Delhi. A girl didn't survive places so perilous without witnessing terrible things and developing protective skills. The net result was that to be threatened by a blade—even one as intimidating as his seax—had nothing on the distraction of being held.

Thought began and ended with Tallis's arms sliding down to her backside.

No.

No!

Chandrani!

Except for her rabbit's-heart pulse, she held perfectly still. Chandrani would find her. Kavya had to believe—and bide her time.

Her feet and calves were going to sleep, but she hadn't wanted this man to lord over her with his height, strength, and the weight of his stare. Not that it had mattered after he'd assumed the same stance. They looked like worshipers at prayer, supplicated before one another.

What he'd done to her . . .

What he *kept* doing. The trace of his lips from the divot behind her ears to the tendon of her neck was like nothing she'd ever experienced. What was this madness? Had his ramblings been a strange cover for his desire to bind her, even ravish her? Sensation shot through her limbs and down her spine. Her thighs trembled—nothing he would see, but she resented her weakness.

"Those people who revere you," he said against the

skin he'd made damp by his tongue. "Do they know how you taste? Do they wonder? Do some fantasize about claiming the body of a living deity?"

Kavya punched her shoulder against his jaw. "Get off me, you Pendray filth. Always thinking with your cocks and your work-worn hands. If you think at all."

He smiled as if *he* were the mind reader. "Stereotypes, eh? Wasn't that my sin a few hours ago? We could play that way all day, but my game is better." He grabbed a fistful of hair. "Tell me, goddess. Do you *like* that they imagine fucking you? Or that I have? For *years*."

Her heart shuddered. He was sick, yet her body reacted to his crude words. No wonder the Indranan lived apart from baser clans, no matter the danger within their own.

"That's why you brought me here? In a camp full of people loyal to me?"

"Ah, so they're loyal to *you*. Not to your cause. You give yourself away."

"No, they have dreams of a better future and hope for the safety of their families. What I offer them is beautiful and pure."

"Pure," he said, the word thick with sarcasm. He sounded English—not the typical Pendray blend of Scots and Norse—but certainly refined and exotic to her ears. "I'm sure the Sun burns away all sin and all thoughts of flesh and desire."

Kavya yanked her head back, but he only pulled her hair taut and dug hard fingers into her hip. He scraped his teeth along her throat. She bit back a cry of indignation.

"I like how you taste, goddess. I even like these twists

and fights. Those are real. You're giving me quite a lot. I'm owed more, but this is a start."

Kavya closed her eyes. His mouth's caress was wrong and ghastly—and yet intriguing. What she knew about sex was . . . vicarious. Being a telepath meant catching scraps of feeling and unbidden images. The first touch of skin to skin, the moment of penetration, the ravage of climax. By comparison, those impressions were ephemeral and distant as Tallis licked her throat.

Yes, he was keeping her mind occupied. He was watching her as if examining the progression of a sick experiment: tempt the untouched with sex and see how she reacts.

The results were obvious. She'd reacted with surprise, a hint of revulsion, and greed. She'd had no idea she could be so untrustworthy. That realization was shocking. She'd always thought herself *above*.

Then he kissed her full on the mouth.

His body bowed over hers. She felt surrounded. Overwhelmed. Firm lips. Spicy taste. His heavy breathing remained tightly controlled. Her breathing and pulse, however, were panicky. More struggles. More casual restraint on his part. He used his arms to engulf her more completely. His strength made her struggles seem as fragile as cobwebs.

"I could do that all night." He broke the kiss and threw her to the ground. "Maybe I will. But I'd just as soon kill you as assault you. I said I don't want you martyred. I want *no* place for you in this world. When I'm through with you, no one will remember you with anything other than bitterness. If they remember you at all."

⋆ CHAPTER ⋆
THREE

Tallis shed his heavy leather jacket and levered over where she sprawled on the ground. He edged his thighs between hers, then shifted so that his pelvis fit snugly against hers. He wore sturdy military-style cargo pants, while Kavya still wore only silk. She would be able to feel his desire taking physical form.

"Should I kiss you again?" He only touched her from the waist down, where he used the weight of his pelvis and thighs as more threat than seduction. Arms straight, he braced his hands on either side of her head. "I'd learn secrets about the Sun you're too arrogant to admit possessing."

"More of the so-called justice you seek? I've done nothing to you!"

"You know my weaknesses better than I do. Every fantasy—even those I can't arrange into thought."

"What are you talking about?"

"You've used that knowledge against me for years," he said, his voice deepening with anger. "If I resisted, you invaded dream after dream like a monster. You'd raid another locked closet in my head to find more secrets. You even profaned the Dragon to legitimize your crimes." He was still aroused. Kissing her had been calculated, but he'd been swept into the vortex where fantasy swirled with reality. "I have the power now. Is it any surprise that I desire to use it against you?"

A clamor of voices came from beyond the tent's dingy white canvas. For a moment Tallis thought she'd managed to telepathically call for help, but she wore no expression of triumph. Then came more voices, more chaos.

He edged away and grabbed the deadly Norse seaxes he'd kept out of her reach. Tallis parted the canvas and peered through.

His sense of hearing gave away her attack from behind, as Kavya swung a cooking pot. The determination and, frankly, the vehemence in her glittering brown eyes were pure surprise. Ropes around her ankles meant she had one chance before losing her balance, but she made the most of it. The bulk of the pot hit his shoulder. One seax with its etched blade and honed edge skidded along the bare rock floor.

She rolled onto her back and grabbed the hilt in both bound hands. A quick slice parted the ropes at her ankles. She spun so that she knelt again, bloodying her knees. Shins braced against the ground gave her more stability. The split skirt of her sari bared the sleek skin of her thigh.

He rubbed the slight ache in his shoulder. "I'd hoped there was more to you than words and specters."

"Why would you think that of an opponent you profess to hate?"

Her eyes were bright and widely spaced, wedded to the high, rounded apples of her cheeks. She had a tiny nose and a chin that, for all her defiance, was softly shaped. Tallis shivered. This was her, *really her*, not the witch who'd infected his dreams for two decades. The real Sun, this woman Kavya, was the perfect compromise between truth and fantasy, virgin and whore—a bound innocent holding his blade.

Although she remained still, ready for the attack he would surely make, she vibrated with near-visible energy. Tallis could practically smell the heady cologne of her fear and focus. He would've bet the rest of his life that she hadn't smelled that way on the altar. There, she'd been focused but unafraid. Her telepathic invasions were vile, even though the surprising resilience of her fighting spirit made him smile deeper.

"I like to think," he said, "that when I break you, I'll have broken someone who deserved the worst I can dish out. Seems you're in the mood to make me a happy man."

"Happy? I want you dead." A look of horror crossed her face. She inhaled sharply, which lifted the supple curve of breasts draped in silk. She appeared ready to vomit.

Tallis chuckled. "You didn't mean to say that, did you?"

Exaggerating the ache in his shoulder, crouching before her, he shifted his weight onto the balls of his feet. Rather than leap, he leaned and swept his right leg. The toe of his boot caught behind her upper thigh with a hard kick. He yanked. Between the blow and the pull, she fell hard onto her side.

She coughed, struggling for air. He pushed forward with two crouched strides and snatched the stolen blade from her bound hands.

"The Sun has some fight. Gratifying, but it won't change anything." The gathering ferment outside the tent renewed its hold on his attention. "Stay. Unless you want to remain unaware of what's happening among your flock."

Her mouth was . . . gorgeous. There was no other word. Bee-stung lips twisted into a sneer. "Do it."

"That's the only command of yours I'll obey."

Intending to piss her off, he took one more taste of the lips he'd never believed could be real. Seeing her in the flesh, tasting and smelling and touching her—those intimacies made her night visits more ephemeral. They were mere shadows compared to the sweet bitterness of the kiss he took without permission.

She bit him. Tallis reared back. He swiped a hand against his mouth and came away with blood.

"That wasn't very nice, goddess."

But he was still grinning.

Both seaxes firmly grasped, Tallis peered outside again. Dusk approached to take the place of full sunlight. Amiable pods of Indranan had been gathered around their fire pits. Now they hurried around wearing frightened expressions.

Strange.

Tallis's own clan, the Pendray, suffered from historic self-esteem issues, but at least they displayed what they felt without pretense. They were boisterous and unapologetic. The Indranan, however, were made of mystery. To see the camp transformed into a frenzied, buzzing collection of scared souls was shocking— so many emotions laid surprisingly bare.

"Let me go," came the persuasive voice at his back.

"Whatever grudge you hold against me, you know I can calm them."

"No. Their panic will remain unaddressed by their savior. Seeing you discredited and ruined has always been my goal, no matter that I enjoyed kissing you." He couldn't help another mocking smile. "But that was absolutely necessary."

"You're crazy and spiteful and, to be honest, a sickening excuse for a Dragon King."

"*To be honest?* An interesting choice of words."

He turned away, chagrined by the power she wielded without thought to the consequences. The fervor had died down, but only because hurrying worshipers had frozen solid, no matter where they stood. Their attention was focused on the altar.

Tallis narrowed his eyes. A man stood where the Sun had delivered her pandering benediction. He was tall, with a commanding presence. His hair was brown, his features sharp, his clothing black on black. Among those gathered in the valley, his layers of leather and protective plates of silver armor stood out like a burn on a child's skin.

The Sun was a warmonger in silks, but this stranger was pure violence. No pretense. Grim lines flanked his mouth. A sharp, narrow nose and brow that was no lighter for its elegance. Those features weren't masked. They were solid and brazen and true to Tallis's every sense. And what he saw was a remarkable resemblance to the Sun.

"You were expecting someone else," the stranger intoned, his words hypnotic. They echoed back across the valley like a one-two punch of spellbinding power. "You were expecting a savior. I'm here to say there is no such thing. And there's no such thing as reconciliation between the factions of the Indranan. There never will be."

Tallis turned and grabbed the Sun by the scruff and dragged her to the tent's opening. Her face had gone chalk white. The color looked sick and unnatural on a Dragon King, but it was especially disturbing when it leeched the soft charisma of her beauty.

"Who is that?" Tallis was more agitated than he would have liked, but the unexpected was always a threat.

"That." She swallowed. "That is Pashkah of the Northern Indranan. My brother."

If skin could turn to ice, Kavya's would have had more in common with the glaciers up the Rohtang Pass.

She hadn't seen Pashkah since she was twelve years old. No matter that span of years, she would never mistake his stance, his face—the face he hadn't bothered to disguise. He'd never needed to. Even as a boy, he'd been able to hold a freakishly blank expression so well that not even she or Baile, their sister, could gauge his emotions. Demons and monsters and ghouls were nothing compared to his uncanny nothingness. Had she been able to understand him, with telepathy or her senses, she might have been able to save Baile.

But in those final moments of her life, Baile hadn't wanted to be saved. Before Pashkah had taken her head, she'd wanted his just as much.

The triplet who wielded the sword gained the power, leaving Kavya unaffected. She hadn't just remained in her childhood home so she could become his next victim. She'd run.

Now, having reduced their family to a series of grim victories, Pashkah stood within a few hundred yards of success. He would take Kavya's gift and add it to the power he'd stolen from Baile. He would become thrice-cursed with his true potential sewn together in violence—while the shrieks of two dead sisters would destroy his sanity.

Tallis shook her by the hair. "What is this, part of your big announcement? Bring in muscle to make sure everyone complies?"

"This is my brother having found me after decades of searching. This is . . . this is the brink of chaos. Worse than you even thought of threatening with two barbarian swords."

She jerked free of his hold and stared him down. At least now she knew who he was. His true identity.

Tallis of Pendray. The Heretic.

She still wasn't able to read his mind, but his seax held residual memories so strong that she'd caught flashes of his true self. His identity. His life on the run.

A man of myth. But still a man.

"You don't need telepathy to sense the panic." She tipped her chin toward where Pashkah owned the altar—the altar she'd hoped would be host to an evening of peaceful triumph. "Those are lambs being herded toward a butcher's knife. This man is fear and danger. Nothing I've done, no matter your delusions, will match the crimes he's capable of committing."

"He's your brother. I wouldn't expect anything less than deceit and mind-warping delusions."

Kavya's heart was expanding with each beat, until it shoved against her trachea. Everything she'd worked for was at Pashkah's mercy. "Do you hate me so much that you deny the obvious? Look at the men at his back. Every one of them is twice-cursed."

"You can tell? You're reading their minds?"

"I don't need to. They're Pashkah's Black Guard. Whole communities have been rolled over by their arrival."

"He kills Dragon Kings? The Council and the other clans would've heard about that."

Kavya shook her head, her eyes filling. "Not killing. Trying to *breed*. The Black Guard was responsible for the Juvine forty years ago, when women were stolen from the South and held captive here in the mountains. Retaliation after retaliation followed, reviving the same deeds and the same hatreds that split our clan three thousand years ago. By trapping me, you've given him unchecked permission. The Black Guard will continue its spree."

Tallis had fascinating skin—smooth except for those places where emotions pushed to the surface. So animated for a Dragon King, he frowned with his whole face until it took on the gravity of a pending typhoon. Finally he seemed to be taking her fear seriously.

"Unbind me," she said, pressing her advantage.

"So you can flee? What do you think I am?"

"An idiotic, brainless *thing*. All I want is to face my brother without ropes around my wrists." She forced strength into her voice just as she'd forced calm into her body. "You wanted me discredited, not martyred, remember?"

"That I can agree with."

"First obeying me, now agreeing with me. You'll be undone by dawn."

"Suddenly you expect to live that long," he said with an edge of a smile.

"You have no idea the consequences if I don't. Forget martyrdom. I'll be the dead soul that gives Pashkah what he's always wanted: the powers of a thrice-cursed Indranan."

He shook his head. "Legend."

"No, *fact*. Just like how the Heretic seems to have graced me with his presence."

That caught him off guard, but only for a moment. "So you admit it. You've known who I am."

"For the last few moments, yes. Your weapon tells tales to a telepath, even if I can't read your mind. But none of it means your accusations hold merit."

He silenced her by dragging a seax nearer to her flesh. Although she shuddered, she appreciated the knife more than his kiss. She could endure pain. Life had taught her those lessons and the means of coping with what no one should have to endure. The surprise of pleasure, however, was still frothing through her veins. Every hair stood on end. Her skin pulled toward his touch and his Dragon-damned kisses.

The conflicting emotions were too much to process.

The tip of the seax was as fine as the point of a needle. Engraved scrollwork along the blade caught the last of the dying sunshine. She recognized the etchings as the ancient language of the Pendray but had no idea of their meaning. Tallis slid the tip between her wrists and sliced the ropes with one swift cut. No wasted motion. Perfect mastery of his weapon.

"Members of the Sun Cult," came the voice that sent

hot dread up her spine and ghostly chills back down. "Your leader is no longer here. Because I am her brother, Pashkah, you can imagine the consequences if I take her life—or if I already have. Perhaps she's merely fled, leaving you to my mercies."

The Black Guard marched to the edge of the altar.

Pashkah didn't smile, but contentment shimmered around him in a swirl of charcoal fog. "I have no mercy."

Additional members of the Guard dragged a pair of men into sight and thrust them to their knees, flanking Pashkah.

Kavya gasped. "No, no, no . . ."

A hand wrapped around her mouth. She struggled until Tallis's words found their way into her short-circuiting brain.

"Quiet," he hissed softly. His arms were strong around her, which was welcome rather than abhorrent. She was ready to shudder apart, disintegrated by fear and utter outrage.

Tallis ducked her back into the tent. They could see through a small sliver that parted the folds of canvas. He kept his mouth near her ear, as if any stray syllable could be a death sentence. Still a Pendray, relying on words. For the Indranan, thoughts were louder.

"Who are they?"

"Representatives to the factions' Leaderships," she replied. "My allies. Oh, Dragon save them."

Pashkah was a man of his sick, malevolent word. He stood over the representatives and spread his hands with a flourish. "These are the presents the Sun was going to offer at dusk. Omanand of the North. Raghupati of the South. She would've stood behind them and smiled that tranquil, happy smile and watched as they shook hands. Ended the civil war. Healed the breach. Wouldn't that have been lovely?"

"Is that true?" Tallis asked against Kavya's cheek.

"Yes," she whispered. "A foundation for lasting peace. But it doesn't matter now. Nothing will matter now."

One of the Guardsmen handed Pashkah a sword that gleamed with a golden sheen.

Tallis drew in a sharp breath. "That's Dragon-forged."

Her lucidity was slipping away, along with her hopes. She was physically ill, so painfully, violently ill. "Yes."

Pashkah lifted the blade. With one blow, he beheaded Omanand. With another, he separated Raghupati's head from a body that flopped onto the altar. Terror echoed through the valley like the shrieks of demons.

Kavya saw only blood.

⇥ CHAPTER ⇤
FOUR

Tallis had witnessed the beheadings of Dragon Kings. He'd dispatched more than a few. Visceral memory would not let his hands forget how the metal hilt would crush the bones of his palm as he struck a Dragon-forged sword through a neck. Neither could he forget the warm spray of the blood. When he'd committed his first murder at the behest of the Sun, that of a long-dead Pendray priest, he'd left behind the ring that bore his family's crest, claiming the kill and marking himself as the target of his clan's hatred. Better that way.

Yet he'd thought about Lady Macbeth. Although he'd wiped clean his armor and his weapons, he would never be able to wash away the stains. The exact temperature of a dying man's blood became an indelible detail.

Subsequent kills had meant less to him. The repetition of it. The rhythm of following orders and detaching his morality. The deaths he'd brought about had created peace in places where Dragon Kings squabbled, where rifts threatened to break fragile alliances. His dirty work had been successful—until it had ruined Nynn's life.

He was unnaturally good at his work.

Pashkah of the Northern Indranan was better.

Had the man felt any emotion about beheading two fellow clansmen, it would be satisfaction. He stood like a triumphant god who, dissatisfied with sacrifices made in his honor, had taken the task upon himself. Two lifeless bodies slumped at his feet. Two heads had rolled away—distended tongues, bulging eyes, matted hair. The pair of Guardsmen stepped back from what remained of the prostrate men they'd forever immobilized. Their expressions were even more vacant. They radiated none of Pashkah's silent triumph.

If Tallis could ever read minds, this was the moment. He sensed more than satisfaction radiating from the murderer. He sensed glee.

The camp was a riot.

The Black Guard descended from the altar and strode through the tents. They grabbed women. *Young* women. Dark robes and saris were subsumed by men in black brigandine armor. Little blackbirds chased by avaricious ravens. In the melee, only flashes of mirrored armor plates distinguished predator from prey.

The Indranan men fought back. Their punishment was that from which a Dragon King could not recover: crippling injuries. Their kind had remarkable healing powers, but they couldn't regenerate limbs. Extreme wounds left scars. Suffering those ramifications could last the length of their two-century life span.

"We have to go," Tallis said plainly. His mission hadn't changed, no matter the hysteria that tainted the air as surely as his nostrils scented blood. "Wouldn't they love to get their hands on you."

"They wouldn't keep me for long. They'd hand me

over to Pashkah and my severed head would lie on that altar within minutes." The Sun had revealed herself as just an Indranan woman, not a goddess, but she shot sparks from her eyes. "*You* brought this on us."

She stood and scampered free of the tent so quickly that Tallis was thrown off-balance. He caught his momentum with a backward twist of his hand. Without wasted motion, he grabbed his pack and tucked one seax into the scabbard crossing his back.

He launched into the crowd, gripping the other blade. The unmistakable swirl of a golden sari was his only means of tracking Kavya through a circus of flailing, screaming, and maiming. She headed toward the outskirts of camp, not toward the round valley's sole exit—a narrow ravine. Likely she'd chosen this place for symbolic reasons. Circles and unions and the security of being held within the majesty of timeless mountains. She'd also chosen the worst place for a group of defenseless parishioners to escape trained killers.

He glanced up. Along the craggy ridges, more Guardsmen stood in anticipation of an ambitious refugee.

Tallis chased the Sun. No lazy pursuit, as if he were the moon tracking across the sky in a never-ending dance. He chased her with the speed of a Dragon King about to lose his sanity.

An Indranan man caught Tallis by the forearm. "Help us, friend. Help us."

"Use what your family gave you. Every pod has a Dragon-forged sword. I've lived among you long enough to know that."

"So few of us remain!" His leathery skin shone with

sweat. The tightness of his creased eyes couldn't hide his distress.

"Then make sure you're one of them. Unless you want to see the Juvine repeated, with your daughters stolen for breed stock." Tallis shrugged free. "The Sun has made you complacent. Peace. Unity. This . . ." He nodded toward the chaos. Two members of the Black Guard held a young man's arms while another gouged his eye with a dagger. Shrieking, clutching the empty socket, the victim was helpless while the guards dragged away a sobbing girl with long honey-brown hair. "This is the world we really live in."

Tallis turned toward where he'd last seen Kavya.

When he couldn't find her distinctive sari, he resisted the urgency of his gift. These people, this riot—followed by the sinking doubt that perhaps he'd been partly to blame. For whatever reason, Kavya couldn't read his mind, but what if Pashkah could? Tallis's focus on her whereabouts might have led the madman here. Those self-recriminations conspired to conceal Tallis's rationality in the steam of a swirling, claustrophobic rage. He needed to find her. No one needed his spinning berserker rage in that quicksand of gore.

Whatever trick blocked his mind from her telepathy didn't protect him from the rest of the Indranan. Their previous, almost polite tap-tap curiosity about a Pendray in their midst had become splatters of toxic confusion. Every mind writhed with the same thought: escape.

The shove and crush of bodies overwhelmed his path. He was tempted to use his seax for more than intimidation. However, the chances that some terrified Indranan carried an inherited Dragon-forged sword put him at a disadvantage. His aggression would appear little different than a Guardsman on the hunt for young female flesh, and he wanted to keep his head. Literally. The body count was currently two—at least.

Tallis of Pendray would not fall victim, too.

There.

Golden silk.

His heart jumped with a kick of adrenaline. The dam holding back his gift was weakening.

Kavya was not alone. A large Indranan woman stood at her side. She wore what appeared to be ceremonial brigandine armor, similar to that worn by the Black Guard. Called "the coat of a thousand nails," its wool and leather padding was backed with rivets. Penetrating that dense overlapping iron with a blade was almost impossible. Pristine and unscathed, the armor was decorated with pale Northern turquoise. Only the woman's posture suggested her clothing and the curved talwar saber she held were more than for show.

A burst of pain shot down Tallis's backbone, from his temple to the base of his spine.

What the hell?

He dropped to one knee and looked up. The female stranger glared down. More pain sizzled his every nerve. Another man might've been crippled by that stinging, blinding blow, but Tallis had nearly lost the Sun. His prize. He wasn't going to lose her again.

"You're coming with me," he said, working past the agony that centered at the base of his skull. He caught the Sun's gaze. "No matter what you and that butcher of a brother have done."

"You blame *me* for this?" Wide, almost innocent eyes

narrowed with concentrated anger. At least the chaos had stripped the last of her ability to draw false impressions from the crowd.

"You've led your people to slaughter," he said. "We won't be victims, too."

Lunging forward, seax at the ready, he attempted to grab her waist with his free arm.

The Sun shot backward. "Chandrani!"

The bigger woman met Tallis's attack with a quick parry and flick of her saber. The curving blade meant his arrow-straight seax was deflected by a swooping arc. It was like trying to stab the center of a blender's blades. Only his speed, which was gathering as his fury increased, dented the skilled woman's defenses. She moved with surprising grace, considering she was nearly his height, made of muscle, and covered in riveted leather armor. A bodyguard. That would explain the pain she continued to shoot through his skull. Some Indranan were better suited to thought manipulation, others to combat. This woman Chandrani was obviously one of the latter.

Tallis spun behind her. He kicked the back of her knee with his heavy combat boots. She stumbled—the opening he needed. The power he harnessed was unpredictable, but he'd been wielding it since its manifestation in his early teens. He let a portion of the rage fuel his movements. Stronger. Faster. His mind slipped behind a haze of red. He managed to restrain his violence only after slamming the hilt of his seax against the woman's temple. She staggered, clutching where blood oozed from between her fingers.

"What have you done?" The Sun rushed forward and

held the woman's head against her chest. "She was the only hope I had of getting out of here."

"No, you have me." Tallis hitched the strap of his pack. "I don't believe you backed yourself into a valley without a way out. Show me how you planned to escape and I won't continue to fight this woman."

"Chandrani comes with us."

He smiled grimly. "If she can walk."

She hated him. Kavya had thought herself immune to hatred beyond her loathing for Pashkah. *That* loathing came from the knowledge that her life was not her own so long as he lived. She couldn't behead him and risk taking two minds into her own. Anyone she hired to kill him could accept double the payment to lead Pashkah right back to her. And she wouldn't risk Chandrani, her only reliable calm in a world of chaos. The woman had offered to kill him several times, as repayment for a bleak night in Mumbai ten years ago when Kavya had beheaded Chandrani's murderous twin sister. Afterward they'd held each other and cried in both relief and grief.

That was an Indranan's deepest burden, to genuinely love and hate one's mortal foe. Kavya lived with the constant dread that the brother she'd adored as a child—together with Baile, the three of them inseparable—was eager to steal her from this world, when she still had so much to do.

But Tallis of Pendray . . .

The Dragon-damned Heretic. She hated him without reservation.

She helped Chandrani stand, although the woman

outweighed her by a good forty pounds of muscle. "I'm sorry," the woman said, her voice rife with pain. "I heard your shout, but your mind flickered in and out. I couldn't focus to find you. Then . . . then there was chaos."

"The fault was mine. I was dazed. Couldn't concentrate after I called for you."

Chandrani offered a watery smile. She only smiled for Kavya, which represented their unshakable bond. "I wouldn't be able to concentrate in the company of that *lonayíp* bastard either."

"I still need you," Kavya whispered, her face flushed. "Please. For me. We need to escape."

Chandrani steadied herself with gratifying efficiency. No one in Asia was a better, more sacrificing warrior. Her honor and dedication had kept Kavya alive far longer than she'd expected as a scared, homeless twelve-year-old girl.

Kavya glared once more at Tallis before turning toward the altar.

Tallis followed. She'd expected his presence, but he seemed unusually willing to *follow*. Not grab and demand. He was connected to her in ways that he resented. What was it about his past that had produced such a strange combination of bitterness and . . . protectiveness? Even affection? An untenable sense of his innate aura was the closest she could get to reading his mind.

Despite the physical bullying, she'd never gotten the impression that he aimed to do her harm. When he called her "goddess," his tone was sarcastic and acidic, but she'd heard something near to reverence. Years of hearing it from her followers meant she recognized unconscious awe. He didn't realize how much he gave away by insulting her with that particular word.

She struggled through the crowd, dodging frantic hands that beseeched her for help—or held her back—but she wore a tight smile. Here she'd thought herself incapable, or more arrogantly, *above* using her physical senses. Tallis was right that she'd become complacent.

What had she expected to happen? That Pashkah would simply let her go? The properties of a psychic Mask—many Masks, in her case—only extended so far. She could've hidden forever had she lived an unassuming life, especially had she emigrated. But because Dragon Kings could no longer bear children, she would've lived day to day without purpose. A useless hermit.

Anger swelled in her chest, fighting for a place where her aching breath huffed. Pashkah would not take this from her, and neither would Tallis of Pendray. Whatever she needed to do to escape, she would do. She was the only person able to reveal Pashkah's treachery and reunite her people.

Raghupati was dead. Omanand was dead. She mourned the loss of two men willing to make a difference, standing beside her and perhaps helping to bear a few of her decades-old burdens.

Thankfully, the Black Guard had scattered into the crowd, leaving the altar a solitary heap of rock.

Tallis grabbed her arm. "Let me go first."

"By all means."

The deepening shadows of evening meant his features were harder to discern. The color was gone. She'd liked his hair, tipped with a silvery sheen, and she'd liked his deep blue eyes. *Too bad.* She was stuck with a deranged Pendray whose looks were a hindrance to her ability to concentrate.

A distracted Indranan courted death by a ready sibling. And so the cycle of death and madness continued.

Creeping through the archway, Tallis kept his back to the altar and circled to the rear. His stealth was impressive. He was in tune with himself and the vagaries of the physical world—typical of the Pendray, as was his stubborn lack of sense. That came standard with their kind.

"What am I looking for?" he whispered over his shoulder.

She caught Chandrani's arm as the larger woman swayed, still clutching her head. "A span of rock with flecks of copper," Kavya said. "It's not sandstone or granite. It conceals a tunnel for escape."

"I knew you weren't that naive."

"Perhaps I was." She glanced back to where the Guardsmen were rounding up women. More and more men had been pushed to the eastern side of the valley, contained by guards holding Dragon-forged swords. That gold-touched gleam on otherwise ordinary steel was unmistakable. They wouldn't be able to fight back, or even flee. Only the Dragon knew their fate. "I had been hoping for unity, not planning for worst-case scenarios."

"The arrival of a twice-blessed sibling is certainly that."

"Twice-*cursed*."

"Do your clan words matter to me?"

Kavya had underestimated the extent of Pendray

rage lurking beneath his cool surface. He radiated the tension of a gale-force blizzard wind. He was different in that he held back what other members of his clan basked in using at any opportunity. At least, that's how the Pendray were described in rumor and disdainful talk.

"If he kills me, he'll lose connection to reality. His mind will be all that matters. He'll live there and refashion the world to match what he sees. That could mean anything." She nodded toward where bodies lay motionless on the altar. Blood had started to congeal around her fallen allies. "I doubt it will be peaceful."

"Turns out you won't need me to discredit you. The Sun led her people to slaughter, with your brother as the heavy."

"You know nothing," Chandrani said with unflinching vehemence. Despite her bleeding temple, she pushed Kavya forward and took up the rear defense. She held her saber with practiced steadiness.

The bubble of relative safety behind the altar muffled sound. Rock protected Kavya from the audible nightmare her people were enduring, but nothing buffered the suffering they shouted in silent, psychic screams. Her stomach was a solid cramp of tissue that wouldn't loosen. Nothing could undo this damage, even if she restored some sense of unity.

How confident she'd been that afternoon.

Too confident. Too arrogant. She'd created a place of spiritual safety that belied *actual* safety. Northerners and Southerners had put aside their differences. There in the valley, when had any needed to use telepathic attacks? Never. They'd been taken by surprise, and they were fighting back, but with two deadly sweeps of his sword, Pashkah had proven all of them to be woefully complacent.

"There," she said. "That block."

Tallis sheathed his seax and dropped his pack. He squatted before the boulder that concealed the exit and pushed.

"Help him or cripple him?" Chandrani asked. "I can do either. He didn't hit me that hard."

"Half your face is covered in blood. He knew just where to hit you, didn't he? Can you read my thoughts?"

Chandrani shook her head, appearing ashamed as if she were to blame.

Kavya touched her friend's cheek—the only skin left exposed by the riveted armor. "Help him. We'll deal with him later."

"I won't let him hurt you." Chandrani's expression remained impassive, but the conviction in her voice was unmistakable. She never lied. She never exaggerated. Her only failing was in thinking she could do everything herself.

They were very alike in that sense.

"Now isn't the time to discuss my fate," Tallis ground out, with his shoulder to the copper-flecked stone. It was half his size. "This was your escape? How did you expect to move this?"

Chandrani pushed Tallis aside. She touched a hidden place along the valley wall. The boulder opened like a door on a hinge. "Brains over brawn, Pendray."

"Too bad for you, sister," came that dreaded ghost-soft voice. Pashkah had intoned for the crowd, but delivered his sincerest threats in whispers.

He stood flanked by two members of the Black Guard. Each held a terror-stricken young woman, while Pashkah was armed with the same blood-drenched sword he'd used to commit public murder. "Brains would've been useful today, Kavya. Now it's time to see what sort of deity you've really become. Come with me or these young women become my next victims."

⤞ CHAPTER ⤝
FIVE

He'll kill them anyway," Tallis said calmly.

Pashkah focused his intense eyes on Tallis. Neither malice nor temper shone in those shaded depths. "Pendray can speak? You learn something new every day. Next I'll expect dogs to write poetry."

Tallis held back his temper at the slight. He focused instead on Kavya. She was more calm in the face of her brother's threat than she had been on the receiving end of Tallis's kisses. What that meant would have to wait. Getting out alive was all that mattered.

"You know I'm right," Tallis said to Kavya. "They're damned by an accident of fate."

"And you believe in fate, you blood-hungry Reaper?" Pashkah's soft voice was mocking with laughter, although his unnerving expression never changed. He reminded Tallis of how Kavya had appeared when addressing her flock—that slippery facade—but he couldn't tell whether it was a Mask or some Indranan trickery. The man was rich with the power of madness. "You're such primitive creatures. It's a shame we're obligated to include you among the Five Clans."

"Go." Tallis had sheathed his seaxes to move the

boulder, which meant he felt damn near naked. He flicked his gaze between Pashkah and Kavya. "Get your woman out of here and go."

"I'm not leaving while he lives," Chandrani said.

Pashkah blinked . . . and Chandrani screamed.

She collapsed onto her knees. She pressed her hands around her skull.

"That's what you get for being a thorn in my side for too long, Chandrani, dear. Anyone who protects or harbors my sister will receive the same." Pashkah trained his viciously vacant expression on Tallis. "I wonder how little effort it would take to lobotomize a Pendray."

The charged-up urges gathering in Tallis's blood had become a hurricane contained within skin. He smiled broadly. "I'm up for it if you are."

That unreserved joy seemed to upset Pashkah more than the words, with his brow drawing into a blink-quick frown. "Try me, Reaper beast."

Tallis let himself go.

With seaxes instantly in hand, the world whirled into shades of scarlet and lead. His peripheral vision became steam. Formless. Irrelevant. His focus trained on Pashkah's sword. In the heartbeat's worth of time between ordinary and extraordinary, Tallis had identified the weapon as the crux of the standoff. Without it, Pashkah could injure but not kill. The Black Guardsmen still held their captives. They might kill the young women if they escaped through the archway, but Tallis wouldn't let their vulnerability influence Kavya. Nor would he divert his energy.

The sword was the key.

He homed in on the glinting golden glow. The power

of the Chasm lived within its luster. Tallis's swords would be cleaved in two if struck by that blade. Nothing commonplace could withstand its potency.

He whipped his body into a greater, faster rage—hyper-focused, yet frighteningly mindless. The part of him that had lived too long among the humans dropped away. He was a creature of energy and the elements. The earth flowed up through his feet. He struck quick-patter steps across the valley's granite floor.

Slicing Pashkah's hand off should've been an easy task. But the fleeting moments before he sacrificed his rationality left him open to telepathic attack. Pashkah lanced his body with pain and filled his thoughts with bile, sugar-spun lies, and dizzying misdirection. Tallis saw images of flowers, bloody teeth, entrails, grains of sand in an hourglass no larger than a child's palm. He felt the wind against his face as if fire and acid had joined with a tempest to flay his face.

His gift fought back. He hadn't given in to its entirety in years. The monster was immune to Pashkah's meddling, because the monster dwelled deeper than consciousness. Whatever Pashkah was doing to his higher thoughts no longer bothered Tallis. Whatever had sparked the confrontation no longer mattered. All that his deepest instincts remembered was the sword.

He spun his seaxes like fan blades. But when he attacked Pashkah, he did so with his teeth.

He *bit*.

A scream echoed down to where Tallis existed, as if his mind had plummeted into a well. His jaw locked. He wouldn't let go. Only when a chunk of flesh ripped free did he rear back. The sword was limp in Pashkah's hand, but he was strong. He held on to it, swung, missed.

Tallis spat the mouthful of flesh onto the ground and smiled.

Clutching his wrist, Pashkah continued to rage in a distant corner of Tallis's mind, but Tallis attacked with his seax. Steel sliced skin and muscle. A crack of bone was satisfying. A second splintering sound was even better. His enemy shrank back. Female shrieks split the air. Only when Pashkah fled through the archway did Tallis turn on the guards.

It was intoxicating to be so pure, so graceful, so at one with his body.

The first guard lost a foot. The second tried what his leader had done—mental attack. Yet he was quicker to give up a useless tactic. He shoved his captive away and drew a broadsword that had originated in the Isles where berserkers ran mad. Did this Indranan expect to best Tallis with a Pendray weapon? He nearly laughed. He was smiling with the contentment of a man who'd been unexpectedly released from prison.

Two strokes later, the guard's sword clanged to the ground. The hand that held it still gripped the hilt.

The women had stopped screaming. They huddled around golden, silken Kavya.

Tallis needed to get them out before his rage subsided. The return to his waking mind promised untold pain. Whatever Pashkah had inflicted wouldn't dissipate quickly. Tallis needed the animal to protect himself from that crippling agony.

"Kavya," he said, like a wolf given leave to speak. He shouldered his pack. "We go."

She glanced at the freed women, who continued to whimper. "They're coming with us."

"We go. Now."

"*With them.*" She was angry and terrified. Disgusted and amazed.

Beautiful.

The animal was honest. Tallis wanted her. He wanted her in every way a man could have a woman. Rough. Fast. Merciless.

With tenderness.

He would take her. One day. She would fight it and love it and he would hold her in the aftermath.

Tallis beat back his animal cravings. He needed to get her free before he could indulge in primitive thoughts. Other than visceral pleasure, a Pendray wanted nothing more than freedom. No walls to keep him contained. There were too many walls in that blood-drenched valley.

The big woman led the way. Tallis surprised himself when he handed a seax to Kavya. She stood up and gripped it, both hands steady. Tallis liked that. He couldn't protect her if she cowered like her charges. Only then did he realize that he'd never lent one of his weapons to anyone.

"Out."

She obeyed, after hurrying the two weaker women through the exit. Had he already possessed her? Claimed her? His animal rage knew the truth. He'd tasted her, kissed her, touched her.

But he'd never bedded the woman called Kavya.

His goal was not to enjoy her sultry charms and resilient spirit, but to make her look a fool. The reasons no longer aligned, especially when he crawled behind her into the escape tunnel. The tight space and his heightened awareness of taking up the rear guard consumed his attention. He couldn't rely on his gift in that tight space. While crawling, Tallis battled to overcome the sense of suffocation that whipped his beastly side into a fit of panic. Two states of mind fought for control, but not entirely because of the necessities of war.

They fought because of a woman.

Tallis wanted Kavya of Indranan as much as he wanted to destroy the Sun.

Kavya didn't like the idea of Tallis following her in that confined tunnel. He was the most vicious creature she'd ever seen.

Yet, hadn't she needed just that? Some ferocity on her side? The women she urged forward, toward the open air, would be dead without him. Kavya would be prisoner to her brother. Would he have dragged out his torture and taunting? Or would he have simply pushed her against the altar for two Black Guards to restrain? One slice later, she'd have met the Dragon in the afterlife.

She shuddered even as she crawled. For the most part, the hollow beneath the mountain was natural. A few of the smaller passages had needed to be widened because none of her armored bodyguards could've traversed the narrow length. A few modifications to nature had created a tunnel she'd never thought she would need.

Her sense of self-preservation had kicked into the stratosphere when faced with her brother's insane placidity. Although they hadn't seen each other in more than twenty years, he'd recognized her as surely as she'd recognized him. The Masks had done their jobs, but now he would be able to track her mind's false persona. He knew what she looked like as a grown woman and knew who accompanied her in flight.

Even if he stopped for the night to tend to his arm, which she doubted, he would be in pursuit. Soon. Relentlessly.

His arm . . .

She shut her eyes for the span of a panting inhalation. Tallis had *bitten* her brother. Her shock had been nothing to Pashkah's expression of agonized surprise. When Tallis had spit and smiled, Pashkah of the Northern Indranan, so insane and formidable, had appeared afraid.

That was a precious memory she would keep as long as the Dragon granted. It softened her hatred of the man following at a steady crawl, behind where she sought purchase on the slippery rock. Tallis of Pendray had saved her life, and he'd done so by terrorizing her brother—a treasure to offset whatever misguided vengeance had brought him into her valley.

She heard Chandrani's voice in her mind. "Almost there. Another hundred meters."

That eased Kavya's anxiety. Chandrani had recovered her telepathy. But what awaited them at the end of their crawl? How fast could Pashkah's men circle around? Would they be able to find the exit in the dark? Of course they would. They'd only need to search for five conscious minds emerging from the side of a mountain. Select few Indranan were skilled Trackers. If Pashkah had tempted one to join his rabble, he would be able to find them at a distance of twenty or more miles—some rumored as many as a hundred.

Locating a half-crazed Pendray mind should've been the easiest means, but during his rage, Tallis had seemed impervious to Pashkah's attacks. Kavya had felt that ambient energy like the heat of an open oven.

Chandrani had hurt Tallis. Pashkah had done *something*. Maybe he wasn't shielded from every Indranan. Only Kavya? Why?

Tallis was a complete unknown . . . aside from his exceptional means of fighting. He'd been able to take down Chandrani without the use of his gift. Kavya had never known a man able to achieve that feat.

Chandrani's mind linked with hers again. Kavya could see what her bodyguard saw, which was near-total darkness. At least the darkness was empty of Guardsmen with glinting swords and voracious thoughts, eager to use their twice-cursed powers on any susceptible mind. Their intentions had been clear enough when holding the young women who continued to crawl through the tunnel. They'd hoped Kavya would go peacefully into her brother's custody, and that in return for their service, they would be awarded the women. They'd each clutched soft flesh a little tighter, greedily, ready to use force.

The Indranan had been damned for generations. Force—force against women—was the heart of their divided, hateful clan, as intrinsic as murderous violence between siblings.

Kavya felt Chandrani withdraw from her mind. She would need all of her faculties to scout for trouble or, worse, to attack if guards materialized from the shadows. Kavya returned her attention to the women she shepherded. She touched their thoughts, one after the other. She was the Sun. Bright. Warming. Such intense focus left her drained, but she wanted them calmed by generous stores of hope. The draining part was concealing how little hope Kavya yet retained.

First one, then the other reached the exit. Kavya quickly followed. When she stood, she recalled the seax in her hand. The mental rigors of the crawl had turned the weapon into an extension of her body. How? She'd never held one other than to face the man who'd given it to her so freely.

The man who crawled out of the tunnel.

Tallis of Pendray.

Whatever remained of his berserker rage was visible only in his eyes. The night darkness was almost absolute. In fact, she was sure that the only clues she collected were drawn from her gift. Could it be possible? To read him at last? But no. It was *his* gift shining in the blackness. His rage was a blue beacon. And his loathing hadn't eased.

He adjusted the strap of his knapsack and held out his hand. "I'll have that back now."

For a moment, she was tempted to hack his palm—an impulse born of frustration and fear. But her hatred had dimmed compared to the terror of standing face to face with Pashkah. How could she have compared the two men?

"I didn't want it in the first place." Kavya swung the sword and presented him with the hilt. The needle tip of the seax pointed directly at her heart. She already bore two cuts on her neck. She knew the blade's lethal potential. But this was a show of . . .

Trust?

And a warning.

She wasn't afraid of him.

"Thank you." He sheathed it behind his back.

"Why?" The tremulous voice belonged to one of the young women. "Why did you do it? You're the Sun. You were supposed to bring us together."

Kavya knelt beside the crouching pair. "You're Sarbani. You share a family pod with Divyesh and his wife."

"That's right."

To the other Kavya said, "And you're Jayashree. Your brother was killed by your husband three years ago. You're safe from that constant fear."

"We have your brother to fear now," Jayashree said. "How is that much better? Sarbani is right. Where were you when he killed those Leaders? I know what it is to be terrified of one's brother, but we were depending on you."

They were too distraught and angry to be consoled now that the immediate danger had passed. "Will you accept my apology and my vow to make this right? Will you come with us?"

A shimmer of thought flitted between the two women. Kavya couldn't tell what they said, only that they were conferring without words.

In tandem, Sarbani and Jayashree stood. "No," said the latter. "We're Northern Indranan. We know these mountains. The last thing we need is a hunted woman and a mad Pendray dog. We'll find the people of the North and let it be known that the Sun has fallen."

⊰ CHAPTER ⊱
SIX

Tallis watched the women walk away, but he saw them as enemies rather than individuals making sensible choices. In the midst of his rage, he'd considered them distractions who imperiled Kavya. Now they were liabilities, and he was glad to be rid of them. Yet the turnabout of opinion after Kavya had just risked her life to save theirs was a biting betrayal.

He shook his head. The rage was still there. His berserker side tended to see things in black and white. There were good and bad situations. Good and bad people. He must still be holding on to that fury, because he should know better without needing a reminder.

"They're traitors," Chandrani said softly.

The bodyguard had rarely spoken opinions aloud. He assumed more virulent thoughts were stored in her mind, or shared with Kavya. Tallis appreciated that she at least thought to include him in her assessment.

"They have free will." Kavya sounded tired and, more tellingly, she sounded disappointed. Grief bowed her posture and tightened the lines around her eyes. She was a woman in mourning, but remorse was not for killers. Tallis had firsthand experience with that fact.

She was so Dragon-damned beguiling that she kept distracting him from his goal.

"They would've been a hindrance," he said tersely. "We need to move."

Chandrani nodded, although she still assessed Tallis as she would a rabid coyote. She pulled her curved saber from a scabbard wrapped at her waist and set out, descending the mountain toward a river far below. "If you strike me again or harm Kavya," she said over her shoulder, "you will never sleep again. You'd awaken missing your legs from the knee down."

"Noted."

Kavya didn't follow. She stood facing Tallis, chin raised high. He wished he could read her eyes. As his gift ebbed, so did his heightened awareness. What would he see in those amber depths? Misery? Regret? Or worse, something akin to Pashkah's sly triumph? Regardless of his personal grudge, he didn't want to learn she was her murderous brother's beatific partner.

"Are you back?" she asked.

"Back?"

She reached up, hesitated, then cupped his cheeks in her icy palms. He would've thought her skin warmed by exertion, but perhaps shock ruled the day.

"Are you Tallis? Or will I have a berserker at my back for the rest of the night?"

"You shouldn't want either."

"I just want to know who or what I'm dealing with." She paused and tilted her head. "Wait, why wouldn't I want the other side of you? You and your gift saved my life."

"Unpredictability."

"I saw that, yes. But something deeper. Your voice . . . *you* didn't mean that."

Tallis made a halfhearted attempt to shake free of her gentle hold, but she held fast. A foreign part of him liked the idea that his skin was warming hers. "Finally able to read my mind, goddess?"

"You'll know when I can," she said with a tart scowl. "Tell me."

"Or?"

"Or I'll ask Chandrani to forgo waiting for you to sleep. How would you use your gift without your legs?"

He placed his hands over hers. Now she was the one gently trapped. "She does everything you say?"

"She has a mind of her own, but she's devoted that mind to my safety."

"Must be nice. A trained Amazon at your beck and call. Why didn't she find you in the tent?"

Kavya pinched her lips together. Her eyes darted aside. "I . . . I don't know. We haven't talked about it."

"Talk." The derision he felt toward her kind spiked. His *rational* anger was returning. "You don't *talk*. You're unnatural."

"And you've nearly evaded my question. Don't believe that will ever happen. Other than the obvious, what do I have to fear from the berserker?"

Tallis tightened his fingers around hers until she winced. He pulled her fists to his chest. "I was able to evade your brother's psychic attacks because nothing logical remains when I go that deep. Just . . ." He swallowed. What was this? He'd never been ashamed of his gift before. Something about this woman made him want to be more than a thoughtless Pendray cliché. "I work by instinct and take on an animal's compulsion to survive at all costs. And . . . to reproduce at all costs."

Confusion marred her soft brow. "We're a dying race. We can't reproduce."

He pulled her closer. Their mouths could touch if he wanted that connection. Or if she did. "That doesn't stop the animal from trying. A primal part of me wants you any way I can get you."

Kavya inhaled. The steady rhythm of her pulse at her wrists pumped with new force. She wasn't a fluttering butterfly beneath his fingers; she was a drummer pounding on a timpani.

"You'd force me? My people have a long, disgusting history of forcing women. I'd never known it was part of the Pendray tradition."

"We fuck like animals, but not by force." He grinned at her look of blatant shock—nostrils flaring, lips parting. "In that way it seems we barbarians have one over your high-handed ways. Anyone who tried to assault a Pendray woman would be pursued to the ends of the earth by her family."

She snatched her hands free despite how firmly he'd imprisoned the wrists abraded by hemp. "I wouldn't know anything about that either. Family means danger."

"So I've seen."

"You . . . you *bit* him."

"I did. I like my seaxes too much to risk them against a Dragon-forged sword."

She straightened her shoulders. "Thank you."

Her gratitude was a surprise. So was the moment she slowly lifted one flowing sleeve to his mouth and used the fabric to stroke his skin. The blood was sticky against the silk, grabbing at it. He must look like the beast he'd unleashed.

Again, that galling sense of shame. He forced it aside, as the last of his primitive temper cooled. He wanted her discredited. That was a given now. Why was he having anything more to do with her? He could take her to the Council to stand trial. But what had she done? There was no proof that she'd broken laws worthy of imprisonment in the high Fortress of the Chasm.

Staying with her had nothing to do with the way she cleaned his face.

Nothing.

Tallis batted her hands away. "Don't try tricks that have worked in the past, goddess. I've learned them, and I don't appreciate being condescended to."

Without waiting for her reply—too stricken by the hurt on her face—he followed the woman in armor. She was a third of the way down the mountainside. The Beas River carved a wide ravine that ran from the highest reaches of the Pir Panjal down to the Punjab Basin. They might camp soon, down among the river-fed trees. Or Tallis might leave soon. He continued moving for the sake of moving.

What if she really had meant to present those Leaders? What if they'd been ready to work toward ending the Indranan civil war?

Tallis was left to his thoughts. Yes, the Sun had fallen. Her reputation among her kind would never be restored. But what if his personal revenge had led to Pashkah's discovery of her presence—and to those murdered men? Would Kavya have been able to protect them had she been readying herself behind the altar, preparing to greet the cult with genuinely hopeful news?

No. She would be dead.

That knowledge was as clear as the river below, and just as chilly. No matter Tallis's actions, she never would've taken to that altar except to kneel and die. Pashkah would've been nauseatingly satisfied and incomprehensibly powerful.

Tallis had saved her life. After all, he hadn't wanted the Sun dead. Only ruined. That sense of having accomplished his mission returned, yet it felt oddly hollow. He breathed deeply and exhaled so much tension. The morning would see his senses clear and his life restored.

That sealed it. He wouldn't camp with the Sun and her bodyguard. Instead he would leave them on the low mountain pass with her shredded reputation as company.

But the animal lurking deep in his soul protested Tallis's decision.

Kavya reached the river's edge in time to see Tallis turn to the south and keep walking. *Where is he going?* she silently asked Chandrani.

He didn't say. Just finished his descent. Didn't even look my way.

"After all that?" Kavya's wrath surged into something powerful and unknown. She'd been angry before, but this was anger born of insult. "Travel on. Put distance between us and the valley. Make what camp you can. I'll be back soon."

With long strides, she strove to catch up to Tallis. The wind whipped through her silk sari, chilling her bone-deep. She had intended to don a heavier sari for the evening's announcement, one without the turquoise of the North or the cobalt of the South, and without her customary gold.

Plain black. Neutral. For a people united.

No longer. She was going to freeze to death, but not before she wrecked Tallis of Pendray.

"You ruined everything, and now you're leaving? What in the Dragon's name sort of man are you?"

He didn't stop. His pace remained even, as if he hadn't heard her at all—or worse, as if he would just ignore her indignation. She wasn't used to being ignored. Arrogance or not, she wouldn't let go of the right to speak her mind and be heard.

"Do you know what will happen now? You said you wanted to discredit me, that you didn't want me martyred, but my brother knows me now. Knows my face and the patterns of my mind. There was no time to disguise my appearance. I can't read you. I couldn't read Chandrani because of your blow to her temple. In the chaos, I had no one else to draw from. I was bare-faced and he *saw* me. He saw all that he'll need to hunt me down."

Jogging the last few steps, she placed her feet carefully. Her ceremonial slippers wouldn't last long on the slippery, muddy shoal. She grabbed his arm with more force than she thought she possessed.

Tallis jerked in a semicircle and clutched her neck—one fluid motion. "Do you court harm? Is that it?"

He squeezed until every fingertip found a pressure point. Black spots flitted against a night sky that wasn't dark enough to compete with the oncoming loss of consciousness. Indranan were helpless when unconscious. They were susceptible to mental influences, or might let a Mask slip. Kavya hadn't slept soundly or for long durations in years. For that reason and many others, she traveled with trusted people like Chandrani, just as they traveled with her. Kavya's youth hadn't offered any assurances. Sometimes she wondered how many of her memories were her own and how many had been left behind by predators who'd used her sleeping mind as a playground.

He tightened. She gagged.

And she kneed him in the crotch.

Tallis let go and stumbled back, cursing. "Is practicing that move a hobby among females?"

"Some old ways are still the best." She rubbed her neck. Her voice was roughened. "Now answer this Dragon-damned question: What do you think will happen to the Sun Cult or whatever you outsiders call it if I'm murdered by my brother? Martyrdom isn't the right word for it. I'd be *sainted*."

"That won't happen. Girls like those turncoats would make sure of it."

"Turncoats, eh?" She threaded her fingers together at her waist and aligned her knuckles. Mountains and valleys. Calm. Breathe. "Does that mean you disagreed with their choice? Interesting."

Tallis stood. She didn't miss the way he shook his left leg, subtly, as if to protect his pride while easing the sting she'd inflicted. "Let's pretend your brother parted your head from that delicious little body of yours. Then what? Just another case of sibling-on-sibling violence. There would always be the suspicions that you'd colluded in that bloodbath. The lure and the heavy. And then—an alliance broken down."

Her teeth began to chatter just when she wanted to appear unrelenting. "'Delicious little body' is even more telling than calling those girls turncoats."

"I already told you that I want you."

They stared at each other. Tallis's expression was generally so open as to be off-putting. He behaved with too many human mannerisms. But with that sentence, he closed off every readable emotion.

"Another slip." She touched his cheek where night shadows made a stripe of dried blood look like dirt. "You'd meant to say something about animals or beasts or Pendray berserkers. *You* don't want me."

He took both shoulders in hand and pinched. His kiss crashed down on her. Lips were enemies—fighting, not working together for pleasure. Kavya found pleasure anyway. She was jarred soul-deep by the aggression of his embrace, with his arms crossed behind her back. She was thrilled by the shock. Telepaths were rarely shocked, which had made that afternoon all the more terrifying.

Some surprises weren't terrifying until after the fact, when thought returned and she would regret enjoying his mouth on hers.

Later.

With more assurance, she took what he offered and made demands of her own. Tongue against roughly pebbled tongue. He nipped with his teeth—a reminder of the force contained within his lean fighter's body. He was a beast in a man's skin.

We fuck like animals.

She shuddered and accepted how he pulled her

more tightly against his chest. He was warm. She needed his warmth. She needed this strangely numbing balm of pleasure. The eager tension of passion overruled every other emotion. All she knew was that Tallis held her.

He angled his head to claim better access to her mouth, then trailed hot, openmouthed kisses down her neck. He licked one of the parallel cuts, then the other. The heat of his tongue was replaced almost instantly by the cold whip of the wind. She shivered beneath that hot cold, hot cold. Every movement, whether feathering or forceful, said he would take her if she lay down on the ground.

It would hurt.

It would be madness.

It would be marvelous.

She moaned, but she couldn't believe the sound came from her throat. He matched her primal desire with a growl of his own. He cupped the back of her head and returned to her mouth. The press of his lips and the welcome invasion of his tongue felt like he'd come home to her.

No.

She struggled. He wouldn't let go. She pressed her hands against his chest and pushed. He kissed her deeper. Panic replaced pleasure. She struggled, fought—

Then bit his tongue.

He reared back. "Dragon damn it, woman."

"I thought your kind never forced anyone. Besides, you're not the only one who can bite."

He wiped his mouth and grinned. "So I've learned. Adding some variety to our real-life encounters?"

"We're back to you being a Pendray in the throes of some delusion. We've never met before this afternoon."

"Oh no," he said, tightness replacing his brief humor. "Don't play coy now, goddess."

"I rather liked when you used my real name. At least then I was a person, not some figment of a lost mind."

"*You* made me lose my mind. That's why I'm here, you witch."

He stalked in a tight circle, then returned to face her. His skin was scented with blood. This man, for all his infuriating delusions, had saved her from Pashkah. That explained why she put up with his erratic moods and accusations. It couldn't be because she hoped for more of what he'd done in the tent—binding her, tempting her. It couldn't be because of moments like these, charged with expectation that balanced between ferocity and passion.

Moments that left her guessing.

She wanted all of it, but just a taste. She wanted it from a man who wouldn't probe her thoughts while doing so, who couldn't manipulate her while she took what she wanted from his body and he took what he wanted from hers.

She'd remained untouched for just that reason. Indranan men could not be trusted.

"Explain yourself," she said. "Please. I might be able to alleviate whatever madness has led you to these extremes."

"There's nothing you could say that I'd believe."

"Try me."

Nothing passed between their minds. Kavya could

only read the grim shadows that accentuated his straight nose, his tightly pursed lips, and the hollows of his eyes.

He bared his teeth before appearing to come to a decision. "You're a manipulative seductress. For as long as I can remember, you've used dreams as a portal into my mind. You've directed my actions for decades, using every method possible—including visions of the Great Dragon so convincing that I'd swear I've looked our Creator in the eye. These kisses aren't new to me, goddess. They're as familiar as the pace of my feet on the ground. They're a base attempt to divert me from the truth."

Despite her confusion and the impulse to defend herself, Kavya refrained. "What truth is that?"

"You're a liar and a user. Your plan for the future of our people is the worst sort of insult. Unite the Dragon Kings through selective murder? It's a beautiful idea cloaked in blood. No more. I'm walking away. Everything between us ends tonight."

With a voice barely strong enough to be heard, she cast a parting sentence toward his back as he walked away. "If I can reach you in dream, Tallis, why can't I read your mind?"

⇾ CHAPTER ⇽
SEVEN

Tallis slept a fitful night on his own. The wooded terrain provided little protection from the frigid wind. He used supplies from his pack to fashion a makeshift shelter, which was mostly additional layers of clothing. His tent was gone. His reason for setting up that tent in the first place . . .

He'd never see her again.

Unless he slept.

Nothing had ever scared him, except for the night when obeying the Sun's first command meant leaving his family behind. He'd never see them again either. That was enough to strike hot jolts of fear into the bravest man. To be alone. No family. Not ever.

He wasn't scared of falling asleep, but he never looked forward to it. Months would pass, until he began to think he was free. Maybe . . . finally. But she haunted him like a peripheral shadow. Some night, when Tallis nodded off—too exhausted to wonder if she'd really left him for good—she would appear. The Sun. Kavya. She had a real name, a real face, a real body that he'd touched and kissed.

A woman's whose life he'd saved. A woman who'd wiped his face clean of blood.

Tallis reclined on his pack, propped against an ever-green, protected from the worst of the wind whipping down the mountain.

He'd walked away, just as he'd said he would. Now he would sleep alone in a forest that bordered the Beas River in the Valley of the Gods. Why did he feel dissatisfied, as if so much remained unresolved? Shouldn't he experience some sense of closure? He hadn't expected her to apologize, beg, justify, thank him—all in the span of twelve hours. In fact, he hadn't imagined what she might do. She and the completion of his goal had been too nebulous. All he'd wanted was to find her. Discredit her somehow. And rid her from his dreams forever.

Huddling into himself for warmth, with the sherpa-lined leather coat buttoned to his neck, he searched through memories and half-remembered visions. Some were so blatantly erotic that recalling them twined with the teeth-grinding, unspent passion he'd unleashed while kissing Kavya. He shifted on the lichen-laced ground, shutting his eyes.

Her scent and her skin were indescribably soft, as was her touch when she'd cupped his bloodied cheeks. Those were real. Images of her naked body on display, her hair long and loose . . . Those were fake, planted by a seductress who'd led him along by his dick and his naiveté for too long.

She blocked out every woman he'd known. None could compare to his fantasies.

Now, the fantasy couldn't compare to the woman he'd kissed.

Why can't I read your mind?

There had to be a reason. She was lying when she

said she couldn't. Or she couldn't access his mind when he was conscious. Or, or, or . . .

He'd lived among the Indranan for months, all in anticipation of the previous day. He'd learned about their family pods—how children ran away as soon as their gifts manifested, escaping their twins, severing all ties with their biological families. Refugee Indranan grew up alone, slowly constructing new families, called pods, from genuine strangers. Strangers meant safety. They bonded over a shared need to protect against brothers and sisters intent on collecting the other halves of their fractured gift from the Dragon.

Their ingrained techniques for self-preservation made Tallis's exile from his family seem insignificant.

Nothing he'd learned could explain what it meant with regard to Kavya.

No, he thought angrily. *She is the Sun.*

He was hungry and growing more furious with himself by the minute. He was rid of her. He'd walked away when staying with her would've meant protecting her, kissing her again. Or worse yet—believing her.

Why can't I read your mind?

He'd thought her inability to be a quirk of luck, a useful aid in finding her. Now that question was the nucleus of a mystery he couldn't solve.

Fuck it.

He'd lived as a human in England for long enough to know that was the perfect expression for what he felt. Angered resignation.

The wind kept howling. His nose and ears were frozen. He had a terrible headache, from the cold and the aftereffects of the rage he'd indulged. There were consequences for dropping that deeply into one's black soul. Returning again was like using slippery vines to climb out of a mud-slicked pit. It always left the slimy feeling of having done something disgusting, as if he'd masturbated in public.

The burden of the Pendray was to live with such power and a disgracefully low opinion of it. Where was the glory in succumbing to one's gift when it meant tapping into the worst, basest impulses? Where was the contentment of a fight well won if an animal won it on one's behalf?

Tallis had bit Pashkah like the rabid dog he'd been accused of being. Years of practicing techniques in hand-to-hand combat and in the use of his seaxes—didn't matter. Just teeth and fury.

He saw her.

Kavya.

No . . .

This was the Sun. She was the woman he'd come to expect in his dreams. This time, she appeared on the back of the Great Dragon without preamble. Normally the Dragon appeared when Tallis most needed convincing, as if the Sun brought their Father into the discussion to ensure cooperation. How could anyone deny her commanding beauty and the unearthly power of their Creator?

Tallis held very still. Somewhere higher up on the plane of his consciousness, he knew he had fallen asleep. He didn't want to wake. He wanted to know what the Sun had to say for herself, now that he'd left her to her own resources, stripped of authority, with two slices from his seax on her neck.

He'd tasted those slight wounds, letting his tongue offer the apology he'd never voice.

"You did well," she said, as softly as the magical swish of the Dragon's wide wings and long tail. "This was how I intended events to proceed."

She was swathed in the turquoise of the North, when she was usually clad in the same golden silk sari that Kavya had worn. The gold accentuated her warm coloring. By contrast, the vibrant blue made her features appear careworn. She was voluptuous, but not with Kavya's innocent sexuality. The Sun's innocence was petulant, like the greed of an insatiable two-year-old. Pleading, then coercing. Coercing, then pleading. He hadn't been able to resist that potent cocktail.

Now he could.

"I didn't do anything to please you," he said. "Your cult is in ruins. You'll only be welcomed into the most warlike pods in the North. Go take shelter with them and watch the last of your reputation rip in the wind."

Amber eyes glowed strong and true, as a corona of light large enough to obscure the Dragon gained strength at her back. Soon her features were cast in shadows. Her body was a silhouette behind layers of flowing blue. Tallis could only sense the Dragon's watchful presence and smell the brimstone smoke of its exhalations.

"It was time," she said. "You killed a priest to unify your clan. That was how the Pendray could become most powerful and lasting."

"It worked. I know that. Other selective murders have had the same effect—bringing peace where none had been. But strengthening individual clans has never been your goal. 'The Chasm isn't fixed,' you said. Unify the Dragon Kings."

"And I will."

"*You* will," he said so forcefully that he sensed his own waking. For a moment, he indulged in the sunshine-warm light emanating from her body. He let her seduce him back to sleep.

"I have work to do, Tallis. The Indranan must be their most powerful and lasting selves, too. That means ending the civil war."

"Peace and unity. That worked out great tonight."

The apparition flew closer. Hot breath scorched Tallis's face. She had never guided the Dragon toward outright intimidation through violence, only ever through awed, calming authority.

"My clan has been cleaving for too long," she said. "North from South. Siblings from siblings. It's time to stop. With all the finger-pointing to come, the factions will resume hostilities. Frightened brothers and sisters will have no choice but to arm themselves. It will be . . . survival of the fittest." Her smile was blindingly beautiful, but unnaturally visible in the shadows cast by the corona. "Those left standing will be few, but powerful enough to rival any of the Five Clans. The *strong* will ensure that the unification of the Dragon Kings becomes fact."

Tallis sat up. He ached from lying on the unforgiving ground. He could still see the Sun and her magnificent mount, so he was still sleeping. He'd expected a more subtle form of manipulation, where the worst possibility would be if he gave in. *When* he gave in. He wanted Kavya too much to refuse what her dream self might offer. This apparition, though, didn't evoke any sense of lust. She'd never spoken to him with such candor or fervor.

Something about this was wrong. Very wrong.

"How would the strong unify the clans?" he asked, his suspicion undeniable.

"That isn't for a good soldier to ask. But it was good of you to walk away. Pashkah and I are grateful for your help, dear Tallis." She reached down to touch his hair, as if petting the fur back from a dog's eyes.

Wrong. So wrong.

His mind was still kicking. Somewhere. He was thankful for it.

As with dreams, when transitions never made sense, the Dragon had disappeared. The Sun was standing before his kneeling form. Tallis took her hand in his and held her palm flush to his cheek. It was hot. Not at all like Kavya's delicate assurance. "You mourn them, don't you? North and South. Those who suffered today."

The hand didn't flinch. He would've felt the smallest movement, no matter how involuntary. "We did what was necessary. What has been cleaved all these years will be united. Fully blessed."

"We," he said slowly. "You and me. You and Pashkah. You and the whole of the Indranan. Or just . . . you?"

The Sun frowned. He'd only seen that expression when she was upset with his reluctance. The corona of light dimmed. Swirls of charcoal and dull pewter invaded the sunny yellow brightness. "You doubt when there is no need. Your tasks are complete. I'll never see you again, but I'm thankful. And so will be the entirety of the Dragon Kings."

He tried to grip her fingers, but they slipped away like trying to hold a cloud. *"You mourn them."*

The Sun blew him a kiss and smiled, even more

childlike now, as if he'd been blessed by a little girl who could never be blamed for anything.

"Why wouldn't I? Good-bye, Tallis."

Tallis jerked away, eyes wide and chest thumping. The dream was gone, but the unnerving truth lingered.

Kavya and the Sun were not the same woman.

Kavya and Chandrani huddled behind a trio of evergreen trunks so entwined that they formed a natural shelter. Chandrani had shed what she could of the padded clothing beneath her armor, giving it to Kavya to stave off the worst of the cold.

But Kavya couldn't sleep.

That old fear had returned, that if she slept, she wouldn't wake up as herself.

I won't let that happen, Chandrani said without words.

Their communication link was whole again, as was the ability to use each other's senses. But Chandrani's powers of attack remained pell-mell and unreliable. Whatever she might accomplish for their defense would be done instead with body and skill. What sort of life had Tallis lived that he knew with such certainty how to incapacitate an Indranan?

Kavya stared into the gentle black as a late sliver of moon rose above the tallest peak in the east. The silver sheen reflected off the river's wide waters. She stared as if watching a flame. Surely Pashkah had recruited a Tracker for his army. Kavya and Chandrani may as well be pursued by bloodhounds. They weren't safe at night, and she couldn't think of a safe place to go come dawn.

I can't sleep, she said. *You know that.*

I know. You've never been very good at letting go.

A moment of levity made Kavya smile at her friend. *Can you blame me?*

The Indranan hadn't been their only enemies when growing up in Delhi and Mumbai. Some humans would've liked finding defenseless young girls on the cusp of womanhood. She and Chandrani had hidden each other with psychic distortion, and they had stayed small and quiet. Only telepathy. Had anyone found them, Kavya harbored no doubt that Chandrani would've died trying to protect her. Her sense of debt to Kavya was infinite.

I'm afraid of Pashkah, she told Chandrani. After tucking her slippered feet more securely beneath her body, she adjusted the armor's padding. Her legs would be numb from lack of circulation, but at least they wouldn't be numb because of frostbite. *And I'm afraid of what that man Tallis said. What if I really have been contacting him in dream?*

Chandrani's outrage was instantaneous. *How? You'd have known.*

Dreams are dreams. And there's no telling what exists inside our minds. So many Masks. So many days where time is missing. Can we really say that our thoughts are our own? Or our memories? Some Masquerade could've planted malevolent intentions when he installed a Mask. I don't know why, or why Tallis in particular, but it's possible. We've known people who've layered too many disguises on top of their true personalities.

As mad as the twice-cursed, Chandrani replied with a nod.

Kavya shivered and tried to keep her jaw steady. Her

teeth hadn't stopped chattering since those moments sur-rounding Tallis's kiss. *That means what he said is possible.*

Even if you can't read his mind?

Can you? Kavya's frustration surged back in force.

No. I could hurt him, but I couldn't find a single thought. Chandrani shifted. Her metal-lined armor didn't make much noise, but it sounded terribly loud in the nighttime stillness. *Kavya, you need to set aside a puzzle you can't solve tonight. Rest.*

Impossible.

Images of blood and ruined flesh—cleanly cleaved heads and a chunk of skin ripped from her brother's arm—filled her mind. A sob choked up from her chest, but her mind was awash with crying that wouldn't stop. "We were so close," she whispered aloud. "So many people trusted me. I trusted that everyone would wel-come the truce. But Pashkah . . . Dragon damn him."

A noise behind the entwined trio of trees stilled them both. Kavya held her breath and clenched her teeth. She couldn't hear beyond the noise in her ears and the squeak of wind swirling through the boughs. If it was an animal, she wouldn't be able to identify it. She could only read the thoughts of creatures possessing a higher consciousness, which fit with what Tallis had ex-plained regarding how he'd resisted Pashkah's attack. If it was a human or a Dragon King, she should've known minutes ago. Maybe longer.

That meant it could be nothing—a trick of the land-scape as it slowly changed its eons-old shape.

It could be a Black Guard trained in tracking.

Or . . .

It was Tallis.

He appeared so suddenly that Kavya screamed in her mind. Chandrani stood and squared off against the infuriating Pendray. "Haven't you caused enough havoc?" Chandrani asked. "I preferred your vow to leave and never come back."

The moon amplified Kavya's ability to see his features. Deep circles curled beneath his eyes. His mouth, so apt to smiling in that disconcerting way, was a grim streak of shadow. She saw worry and extreme fatigue as plainly as if he'd spoken the words—as plainly as if she'd taken up residence in his mind and experienced his exhaustion.

"Put it away, Chandrani," he said nodding to her saber.

"She's right, though, about you vowing to leave." Kavya forced her voice to remain even. "Why not stay gone? Pashkah did what you'd set out to do—to ruin me. There should be nothing left between us other than my extreme regret that I ever met you."

"Look at me."

She stared once again, indulging his command because she wanted to. He was handsome to the point of stabbing pain in her chest. A man had never figured into her plans. She was too vulnerable. She could barely sleep, let alone lie beside another. So much vulnerability was terrifying. Tallis made her want what she'd never even imagined. That should've been enough to raise her defenses and cast him from her thoughts.

He was dangerous.

Except, she'd never considered lying with a member of a different clan. Tallis couldn't creep into her mind. He'd find the idea repulsive.

Instead he would touch and stroke her with his strong, work-worn hands.

So she looked, memorizing the way the moon added deeper luster to the silver sheen of his dark hair. That heavy mass was tempting. She could bury her fingers in it and pull his mouth down to hers.

"Kavya."

She blinked. "Yes. I looked. What about it?"

"I slept." He shouldered past Chandrani, who made a token protest both mentally and verbally. "Do I look like I've slept?"

Kavya pushed free of the trees as she stood. The moon wasn't strong enough to help answer his question. She placed cold hands on his cheeks. Only when skin met skin did she realize that her touch was an echo of how she'd held his blood-streaked face. His eyes closed briefly on a sigh. That wasn't possible. He was too angry for sighing.

"I knew it," he whispered.

Rather than question him—because he was still a *lonayíp* bastard who spoke in riddles—she turned his features toward the moon. The circles under his eyes were so deep and dark as to appear agonizing. He looked ten times as tired as when they'd parted.

"I don't understand." She pulled her hands back just enough for him to grasp them, fingers twined, holding each other again. She was afraid of repeating these intimate things—making patterns, finding familiarity she didn't want to feel but couldn't deny.

"You came to me again. In a dream."

Kavya jerked away. She wasn't touching him, just the sharp bark of the trees at her back. "I've been here with Chandrani the whole time. Linked with her mind. Very much awake. I . . . I—"

"You what? The only way you can convince me of a Dragon-damn thing is to tell the truth. It has to *sink into my bones* as the truth. I don't have any other way to judge what you say. So say it."

"I would've found you had I been able." She swallowed, grateful for the darkness that concealed her embarrassed flush. "I wanted to know where you'd gone. I would've cheated. I would've searched your mind for clues as to why you'd really gone."

Tallis of Pendray bowed his neck. He looked like a supplicant, which sent shivers of satisfaction up her spine—then dread. She didn't want this man to be just another admirer.

"Do you believe me?"

"Yes," he said quietly. "Now, one more question."

He lifted his head and stepped to within a breath of her body. He'd never stared at her with deeper concentration.

Kavya wanted to look away, but that would be tantamount to running. "Ask me."

"Do you mourn those who were hurt and scared and stolen?"

Tears were sticky like gelatin in her throat. "I do," she managed to say. "A piece of my heart died at dusk."

"And if you were able, what color would you wear to express that mourning?" Surely he had other features, but she was riveted to his tortured eyes. "Tell me, Kavya. What color do the Indranan wear to mourn their fallen?"

"The same color we gave to the humans here in India, Pakistan, Tibet. No matter the faction, North or South, we wear white."

→ CHAPTER ←
EIGHT

Tallis stared at her face, her honest face, and ducked into himself. He didn't move, but there was no denying his withdrawal from Kavya's simple words. It shook everything he knew to its bedrock.

He'd rebelled against the Sun—the dictator who'd turned him into a killer. He'd plotted against her and hated her. She'd been using him, and he'd been right to rebel. He only regretted that he hadn't started to revolt years ago. It was past time to break free of that false prophet.

That the apparition happened to look like Kavya, happened to use the name her innocent followers had bestowed . . .

He was mad.

Or Kavya was even cagier and more manipulative than he'd believed.

No, he couldn't hold on to that logic anymore. Kavya was an optimist in a time of despair. She manipulated people, but he'd never seen what might qualify as malevolence, only subtle pushes toward the hope and courage few dared dream: peace.

All that remained of his antipathy toward Kavya was

that her goal of unification aligned with the woman who'd directed his violent hands. That *thing* was not optimistic or innocent. He'd felt only selfishness and ambition.

For the sake of the Dragon Kings as a whole, that ambition could not come to pass.

Part of him had grudgingly come to respect Kavya. It seemed a shame to find a reason to continue thwarting her noble endeavors. But his intention remained the same. He would rid himself of the demon in his mind, even if it meant keeping Kavya from accomplishing her mission.

"I dreamed of you again." Throat tight, he cut off her protests with a stiff sweep of his hand. "It wasn't *you*. Nothing fit. She was a warped version of how you appeared before your followers. Something to please everyone. Only . . . more exaggerated. It was the first time I could see through the illusion. She said she mourned the dead, but she wore turquoise from the North."

"That would never happen. Ever. It would be an insult, not to the South, but to the people we used to be. Long ago. A people who shared the same name, without qualification." She forcefully shook her head. He'd known as much, no matter his unanswered questions and fury at having been used. "What else did this . . . Sun tell you?"

"She claimed that peace between the factions would mean unification of the Five Clans."

Kavya's brows drew together. The more she revealed of her authentic personality, the more animated her features became. She exposed more with her frown than she could have with a hundred words. At least that was reassuring. Toward the end of his dream the phantom in his head had gazed down at him with an eerie blankness that reminded him too much of Pashkah.

"That has never been a facet of my hopes," she said. Her fingers compulsively itched the evergreen's shredded bark. One foot tapped the needle-strewn ground—a soft patter of sound he identified despite the steady, growling flow of the Beas at his back. "How would the end of our civil war unify all of the Dragon Kings? I can't even comprehend the power someone would need to make that happen." The drain of hope from her eyes buried pain behind his sternum. "To force compliance? By any means?"

Tallis nodded. His eyelids felt lined with grit. "The Sun I envisioned said that the factions would unify when twins stopped resisting the inevitable. A gift split between two people was a gift that hadn't been allowed its full potential."

"So just start killing each other?" Her melodic, softly accented voice pitched toward hysteria. Whatever tricks she'd used when speaking to the assembly, none had been to modulate the musical rhythm of her speech. That rhythm was choppy now, made staccato by her mounting outrage. "Murder your twin? Your triplet? Was that her message? She might as well advocate brinksmanship among human nations that stockpile masses of weapons."

"'Survival of the fittest,' she said."

"And those who survived would be powerful and *insane*. Can you imagine the upheaval? For the most part, our kind blends with the human population. You have, haven't you?"

"For years."

"Do you think our relative anonymity would last if we started killing each other in the streets? Or bringing innocent humans into the fray?"

The jab of guilt made Tallis look away. He'd led the Asters to his niece's home. *Just for questioning*, they'd claimed. Only, Tallis had watched in horror as her unassuming life had been shattered by the Asters' men and a few of his warped Cage warriors—those Dragon Kings who fought to clear debts or, for some, to earn the right to conceive children. Dr. Heath Aster, son of the cartel's patriarch, was the only person in the world to have discovered a method of circumventing the barrier that had hampered natural conception for a generation. Fighting for the survival of one's bloodline had driven some Dragon Kings to the underground world of the Cages.

Then how had Nynn been able to conceive a natural-born Dragon King son?

Just for questioning.

He'd never wanted them to invade Nynn's home and murder her human husband with a shotgun blast to the chest.

"It's happened already," he said. "I know of at least one human who's died because of this increasing need to consolidate power."

"You thought by discrediting me and keeping the Indranan split into factions, that power would never come to pass?"

"Yes." He paused, glanced at a very grim-faced Chandrani, and decided to tell the truth. "And because I genuinely hated you. I wanted revenge for twenty years of having been manipulated toward a goal that held no more substance than my dreams."

Kavya was a strong woman. Any other would have railed and cussed and blamed him—rightfully so, it seemed. Layers of guilt. Soon he would be buried beneath them, with only a life of berserker mindlessness to swirl free of the cloying dirt.

She was strong because she nodded. "You hated the wrong person."

"Seems that way."

"Are you crazy?"

"I don't know. And believe me, twenty years is a long time to ask the same question."

She drew back and did that odd thing with her fingers. Hands clasped at her stomach. Some particular adjustment to the alignment of her fingers. What followed was an expression of serenity and steady calm that Tallis envied. He coveted it more than he'd ever coveted anything.

What would it be like to go through life again with a sense of rightness and certainty? He'd known that feeling once, but he would never trust it again. Too much damage had been done when he'd relinquished free will in favor of blind faith.

"I don't think you're crazy," she said simply. "But I do think we need to go. A telepath must've driven you to these extremes. If she—or even he—has been feeding you these lies for two decades, then it must be someone with a great deal of power." She paused. Her gaze darted all around, as if the trees might come alive. "Two decades . . . My brother killed our sister almost exactly twenty years ago."

Tallis swallowed, his throat clogged with bile. In those dreams, he'd experienced some of the most erotic moments of his life, waking up in a flush of sweat and infuriatingly dissatisfied. Sometimes he'd wanted to stroke himself, with the image of golden flesh behind closed eyes. But the morning always brought the same nauseating doubts. Was he insane? Had he killed for no reason? Those questions cooled his ardor within moments of waking. More frustration. More mounting anger.

"I . . ."

He stopped himself. He clamped his lips shut and shook his head. Some shames should never be admitted. This was one. Hurt, revulsion, betrayal—he couldn't separate his emotions. They welled up in him and tempted the animal. The berserker dwelling in his marrow, sinews, and the deepest recesses of his mind had known the truth as soon as Kavya, *the real Kavya*, had lain beneath his body.

"I hope that isn't the case," he finished, knowing his words wouldn't gratify either of them. "But I can't deny it's a possibility."

"Then we may have found ourselves a common enemy, Tallis of Pendray." Kavya offered a smile. Too bad it was tinged with sadness and fear. "Until we have the answers you seek, nothing will come of my attempts to heal the wound Pashkah inflicted on my people. If he catches me, he will kill me. And if you insist on revealing the tricks played on you in dreamscape, he'll kill you, too."

They didn't resume camp, although Kavya was weary. So weary. But fear of Pashkah's retaliation propelled her onward. They trudged south. Although humans had built a highway that extended down from the Himalayas, following the deadly Rohtang Pass through the Valley of the Gods, past where her followers had encamped outside of Manali, the Beas River was Kavya's guide. She knew these foothills like she knew the sound of her breath. What she didn't know was whether Pashkah had remained in the Pir Panjal after killing Baile. Had he traveled, or had he stayed to learn these mountains as well as she did?

Had he ever followed her? Had he been there with her in Australia, where some of the Southerners had emigrated?

Not that it mattered. He could follow her anywhere now.

"I'll need another Mask," she said in the hours of early morning.

"Why?"

Tallis sounded strangely agitated. She was beginning to learn the expressivity of his voice, which was almost as animated as his face—if one paid attention. That she couldn't read his mind meant he was the first person she'd needed to understand by sense alone.

"Because Pashkah knows what I look like now. Even worse, he'll recognize this version of my mind. Night or day won't matter."

"He'll follow what he knows of us," Chandrani said. "His pursuit will be entirely psychic now."

She had stopped speaking directly into Kavya's mind—a deliberate means of including Tallis in their plans. That was new. Chandrani trusted no one but Kavya, and vice versa. Voicing her opinions to Tallis was smart, for now, if only to fold his canny strategies into theirs. He was skilled in the use of his Pendray weapons—seaxes and berserker rage, both. Beyond that, Kavya knew he was an unacceptable liability. How could anyone be so susceptible to suggestions pushed into his dreams?

But she knew the answer. The mind was a fragile place. With the right whisper from the right person, that whisper could become the truth.

"A Mask would disguise you," Tallis said without question. "What does it do to who you are now? Or who you really were? I assume you've used them before."

"Yes."

"How often?"

"This will be my fifth."

He stopped. His boots made a squelching sound on the damp rocks along the river. "Your fifth? Who the fuck are you, really?"

Kavya jerked. "I'm *me*."

"Layered with four other versions of you."

Why was he making this sound so wrong? It was the way of her world.

"With the right Mask," she said, "a Northerner could live alongside a Southerner in the same neighborhood. No fighting. No fear. Only the most visible, like our politicians, need them more frequently."

"And cult leaders."

"You're not one to judge. For centuries, we've needed Masquerades to save us from aggressive twins, and to keep the peace between the factions." She huffed a frustrated breath. "Disguise is better than fighting and dying."

Tallis continued their trudge, leading them down the

mountain. It was roughly thirty-five miles to their destination, Bhuntar, but a four-thousand-foot drop in altitude. Kavya felt renewed strength in her lungs as the thin air gave way to stronger bursts of oxygen. She eyed Tallis. The tension in his shoulders gave away that he shared none of her invigoration, as did the way stiff steps spoiled his warrior's grace.

"What are Masquerades?" he asked.

"Back-alley merchants. They're generally considered unclean. No one acknowledges a Masquerade as a family member, and none I've ever met live in pods. They hone their gift to provide Masks for the right price."

"Like human moneylenders of old—necessary but exiled."

"Yes."

He seemed bitter, even repulsed, despite nodding. Again, she felt the need to explain Indranan culture. How could Dragon Kings know so little about the rest of the Five Clans? How had they become so insular?

"Your gift is too dangerous," he said softly.

"That's rich coming from the man who used teeth rather than steel. Is a Pendray berserker any less dangerous?"

"There's no hiding what we do. You hide behind party tricks and layers of lies. I know who I am. You don't have a clue."

"You know, do you?" She heard the sneer in her words, which was new. Surprising. When was the last time she'd given over to words so pure in meaning and tone? "You're the man who doubts his sanity. You're the man who dresses like a human but hides a raging beast. You might as well be Jekyll and Hyde. Admit it and feel better for it. 'Yes, Kavya, I'm half of myself when I'm a regular man.'"

He spun and grabbed her shoulders. The sound of Chandrani's saber drawn from its scabbard should've been reassuring, but Kavya didn't want her friend's protection. She wanted to push Tallis. To learn more about him.

"I'm both," he snapped. "There's no need to choose."

"Liar. And if you keep lying to me, we'll part ways no matter how useful you might be in defending me."

"You think that's the reason why I'm traveling with you?" He clamped tighter on her shoulders. "Dragon-damned woman. You're the most perfect bait a fisher-man could want. A wiggling little worm to drag Pashkah out of hiding. If he's the person who's been manipulating me, or if he can provide any information at all, then with him is where I need to be."

"So you can, what, bite him again? That must be *your* hobby."

"I'll kill him. Get him out of my head."

"I'm a worm," she said with disgust. "Bait. You *are* as delusional as you fear."

His mouth was a sour pucker, when she'd felt it softer and more pliable, capable of moments of tender-ness. "Delusional, says the telepath who can't tell Masks from reality."

"You're a hypocrite, too. Or a stubborn moron, just like everyone assumes of the Pendray."

She actually grinned when all he could do was shake her. That snap of leashed aggression was welcome. It distracted her from Pashkah—the real danger she faced—and revealed another aspect of Tallis's character. He could've unleashed that aggression at any point in their association, but he'd held it back until the last possible moment. Then he'd possessed sense enough to use it against genuine evil.

"You hate your rage as much as you revel in it." Conviction strengthened her voice when she should've been speaking in whispers, if at all. "Gifts come with tremendous benefits and terrible consequences. The humans have gained free will as they've matured. Our kind claimed that right centuries before. That meant and still means deciding how best to use one's powers."

"Fair point. You win. This is me exercising my free will."

He stalked away. Again.

"You're used to running," she called. "That's the solution to conflicts you can't resolve. Tell me I'm wrong and I'll shout for Pashkah right now. I'll bring him down on our heads and we'll duke it out right here. Tell me I'm wrong, Tallis, that you travel the world because you *want* to."

He stopped. Rather than reply or even turn, he bowed his head—just a fraction. He didn't contradict her, but neither did he agree. She couldn't have gone through with her threat, just like he couldn't have replied. Both were obvious.

She jogged to catch up to him. The hem of her sari was soaking wet and coated in mud.

A breeze touched her face when she stood at his back. That breeze smelled of cold and earth and water—and Tallis. The leather coat made him look bulkier, more intimidating, but she knew what lay beneath those layers. Could she say the same about the mind she hid under layers of Masks?

"I know two things," she said quietly. "First is that a berserker saved my life. No matter what you think of that side of yourself, or how you resist it, I won't forget what you did for me."

"And the second thing?" His voice was roughly seductive.

Kavya inhaled deeply and focused on the swatch of skin between his hairline and the coat's collar. She wanted to touch him there. "To survive against Pashkah, I'm going to need your help."

⇒ CHAPTER ⇐
NINE

Tallis stood at the northern outskirts of the city of Kullu, where the valley pass dipped sharply down along the course of the Beas. The sun angled over the eastern ridge of mountains and banished the shadows. Likely it would've appeared over a flat horizon several hours before, but it had to climb that rocky barrier before casting its rays over the river.

"The Valley of the Gods," Kavya said reverently. She stood beside him, her eyes both sharp and somehow unfocused. She seemed to absorb the energy of that scene in a way he would never understand. Perhaps the same would be true of him if he again stood on the Highland moors and looked down over the North Sea. His homeland.

This was hers.

"Did the Indranan inspire the name?"

"Long ago, yes. Before the fracture. We roamed throughout the mountains and down to the Indian Ocean. Later, the Northerners came up this pass and continued on to China. The Mongols were quick learners. Many Indranan stayed with them. The Khan must've appreciated having telepaths among his number." She smiled softly. "Historians get so much wrong."

"Like Alexander and the Tigony," Tallis said, matching her small smile. He'd wanted to see the real one again, genuine and full of joy, but this would suffice. A subtle truce. "The arrogant son of a bitch thought he'd done it on his own. The Tigony are a vengeful lot, despite their airs. When he got too full of himself, they made sure his conquests came to an end. Period."

"How do you know so much about the Tigony? They're like you said—full of airs."

"You can't imagine them telling war stories with a Pendray?"

"The clan that backed the Greeks and Romans, who tried to impose their beliefs on Pendray-backed victims—Celts and Norse and the like. Not the best recipe for heart-to-heart chats."

"I have a Tigony friend in high places." Probably an understatement, considering that he referred to the Honorable Giva, the leader of the Dragon Kings' elected Council. Then again, to call Malnefoley a friend was an exaggeration. They tolerated each other because of shared family connections. Distrust meant they would never be close unless their ambitions aligned. Basically, Tallis was bragging. *Idiot*. "Let's just say my brother married a hundred times better than he deserved."

"You? With secrets? I'll never recover from the shock."

With a chuckle, Tallis turned away from her profile. Now that he knew the difference between the Sun and Kavya . . .

She was flesh and blood.

He'd been infatuated with a vision. The best scenario was that the vision was of his own making, but that would mean shouldering the blame for the damage he'd wrought. The worst case was that he'd played puppet to the likes of Pashkah. What he'd revealed in his dreams, what he'd done—Tallis didn't want to think of sharing that with a vengeful stranger.

Kavya was different. Out here in the wilds of the Pir Panjal, she was well away from her people. She couldn't read his mind. She was forced to be herself, and that was even more tempting than an image of perfection. He liked how he could unnerve her with his dry humor and even his silences. He'd needed to learn English sarcasm like another language, but it was useful when sparring with a woman who used thoughts more than speech.

His people, however, told stories. Huge, rambling, straightforward stories. Subtleties such as irony and sarcasm hadn't made sense. Tallis had arrived in England as an exile, completely unprepared for the cultural difference of a few hundred miles.

"What about the Southerners?" he asked.

"What about them?"

"If you in the North managed to mingle with the Han and the Mongols, where did the Southerners go after the split?"

"The coastline and the islands—Indonesia and the like. Some even colonized Australia. Every religion in this region is so fractured. Tiny pockets of belief. We migrated and split and kept splitting. Pods became villages, and villages became cultures. And we'd split again, always so distrustful and willing to move on, start again, if it meant the chance of being safe."

The Pendray way would've been to stand and fight, not run, hide, change, live in fear. He understood the desire to have one's gift from the Dragon made whole, but the cost was a civilization that resembled a petri dish of bacteria dividing and dividing.

Kavya led the way into a seedy, run-down area of Kullu. The idea that she would assume another Mask turned Tallis's stomach. He followed, with Chandrani at the rear. He knew they talked to each other. That shouldn't have bothered him, because they'd taken to voicing important decisions about direction and timing. The remaining, unspoken little things *did* bother him. For the first time in longer than he could recall, he was keeping company with Dragon Kings. They challenged him. Kavya in particular. As if his mind had tipped sideways, he was confused, angry, and uncertain of his purpose.

Find Pashkah?

Run from him?

Worse, it had been nearly thirty-six hours since he'd eaten. Hunger tended to bring out his less desirable traits. He was irritable and prone to snap harsh phrases. The beast needed to be appeased. Now that he'd called it out of its cage, that dark and raging animal was making more of his decisions.

"What happens after?" he asked.

Her strides were short but quick. She'd had no trouble keeping up with his pace, probably due to her familiarity with these daunting mountains. "After what?"

He needed to stop admiring the way the morning sun turned her golden skin to bronze. She glowed as if she really were the Sun of his dreams. "After you take on another Mask. Can he find you at all? Will you go into hiding? We've had different goals from the start."

"The start being when you kidnapped me among my own people for reasons that seem founded on madness?"

"Yes. That."

"At least you can admit some of what took place yesterday."

"What happened to how much you appreciated my saving your life?"

Kavya brushed long chocolate-brown hair back from her shoulders and used a sleeve of her sari to wipe her face. Only then did he realize that yes, she was rather a mess. He must look worse. "I thanked you once," she said, not breaking stride. "Don't expect more gratitude until you do something new to deserve it."

The October morning gave way to surprising warmth. Tallis unbuttoned his coat. He couldn't imagine the snow and winds this place would withstand come winter. Already, preparations appeared to be under way. Chopped wood lined each building in great stacks. The faces of these hearty humans spoke of survival. Deep wrinkles were born of squinting against snow and ice made into beacons by the high mountain sunshine.

Kavya lead them deeper into the crumbling neighborhood, to a few rickety buildings. This city itself was a destination known for attracting adventurers who sought guidance up the valley toward the infamous Rohtang Pass. The natural wonder, which was so dangerous that humans closed it from November to May, was a temptation to those whose lives lacked mortal thrills.

Tallis resented them, pitied them, envied their innocent cares.

But this was no tourist area. They approached a small pine building. It was daubed with mud and listed toward where the valley continued its downward slope. Kavya closed her eyes. Although he heard nothing, Tallis felt a pulse of energy flow from her body. Why had no one ever talked about that facet of the Indranans' gift? It didn't have to be audible for him to know it was there.

A man appeared in the doorway of the listing little building. He matched the pine shelter that surrounded him, as if a rough wind would send him twirling into the sky. He had to be pushing the upward limit of a Dragon King's life span.

"A Mask, eh?" He rubbed a chin covered in bristly gray hair. "That will cost you."

Kavya nodded. "It always does."

The man's name was Nakul. Kavya had known of his existence in Kullu for several years, because she'd thought she might need him one day.

"You're really going through with this?" Tallis asked.

He stood with his hands in the pockets of his leather coat, so Dragon-damned handsome that she was dazzled. People called her the Sun, but nothing compared to how the dawn graced him. Pink and gold were blessings that washed over his features. His skin was luminous. The cold ocean blue of his eyes was lightened without dissipating any of his intensity. Even his lashes were tipped with a silver sheen that matched his thick hair.

The berserker rage had spun everything about him into a wild creature, ragged and worn, but with so much strength that his casual posture couldn't disguise his vigilance in watching the trees, houses, and high mountaintops. He wore the weariness of a man who'd been at war for years. A man without faith. A man without allegiances or a home. A man who'd seen something terrible, unspeakable, and would never be the same again.

She wanted to hold his head to her body and stroke his hair until it was free of wild tangles and his mind was free of old, sad pains.

Frustrated by her capacity to be distracted by Tallis, she turned to face Nakul.

The old man scared her.

How many Masks had he dispensed through the decades? How many had he cleanly installed? Would age affect his work? Her mind already verged on having been soaked in too many artificial details. It would take a patient, skilled Masquerade to pick through those false touches and places new ones in between.

Pashkah would find her. She would never be able to reverse the damage to her people. Out there, women had been kidnapped. The Dragon only knew what was being done to them. The Dragon only knew what repercussions would come of their abuse.

"Yes, I'm really going through with this. You can step inside, or you can stand watch."

"I don't want to see any more witchcraft. I've had my fill for ten lifetimes."

Head high, she walked the small distance to Nakul's half-falling awning of tattered, dirty canvas. He'd bring it in before winter. Some internal sense of being in tune with her homeland said the snows would be soon in coming.

"I know who you are." Nakul's voice reminded her of his gnarled old bones. He was stringy with exposed tendons and veins. Whatever was left of his flesh hung in saggy pantomimes of a man's muscles. "The whole of mankind and the Dragon Kings would lie here in the dark, confused and freezing to death, if the Sun abandoned us."

A shiver turned her skin into a field of goose bumps. She didn't know which sun he meant.

"I will give you anything you like." Her peripheral vision found Tallis edging slowly closer. Skepticism tainted the air around his lithe body. "Just name the price."

"Come inside."

The interior of the shack was no surprise. It matched the slumping, resigned way the outside seemed ready to tumble down the mountain, consequences be damned. A tiny cookstove was all he had to fend off the chill. Behind the stove, in the scant space between it and the far corner, were blankets and stuffed burlap. Puffs of wool and cotton poked out from the rough stitching like a seeping wound. There was no order to his living space. Even aligning her knuckles did nothing to alleviate the tension festering along the path of Kavya's spine.

I shouldn't be here.

No choice.

"My price is, I want to leave this world."

Kavya's heart picked up speed. Tallis entered through

the only door. Negative judgment was written over his face, shadowed by the shack's grim, slimy darkness and obscured by the floating dander of neglect.

"I can't do that," Kavya said. "I have no Dragon-forged sword, and I have no intention of taking a life."

"You have other ways. *We* have other ways. You're the first Dragon King to seek my aid in more than ten years. That's ten winters of a chill I can't get out of my blood. I face another ten at least." His voice grew more impassioned. "I'll be a madman. A telepath alone with one's thoughts is a pathetic thing."

"Hey, now," Tallis said. "What does he mean that you have other means?"

Nakul looked as if he were already dead inside. He only needed a means of making it happen.

"We're Indranan, and we have our ways. I want Kavya to turn off my mind. Leave me uncaring. Let the elements ravage my body, but without the faculties to drive a Dragon King mad. I'll live out the rest of my life with frostbitten limbs and a stomach begging for food, but I won't be of this earth." He nodded firmly. "That, Kavya of the Indranan, is the payment you will give to me."

⇒ CHAPTER ⇐
TEN

Tallis grabbed Kavya's arm, which was honed of slender, resilient muscles beneath the sleeves of her sari. "Especially now, you can't consider this. A Mask is one thing. Lobotomizing a fellow Dragon King is repulsive."

With a sour mouth and rebellious amber eyes, she looked him up and down. "Better to kill them outright, Heretic? Your sins precede you."

"Sins that haven't been of my making."

"Bathatéi."

The worst curse a Dragon King could spit sounded particularly vicious when coming from a soul as placid as Kavya. Part of him was glad she possessed that much fire. They would both need it.

The Chasm isn't fixed.

He banked a shudder. He hadn't been reminded of that warning in months. Only his dream of the Sun had brought it back to mind. At least that much of her prophecy rang true, although he couldn't begin to know why.

"You can curse all you like, goddess," he said. "It won't change what you're contemplating. It's *sick*."

Nakul pinned him with eyes made watery and colorless by age. "Determine your own fate, Heretic. You're able-bodied enough to make that possible. I want the privilege of determining mine."

"Why not leave the mountain? The Punjabi plains are within reach. Instead you want to stay where the elements will maul your body? It's wasteful."

"Determine your own fate," Nakul said again. "Let this woman determine hers and me, mine."

"Tallis, tell me what you'd do in my situation. Risk death by Pashkah—"

"Or risk insanity." He smacked a fist against his palm, then turned sharply to jab an angry finger at her face. "You have more choices than that. Tell me you didn't have to fight your way free as a kid."

Kavya bowed her head as if it were an unbearable weight. "I did," she whispered. "You'd have me go back there?"

"At least then you had some control. There's no control in giving yourself over to this man. He's begging you for death, and you'd let him apply another Mask?"

Tilting her head, she assessed him so intently that he suppressed the need to look away. The Sun could be persuasive. She had that much in common with the beautiful demon in his head. He hadn't realized how many variations persuasion could take. He'd only been privy to what appealed to his sense of chivalry, reverence, and quite frankly, his lust.

"Why does it matter to you?" she asked.

Tallis flared his nostrils on a long, tense inhale. "I want Pashkah to give me answers. Worm, remember? Bait. He won't find you if you're some other person."

She'd be another person.

That thought ricocheted through his insides like a bullet, hitting vital places along the way: his accelerating heart, his struggling lungs, his closed fists that wanted to open and take hold of her—or remain fists and pummel anyone who tried to do her harm.

"Great." She shook her head with sharp movements. "The only time you defend me with words rather than weapons and bare teeth, and it's to use me as a means of getting back at Pashkah. When was the last time you did anything because it felt right?"

"When was the last time you did what you wanted? You've been guided by your cult's needs for so long."

She turned away from him and settled more firmly into her seat. "I'll do it," she said to Nakul. "I'll release your mind from this world. All I need is another Mask."

As Tallis watched, he pondered something despicable. What would be the harm in letting her wear another Mask? Her madness would mean a permanent split among the Indranan. She'd never be able to affect a new peace. The dreams would end. The prophecy would be undone.

Then what?

He'd have left Kavya to an abyss   the same abyss he was trying to escape.

A surge of primal instinct said his future was bound with this woman. This was Kavya. She was still his prize, and his baser nature still wanted her. He was beginning to agree with the animal in his soul.

Kavya yelped when two strong arms grabbed her out of the chair. Tallis's force and the rotting wood combined to splinter the chair into shards.

"What are you doing?"

"The old man said as much. This is me determining my fate. It involves you. I could apologize for that, but I won't. I'm being selfish."

She struggled against the hard, muscled forearm that wedged between her diaphragm and lowest ribs. "What are you talking about, being selfish?"

His mouth nuzzled the shell of her ear. "Remember what the animal wants."

A shiver of dread and, Dragon help her, unchecked desire was absorbed by his firm hold. "Are you about to go berserker?"

"No. I'm as clearheaded now as I've ever been."

He pulled her into the sunlight. The heels of her slippers shredded against the wood floor of the make-shift porch. Kavya used her nails to flay small strips of skin from the backs of his hands, but nothing stopped the frightening, arousing power of his demand.

Arousing.

No, no, no.

She twisted her torso and kicked her feet. "You want Pashkah to kill me, don't you? Or maybe you don't care. I really am some dangling piece of meat. A *worm*. You wanted revenge when you thought I'd infested your dreams. Turns out it wasn't me. Instead you'll settle your grudge on the woman who's the best fit."

"You weren't listening." He dragged her down the alley and pushed her against the wall of a weatherworn trailer. "I may be a Pendray dressed up in an English accent with too much knowledge of the world, but I am able to multitask. That means wanting you, no matter how else I'm occupied."

Chandrani's shout manifested as adrenaline-fueled fear at the front of Kavya's skull. It was all the warning she offered. Kavya twisted, slipped, slid—onto her knees, rolling away from Tallis.

Chandrani's saber sliced across his shoulder. Only the thick padding of his leather coat kept his skin free of the blade's cut. He spun and shrugged from beneath his pack. The seaxes became an extension of his limbs. He didn't hesitate. Saber and seax clashed in a shriek of steel against steel. Chandrani ducked, parried, attacked anew.

"Respect Kavya's wishes or this fight will continue."

Sweat lined Tallis's hairline and the back of his neck. His frown never eased. Although he held two weapons with the elegance of a man long trained in their use, he didn't have Chandrani's loyal determination, nor the ability to shoot spikes of pain down her spine, as she was doing to him. He hissed with each one. Her momentum edged them toward the outskirts of the small town. People had emerged from their trailers and shacks to watch.

"I don't want to hurt you," Tallis called. "Not the way I could. You've seen it."

"You'll never get the chance." Chandrani's face was a picture of concentration. She was a warrior to the core. Wielding her saber and forcing telepathic jabs into her opponent's brain was difficult to coordinate, but she did so with great skill. "The old man begs for a lobotomy I'll give you one whether you want it or not."

"Didn't you hear me? Do you want to be torn apart?"

Again he appeared on the verge of something *other*. The light in his eyes winked out. His features slackened, as if easing toward sleep. Kavya had seen that look when her brother's blood had streaked Tallis's mouth. How intent was he on keeping her from wearing another Mask? Would logic even matter if he skidded past a berserker's invisible threshold? It would be like talking a wolf back from his latest kill.

"Stop!"

She couldn't let them hurt each other. Chandrani, for all her determination and loyalty, would not survive this confrontation. Soon Tallis would slip beneath her ability to hurt him with telepathy. The animal was immune. Chandrani wasn't immune to the fury Tallis could bring to bear.

Chandrani, he's already proven that he can hurt you. And he did worse damage to Pashkah, of all people.

He's bastard Pendray scum.

I know. Kavya blinked as Chandrani's attack lessened by slow degrees. *I won't let him ruin our plans. Please. Too many have been lost. To lose you would break my heart.*

Chandrani jumped back and lifted her saber. "I yield, you Reaper shit!"

Tallis seemed to flip a switch. The light in his eyes returned. He sheathed his seax. "You're done being an idiot?"

"Not if you keep insulting me."

"That's all I've got," he said, picking up the other seax and slipping it into the second scabbard. "Because you fight damn well. I'd never even try if we were human."

Chandrani frowned and studied him. "Some new trick?"

With a tight smile, Tallis shook his head. "We Pendray aren't up for tricks, remember? You gave me one helluva headache back in the valley."

"And you the same to me." She assessed them both. "Will you let Kavya do as she wishes?"

"Wishes and dreams and useless optimism," he sneered. "You're quite the pair. Even when faced with Pashkah's rage, you'd climb back into the hills and start again." What began as a glance toward Kavya intensified into a full-out stare. "If you wanted to settle down with a quiet pod, I'd encourage you to walk back into that shack and accept a new Mask. They'd never know you were the Sun. You'd never remember that you weren't Kavya. And I'd take my fight to Pashkah, Dragon damn the consequences."

Kavya swallowed past the dry lump in her throat. "I wouldn't stop."

"Then you need every bit of the brains you have left." He stalked toward her. Rather than touch her with what so plainly remained of his ferocity, he swept tangles of hair back from her face. The light in his eyes was magnetic now—that undeniable ocean blue. "Don't do it, Kavya."

He held her face and rubbed a thumb across her lower lip.

"Don't do it," he said again.

Had he repeated it as a command, she might have kept up her resistance. Instead it sounded like an entreaty. He wasn't begging, but it felt rather close.

Remember what the animal wants.

She saw it across every blindingly handsome feature. He was waiting as if his next breath depended on her reply. When had she been on the receiving end of such a plea? This man truly didn't know her decision. She couldn't read his mind, and he sure as hell couldn't read hers. She'd never been at such a loss.

"We'll find another way," she said softly.

A soft exhalation rolled down his torso. "Then we need to go."

"Not yet." Kavya faced Nakul's shack.

"What are you doing?"

"Honoring a vow."

"You didn't get the Mask. You don't have to do that now."

"I'm an idealist, but I know that my battle against Pashkah will not end peacefully. Nakul's battle is at an end. He wants to surrender. Unless you have a Dragon-forged sword hidden under that coat, I'll help him."

→ CHAPTER ←
ELEVEN

Tallis watched as Kavya emerged from the old man's shack. Her face was grim, her shoulders stooped. He couldn't imagine doing what she'd just done, but maybe that's because he couldn't imagine taking on that responsibility. Odd. He'd taken lives in service of a higher calling, but never because a man had begged for relief.

She trudged up a small hill that overlooked the hovel.

"Is it done?" he asked.

"I wouldn't be here if it wasn't." Kavya's gorgeous sari was ripped and muddied. She was a fallen angel. "I stand by my commitments."

"I'm seeing that."

"I can never tell when you're being serious or mocking me," she said, sitting on the cool, rocky ground beside him.

"One-on-one verbal communication can't be among your strong suits."

She didn't argue, which was an improvement in their ability to stand each other. Then again, perhaps her thoughts were still in that shack. "I don't agree with what I did."

"I didn't think that." He ducked his gaze toward where his fingers shredded a palm full of pine needles of their own accord. "Had I a sword, I would've taken off his head out of mercy. To know his body will live on for years is . . . harder to stomach."

Dark hair streamed over her shoulders in messy clumps. It didn't matter. She was herself, and he enjoyed looking at her profile. He'd come to doubt almost everything else.

"It was what he wanted. *All* he wanted. How many people can articulate that without doubt, and be granted their wish?"

"Few." Once again he regarded the city where it sat nestled along the Beas. Chandrani had taken it upon herself to find a marketplace of some kind, no matter how rudimentary, to procure provisions. "Your guard. What will she use for trade?"

"I don't know. It will be a testament to the value of her armor or the intimidation of her bearing."

"She has both in excess," he said dryly. "You know, I'd developed the impression that the Pir Panjal were the exclusive domain of the Indranan. The Sun Cult was all I sought. To realize that humans without gifts other than ingenuity and community can also weather these harsh climes is . . ."

"Humbling? Don't say it. It doesn't fit you." She sighed, which sounded more weary than a woman should ever sound. "Are you one of those Dragon Kings who thinks us better than human beings?"

"I've known too many good people to class them all as inferior. But perhaps I've taken aspects of their culture for granted."

"That's quite a concession coming from you. Practically admitting a wrong."

"It's the best I can muster, goddess." He grinned at her perturbed glare. He'd use the epithet over and over if it meant gathering more of her rare expressions. But he sobered. Maybe part of him remained in that shack, too. "Was it difficult? What you did to Nakul?"

The answer was etched across her soft features before she replied. "Yes."

"Then I'm proud of you."

Kavya stood abruptly. "Don't condescend, Heretic. It's beneath even your low opinion of me."

"My opinion of you is . . ."

She stared down at him. For all his strength and the thunderstorm of his gift, he was beneath her in unnerving ways. "Is *what*, Tallis?"

"Changing."

Chandrani climbed the slight rise. "Kavya, I brought food."

The women quickly embraced and continued up the slope toward a clump of evergreens. Kavya briefly looked over her shoulder—the most minute invitation. Tallis had been waiting for it.

"He doesn't deserve any more from us," Chandrani said coldly.

"He saved our lives."

"And put yours in danger."

Kavya shook her head. "I put myself in danger. What did you find?"

Chandrani unloaded a burlap sack of crusty bread, hard cheese, fruit, a hairbrush, homemade soap, and bottles of water. "It was the best I could do with what I had."

With a hearty clap to the woman's back, stronger than Tallis would've imagined, Kavya smiled. "Don't apologize. This is far more than I expected."

They ate in silence, before each descended into town to find water for washing. Tallis's urge to follow Kavya was strong.

Chandrani stood overlooking the impoverished houses below. Her face was blunt, with a square jaw and a strong nose. A graceful brow was all that saved her from appearing overly masculine.

"Will you tell me more about her?" he asked.

"If she wishes to tell, then you'll learn who she is." Chandrani readjusted her scabbard and checked the position of her saber. The curving blade was so long that it reached below her knee. "But know that she keeps secrets even from me."

Tallis couldn't help a rueful smile. "You'll probably be insulted, but that doesn't surprise me."

"I . . ." The woman glanced around. Even in the midst of their conversation—seemingly as awkward for her as it was for him—she kept her eyes alert for trouble. They were allies paired for but a day.

He picked up another handful of pine needles to shred. "What is it?"

"I'm glad you stopped her from assuming another Mask."

"Oh?"

"In the days after she takes on another, I hardly recognize her thoughts. Only pieces of her come through. Until she gets a handle on the new layer, she isn't herself." Chandrani looked down. A bowed head didn't suit her. "I've feared that after another Mask . . . she might not find her way clear."

Tallis nodded with an expression that suited the woman's frank admission. "Then I'm even more glad I did what I did."

Revitalized after a good washing, Kavya wanted to squirm because of the steady attention Tallis paid her. He was infuriating—strange, uncomfortable, wholly unknown. He was speaking some other language. Not the guttural force of the Pendray's incomprehensible words, nor her own people's elegant tongue. He spoke with his intense expression and the temptation of his azure gaze.

And those unnerving silences. He'd hardly said a word during their descent. She could barely keep herself from shouting, "Say something!" Anything to better understand the man who was both enemy and ally.

So . . . she would learn to speak his language. Verbalize her thoughts. Spar with him. Try to keep up. No way was she going to be tied into knots by this man.

"You were right," she said plainly, standing before him.

He crossed his arms. The leather of his coat creaked around the motion. He was intimidating, with scaxes crossed behind his back and no softness in his perfectly symmetrical, perfectly formed features. "This I must hear."

"Do you want to make swallowing my pride any more difficult?"

"I want you to remember it, so it's not so difficult next time."

"You expect there will be a next time?"

"I may be confused out of my skull, but on occasion, I make the right choices and say sensible things. What did I do, goddess?"

"Pashkah would've killed me had he found me alone behind the altar."

Chandrani made a sound of protest in her throat. "Kavya, you can't think—"

"I don't mean it as an insult to you, my friend. Against what appeared to be twenty Black Guards, even you and the rest of my protective force would've been hard-pressed to save my life." She nodded toward the man whose smirk had eased into a wary sort of appreciation. "Tallis managed. And he reinforced your fears about my rash intention to wear another Mask. I don't want to hide again. Pashkah will always come for me." Feeling more put-together after the cold sponge bath, she straightened her spine. "I can't lead anyone if I'm running from him."

"You sound different, Kavya," Chandrani said softly. "What is it?"

"He's been a twenty-year boogeyman with the power to kill me. Many people might want to kill me, including those I never suspected." She quirked a smile toward Tallis. "So why make decisions based on fear? I need to take the offensive."

"Are you giving up on our goals of peace? Kavya, you can't."

"No, but I won't be caught out like that again. I must protect myself before I consider bringing others with me. They . . ." She swallowed so hard that tears gathered at the corners of her eyes. "They trusted me, and that

I knew what I was doing. I *didn't* know. Pashkah could've been anyone—one of the human cartels, or gangsters from the North or South who benefit from our continued feud. The longer we fight, the better the trade in Masks and other so-called remedies for our gift." She met Tallis's eyes with what felt like a dare. Why did she care what he thought of her plans? Or her deep regret? If anything, she should be hiding her plans from him. "I'm not stopping what must be done on behalf of the Indranan."

A twist of emotion shaped his mouth, which was a restrained reaction coming from him. Such a finely shaped pair of masculine lips. She'd felt that soft, damp skin against hers and wanted more. Rational thought didn't change what her body craved. And she'd be lying if she thought it was merely physical. Held in Tallis's embrace, her worries had melted like ice in the spring.

"Don't look at me, goddess. I'm not one of your true believers. I have plans of my own. If they conflict with yours, then we should move on."

"I tried that after escaping the valley. You came back."

His smirk flashed. She was coming to like its appearances. That meant she'd caught him by surprise.

Yet a task harder than dealing with Tallis still remained.

She turned to Chandrani and took hold of the woman's upper arms. "I have a favor to ask, my dear friend."

"Again, you sound different. That old Masquerade didn't do something to you, did he?"

"No," Kavya said firmly. "Come see."

She invited Chandrani into her mind. They shared

old memories. Good memories. The memories both trusted as genuine. Even painful recollections held truth—perhaps more than those of laughter. Any Mask could falsify happy impressions: sunshine, a child's smile, the hand of a friend entwined with one's own. But what Masquerade was skilled enough to create terrors and heartaches that felt undeniably *real*? Those were particular to the soul's darkest places.

So she gave Chandrani their first night together in Delhi, and she offered the tears they'd shared after Kavya had killed Chandrani's sister, Leela. It had been the only way to keep Leela from taking what didn't belong to her. Chandrani's gift. Chandrani's life.

"I need you to go," Kavya said, voice rough. "Go home to your pod. Marry Nirijhar. He's been as faithful to you as you've been to me. Time to honor your promise."

Chandrani shook her head. "He would understand. He knows I need to protect you."

"No." Kavya firmed her voice. She'd rarely used her gift against Chandrani—only *with* her, to exchange information and comfort. But she did so now, adding mental persuasion to her words. "You need to stay here. We're from the North. Our people may listen." She concentrated harder. "Marry Nirijhar and indulge in the reward of his comfort. Talk among those who'll listen. Tell them about Pashkah and how I'm not giving up. Those who will listen will also be those who talk. They'll pass on what they've heard. Peace needs to come from the people or it will never stick. Our hopes cannot hinge on what might appear to be the dogma of a single woman."

"Leave you." Chandrani's words were flat.

"For now."

That lump had returned. Rarely had Kavya spent a day without Chandrani, not since their first introduction when they'd both eyed the same loaf of bread from an unsuspecting vendor. Kavya had snatched it first, only to be chased down by a much bigger, stronger girl. In the end they'd laughed at the vendor's sad attempt to shout for police, and they'd shared the bread.

In the years since, they parted only when Chandrani returned to visit her birth village, even higher in the Pir Panjal. She and stout, strong Nirijhar had fallen in love. It was time to let that love run its course.

"I'll return," Kavya said. "I promise."

Chandrani eyed Tallis with dark suspicion. "And if I go?"

Kavya's smile was sardonic. "Then I'll have a man at my side, too."

"I still don't trust him."

"Don't think that I do. But he and I are bound by mysteries neither of us want looming over our lives. Until those mysteries are solved, I doubt he'll let me be harmed." She slid her gaze toward Tallis, whose averted face spoke of disinterest, but whose posture leaned toward their conversation. "Isn't that right, Reaper?"

"Yes." The quickness of his reply confirmed Kavya's guess. He had been hanging on to every word of the conversation. She liked knowing that her guesses about his physical cues were becoming more accurate.

"See?" She returned to Chandrani. "You want to do what's right, not just what's best for me. So you have new orders, Chandrani of Indranan. Hug me. Promise you'll marry the man you adore. And bid me a loving farewell."

✦ CHAPTER ✦
TWELVE

Tallis stood at Kavya's back as her bodyguard trudged away. The only dejected thing about the woman was a sense of having failed to win an argument. Her back was straight, her strides confident. If he hadn't been privy to the spoken portion of their conversation, Tallis wouldn't have guessed she was anything but a determined soldier. Off to do her duty. And apparently off to get married.

"Where does she live?"

Kavya touched the bottom curve of one eye. A tear? Tallis didn't want to be moved, but if this was real, he wanted to know what it looked like and how it felt. Whatever was blocking her telepathy might not last. He wanted as many details as possible about her true self.

"Far north of the Rohtang Pass, in a city called Leh—nearly the northernmost city in India. Her family believes themselves personally touched by the Dragon because of their proximity to the Chasm. I don't know of any other Dragon Kings who live nearer."

"Yet she followed you?"

"No, she fled. As we all do. Mumbai and Delhi are cities where one can blend in and start new lives." She shrugged—a jerky motion, as if yanked by a careless puppeteer. "There's nothing else we can do. As a people. Unless I . . ."

She shuddered. When Tallis moved nearer, she held out a warning hand. "No," she said. "I don't want you near me."

"What was that you told her, about how you could count on me to keep you safe?"

"What else would I have told a friend who didn't want to leave my side? That I think you're delusional and dangerous? That as soon as you've untangled the brambles in your head, you'll do something stupid like maul me in my sleep?"

"Depends on how you define *maul*."

Her expressions were gaining so much candor. Right now her face showed a combination of disgust and embarrassment. "Chandrani had to go, and I'll leave as well. Heading south. Hopefully Pashkah will assume I've gone to Delhi, back to the streets where I grew up. He'll have learned that much about me now."

"After just a few minutes together?"

"Do you have siblings, Tallis?"

"Five." He twitched down to the bones. "Well, four now."

Kavya's brows drew together. "Four?"

"Leave it," he said sharply.

Just when Tallis was convinced she'd keep probing, Kavya only nodded. "Would you know their thoughts and feelings after only a few moments?"

He closed his eyes and remembered green—so much bright, kelly green touched with the mind-blowing purple of heather in bloom. He remembered his brothers and sisters. Then he tried to imagine telepathy between them. He couldn't do it, but fact overlaid his sudden, choking flush of memory. "Yes, I could. A long time ago."

"Then know that even in combat, Pashkah learned more about the last twenty years of my life than I'll ever know about another person."

"Did you learn the same from him?"

"Yes." Her face paled. It looked sickly, unnatural compared to her usual golden coloring.

"And you'll keep that to yourself?"

"As a kindness." She shuddered and pulled deeper into the under-armor padding Chandrani had left behind. "So . . . anywhere but India."

Tallis exaggerated his movements as he looked up and down the valley. "How do you expect to get out? By sailing down the Beas?"

She tipped her head, frowning. "How did *you* get here?"

"By sailing *up* the Beas."

Her laugh was like the soft song of birds or the ringing of church bells in celebration. He was transported back to an evensong performance at Bath Abbey. The unfiltered waters of the Roman baths had still flavored his tongue with salt and oil. Children's voices had raised in song. He hadn't believed the words intoned by the vicar, but his cadence had calmed Tallis's soul.

That was Kavya's laugh.

"There's an airport ten kilometers south of here, you ridiculous lout. Outside a village called Bhuntar."

"An airport." Tallis laughed, too. He let out the sound, as if grinding tension could be released so easily. Maybe it could be.

"Did you think we use magic spells and rafts made of inflated animal hides?" She shared his grin. "Not anymore. Unless you'd rather walk or sail, I suggest you get your mind out of medieval times. We're not all Tenzing Norgay helping Englishmen climb Everest. Come on." She nodded to indicate the heart of the city. "We can take a shuttle to the airport and decide where to go to regroup."

Tallis shook his head and followed the Sun—who'd suddenly decided to find a sense of humor.

She turned to glance at his profile. He could feel the weight of her inquisitive eyes, not just then but every time her gaze sought his face. There was curiosity and confusion and wariness. He wanted other reasons for her to look at him, but Dragon be damned if he could name them.

"You really think we're banished up here in the peaks, backward people like Sherpa herders and folks bunkered down in Himalayan igloos . . . don't you?"

"No," he said. "Just because I trekked up from Punjab and missed what I assume will be a five-star deluxe airport doesn't mean I'm ignorant of your people. I've been here nearly three months."

"Stalking me?" Although Kavya's eyebrow was arched with sarcasm, he couldn't return her jest.

"Yes. I was actually surprised when I found your followers' camp. I hadn't expected anything so organized. I'll admit to expecting little burrows or hideaway shelters in a forest like this."

Kavya's mouth tightened until the blood drained away. "I should have. That would've been safer."

"How? It took me months to find you because I don't follow brainwaves and Indranan witchcraft."

"I'm not a—"

"In other words, I didn't have the gift Pashkah does. All he needed to do was open up his mind and fish out the largest collection of Dragon Kings in India, Nepal, wherever."

Late rays of light shone on her face, adding artificial color while she was still pale. The ground was slippery and steep. He instinctively reached out to steady her with an arm around her waist. She flinched. "I don't need your help," she said.

"Look down."

Kavya at least listened that much. She inhaled quietly but sharply. The instep of her slipper was mere inches from landing squarely on a broken bottle's sharp edges.

"We're not the Garnis with their senses and reflexes," he said, "but the Pendray aren't too shabby when it comes to the physical world."

"And all without telepathy."

"None. Just . . . looking. Keep your eyes open, goddess. We're going to need it for both our sakes."

She glanced down at where he still held her around the waist. "Think I can walk now?"

"Remains to be seen."

Relinquishing her small, warm body was harder than he would've liked, and it was certainly harder than he would admit to her. She was like holding fire. Not for the first time, he was glad she couldn't parse his thoughts.

"Do you still want me?" she asked.

Now Tallis was the one to stumble. He let go so as not to drag her down with him. That meant he landed alone on his ass, smearing his coat in the gooey pavement grime left by the end of the rainy season. "That was mean."

She laughed again and headed down the slope without his assistance, although she watched her steps with more attention.

Tallis pushed himself up. He pulled the tail of his coat around and grimaced at the slash in the leather. But he couldn't bring himself to raise a temper. There were so many other reasons to let his temper off its chain. Right then, Kavya wasn't one of them.

"Yes," he called. "I still want you." He caught up with her in a minute. "Besides, I bet your impression of the Pendray homeland is little better than my misconceptions."

"Let me see . . ." She posed her head as if in deep thought. "Highland people wearing skins and living in grass huts. Sacrificial lambs. Faces painted blue before battle where the field of combat is overrun with berserkers spinning like helicopter blades. Oh, and some live by the sea. Boats that withstand the worst storms. Myths of gods that say only the bravest make it to . . . where is it?"

"Valhalla? Depends on who deified us." He cocked one brow. "Withstand the worst storms? That sounded almost appreciative."

He took her hand, just because he wanted to. Let her fight him off.

She didn't.

"Assume the worst if you want," he said. "I'd rather you keep that note of admiration. It does a poor dumb Pendray's soul good."

Taking the shuttle to the airport should've been a simple affair. Short. Bumpy. Full of people. It was anything but simple with Tallis crammed beside her on a seat upholstered with ripped, stiff leather. Springs stuck into Kavya's back. She tried to arrange tufts of stuffing to cover the worst of the metal, but it didn't help. She sat very straight and tried to focus on the scenery that passed through a mud-splattered window.

She'd been born near here. These foothills had once been her home. An innocent home, despite the tension that warped her parents—the parents of triplets. She wondered how it must've been for them, counting down the days until their children's gifts manifested. For years, Kavya had lived in blissful oblivion. The sensible thing for Indranan parents to do would be to separate their children at birth, and some did. Most lived in hope that history wouldn't repeat itself. For their clan, however, history meant making the same mistakes, no matter the generation.

She, Pashkah, and Baile had been raised together. Played together. Loved one another. Baile had been the princess, always dressing up in their mother's saris and insisting on flashy decorations in her long, long hair. Pashkah had been rough-and-tumble, with a smile no one but his sisters could resist, even when strange moods had distanced him from everyone. Kavya had been the quiet one . . . especially when she learned of the trials that would await them. No one had told her. She'd learned in that way children learn things their parents aren't prepared to explain: through rumor and whispers. She'd even warned Baile and Pashkah.

They would never hurt one another. At the age of ten, they'd sworn it. They'd even gone so far as to tell their parents of the oath they'd made, in hopes of relieving the palpable anxiety ballooning in their home.

Two years later, Kavya had found Baile and Pashkah fighting. At first she'd been able to convince herself it was play. Jest. Fun. Their thoughts, however, had been black with rage and burning hot with the need to survive—and to *take*.

Baile lay dead. Pashkah stood triumphant. Kavya ran.

Now she was leaving again. This time felt different, as if she was being pulled toward a conclusion that would mean ending the last of her old life. One way or another.

"Are you scared of him?" Tallis's query dragged her free from that downward spiral of thoughts. The topic, however, was still Pashkah.

"I'm not scared of dying, if that's what you mean. But this is my life, my gift. I won't give them to him just because he's a spoiled bully. Two-thirds of a gift from the Dragon isn't enough for him, but it's twice as much as he should have."

"What was her name? The triplet he killed."

"Baile."

Maybe her delivery stalled further questions, as had his warning tone when he'd discussed five—then four—siblings of his own.

Or maybe he was looking at the sky.

Tallis had leaned over her lap, supporting his arm against the seam where the window met the metal frame of the bus. Cold air seeped in through that poorly sealed crack. He dipped his face low, as if he were preparing to lay his head in her lap. Kavya lifted her hands. Fingers spread wide and tingling. She forgot to breathe. Although Tallis's clothes still bore the grit and pungency of the forest, she caught the scent of his freshly cleaned skin. Again her attention was drawn to that strip of skin between his hairline and collar. That's what she smelled, what made her mouth water. She wanted something as reckless as it was elemental. Just . . . *Tallis*. She swallowed and banked a heady shiver, unsure whether to push him away or touch the wild mass of silver-tipped hair that had fascinated her from the first.

Yet he hadn't been seeking refuge in her body, even if she'd been willing to offer it. Instead he peered through the glass, toward the rocky mountaintops and on toward the sky. Gray layered over his features. The shadows were banished as he stared straight up toward the light source, but the light wasn't clear.

"Tell me, Glinda, Good Witch of the North, what does that sky say to you?"

"Glinda?"

"Never mind. Just look."

Only, Tallis didn't shift position. He didn't retreat to his half of the seat. Neither had he let go of her hand while they'd traversed Kullu's knotted yarn streets and surrounding forests. Apparently once he pressed into her space, he decided to stay there. She should've minded. Instead she stared at the strong, corded tendon that angled down from his arrogant jaw to his throat. A glimpse of collarbone and a touch of masculine hair were visible where his shirt gaped.

Tallis had touched her bare arms, which had been surprising enough. The rush of heat circling like blood through arteries and veins said touching would be very different than being touched. Already she'd learned that kissing was different than being kissed. She wanted that control and to let her curiosity seek what it would—to solve the mysteries of how a man's skin felt beneath her hands.

Tallis's skin.

"Kavya," came his sleek, low voice.

She blinked to focus on his face, which remained brightly lit by the pallor of pale light. Gray over blue intensified the notion that his eyes would match the color of an icy ocean she'd never seen. Her hands were still poised above his head. Being bold and without asking permission—*he never had*—she lowered one to his temple and petted silken hair back from his face. Briefly he closed those haunting, haunted eyes.

In doing so, he released her from his spell. She still stroked his wild, gorgeous hair, luxuriating in her reward for being bold, but she glanced up as he had.

The sky was filled with snow.

It wasn't falling yet, but swift clouds were sweeping across the valley. The sun was just as powerful but hidden behind a layer of icy mist the color of dirty cotton.

"That." She tightened her grip on his hair, only noticing when he winced and laced his fingers through hers. "That's trouble."

"How long?"

"Thirty minutes. Maybe."

"How much longer till the airport?"

"Not enough time to commission a plane and take off today."

"Commission? What, no tickets? No cute stewardesses?"

"No *flights*. The runway is short and dangerous. Air

India and Kingfisher no longer offer regular service. It's all private pilots."

"I told you it'd be five-star deluxe."

"I could push you into the river so you could float to Karachi. The Beas makes it there eventually. *You* wouldn't."

"Been to Karachi. I'm just a tourist, goddess. Wouldn't want to waste time repeating the same sights."

"You're a jester without an audience."

"You're here with your hands in my hair." He glanced up through the window again. "What's your strategy? Personally, I don't like the idea of a blizzard. Wasn't on my travel brochure. Not in mid-October."

"We won't freeze. We'll get to Bhuntar and stay the night. If it's a blizzard, we stay a few nights. The runway is hazardous enough without snow and ice as an added dare to the Dragon's mercy."

Tallis sat back on the creaking old seat and crossed his arms in that defiant gesture of his. He adjusted his shirt collar and the layers of his coat, while Kavya coped with the loss of his warmth beneath her palms. His mouth was motionless now, locked in a mocking expression that said she was going to regret his next words. Regret them, or be angered beyond the ability to retaliate.

"Please tell me Bhuntar is smaller than Kullu."

She frowned, wary. "Why?"

"Because I want a tiny bed-and-breakfast. Breakfast optional. And I don't want there to be anyplace else for you to sleep other than in my bed."

✧ CHAPTER ✧
THIRTEEN

Bhuntar was even smaller than he'd pictured. Tallis decided that was a very, very good thing. The snowstorm struck with speed more akin to lightning than a blizzard. Then again, he had no experience with the ferocity of a blizzard in the foothills of the Himalayas. He was a man of the Highlands and a man of the sea— even a man of the world. He was not born to storms that sounded like planes crashing into tarmac.

Great analogy.

The shuttle had only just crested a hill overlooking Bhuntar when the storm obscured everything in a blast of white. The driver pumped what sounded like brakes forged during Clan Sath's reign as lords of the Egyptian Bronze Age. Ice beneath the wheels, or perhaps snow in the treads, made the bus fishtail. A car climbing the steep road swerved to avoid the collision. Several on the shuttle gasped. One woman screamed, and a baby started to cry. For the most part, the occupants were silent.

"This happens to them all the time," he muttered. His knuckles were white as he gripped an armrest. "Tell me that."

"Not *all* the time." Kavya's voice held the intention of humor, but taut skin across her cheekbones gave her away. "Sometimes we close down the highway and ski down the ice. Much more efficient."

"I nearly believed you. Your sarcasm is getting pretty good."

"I wasn't being sarcastic."

The bus didn't move. The driver pumped the accelerator as the engine turned over and over. It was the sound of helplessness: a vehicle that wouldn't start, when a half mile separated them from the nearest shelter.

Tallis wanted to smack himself in the face. *What in the name of the Dragon and the Chasm am I doing here?*

He was sitting next to the Sun, who was a flesh-and-blood woman unlike any he'd ever known. He was enjoying her company. He remained suspicious as hell as to her motives—and suspicious as to why he felt such an attraction. He couldn't trust whether his reaction to Kavya was of his own making, or some wiggling, undetectable nudge of an idea that wasn't his at all.

But . . .

The beast inside him had not lied and could not be deceived. Rather than spend the next twenty seconds listening to the driver try to resuscitate a dead engine, he closed his eyes. He let his mind reopen the memories he'd accumulated during his berserker fury—the feel of teeth sinking deep, the foul taste of Pashkah's blood. Spitting out the piece of flesh would be an insult too disgraceful and revolting for Pashkah to forgive.

Tallis wasn't in the mood to forgive him either.

Past that, through that, he remembered kissing Kavya. Yes, there had been lust and need. But his soul, if he still had one, had experienced a soothing rightness he'd never thought possible. It was as right as coming home. Maybe that's why he couldn't even depend on his deepest instincts. Tallis had no idea what it was to go home, or to be accepted with open arms. Why would he equate that fantasy with a woman he couldn't trust?

Fanciful, ridiculous bollocks.

"How much time before we're snowed in and can't leave this bus?" he asked.

Kavya searched the sky. Eerie pewter clouds lightened her amber irises. Flecks of gold glowed like burning flames. Her lush lips parted.

No matter the reason, no matter the insanity of bedding the woman against whom he'd sought revenge, he *did* want her.

So he would have her.

"This isn't good," she said. "The snow's collecting too fast. We stay or we go. Your decision, Pendray. You seem to think you and the earth are on friendly terms. Figure out her intentions, and make a choice."

"You're no fun when you're being condescending."

"Just returning the favor."

He frowned and took a deep breath. "Advantages of staying?"

"Warm for now. Lots of bodies. Guaranteed shelter."

"Disadvantages?"

Kavya glanced around the bus. "Lots of panicked minds if things get worse and stay that way."

"Is that the likely way of things? Get worse and stay that way?"

"October storms are freakish. No gauging if they'll stay for a few minutes or a few weeks."

"Then we go."

"Agreed."

He grabbed her hands—then hesitated. She was dressed in a patchwork of silk and cotton padding. Slippers. No gloves. Skin exposed to the elements.

As a species, the Dragon Kings feared the inability to continue procreating. Extinction by slow measures. No more babies. No powerful future generations. They certainly didn't fear a bit of cold. But pain was still pain, even if their bodies quickly healed.

"You keep your mind trained on the town," he said. "Find us minds. Guide the way."

"And you?"

"Wind block." She laughed with a mocking tone he didn't understand. "What?"

"You'll see," she said, still smiling, but the tautness across her cheekbones had claimed the corners of her eyes. On the inside, she wasn't laughing at all.

Tallis hefted his pack, checked his weapons, and headed toward the front of the bus. Other passengers started talking in that low buzz noise of gathering panic. The hairs along the back of his neck lifted. He'd heard that same buzz when Pashkah had stepped onto the altar. Worry, building on worry, building on worry . . .

The snow was going to be ball-bustlingly cold, but he didn't want to be stuck in a group of freaked-out innocents when his sense of claustrophobia kicked in. The Pendray loved open spaces and sweeping Highlands. Tight little shuttles crammed with panicking humans was enough to spark a flare of red across his vision.

The bus driver said something he didn't understand. Tallis glanced back at Kavya for explanation. "He says he'll have it started any minute now."

"Does that change your decision?"

She shook her head. "Out."

He yanked on the lever to open the bus door and jogged down three steps. Wind smacked his face like a punch. Unlike any Tallis had ever known, this wind held nothing back. If he hadn't been gripping Kavya's hand, he'd have thought himself alone in a swirling maelstrom of pure ice.

She pressed her mouth against his ear. "Block that wind, Pendray. Dare you."

Tallis grinned into the worst of the snow. "I'm doing a piss-poor job at it. I admit it. Lead on, goddess."

Her fingers became five small vises. She wasn't letting go, and neither was he.

"You find our direction," he shouted. "I'll guide against the worst of the here and now." He caught his foot on a rock that poked out of what was already a half inch of snow.

Kavya rolled her eyes. "Like that?"

"Shut up."

The next thirty minutes were longer than they should have been. Tallis was certain they'd walked for at least six days. The hairs in his nostrils were frozen. He knew he should breathe through his nose, to better protect his lungs, but he was panting. Pain gathered in his chest. The cold pounded a beat meant to rip him open from the inside out. He focused on keeping Kavya from harm as she focused her gift on the tiny speck that was Bhuntar. Sometimes the fool woman closed her eyes.

Sometimes she talked to herself in the strangely sing-song language of the Indranan.

He was equally strange in thinking he'd like to hear her talk to him with those melodic syllables. Warm and safe and close.

Frostbite must be reaching his brain.

She swayed. Tallis reached out to find soft skin caught in a deathlike chill. "Dragon damn, Kavya. You think not saying anything will keep it from happening?"

"Hmm?" Her eyes were glassy, although he couldn't tell whether it was from concentration or the hazy sleepiness that preceded losing consciousness. "Damn you? What?"

Tallis wasted no time in opening his coat. The cold shocked his body like machine-gun fire. He hadn't realized that being cold and being cold while wearing a big leather coat would be so different. He swept her into his arms and tucked as much of the wool lining around her limbs as he could. Too much of her skin remained exposed.

"Go," he said near her ear. "Tell me the way. Pound it into my brain with a hammer if you can. Just show me the way and I'll get you there."

Kavya focused on two things: the collective warmth of hundreds of active minds in Bhuntar, and the very personal warmth of being held by Tallis. She couldn't decide which was more seductive. She only knew that to have more of his warmth, she needed to get them to safety.

Passing images into his mind would've been simpler. Half out of reflex, she tried twice before giving it up as a lost cause. She didn't want to risk losing the way. Instead she had to make her numb lips and stiff cheeks form words.

"Close," she said, teeth chattering so badly that her temples hurt. Her eyes stung, and a headache burrowed into her skull, using her ears as convenient entrances. "Another two hundred meters. First building."

"Dragon-damned, *lonayip* sonofa*bitch*." Rather than stop, he picked up the pace and held her even closer.

Winding her arms around his middle, where the coat retained the heat of his body as it worked to its maximum potential, Kavya nestled close. She offered words to guide him. When was the last time she'd spoken so much to one person? To groups, sure. They needed a clear, sure tone to rise above the din of other voices. Otherwise she spoke with her mind. Another mind would speak back. Here it was the intimacy of how his chest rumbled when he replied, and how his breath was a welcome flash of damp heat against her temple. This was the intimacy of speaking with bodies—tongues and lips and the thousand other things that went into verbal communication.

A different sort of gift.

Tallis followed the long line of what appeared to be a warehouse. At least for those moments, they were both protected from one direction the wind used to attack. Kavya rubbed her ears. The blizzard lived there in a perpetual cacophony. She would scrape it out if she could—grab one of Tallis's seaxes and hand it to him with the command that he dig out the mind-numbing sound.

"Cross to that building with the high gable," she said

past numb lips. "People eating and drinking. There's a fire. A couple is . . ."

Another chuckle rumbled out of his chest, where she pressed tighter with every step. Only his embrace kept her from shattering into chunks of ice. "A couple is what, goddess?"

"Naked together. Upstairs. There must be rooms."

"Is that all? Naked?"

Even as he teased her, he crossed the wind-whipped street toward an inviting orange glow. A few more strides and she could make out windows lit from within. A tavern? A bed-and-breakfast? Dragon be, just *anything*.

"Not just naked." Her relief was so close and potent that she said aloud what she'd only ever thought. "They're fucking."

"Very nice." Surprising admiration shone through Tallis's wind-scoured voice. "I didn't think you had it in you."

"I have a lot in me. Your thick Pendray brain can't hear much of it."

He gave her bottom a quick pinch. "Then you'll just have to show me instead. The Dragon Kings play charades. The world's worst potential game show."

Kavya giggled, made half hysterical by their intimate, dangerous trek. "The Tigony would refuse to play because it would be too debasing."

"If they did, they'd charm the audience and win hands down."

"Garnis, of course, wouldn't show up."

She could become addicted to the way he laughed, with the whole of his body, yet centered where her ear pressed against his sternum. She didn't like admitting such vulnerable thoughts, but they remained front and center.

He laughed that way now.

"The producers wouldn't even put out a chair for them," he said. "The Sath would know everything because they'd have found out the questions in advance."

"Thieves," Kavya said without malice. Yet she knew their kind. A Sath would trade just about anything for a secret. "The Indranan would either learn the answers telepathically or kill each other trying."

"I like that you can laugh at your own people, no matter how grim." Tallis kissed the top of her head. "And the Pendray would tear the place apart in a child's tantrum when they didn't get their way."

He put her down as they reached the building. The snow was cold against her feet, which remained barely covered by her shredded slippers. Her knees were unsteady after having been carried. She righted herself using the solid steel of Tallis's upper arm. "And thus ends our attempt to cast the Five Clans in a game show."

"We didn't do very well." He smoothed hair back from her temples. The wind took it, scattered it, and he smoothed it again.

"No, but everybody needs a hobby," she said, returning to their first shared jest. "And we saved ourselves the embarrassment of looking like fools in front of potential investors."

"We'll save our skills at persuasion for getting a room at this inn. I'm *not* sleeping in a manger."

"You're going to be picky in this storm? I'd trade your seaxes for a chair next to the fire."

"And then I'd trade you and the chair back for my weapons."

They pushed in from the storm. What had been frigid and noisy became fireplace-warm and relatively quiet, filled with the soft chatter of two dozen voices. Kavya felt as if she'd been sucked into a vacuum. No screaming wind. No biting ice. She was standing on her own, but she didn't let go of Tallis's arm.

"Witchcraft," he whispered. "Have at it."

His expression was unexpectedly bright and teasing, with a dark pink flush across his features. He was half-sweating, half-covered in melting snow. His dark, silver-tipped hair was sprinkled with ice crystals that were quickly turning to gleaming droplets.

"On a small scale, maybe. Unless one of your hobbies means you've learned to pilot a Cessna off a short, slick runway that leads right over the Beas—you take off, or you drown—then I suggest we stay friendly with the locals. That means as little obvious manipulation as possible. I can't force them to behave out of character, or someone will notice. The more they notice, the more foreign and threatening we'll appear."

"Wait, how do you know it's not one of my hobbies?"

"This isn't the time for sarcasm. We need a pilot. That means being fair to the innkeeper and getting recommendations."

Tallis made a face that was complete slapstick. Scowling mouth. Deep frown. He looked like a child on the verge of a fit . . . until he grinned. "Very well. Play by the rules. You'll be the first Indranan in the history of our race to do so."

"Pig." She slugged him on the shoulder, but his heavy

coat protected him. So did his strength. Dragon be, his *strength*. He'd already recovered from carrying her down half of a very steep slope. "But that's not to say persuasion isn't in order."

"How are you going to manage then?"

"I . . . I have a favor to ask."

Wariness crept over his features. *As well it should*, she thought.

"What's that?"

"We know I can't read your mind. Maybe because you've been able to resist. I don't know how. All I know is that an unwilling mind is harder to read. Can you try? Try to give me something from your thoughts?"

Tallis's brow was furrowed again, with no playfulness this time. "Give you what?"

She inhaled. "Anything . . . *interesting*. Anything to distract the innkeeper and make him curious enough about what goes on between us to let us stay."

She knew how she must look. Ruggedly used. Wind-whipped. Exhausted. Some blood still splattered her sari in gory, dark brown constellations. She was desperate, and she'd do what she needed to find them shelter, but part of her knew this was important. Had she spent two days with another Indranan, she would've known what to believe . . . to *trust*. Until they fulfilled their respective ambitions, she and Tallis were bound. She couldn't decide whether to take comfort from that fact, or to steal a knife from the inn's kitchen and keep her eyes open all night. Knowing what kind of man had carried her through a blizzard was as important as food and a soft, warm place to sleep.

"Show me what you see when you look at me," she said. "Let me give him that."

"Right now? I see a freeze-dried rat."

"I mean, how you think of me in my best light. How you think of me when you imagine us upstairs."

"Upstairs like that couple? Fucking? You want me to imagine you that way and just hand it over to you?"

Swallowing her embarrassment and anticipation, she swallowed tightly. "Yes."

"I'll try," he said with a dark smile. "But I won't be doing it to buy a little goodwill from a horny innkeeper. I'll be doing it to seduce you."

⊹ CHAPTER ⊹
FOURTEEN

Tallis knew there was a practical purpose behind her request. It made sense to gather as little notice as possible in a town that small. These people might never have met a Dragon King, which meant he and Kavya would walk as gods among mortals. In bigger cities with more jaded populations, their kind didn't stand out so prominently.

They needed a room for the night. Tallis really didn't want to search the storm for another. This place had the rustic charm of a pub back home, inviting in the sense that anyone could walk in, order a pint, and start a conversation about politics or sports on the telly. Conversations might turn to good-natured fights, but that was part of the appeal. A little roughhousing never hurt anyone, or else he and his brothers wouldn't have escaped childhood.

He shuddered when he compared his upbringing with the actual terror Kavya must have experienced—or all of the Indranan, for that matter. No roughhousing. Life or death.

Beyond the practical, he was going to make Kavya work for access to his mind. Maybe it was possible if she focused hard enough while he made an effort to let her in. But he'd only just started to differentiate between the real Kavya and some dreamscape figment. He didn't want to start losing track of the real woman while she rattled around in his thoughts doing Dragon knew what sort of damage.

Her expression said doing damage was the last thing she was considering. Dark, gently widened eyes stared at him as if he'd asked her to disrobe before curious patrons. Some had stopped talking to watch their interplay. But Tallis hadn't asked her to disrobe. He'd told her the truth. She was the one who wanted to bare his innermost thoughts—fantasies, actually. So he'd give them to her. Any way he could manage.

"Imagine what you like," she said at last. "If I can get a glimpse of anything, I can use it."

"*Use*. That seems to be a common theme for you."

"Do you think I like this? I've *never* used my gift to manipulate anyone for personal gain."

"All for your altruism, I suppose."

She stared up at him with eyes so luminous and pleading that Tallis's heart jumped. "Yes. The idea of manipulating people for personal reasons . . . repulses me."

Her shudder was strong enough to affect him physically, adding a touch of nausea to fantasies and strategy.

"And you're not making it any easier," she added. She glanced around, nose wrinkled like a rabbit scenting an approaching predator. "They think we're making a scene. Is that what you want? Just do this, Tallis. We have your seaxes to barter, or we have whatever image you can conjure. Otherwise we're back out in the snow."

"And if you're just as incapable now as before?"

"Do it," she hissed.

"Fine." He pulled her aside, to a far wall banked with shadows. Although what appeared to be the innkeeper still eyed them, they had relative privacy. Tallis held Kavya's wrists in his palms, all of which were just beginning to thaw. He pushed past the white chill memories of the past hour and focused on the soft curve of her luscious lower lip. "You want it? You got it. Try to keep up, goddess."

He stared into eyes shaded to resemble freshly tilled earth, fertile and ready to welcome the spring, just as her body would welcome his. The pulse at her wrists accelerated along with his heartbeat. Kavya licked the lip he couldn't ignore—would never forget.

"Show me." But after breathless minutes, she began to shake. Those inviting eyes pinched shut. "I can't read a Dragon-damned thing," she said, her voice jagged with frustration.

Although he shouldn't have felt anything but relief, Tallis shrugged off a surprising sting of disappointment. His mind was filled with visions and dark fantasies. She couldn't see any of them. Their closeness was what had her pulse racing, and he should've been just fine with that.

Forget it.

Telepathy as seduction? Never again. He was Pendray—a man of the earth, of base things, of sexual appetites that surpassed those of the other clans. Besides, he'd had enough of temptation that began and ended in dream.

"Then we'll do it the old-fashioned way," he said.

"Here?" The word was a quick squeak.

He touched his mouth to her neck in a kiss meant to torment as much as arouse. She had him caught in tangles and brambles, and he wanted her just as trapped. "No, with words. I'll start. Do you feel my breath on your skin, Kavya?"

"Yes," she whispered.

"I'll tell you my thoughts here against your neck, and you can give whatever you like to our unsuspecting, soon-to-be innkeeper."

"You'll tell me what you want?" Her voice was quiet as the softest snowfall, not like the fire raging between them as fiercely as the blizzard they'd escaped.

"I'm lying on a bed, completely naked. Vulnerable. You're bare, straddling my hips, both of us bathed in light. My cock stands away from my body, aching for you. I'm cupping your breasts, exploring your sensitive nipples. You beg for more. You sound so desperate—until you demand more. My hands tighter. My touch rougher. You *say* you want me thrusting deep, but you never sink down. You never give me the release you promised time and again. No, you only want me violent and mindless, and you tease the fuck out of me until *I'm* the desperate one."

He swallowed tightly, breathing in ragged gulps. That particular dream left him furious and feeling violated all over again. He'd tried to remain distanced from the recitation, but he couldn't help drawing new passion from Kavya's reactions. She was panting against his temple, then against his neck when he straightened. He forced her chin up. Her eyes were wide, dilated, filled with delicious cravings.

"Now give him what you think of yourself." His voice was gruff, still affected by his agitated bitterness.

"I'm no enticement," she said quietly.

They'd only washed that morning, but they were both haggard from the most recent leg of their journey. Tallis would've given a good ten years of his life to kiss clean, pure skin and for her to kiss his scrubbed skin in return. Instead he closed his eyes and enjoyed the primitive scent of woman, mud, snow, even blood and the tang of fear. Beneath the brutal notes of that fragrance was Kavya, and she was aroused. Pheromones might as well have been 80-proof liquor.

She had the power to ease the sting of having opened himself so completely, so foolishly to a manipulative figment.

"Forget reality." He was so near to her cheek that the damp warmth of his words petted back against his lips. "Show him how you'd like to appear for me."

By the downturned lashes framing her eyes, he didn't need to be a telepath to read Kavya's embarrassment. "I know the facts. I've seen details in others' minds—too many, really—out of my own curiosity. But for myself? I wouldn't know where to begin." She shuddered and gripped his waist, as if the wind threatened to knock her down. "I've never had a lover."

Tallis wouldn't have heard her soft words had he been any farther from her neck, her jaw, her mouth. As it was, that lone sentenced rocketed through his body and pooled where his erection was losing patience.

"A virgin?" he breathed.

"Yes."

Old images of having been left continuously unfulfilled by a skillful, seductive dreamtime version of the Sun finally cleaved truth from fiction. Whatever entity had invaded his dreams, whatever had made him wild with the need to take, whatever had left him howling his frustration come morning—it hadn't been Kavya. She couldn't meet his eyes, let alone force erotic fantasies into his unconscious mind.

Outrage surged back to the fore. He'd been played the fool so often. Kavya wasn't to blame, but she was all he had. She was his only link to discovering the real culprit.

"Then give it your best shot," he said tersely, pushing her back against the wall. "Use what I told you, if that's all you have. We stay here or we don't. We sleep upstairs or we find a corner by the fireplace. I don't care. I'm done playing toy to an Indranan woman."

Kavya jerked her chin to level. Her expression was . . . agonized. "Do you have any idea what it's like trying to say something so personal out loud? We don't have to. Ever. Fantasies are whispers and glimpses at the back of a willing mind. Then when I actually *speak* a secret I've kept close for years, you ridicule my honesty? How is that fair?"

She aligned her knuckles in that peculiar way, pushed past him with a backward glance, and went to speak with the man behind the bar.

Tallis was left chastened. Nothing much about his time in India made sense. He couldn't imagine communicating as she described, but that didn't make him a complete idiot. She *had* given him something special—a confidence that didn't seem to be common knowledge. He'd fallen back on the familiar anger she didn't deserve, which meant he'd given her no reason to trust him with another secret in the future.

But what a secret. He pushed the heels of his hands against gritty eye sockets, where erotic visions changed. Making love to her would have nothing in common with being tempted and teased by the Sun. Instead he would lie over Kavya, lavishing her tense body with attention until she relaxed. Until she gasped, writhed, opened. For him.

A virgin.

As if she needed to be more intriguing, more compelling. He was an idiot with a mission. Suddenly that mission wasn't nearly as important as making sure no one but Tallis ever touched Kavya of Indranan.

While speaking with the innkeeper, Kavya felt the moment when he gave in to her request. It was the same moment her thoughts flashed back to Tallis's description, as hot as a red-tipped branding iron. Almost against her will, she gave the innkeeper the story she would never forget—the erotic story Tallis had tersely whispered against her throat. His apparent anger hadn't lessened Kavya's arousal. Instead she was intrigued by the potential for a pleasurable sort of brutality. He had her turned inside out with wanting and curiosity.

She gave that curiosity to the heavyset man with stiff black hair that stood on end. Knowing she shared something so intensely personal and *new* as a means of barter made her ill. Her stomach crushed into a pebble filled with bile and acid.

"Your anklets," he said simply, although his eyes were voracious and his mind begging for more. He crossed from behind the bar, pushing into her space. "I'll take them."

Tallis placed a hand on her shoulder. She jumped, then turned toward the thick shelter of his chest. "Your anklets aren't much to part with. One night's boarding and a meal for us each?"

The innkeeper's greedy gaze flipped between them both. Maybe erotic thoughts and a bauble of jewelry was the right mix, because the innkeeper nodded. His heavy jowls nodded after him. He was human, and ready to make concessions she wouldn't have thought possible.

Soon she and Tallis carried plates of rice and palak paneer up to a room with a single bed and a washbasin. Stark, cold, with one window, it was the closest thing to sleeping outdoors in the flash blizzard. But the food was warm and smelled delicious, and they were safe for the night.

As if the conversation about sex and Kavya's virginity hadn't taken place, Tallis shed his weapons and his pack. He kept the filthy leather coat on. Kavya shivered all the more for remembering how that coat had felt when wrapped around their bodies. He'd held her and carried her and made her feel small, sheltered, cared for.

The smallness didn't offend her, despite that irrationality. Had she needed to portray Tallis by telepathy, she would've used her gift to transform him into a living god. One touch handsome man. One touch skilled warrior. One touch raging beast with a pulse-pounding undercurrent of violence.

A protector.

But Tallis only sat cross-legged on the bare wooden floor and started eating.

"Not going to wash up?" she asked.

He cocked an eyebrow while inhaling another bite. His throat tightened over a swallow. So many new responses to how he behaved, and she didn't understand any of them—not truly, not physically, not in person. The perceptions she'd collected through the years were like a child's primer. The basics. Tallis could teach her so much more.

"Your food will get cold," he said. "Then when you're ready, there's a change of clothes for you in my pack."

"How . . . ?"

He grinned. "Don't ask. Kullu's a big city and we walked a lot of streets. We're not going to Karachi or wherever with you standing out like a vagrant at a wedding. Or me, for that matter. But eat something first. You look ready to blow away."

Her stomach agreed with a loud rumble. She dragged a thin blanket off the bed and sat beside him, her legs outstretched. Both of their backs were against the wall, with a clear view of the door. The room was small and spare, but taking up that position seemed automatic for Tallis—with his eyes trained where an enemy might invade. Kavya's caution came from how she thought about the world, constantly tripping from mind to mind in search of hostility.

That means of defense was so draining. She was exhausted.

Finding no present threat, she finally ate. No, she *savored*.

And she pushed her thigh against his.

Tallis shifted his shoulder so he could face her. She expected to see sardonic mockery, and in that, he didn't disappoint. "Hello there."

"It's for practical reasons."

His grin was cheeky, daring her to make thigh-to-thigh touching into something practical. "Do tell."

"Remember how you kept me disguised from those gathered in the encampment?"

"I liked that part. The rest of the day not so much. But those few hours in my tent are well worth remembering."

"You kept my mind occupied."

"I did."

"So . . ." She ate another bite, chewed, hesitated, procrastinated, and finally swallowed. "So do it again. Keep touching me. My mind will stay with you. Pashkah won't be able to find me if I'm disguised that way."

He affected a contemplative look. "You're telling me that the best means of keeping you safe is to have my way with you, until you can't think of anything else? Just complete focus on the man who wants to seduce you?"

Kavya forced calm into her next deep breath. "Yes. Keep me distracted. But I need to know I can trust you."

"I can do that." He set his plate aside. "Just remember you're the one who mentioned touching. But I won't need to if distraction is the goal."

Kavya stared into his ocean-blue eyes and tried to imagine what tricks he intended. He was a Reaper but he had a great deal in common with the Tricksters of Clan Tigony. He was smooth, cultured in the ways of human beings, and had no sharp edges. Everything about him said, *Calm down. Trust me. I can make this happen.*

Only, she knew the difference between his slick exterior and the monster that lurked beneath. She knew the difference, and she liked it.

"Very well," she said. "How would you distract me without touching me?"

"We could always talk. Stay concentrated on my accent, which I've been told is marvelous for lulling women out of their knickers and into my bed."

"*Arrogant* isn't a strong enough word for you."

"We could fight," he said, grinning. "That worked well last time, too."

"That's a given, not an option. It'll happen no matter what you do."

"True, that."

He stood and left the room. Kavya waited, finishing up the palak paneer that was, indeed, growing colder by the second. Only a sliver of heat remained under the deep center of the rice. The whole time, she watched the door. Waiting. He wouldn't leave—not when he had hooked her with intrigue and attraction. Maybe this was part of his intention. He was distracting her by causing her to wonder where he'd gone and what he was doing.

After finishing her food, she used water from the basin—water that may as well have been ice cubes—to wash up. True to his word, Tallis had stashed a modest maroon sari in his pack. She felt almost feminine again when she wrapped the intricate folds around her chilled body, and used the comb Chandrani had procured to untangle her hair.

She was sitting on the bed, impatient, huddled with a blanket around her shoulders, when Tallis returned. He held a steaming cauldron of water, with his hands protected by two mitts. He took one look at Kavya and laughed. "Impatient, were you? Too bad. But for me, ice baths are only for those intending to get rid of one's arousal. I want to stoke mine." He set the cauldron on the floor and dunked a washrag. "Kavya of Indranan, I'm going to strip for you."

→ CHAPTER ←
FIFTEEN

Yes, taking Kavya of Indranan by surprise was quickly becoming the highlight of Tallis's time in the Himalayan foothills. Using the word *strip* before an admitted virgin elicited the surprise he'd sought.

Then again, she'd stolen his breath by transforming from a bedraggled traveler into a stunning, freshly scrubbed woman. She wore the sari he'd snatched from an unsuspecting merchant. Tallis had meant to be quick, grabbing the first he found, but the sari complemented her coloring to perfection. She was painted in shades of gold, bronze, and carnelian red, like sunrise over dark granite streaked with clay. With wet hair and her shoulders swathed in a rough wool blanket, she was the most exciting blend of innocence and sensuality Tallis had ever seen.

A wide-eyed temptress.

As if she'd been practicing the facial expressions that were so new to her, she shifted from curious to wary to flat-out panicky in the span of a heartbeat. "None of what we said downstairs needs to be fact. It was a means of getting us a room for the night."

"Will you use the same techniques when securing us a flight out of here?"

She looked away, etching her thumbnail into the wooden headboard. That word *use* made her so uncomfortable. Even sickened. Could she really have been so altruistic all these years? If given the opportunity to influence people's decisions, would Tallis have been able to resist the temptation? No matter how formidable his berserker, he didn't think he was that strong.

"We have days to figure that out," she said, still picking at creases in the wood. "The storm won't break soon. The runway will need to be cleared. The villagers won't make that a priority compared to making sure the roads are plowed first."

He grinned and wrung out the washcloth. "So what you're saying is, we could be stuck here for days?"

"Days—" She cut herself off, eyes darting from the basin of water to the white-pummeled window. "Perhaps."

"By the third or fourth night, we'll have to let the innkeeper watch. He won't settle for your mind games."

"Quit being crude."

"Fine," he said with a shrug. "I can always touch you as a distraction. I'm quite fine with that approach."

Shaking her head, she backed tighter against the wall. The blanket dropped down from one shoulder. Only then did he realize that she'd slipped a flannel shirt from his pack over her sari. She was silk and flannel. Sleek and warm. Completely alluring. He liked it too much that she was wearing something of his. Or, he liked it just enough, considering what he was prepared to do.

If he could go through with it.

"Do what you want." Her voice was resigned but her eyes still quick, darting, wary. Interested.

"I plan to."

He unfurled the rag and scrubbed it across the back of his neck, around the front of his throat, and up his face. The tattered washcloth didn't have the bite of a stronger rag, but the hot water made up for it. Tallis couldn't help but exhale in a shuddering sigh of pleasure as the warmth soaked into his skin and assuaged tensions he hadn't acknowledged. He'd been too tense for too long. As the tendons of his neck softened and relaxed, he only wanted more.

Meeting Kavya's slack-jawed expression of amazement added to his hunger. He was a man of the earth and the sea, but he'd lived among the human world so long that luxuries had become part of his definition of a good life. Circumstance meant he didn't have many opportunities to indulge. That made moments such as these more precious.

"Are you watching, goddess? This is only the start."

"You're not . . ." She pressed the back of her head against the wall. She couldn't get any farther from him unless she made a run for it, back into the snow. The amber flame in her eyes promised that wouldn't happen. "You're not going to go through with it," she said with more conviction. "I don't believe you."

"You don't believe me? Which part of my behavior has led you to think I don't follow through with threats? Or that I don't have it in me to be more nasty or underhanded than you can imagine?"

"I don't have to imagine nasty or underhanded." Her voice was tart and her expression fierce. "I've seen it and lived it. Give me softness and promises—*that* I wouldn't imagine."

"Alas." He banked an impulse to take her by surprise yet again, by giving her exactly that. "This is the best I can come up with. And for inexplicable reasons, you want to think the best of me. Strange, I know. So watch and enjoy. A living god is going to do his best to keep your mind thoroughly occupied."

"A living . . . Wait." She stood and crossed her hands as if to stop anything and everything happening in that small, drafty room. "Why did you call yourself that? 'A living god.' Why that phrase?"

"Not a clue. You're my false goddess. I might as well return the favor."

"No. I don't . . ." Frowning so fiercely that Tallis wanted to ease his thumb between her brows, she backed flush against the wall and tucked her hands out of sight. "Never mind."

Tallis shrugged, although her behavior set him on edge. Fuck it. He *wanted* her on edge, and he wanted to get clean. "Suit yourself."

He pulled off layers of shirts and basked in Kavya's quiet inhale. The water was still hot enough to numb the ends of his fingers. He rinsed the cloth, then set about rubbing away grime and sweat. The aftermath wasn't as pleasant, as drafts skittered chills across his skin. Whenever he closed his eyes to better absorb the sting of heat and the shudder of cold, he wondered what she was thinking. Was she equally affected by the moment? For all he knew, he could strip naked while sporting the hard-on to end all hard-ons, and she'd only stare at him with an expression of disdain and wariness.

Kavya was a hard woman to understand. Rather than

feel vulnerable, as he often had during dreams of the Sun, he was excited by the unknowns she presented during every minute of their acquaintance. She was the virgin, and yet as he washed more of his body, *he* felt inexperienced. Adrift.

This was supposed to be about distracting *her*. Seducing *her*.

Tallis opened his eyes and was surprised to find Kavya had stepped away from the wall. She was within touching distance. Had he been so lost in his thoughts that her quiet steps went unnoticed?

"You want something?" he asked with a lift of his brows. "Have you come to help me out or to hit me?"

"Both?"

"I like that, although it might depend on the order."

"Give me the rag." She snatched it before he any chance to reply. "Turn around."

Scalding cloth met the stretch of flesh between his shoulder blades. He hissed, then let the breath out slowly. She didn't caress him; she definitely meant the rough up-and-down to be a hearty scrub. But Tallis smiled to himself. She was washing him. Life had turned unexpectedly sunny, despite weather and terror and confusion that demanded he think otherwise.

"I didn't know I'd be getting help," he said. "Shall I offer to return the favor?"

"You know I already washed."

"In the equivalent of a glacial stream." He bent at the waist and shucked his cargos without pretense. Kavya gave a little squeak. "Now keep washing, or give it to me before you pass out."

She slapped the cloth into the water, splashing droplets of fire across his stomach. "I was only doing you a favor."

"Keep telling yourself that."

Kavya retreated until she once again connected with the wall. She was looking at him—all of him, with particular attention to his ready cock. That she remained clothed was lamentable, but she remained luminous. He'd never met anyone who seemed made of light. He was only thankful he'd discovered that she was a genuine woman with a temper and a hefty dose of arrogance. She was real. And she was still made of light.

Tallis continued his wash. He rinsed and scrubbed, rinsed and smoothed. She never took her eyes off movements meant to be practical yet provocative. At least he'd reclaimed his self-control, especially when he wrapped his cock in the hot cloth. Had he been alone, or had she been any more experienced, he would have stroked more than the once, twice he permitted.

Back around to his balls.

Back up to his aching, swollen head.

Then two more strokes.

As such, he managed the one part of his hands-off seduction he'd known would be most difficult—washing the physical expression of his desire—without indulging too much.

He turned away on a heavy exhale and washed his hair with their sliver of soap, rinsed out the cloth, and dried himself with his last clean flannel shirt. He stood naked before her for an endless span of seconds.

She only pulled the blanket more closely around her shoulders.

"Now, unless you want to stroke my prick as well, I suggest you lie down and get some rest."

Tallis grabbed the blanket from her slack hands and settled onto the single bed, his body crammed against the wall. There was plenty of room for her to join him, and they'd barely need to touch. Yet whether she joined him or not, he wouldn't be sleeping that night. Either he'd stay awake listening to her little sounds and intakes of breath, or he'd lie stock-still with her body tucked against his. Not touching. Only imagining.

She didn't seem ready to sleep either. She dimmed the room's one lamp, walking and moving as if in a daze. Using his coat as padding, she lay down in a corner of the room and made herself into a tight ball.

So he spent the night listening—dreading, hoping, wondering when she'd relent and come to bed.

Kavya sat in the corner wrapped in Sherpa, leather, flannel, and silk. So many textures, and so many scents. The scent of one man in particular would've kept her awake all night, had she been inclined toward sleep.

She'd never seen anything so erotic, all the while knowing Tallis had performed his taunting striptease for reasons that had nothing to do with enjoyment. He'd been distracting her; that much was legitimate. He'd also been mocking her, with his curling smile and arrogant stance. Everything about the casual grace of his body said he knew what it was to touch in ways she'd never experienced. He had kissed her, and now she knew what had been hidden under the bulky coat she used as bedding.

Male perfection.

She couldn't think past that word. *Perfection*. His limbs were long and strong, with muscles defined by lithe, sweeping curves. He reminded her of an acrobat or a dancer, where bulk wasn't prized so much as agility. Lines bisected his abdominals and marked the boundary of each cluster of muscles. His pectorals and lean, strong thighs were dusted with dark hair. She could see his power in the flex of every movement, and in memories of how he'd carried her through the blizzard.

And his cock.

Kavya pressed fingertips against her eyelids and kept pressing. She'd never seen its like. The male anatomy was not a mystery, telepathically or physically. Even aroused men were familiar to her—too familiar, in some circumstances. To stand in such close proximity, so that she could see every ridge and vein, was entirely new. He pulsed with energy that built and built and gathered *right there*. Yes, that was new indeed. That was new like seeing fire for the first time.

The sight of fire wasn't as impressive as its warmth. Feeling its warmth wasn't as daring as getting closer, closer, wondering how it would feel to be consumed by something so beautifully elemental.

Had she been some other woman, perhaps, she would be lying next to him—or beneath him, or straddling him. Huddling deeper into the safety of his coat, tucked in a corner beset by icy drafts was perhaps . . . oh, she didn't like the word, but it was cowardly. She was hiding from him. She could come up with a thousand protests as to why enjoying this man was a bad idea.

But she couldn't think past one. If she gave her body to Tallis of Pendray, she would want to give her heart as well. At least she knew that much about herself, even if her naiveté and arrogance had taken her by surprise.

She led with her heart.

The Indranan were supposed to lead with their minds, with thoughts always the first into the fray. In any conversation, in any battle, the mind over body and heart and soul. In that, she'd always been different from her clanspeople. Perhaps that was why she strived to bring her people together in peace and with hopes for the future—hopes that had everything to do with letting the heart have its say.

Love. Trust. Families without fear.

"You're not sleeping." Tallis's voice was so low that it blended with the moan of the storm's wind.

"I don't sleep if I can help it."

"Stubborn?"

"Self-defense."

He shifted on the narrow bed, where the springs composed songs to the slightest shift of his body. "Tell me?"

Snow-white light stripped the room of color and replaced it with shadow. He was hugging a pillow. The tops of his shoulders and upper back peeked out from beneath the covers. She couldn't see his eyes, but she felt their keen interest. Perhaps that layer of darkness allowed her to think of his interest as genuine, rather than a prelude to more ridicule.

"If an Indranan sleeps, she's vulnerable to suggestions from outside minds. It's an invitation for others to come play. I could wake up with totally foreign impulses deciding my life."

"How do you know you're not already under the influence of those impulses?" He sounded genuinely curious, speaking words touched by wariness.

"I don't, necessarily. A Mask is one thing. It's a canvas to disguise pieces of a personality. But thoughts born of a Mask can slip deeper during sleep—I've felt one or two. They don't ring true. Like a splinter in my brain. Usually I can root them out and categorize them as *not me*. Not me," she repeated softly.

"But you still avoid sleep?"

"If I can help it. Or I had allies like Chandrani. We'd sleep in shifts. One would protect the other."

"Like having each other's backs?"

"Something like that, yes."

"Your people . . ."

Kavya sat up. "You've lived among the Indranan for what, a few months? And only in an attempt to find me. That doesn't mean you're any more accepting of our ways. You only collect information to search for weakness."

He chuckled, like a teasing caress emerging from the blackness. "So quick to assume, goddess. I meant nothing cruel."

"Then what?"

"Your people—I don't know how you've survived. All gifts come with a price, but the Dragon chose the Indranan to suffer most. Nothing is as sacred as the mind, yet you have access to everyone's innermost fears and desires. To be honest . . . I'd read your mind right now, if I could, when I've thought the practice despicable." He shifted again on that telltale mattress, still hugging the pillow, biceps flexing in stark relief. "It's that tempting. Why speak, when I could just peek in and *know*?"

She needed to be closer. Elementally, she'd known this would happen. The compulsion to read any aspect of his body for truthfulness joined with her physical curiosity. Tallis of Pendray was a snake charmer—just charming enough to overcome her fear and frustration.

Kavya crawled the two paces toward the bed, dragging her makeshift bedding as a turtle would its shell. Hands shaking, she reached out and touched his forearm. His breath was sharp. He covered her hand with his and brought it to his face, where micro twitches of tiny facial muscles revealed so much. She was coming to think of touching his face as the sincerest means of knowing what was true and what was placating mockery. Coming from Tallis, the two were sometimes one and the same.

"What would you want to know?" she asked softly. The blizzard's winds kicked up in a frenzy of force and tiny, pelting ice crystals.

"What you thought of my body."

A laugh huffed out of her lungs. She was smiling when he cupped her cheeks, too. "How egotistical is that?"

"Very," he said. "I wanted to impress you as much as I wanted to distract you."

"And intimidate me. And tease me for my lack of experience."

His smile bunched beneath her palms. "Yes. All that, too."

"What else?"

"I'd want to know why you hadn't come to bed. Why is a cold corner better than lying with me?"

"You just admitted it: because you wanted to intimidate me and tease me. If I lie with any man, it will be because I'm desired, not the object of a dare or vendetta."

Tallis threaded his fingertips into her still-damp hair, tunneling down to her scalp. He tugged, gave a little shake. "This has nothing to do with vendetta."

"Then . . . what?"

"We're back to that pesky beast in my blood." His chuckle shone a light on his own failings. "*Wanting*. I'm not used to being denied."

She pulled back and sat on her haunches. "I don't believe that at all. The man known as the Heretic? I think your choices have denied you a great deal."

He withdrew the warm gift of his touch. The room went cold for reasons that had nothing to do with the storm. "Go to sleep."

Another burst of the blizzard's power slammed against the loft's window. Ice and terrible winds and the unpredictable nature of a squall. Tallis slipped from her thoughts. She couldn't stand remembering how much distance remained between them. No trust. No affection. Instead she reached out to find Chandrani. Was she safe? She couldn't have made it home over the Rohtang Pass so quickly, but maybe she'd been able to find shelter.

Kavya closed her eyes, reaching out, concentrating. Searching.

Chandrani.

She exhaled softly when she found her dear friend well on her way to Leh. The snowstorm had passed to the south of her path. She would be home with family soon, perhaps free of the scandal she'd face if associated too closely with the attack in the valley.

But then . . . another mind found her.

Kavya flinched in pain. She pushed her fingertips against her temples. *Dragon help me.*

By searching for Chandrani, she'd given away their location. He must've been waiting for any opportunity when Tallis wasn't dead center of her thoughts. Aside from the shocking pain, Pashkah's invasion came in the form of a single sentence.

I'm coming for you, sister.

✦ CHAPTER ✦
SIXTEEN

Tallis jerked upright when Kavya screamed. "What?"

"Pashkah."

"What? What happened to keeping you distracted?"

"I . . . The storm . . . I wanted to know if Chandrani had made it to safety."

Tallis jumped out of bed and stumbled until he found the lamp. A turn of the wick and he could see where Kavya knelt on the floor. She'd been touching him. They'd been sharing barely formed ideas. Now panic turned her usually placid expression into one of abject fear.

"What happened, exactly?"

"I searched for her. Out in the world."

"I thought only Trackers could search that far."

"In most cases. But if you knew someone for twenty years, you'd know how to communicate with little more than raised eyebrows or a blink. Chandrani and I are that way with our minds. I have more range with her than with anyone I've ever known. But Pashkah . . . He barged in. Cut us off. He's so powerful, Tallis. You have no idea."

He kicked into what remained of his clean clothes.

The rest he stuffed in his pack, along with their scant provisions. "Next time I'll distract you with a game of twenty questions. Might be more effective than keeping the interest of a frigid snob who volunteers for trouble whenever she can."

"Frigid?"

"*That's* the word you focus on. Fantastic." He pulled on another shirt, then shoved tired feet into his boots. "I hope whatever scattered bullshit is in your head has to do with surprise and being frightened out of your wits. The relative state of your sexual experience and my effect on it ranks well below getting the fuck out of here."

"You're vulgar."

He thrust the blankets into her hands. "And you're a dead woman if you don't figure out some way to duck under his radar. How much does he know?"

"Where I am."

"Dragon damn it. And there's no way you can confuse him now? Focus back on me and my enthralling body? Maybe if I slap you for being such an idiot, I'll scramble your gray matter."

She surged to her feet. Anger hardened her features like a warrior being frozen by Medusa—Medusa, that ancient Trickster of the Tigony. The tale of a trusting, ridiculously empathetic young woman who didn't account for her own safety wouldn't become a story told through the ages. Instead Kavya would be a cautionary tale and a reason why the Indranan should remain a people divided.

Tallis wanted that. He wanted any attempt at their reconciliation thwarted, because it ran contrary to the figment infecting his mind. But he didn't want to do so at this woman's expense—unless it was absolutely necessary. She was still too much a part of the mystery of his dreams and, increasingly, the mystery of his waking hours.

"If you slap me," she said, "we'll be right back at the beginning. You'll be facing off against one of your own seaxes."

"You and what training, goddess? Get moving and think us a way out of this hell."

"We stick to the plan." She layered a blanket in imitation of her sari, using the same pattern of tucks and pleats. "We fly out."

"Insane." He shoved a finger toward the window. "Blizzard." He shoved the same finger toward Kavya. "And you're a head case. Forget being Indranan or a mind-witch or whatever. You're not rational and you're not stable."

"Says *you*, of all people! Then go. Leave me to Pashkah and see what happens."

"I can't and you know it." He threw her a spare pair of socks. She quickly stripped her slippers, donned the socks, and shoved the delicate shoes back on her feet. Better than nothing until he could steal her a new pair of shoes. "I'll have wasted months here in India," he said. "Worse, I'll never learn the truth about the last twenty years. Forgive me if I find this topic worth pursuing. I don't intend to die in a fiery crash before that happens."

"So selfish. He will *own* the Five Clans if he kills me."

"*Bathatéi*. He's not more powerful than the Giva.

He's as insane as you are, apparently, although with a penchant for chopping off heads. That doesn't make him invincible."

Kavya shut her mouth, but Tallis could practically see the effort she expended to stop arguing. The silence between them was knife-sharp, honed with worry and the threat of danger. Tallis didn't like it. An enemy should be seen. Faced. Defeated with the whites of the eyes in clear sight as the life drained away. They were being pursued by a phantom. He wouldn't see Pashkah of Indranan until the man appeared out of thin air to kill him and Kavya both.

Tallis strapped on his seaxes and threw his pack to Kavya. "It'll help keep your back warm, at least."

"We're going. To the airfield."

"No, you're going to lead us into the snow and play rabbit. You'll hide. No more calling out for lost friends like using a ham radio."

She shook her head. "He's nearby. Otherwise there's no way his voice could be that strong and clear. Either he tracked me himself, or he had help. Doesn't matter now. I'd never be able to construct an effective disguise with so little time."

"Out in the woods, then. You'll at least be distracted by the snow."

"Are you being intentionally thick? *He knows I'm here*. He'll only need to search for a woman shivering in the snow, cursing the cold."

"That worked *so* well. As will flying away in a blizzard. How did you gather such a following? I haven't seen a Dragon-damned thing to say you can take care of yourself, let alone lead hundreds."

Eyes blazing, she struck him hard across the cheek. Caressing his face was one thing. Having his head rattled by a woman's hard slap was another sort of provocation—toward violence rather than sex. "I am the Sun."

"You're a sham. Scared and running. *Always*. I wonder if that'll ever change. Maybe I've been paying you far too much attention, trying to make sense of a girl's game of make-believe." He opened the door and shouted over his shoulder. "You're not beautiful enough to make it worth the effort, goddess."

Kavya's padded footsteps chased his down the stairs. "And you're not so charming as you think, you *lonayíp* bastard. Arrogant. Stubborn—"

"But not fearless. You want to end up like Nakul? Our bodies broken and burned at the bottom of a chasm, until you're practically begging Pashkah to come take your head? Just my luck, he'd leave mine intact."

"Not before he chewed a chunk of your arm off."

"Bring it," Tallis snarled.

He stalked through the pub, which was quieter at that late hour. From the small, almost primitive kitchen, he retrieved two loaves of bread, several hard sausages, cheese, and more bottles of water. Kavya stood in the doorway. He spun her, unzipped the pack, and shoved the provisions inside.

"That's in case we live to see morning. I'll be hungry."

Kavya glared, which he could clearly see in the strange orange and silver light that emanated from the pub's main room. Someone had banked the fire, but the snow added a sheen to every surface. "You're optimistic all of a sudden."

"You're rubbing off on me," he said dryly. "Or maybe

it's that a man like me has seen worse and survived worse. That I'll live till morning is a given."

"And me?"

"That depends on your brother and the state of your brain." He glanced around as if the man might materialize out of the shadows. "I'd ask you to look for him, but I'd rather you stay pissed at me. Mind on me, goddess."

He grabbed her upper arm and trudged out into the snow. The cold sucked air from his lungs and replaced it with the burn of ice. Kavya gasped a curse under her breath.

"Watch it. A woman shivering out in the open, remember? Let's go back to arguing about airplanes and fiery crashes."

To his surprise, Kavya yanked free of his hold and headed . . . south? The best he could figure, with direction as hard to discern as her swiveling moods—and how she made his moods swing from ecstatic to furious with just a few words.

Hate you.

"No, you don't," she called back through the wind.

Both of them stopped. She turned. They stared at each other through a snow that blew in flurries like cotton in a fan.

Tallis shook his head. "Well, well. So much for keeping clear of your tricks."

Kavya couldn't explain it any more than she could look away from accusatory blue eyes made black in the night shadows. A few errant streetlamps made the snow sparkle ominously, but that overhead light only deepened the dark hoods beneath his brows.

"No tricks." She twisted her hair into a long rope and shoved it beneath the straps of the pack, out of the way of the wind. "I just think it's the strongest thought you've had since we met. I dare you to say otherwise."

"So you can hear psychic shouts now? I have plenty. One of them is *keep the fuck out of my mind*."

She strode toward the airfield. The vehemence of his hatred remained an indelible imprint, like a brand in the folds of her brain. She didn't want that. She shouldn't care, but she didn't want that at all.

The airfield wasn't far. She made quick time, with a malevolent ally tailing every step. She could be distracted by him, but she didn't want to hear his thoughts. Not ever again. He was a Pendray cretin. More than that, he was *Tallis*. She only just learned to read the truth of his words while cupping his cheeks and hearing the scratch that added emotion to his voice.

Being able to hear his thoughts was almost a disappointment. He'd be just like every other man.

But if she didn't think about Tallis, she'd be assaulted again. Already she could feel the press and prod of a hateful, violent mind bearing down on hers. The moment she lost concentration, she would become her brother's next victim. So she focused on the man whose bed she could've shared but hadn't. Why hadn't she?

It was a moment wasted.

Illuminated by industrial lights that trailed down the runway, the airfield looked like a grave waiting to be dug. Maybe it was panic driving her actions. Maybe it was the understanding that she'd rather take her chances against the elements than against Pashkah.

"I've faced him before, Kavya," came Tallis's call. "I can take him again."

"And if he has reinforcements?"

"You could find out."

"I won't *look* for him!" She kept up her quick pace until she reached the hangar.

Tallis grabbed her hands just as she'd wrapped them around a rusted, icy padlock. "If he's on his own, or close to it, then we stand our ground. If he has a dozen Black Guardsmen at his back, then we take our fool chances against the storm."

"Can you fly?"

"*Now* you think to ask?" Unexpectedly, Tallis laughed. The storm had relented enough that she could hear him perfectly over the steady wind. "Yes, I can fly." His laughing expression melted in a heartbeat. Angered resolve took its place. "But I'm not letting you back in my mind."

Kavya stood toe-to-toe. Although she needed to arch her neck to look in his eyes, she didn't feel the least intimidated. "If I find a way, I won't need to ask permission and you won't be able to stop me."

He stilled. He touched her chin with frozen fingers. "You really are a witch."

She'd never heard such disdain.

"Lucky for you, I am. I'll look for him. Just to see which odds are better."

"I'm guessing they're an even split."

"Shut up and hold my hands. I need something to physically ground me, in case he's close enough to assault me. Slap me if you have to. Anything to pull me back to you."

"Slapping you will not be a problem."

Tallis snatched her hands in his and threaded their fingers. She looked down. Whether by conscious action or accident, he aligned their knuckles in even rows. Mountains and valleys. Perfectly spaced. Perfectly synchronized. Kavya blinked once in disbelief but quickly took the alignment as a sign—of what, she didn't know, but it was calming and auspicious. That's all she needed.

The snow gave way as she reached past her body, drawing on her gift to search for the black force that had been chasing her since the age of twelve. A gray fog swirled around her as if she were being swallowed by quicksand that was no less deadly for its gentleness. Somewhere outside of herself, she felt the solid grip of a man's hands. They were cold. Hers were cold, too.

Tallis was too important to let go of. He was the first person she'd ever known who hadn't treated her like a victim or a deity. No matter that he called her *goddess*, he challenged her at every turn—good and bad, stubborn or constructive. She liked it. She liked seeing him naked, and she liked that he held her hands.

The agony of scalding metal slid from the back of her neck to the base of her spice. She cried out, swung out, spun in circles—all with her thoughts. She fought the swirling gray quicksand to find her brother. He stood on the other side of a massive divide that spouted fire.

It's what needs to happen, Kavya. He was as sober as she'd ever heard him. *The Chasm isn't fixed. The Dragon has summoned me to be the one to make it whole. Can't you see? You're as important to this calling as I am.*

By being murdered.

By dying, yes.

She shuddered, then screamed as he lanced another sharp stab down her spinal column. Every nerve sizzled. *I'm not going to die by your hand. I swear it.*

The mists evaporated until she peered beyond the physical world to find Pashkah silhouetted against a grouping of evergreens on the outskirts of the village. He seethed with rejection. For a moment he'd been calm, as if made so by a higher power. He'd spoken reverently of the Dragon, but that calm was quickly overpowered by the violence she'd feared since childhood. Around him in the trees gathered more Guardsmen than she could count.

Too late for that vow, sister. We were children then.

Pashkah pierced psychic fingers through her skull, as if her brain was being touched, handled, turned over between careless hands. Kavya swallowed a thick glob of bile as she kept from vomiting. It was the worst sort of vertigo.

The only name—the only word—that would pull her free of hell.

"Tallis."

Warm lips crushed against hers. He tasted of the snow. Strong hands framed her face. Tallis gave her a little shake, then pushed his tongue into her mouth. Kavya wound her forearms around his neck and dragged him closer. She opened her eyes. The snow had salted his silver-flecked hair and the winds had tangled it into a wild mass. He would never be anything but a wild creature, no matter the trappings of his human clothes and world-weary ways. Men with sharp minds became jaded. Men with instincts and a connection to the base power of their animal selves—they thrived, leaving sharp minds behind in favor of sharp claws.

And sharp teeth.

He nipped her lower lip. Kavya yipped and pulled sharply away. Their arms, however, were still entwined around wind-chilled bodies.

"There you are." His voice was a childish tease, which didn't obscure the worry deep beneath his usual sarcasm. "Status report, please."

"Other side of town. He's crazier than I thought. At least twenty guards." She shut her eyes and gripped Tallis harder, stemming another tide of vertigo. "He played with my brain like tossing a ball."

"Any Tracker?"

"Don't know. Couldn't tell when I was fighting him off. He . . . Tallis, he's vicious. He might not need one anymore." She nodded toward the hangar door. "You going to help me steal a plane? Or a helicopter? Or a Dragon-damned hang glider?"

"You keep making this more interesting. Is that your real skill?"

"Hobbies, remember? It certainly isn't sex."

His expression was reward enough for being bold. Blue eyes could burn like fire, even in a white squall. She had proof when Tallis looked at her as if the rest of the world could go to hell, if only the Dragon granted them a night together. "I think you need a new hobby. Soon."

She briefly touched his face. They had time for nothing more than an exchange of heat from skin to chilled skin. "Don't you know? I already have my eye on one. Extreme mountain aviation."

⊹ CHAPTER ⊹
SEVENTEEN

A prickle of urgency climbed the hairs along Tallis's forearms. He could've attributed the sensation to yet another spray of snow and lick of wind. With Kavya at his side, however, that wasn't likely. Her gift was beyond his comprehension and beyond his senses—or it should've been. Instead he'd known when her distress had reached its height, when he'd needed to drag her back to the physical.

When he'd needed to kiss her.

That was becoming more frequent.

But this was trouble. Pashkah wasn't up the pass somewhere, creeping through the white-out conditions of the Valley of the Gods. The man was single-minded. There would be no broken-down buses and feeling through the snow for an inn. Not for Pashkah.

Tallis used to think of himself as a professional of sorts. He had a job to do, no matter that his occupation paid nothing. Its benefits package included ostracizing him from each of the Five Clans, as well as occasional visits from a feminine entity that seduced him into thinking the sacrifices were worthwhile.

Yet that odd, misguided professionalism had been a

point of pride. He discredited, upended, maimed, and, on occasion, killed. He sliced malfunctioning systems into pieces, at one point believing the Great Dragon actually blessed the deeds, and that the Dragon Kings would eventually thank him for his surgical rage. They'd demonize him, but they'd thank him for doing what no one else could.

Pashkah seemed to be under that same delusion. It looked more pompous and ridiculous when someone else wore that cloak.

Besides, Tallis had an ally now.

She was sexy as hell and even crazier than Tallis. After all, Kavya was the one who barged into a hangar and starting pulling tarps off vehicles. She assessed the machines with what appeared to be an eye for their soundness—not that he believed any vehicle could be considered sound in these conditions. They were sheltered by the hangar, but the storm sounded like a dozen growling bears, each of them with a different grudge.

He sheathed one of his seaxes and glanced down at the lock he'd split. "I can feel him, can't I? That . . . pressure? I don't know what else to call it. In the valley, when people were curious but peaceful, it was nothing but a friendly tap. Just checking me out. This . . . *Bathatéi.*"

Kavya flipped on a glaring overhead fluorescent light. The unnatural brightness bleached her skin and added shadows to the hollows of the cheeks. She rewound her chocolate hair. "It's not pressure for me. He's beating me across the back of the skull. Soon you'll be back to having psychic shocks shoved down your spine."

"I didn't like that," Tallis said. "Think I'll pass."

"What, go for full berserker from the start?" She nodded to a corner filled with stuffed burlap sacks. "Use it as ballast. If we manage to take off, we'll need the weight to fight the wind. I'll find fuel."

"So bossy," he said, doing as she'd commanded. Self-preservation trumped pride. "Besides, a berserker needs to be provoked. Not zero-to-crazy. This is good, though. I feel like we're making real cultural strides, you and I. One day I can talk to others about the Indranan and their capacity for distraction—"

She shot him a nasty scowl, although a blush brightened her cheeks.

"—and you can espouse how sensible the stubborn, uncouth Pendray can be."

"Sensible? That's not the first word I'd choose."

"As long as you don't use it to describe what you're planning, I don't care what you do." He crossed his arms as she opened the door to a battered four-seater Cessna. "I take that back. I care to avoid getting in that thing."

"Open the hangar bay and get in. You're the pilot, remember? Just be prepared to listen to my navigation very, very well."

The utterly frigid metal of the hangar's wide sheet metal door stuck to his palms as if coated with glue. He shook free of its unnatural grip and looked down to find a strip of abraded skin across each palm. The wind struck him as it whipped through the open hangar. "It's amazing you didn't badger your followers into compliance."

"Don't start."

Tallis jogged across the hangar, stowed his weapons in the scant space among the burlap ballast behind the passenger seat, and climbed in. Kavya quickly followed as he buckled up. "This *will not* work."

"Your nickname should be Faithless. Heretics have to believe in something contrary to the common canon. You don't believe in anything." With a flick of the controls, Kavya turned on the Cessna's safety lights. "Let's dare the Dragon, right here in the foothills of where our Creator was born and died. See if you're a heretic or a nihilist. In four minutes, you'll be full berserker and fending off my brother again, or you'll be praying like you've never prayed before." She grinned. "Maybe both."

"When did you become so obviously insane? Forget Masks. This is all you, Kavya."

"And you're already addicted."

Tallis smiled right back. "I knew you were unnatural and downright shady, but this is new. Your brother's in town so you hope to sink to his level of obvious mental degeneration."

He kicked the engine to life. Propellers swirled with patterns of air, whereas the blizzard made random swoops and threats. Tallis watched, as if out of body, as he wheeled the tiny plane into alignment with the wide, gaping exit.

Vibrations that had nothing to do with the accelerating propellers shook the small craft. The Dragon was angry at their arrogance—the Heretic and the Sun, both of whom were trying as fervently as Pashkah to change the way things had been for generations. What hubris! What gall! The sort of hubris and gall that deserved punishment.

"You know, maybe it's a parable." He felt happily

sardonic and that contradiction was reflected in his tone. This was merely another reckless step in an otherwise misguided, risky, worthless life. No, this was a cataclysmic leap. "Maybe we're meant to crash where the Dragon died. Swords forged in the Chasm, fire, tons and tons of lava."

"You're talking, not flying."

"Is this where you said I need to concentrate really hard?"

"Yes."

"Without telepathy?"

Kavya shot him a prickly glare. "One set of controls, but two sets of eyes and two sets of everything else. We can make this work *if* we work together. Don't sit there making jokes about reading minds. You're the one always espousing the virtues of living in the physical world and being one with the earth."

"*One* with the earth. Not plummeting toward it."

For all his protests, Tallis didn't hesitate anymore. The pressure against the top of his spine was becoming more like how Kavya described it: the pounding of a mallet, only that mallet had been studded with nails. He resisted the temptation to touch the back of his neck, where he was sure he'd find dots of blood. At that moment, there were so many ways to risk death and dismemberment.

He went all in with the Sun's method of choice.

"Aw, fuck it. Let's do this."

She slid him a sideways grin. "About time."

Throttle back, he navigated the plane out of the hangar. Almost instantly a gust of wind caught beneath the wings and tipped the cockpit starboard. Kavya gasped.

Her skin had paled, but she bit her molars together so hard that Tallis saw the bulge of muscle and determination along her jaw.

"I got the steering," he said. "You watch . . . the other stuff."

The blizzard was a complete and total sonofabitch. Tallis fought the controls with his whole body. Layer upon layer of white made him curse the lack of color. He wanted green and blue and bright sunny yellow—anything but white, or the orange and red flames of a fiery crash. He angled the nose of the little plane toward the runway, which was surprisingly clear. The wind hadn't allowed snow or ice to accumulate across that long, flat surface. The snow had no building walls to settle against. Instead the runway looked like a winter desert where the sands flew right to left. There was more consistency without the interference of structures from town.

A straight shot.

Him against the wind.

Could be worse. He couldn't think of an example of how, but he was sure there had to be one.

Judging the direction of the gale and the way the plane pitched, he adjusted the flaps to compensate. They weren't taxiing straight. More like a sidewinder. Rear wheels skidded and slipped. A sneaky gust lifted the nose off the ground.

"They're coming," Kavya said, almost in a trance. "At the hangar. Snowmobiles."

"Then airborne it is."

He pulled back the throttle and begged the little two-seater to gather her nerve. More speed. *More.*

Kavya cried out, clutching her temples. She shook in her seat, as if whipped side to side by unseen hands.

Tallis didn't dare let go of the yoke, but he needed his copilot. He needed Kavya as his partner.

"You're a lying bitch, goddess. You hear me? Get your ass back here so I can tell you what I really think of you. I want the chance before we smash into the Beas." He risked a sideways glance. "I mean it. I'll slap you in the face right now. And if we do get out of here, you won't believe what I have planned. *You* get to strip next time. I want a show like you've never given another man. Don't piss me off or I'll be the one to rip off your Dragon-damn clothes."

She shivered again, then nodded. Her voice was an ancient album that had been scratched to hell. The song was still there, but obscured by damage. "Promises, promises, Tallis. Now fly this *lonayíp* thing."

Kavya fended off Pashkah by distracting him with her own vulnerability. She imagined herself a child of only twelve. *You should've killed me then, you monster.*

The pain kept coming, but better to aim it at her than at Tallis. He was operating at the highest mental function. Total concentration. That meant he'd be vulnerable to Pashkah's psychic attacks. She couldn't let that happen, when flying in the storm required as much brawn as skill. She focused on Tallis's verbal tirade. He kept taunting her, saying things that no longer rang true, but that served as an escape route.

Escape. Again.

She wanted to turn around and face her brother once and for all. That wasn't possible.

Not yet.

She took refuge in watching Tallis work. The tendons along his neck tightened, as did the set of his jaw. He was a rubber band about to snap. Except for his hands. She fended off the agony that bored into her bones by watching his hands. His knuckles were white with the pressure of gripping the yoke. Every vein stood in relief. The light dusting of hair across the backs of his wrists seemed exotic. She wanted to touch him there. She wanted to touch him all over.

"Kavya, Dragon damn it!"

The plane suddenly slid to the left. "I'm here."

"Don't know where the fuck you went, but don't do it again."

"I'm trying to keep him out of your stubborn, perverted head."

"I like my head a little perverse, thank you."

"A *little*?"

"Hush. Hold on." He grimaced. His nostrils flared over lips taut with concentration. Blue eyes had narrowed to laser beam intensity.

The plane skittered and slipped and insisted that it would never get off the ground. The small Cessna didn't have enough speed, but the wind had enough power. An upward surge caught the wings about a hundred yards from the end of the runway. Tallis didn't miss the chance. He hauled up on the controls until the nose lifted and the rear wheels left the ground.

Kavya screamed, partly out of triumph. Tallis's grin was maniacal and transformed his entire face. Mad, but in the best way. Mad in a way she wanted to share—without fear and without regret.

She sent a parting psychic shot back toward her brother. She wasn't a trained fighter, and she didn't have his twice-cursed power, but she had a moment of pure adrenaline. Fused with her hatred, she flung her worst back toward the man who'd warped her life for too long. She pictured his joints. Knees. Shoulders. Hips. Elbows. She burned fire into each one. There was no way to hear his bellows over the sound of her heart, the storm, the propellers, but his telepathic scream resonated behind her breastbone with a satisfying rush.

No wonder he sought so much power—heady and dangerous.

She broke from that seductive trance by reveling in the intoxicating thrill of the elements. The storm played games with the little plane, up and down and listing like a rowboat in a froth of whitewater.

"Shit," Tallis grunted.

The craft spun twice. Kavya was dizzy and nauseated. "What in the name of the Dragon was that?"

"We either spin with the wind, goddess, or see what happens when our wings sheer off."

"Spin, then."

"Only when the storm says so. Surprisingly, it doesn't respond to your bossy orders."

"You've taught me to cope with that disappointment."

He grinned again, although his knuckles were still bone beneath skin. No blood and no color. "Does that mean I'm a force of nature? I could get used to that."

"As infuriating as one," she said.

"Bollocks. You like it. Besides, I obeyed you when I climbed into this— Whoa!"

The plane rolled again. The wind-tossed waters of the Beas were all Kavya could see out of the front cockpit windows. The g-force against her face meant gravity wanted them. The earth wanted them. And the storm didn't want them sharing its sky.

Tallis's desire to live trumped them all.

He steered the Cessna out of its downward plummet. He growled with what sounded like Pendray curses. She joined in using the Indranan tongue. Somewhere in time, however, they crossed from those separate languages and slipped into the mutual language of all Dragon Kings. Like the humans' story of Babel, the Five Clans had fractured, too, each with its own means of communication. She liked sharing what might be their final words as if speaking directly to the Dragon— prayers and curses mixed, in complete understanding.

A headache that had nothing to do with Pashkah's mental bullying pierced her temples. She rather liked that. Physical pain, not mental. But not *too much* pain. Crashing would mean agony beyond imagining. She and Tallis would wind up as he'd described: stuck in useless, broken bodies, unable to die. She'd obliged Nakul's final wish, yes. This would be different. Their minds would remain intact. She might have the strength to put Tallis out of his suffering, although the idea of lobotomizing him added a layer of gut-wrenching sadness to her fear.

She wouldn't be able to do it to herself. Endless suffering.

Hating her helplessness, she gripped the armrests until she thought her arms would splinter. She was panicking, and that was never a good thing for an Indranan. If Tallis was holding his fear response at bay—the berserker that almost certainly wanted to overrule his thinking mind—then she could.

"You threatened to strip me." She grinned to herself, knowing Tallis would be smiling, too. "Think you can manage?"

"I'll manage just fine."

"A lot of experience in that department?"

"A lot more than you."

She wanted to wipe the sweat off her brow but couldn't find the courage to let go of the armrests. "You think you can handle seducing a virgin?"

"Seducing? We were talking about the forceful removal of your clothes."

"That's part of it, I'm sure," she said with a shiver. The adrenaline, the physical anguish, the absolute terror—they were blending with their ribald conversation until her body felt molten. She was a bundles of nerves contained within too-tight skin. "But I don't respond to violence."

"Says you. The right kind can be amazing."

He said that last with a gasp—sexy and breathless— as the plane righted and swerved sharply to port. Had they been any nearer to the ground, the wing on Tallis's side would've shredded into the earth.

"We're lucky to still be airborne," he said after a hard, telling swallow.

"Every second is a victory."

"We're agreeing on so much, goddess. You'll come around. I know it. Strip. Kiss. A little rough play—you'll enjoy my definition of seduction."

"Can a man be that assured and actually manage to be amazing?"

"Kavya, right now I'm flying a paper airplane in a turbine." His neck was rigid with tension. "That means I can spin straw into gold and level mountains. Pick what impossible deed you want me to accomplish next."

"Make me feel safe enough to sleep beside you."

Where in the world had that come from?

Tallis glanced toward her, eyes aglow with hot blue fire. "Safe. With me. You have no idea what you're talking about."

"Fine." She returned her attention to the window and tried to ignore the creaking protests the plane made—and the sudden frost in Tallis's bearing. "Just stick with calling me by my name. Not goddess. I'll consider that miracle enough."

⊹ CHAPTER ⊹
EIGHTEEN

Perhaps the Dragon wasn't angry at them after all. Maybe he just wanted two troublemakers the hell out of the Himalayas. Fine with Tallis.

Through some combination of skill, luck, and complete idiocy, they belly flopped the Cessna in a cornfield. The stark Pir Panjal peaks had given way to less formidable hilly terrain, as well as grasslands, lakes, and abundant population centers. Kavya had navigated along the national highways until final sputters of fuel, as well as a suspiciously freaky sound coming from the port propeller, meant her goal of a landing at the Jaipur International Airport was too ambitious.

That the plane's nose hadn't dug a trench was a minor miracle.

As it was, Tallis's door was jammed into the dirt. The plane was tipped sideways, with the wing on his side snapped back like a crippled bird. The temperature was sweltering and humid. Apparently they'd dropped into hell as a nod to the fate they'd courted. He shed his coat and handed it to Kavya, who padded the door frame where a jagged piece of metal waited to slice her palm. She crawled the upward angle out her door, then turned to take the pack and seaxes from Tallis. Their fingers touched. Hers were still shaking, after nearly five hours in the air. Eyes assessing each other, they must've made a strange tableau in the middle of that field.

Tallis blinked and Kavya turned away. After climbing out, feet back on solid ground, he leaned hard against the half-wrecked cockpit. "Any head cases coming after us?" he asked, angling his question toward where she'd taken a seat on his pack.

"No. Coast is clear. Plenty of Indranan in Jaipur, maybe ten kilometers from here. But we'll blend in better."

"Good." He stood back from the plane and gave it a solid looking over. "I'm quite proud of that, you know."

"Crashing?"

"Landing. A very creative landing." He walked around to the ruined port side. The wing was like a hangnail—a clinging piece of something that had once been part of the whole. One of the propellers was twisted into the stripes of a candy cane. No wonder it had grated so badly. "And a lucky landing at that," he said to himself.

"Do I want to take a look?"

Tallis emerged from around the rear of the plane and smiled. "Nope."

"Then I won't."

"You'll lose that green tinge any minute now and realize that extreme mountain aviation is a completely shite hobby. Tell me this was the one and only time you planned on giving it a go."

"One and only time." She stood, strapped on the pack, and arched her neck to a particularly defiant posture. "I'm never running from him again. You should know that. Whatever distance we put between us and him now is for strategy. But . . . there will be a reckoning."

Tallis watched her with nothing short of complete fascination. Her insides should be jelly. Her mind should be some fog of pain or confusion or madness. But she was still Kavya, the Sun, the goddess who dogged him while waking, not sleeping. Her resolve made him feel invincible.

He walked toward her, slowly, just as she'd approached him when he emerged from his berserker fury. Wild animals required patience and caution. Kavya seemed like just such an animal. She was not the pristine cross between deity and politician who'd spoken on that distant altar. Only days had passed, but already that woman seemed years distant, consumed by danger and circumstance. The woman who'd shouldered his pack and stared at him eye to eye was more primal. She'd shed the constraints of her role.

After kneeling to pick up and sheath his weapons, he touched her chin. His fingers wanted to wander, so he let them—along her hairline, over her cheekbones, down to the lower lip that would never fail to arouse him to his core. "This is closer to who you used to be," he said quietly. "Isn't it? This adaptability and resolve. You weren't always untouchable and perfect."

"I've never claimed to be either."

"Your followers believed otherwise." Rather than start another argument—he really didn't have the strength—he turned to survey where they'd landed. They were surrounded by cornstalks taller than Kavya. "Ten kilometers to . . . what was it? Jaipur? How many people are we talking? Because this doesn't look promising."

"I don't know. Maybe six million?"

"Well, well. A welcome change from Bhuntar. A city means food, new clothes, a bath, shelter."

She started walking. "You had a bath last night, if I recall."

"*If* you recall?" Tallis caught up with her swift steps. "You'll recall that particular bath for the rest of your life." He dropped his voice an octave. "And so will I."

"It's best to get away from the site of the crash," she said, apparently ignoring him. "People will come to investigate. We'll find a little town and transportation that doesn't involve walking."

"You want me to steal a car?"

Kavya's laugh was beautiful, even brushed by a hint of leftover hysteria. "No. Not a car. Never mind. You'll see."

It was midmorning, and the blazing sun made the snowstorm up in the Pir Panjal seem like a horror movie villain they'd barely escaped. Every ten minutes or so, Kavya would stop, turn her head some direction or another, and close her eyes. She might make a minor course correction. Tallis bit his tongue to keep from asking questions.

Companionable silence was a good thing after all they had suffered, escaped, and heaped on each other. Soon the monotony of the walk was poking holes in his conscious thought until higher function dribbled through. He was a walking reflex. All instinct. Rather than sink into that seductive trap of action and reaction, he took Kavya's hand.

"What's that for?" she asked, staring at where their fingers interlaced.

"Because I wanted to. It'll give me something to think about other than how tired I am."

She smiled with that quiet, teasing humor he was beginning to anticipate. "I'm glad you admitted it first. I wasn't going to mention it at all."

"Being so tired that the ground looks as comfortable as a feather bed?"

"Something like that." Her voice was dreamy and soft.

"But you can't sleep. That whole Indranan thing."

A heavy sigh lifted her shoulders. "I can't sleep."

"Wait." He pulled her close, guiding her by tense upper arms. She felt even more frail than she looked, although she'd survived several circles of hell. "Are we safe here? There may be loads of Indranan in the city, but can you sense any nearby?"

"What does it—?"

"Let's call this 'question time,' and that's my first. When we're done, we can discuss another topic, perhaps one of your choosing."

Her lips twitched into a smile, as if a feather had tickled her lower lip. "We're alone. I can't search too far without giving us away again, but—"

"Good enough."

"When it's my turn to speak, will you interrupt me?"

Tallis chuckled and kissed her forehead. It was becoming so easy to touch her so casually. Good? Bad? Didn't matter in the middle of a sun-drenched cornfield. "We'll see. There's no telling when one might need a good interrupt—"

"Are you done yet?"

"You think you're so clever."

Kavya's mouth softened around a deeper smile. "Even *you* know I'm clever. " She exhaled softly. "Too much for my own good? Not clever enough? No telling."

"I protest. You're talking again." He rubbed his thumbs along her upper arms. "So there's no one around who might play roulette with your thoughts. Time for a nap."

Her expression of panic reminded Tallis of all he hated about her relationship with Pashkah. No, the *only* thing he hated about it. Pashkah made her less of a woman. He made her scared and small and doubtful. What the man had done at the assembly in that hopeful little valley was horrific. In doing so, he'd layered disappointment over her existing fear.

That wasn't what he'd grown to expect from a member of the opposite sex. Pendray women were indomitable. Boudicca had drawn her inspiration from the Pendray, revered in myths as Valkyries. Kavya had that spirit in her, but only glimmers shone through at any time. When she'd uncovered that airplane and began filling it with fuel—that had been strength to the point of suicide or legend, depending on the storyteller.

Yet when Tallis mentioned a mere nap, she shrank into herself like some darting sea creature seeking shelter among the coral, although that was probably an analogy better suited to the coastal Southern Indranan.

"I'll be right here," he said. "I have two rather vicious weapons, I have a gift that makes grown men weep in fear, and we are relatively free of Heartless mind-fuckers who'd keep you from getting rest."

"Where do you mean, 'right here'?"

Tallis smiled. He slid his hands down her arms as he folded back onto his haunches. He looked up at her, while still clasping her hands. "Here."

"In a field."

"That's wasn't a question. Good. I won't need to remind you of the rules."

"There are no rules with you," she said, slowly shaking her head. Shining dark hair tangled around her shoulders.

"All I know is that we'll both be more zombie than conscious if we keep walking." He let go of her hands and spread his. All around them was a field of sheltering green. "I'm going to sleep. Should you wish to continue zombie-crawling to Jaipur or wherever, be my guest. But think about that. If you're caught alone by yourself, what would you do?"

Kavya's eyes burned. The underside of each lid felt lined with the silt of a riverbed. She looked down at Tallis, who had cut a pile of stalks to assemble a makeshift bed. The ground still held the moisture of the monsoon season. He draped his coat over the top, stretched his long legs, and sank onto the vegetation with a sigh. Logically she knew those pointy stalks couldn't be comfortable, but he might as well have been lying on a cloud. She longed for that calm, and for the calm she would find against his body. Those hindering layers of clothing would provide softness for her bed, with his strong muscles revealed for her pillow.

"Dragon damn it." She sank to her knees. "Don't say a word."

Apparently Tallis was self-aware enough to try to stifle a smile, and when that didn't work, he covered his mouth with the back of his hand.

She raised her brows. "Are you going to sleep with those blades at your back?"

At least there she'd caught him off guard. He frowned briefly and sat up. He unsheathed one seax and dug the blade into the ground at his left hip, halfway to the hilt. He would only need to reach across his body with his right hand to grab it from its concealment alongside a stalk. Holding the second weapon, he eyed its shining blade, then Kavya. "You handled yourself well with this. One day I'll teach you how to use it properly."

He shoved it into the ground next to its duplicate.

"One day," she whispered. "I don't think so."

Without warning, he closed firm hands around her shoulders and pulled her stiff body toward his, alongside his, touching his. "You didn't think you'd be taking a mid-morning nap with a Pendray exile in a cornfield either." His voice was playful, as were his ocean eyes. "With all those minds at your disposal, I'd have thought you would have a better imagination."

Tallis arranged their bodies so that one shoulder each dug into the thick, tall, sun-warmed bale. They faced each other, lying on their sides. Wrapped together. Legs extended. Hips paired, touching. No part of her could deny notice of any part of him. His torso, clad in only a lightweight cotton shirt, was hers to enjoy.

Kavya didn't want to hear him talk anymore. She didn't want to bicker or even joke. That allure of the physical was too powerful. So she kissed him. It was the first time she'd initiated a kiss, but she was too pent up to take it any further than a brush of sensitive skin.

Tallis picked up where she left off. He wasn't stopping.

And she didn't want him to.

She shivered and wrapped her arm around his firm abdomen. He was made of hard planes, like a man pieced together from scrap metal, yet with the grace of a finely honed blade. He was the living embodiment of his weapons—hard, graceful, vicious, beautiful.

Tallis shifted until he pressed her back against their makeshift bed. She soaked up the sight of him as he loomed so powerfully above her, blocking out the sun, replacing it with the need for him. Just him. He exuded the gorgeous, intimidating strength of monsoon clouds ready to part with curtains of rain. His eyes were narrowed, intense, greedy, but his lips appeared vulnerable. They were reddened and slightly swollen from their kisses.

I did that.

Tallis smiled.

Whether he heard her thought or not didn't matter. Not when he pushed his palm up between her legs. "I'm going to give you something, Kavya."

She swallowed tightly, then cried out when his fingers brushed the sensitive skin between her legs. Panic caught in her throat when she managed to reply. "What?"

"The gift of my restraint, and your first taste of pleasure." He smiled again, this time with salacious humor. "Actually, I'm the one who gets to taste."

"Tallis?"

He stilled and took a deep breath. "Tell me to stop. If you want me to."

"Are you going to have sex with me?"

"No," he said, his expression surprisingly neutral. "If the time's ever right for sex, you won't have to ask for clarification. You'll make it happen. I know you that well, at least." He bowed his head against her stomach. His hair caught the sunlight. The silver tips were filaments of precious metals, glinting like tiny, tiny mirrors. "But for now, I want to kiss you. Everywhere. Will you let me?"

Kavya's head spun with a flickering slideshow of images. Where could he kiss? He cupped her mound and began to explore with his fingertips. She yanked her head from the ground. They locked gazes.

"Yes," he said. "There."

She gulped a breath. "Do it."

"So bossy . . ."

He pulled her inner thighs wide. With a surprised gasp, Kavya adjusted her position on the bed he'd made—and she dug her heels into the soft earth. His shoulders became her handhold. Tallis slipped between the silk layers of her sari, then used roughened thumbs to part her folds. He dipped closer. He licked. He *sucked*.

Kavya paired a hoarse cry with a slap against his upper back. Her palm landed with a hard thumping sound. Beneath her palm, Tallis shuddered—long and uncontrollably.

"That's it," he said against her inner thigh. "Give me your aggression. I can't take it out on you, but you can give it to me. Don't close your eyes or bite your lip.

Don't keep quiet, Kavya. Take your frustrations out on me. I want all of it."

Every nip of lips and teeth against her sensitive nerves wound her body tighter and tighter. Once she had been all supple ease and grace. Now she was a series of reactions to what he wanted. His pace. His direction. She gave him everything.

"Breathe. Breathe, Kavya. Watch me as I take you."

Fighting the sensual lassitude that made her head heavy, she did as he ordered. His face was centered between her legs, with his mouth nestled against her private core. She caught sight of his tongue when he licked upward. Then flashes of teeth when he smiled, or the grim set of his lips when another shudder overwhelmed his broad shoulders.

Now she knew truly what he'd meant. He was enjoying this just as much. What must the effort be costing him, to keep from giving in to the animal desire to lever over her body and *take*?

Oh, that thought. She rode that thought until its rhythm matched the flick of Tallis's tongue, until it crested and broke. A gasping cry ripped from her throat. Tallis gripped her backside when she thrust up, seeking more—and he gave her more. The pressure of his lips and mouth intensified her climax, while that maddening tongue prolonged it. Every time she thought she couldn't ensure another moment of such intense ecstasy, she was convinced that she could. *He* convinced her.

Only when her thighs wouldn't stop shaking and her throat ached from sharp, endless gasps did Tallis ease her from that wave of climaxes. He slowed his kisses. He caressed and soothed. Kavya couldn't have moved for all the world, but he arranged the draping silk of her sari back around her legs and pushed up to his knees. After lying down, he urged her to tuck her head in the hollow between his chest and shoulder.

Long, languid moments passed as their breathing approximated a normal pace. Tallis idly petted whatever skin he could find, although his energy, too, seemed to be waning.

"I meant that as a joke, by the way," he said, still hoarse. "You have plenty of imagination. But who could've foreseen this? Where we are?"

The last vestiges of pleasure worked down her spine. He pulled her closer. "Not me. Not ever."

"I choose to take that as a statement of wonder and awe."

"Exasperation and confusion." She kissed his neck. "And yes, wonder and awe."

"That works." He smiled, then tucked loose tangles behind her ears. His touch—how could a Pendray berserker be so gentle?

She smiled tiredly, with the effort costing her what felt like the last stores of energy. "But . . ." Trembling with curiosity as more and more possibilities came into focus, she tightened her fingers against his outer thigh. "What about you?"

"Later, after we find a hotel. I'm very discerning." He glanced up toward where green leaves created an awning against the blue of a clear sky. "Truly discerning."

She leaned forward and kissed each eyelid. "Are you sure? After what you gave me . . ."

"I'll hold you to it," he said, eyes gentle. "Sleep now.

We'll reset this whole mess. When we wake up, we can revisit the tantalizing possibility of you choosing a topic of conversation."

Kavya's heart shoved into her throat. "I want to trust. I want to be prepared the next time my brother comes for me. But I don't know if I'm capable of any of that. Not yet. Not even after what you've shown me."

"What's changed when it comes to your ability to fight? You came up from the streets."

"Maybe it's a matter of faith. I think back on the young woman I was, cobbling a life together out of mud and trash."

"Not a bad thing. Admirable, actually."

"I got caught up in the myth of my own resilience. Not everyone comes out unscathed."

He tapped her temple. "You call yourself unscathed? Woman, you're a head case, and I mean that with a surprising amount of affection. Remember, that's coming from a guy who's been talking to dreams for twenty years."

"That is pretty messed up."

"I don't think *unscathed* is a word for people like us."

"This won't last, will it?"

"What?" He half grunted the question.

"This. Us. A moment like this when we're not fighting anyone and we're actually . . . serene. Good things don't last." They were hot and sticky, but Kavya wouldn't have let go even if he gave her the opportunity.

"You need to know what a good thing is before you can figure out it won't last," he said. "This, goddess, this is a very good thing. Now do me a favor?"

"Hm?"

He smiled in that antagonistic, endearing way she was beginning to relish more than hate. "Question time's done. Be quiet. Be still. The sun's on your face. A man is holding you as if you're the last piece of driftwood in an endless ocean. I'm that tired, and you're that nice to hold."

Long years of panic and habit screamed that sleep should be easy. But even there, feeling more protected than she had in years, she couldn't.

"Kavya?" His voice was thick with the drug of fatigue. "You'll be here when I wake?"

She kissed his lips, which smelled and tasted of her own body. Wholly erotic. "Yes, I'll be here."

⊹ CHAPTER ⊹
NINETEEN

If Tallis had slept, he'd done so in quick snatches like chasing birds, clutching a few feathers, and watching them circle back into the sky.

He jerked awake, but his body stayed still except for the flutter of his eyelids. The colors of the piercing blue sky flickered between his lashes.

The plane. The crash. The cornstalks and his seax at his hip.

Kavya.

The strange contortion of his body registered next. He had shifted again. Kavya was curled into him, her spine curved to make the letter *C*. Her head was tucked beneath his chin and her knees were drawn up to his hips. One foot negligently draped over his thigh. He still lay on his back, mostly, but he'd managed to encircle her with both arms. In the heat, she'd kicked free of silk from the hip down, exposing lush bronze skin.

The sole of Kavya's foot was blistered, her socks and slippers victim of the elements. Slices stepped like ladder rungs up her arms and down her legs—the physical trauma of flight after flight. That he was only noticing now set a strange current to work inside of Tallis. He should've noticed. And *that* set off an argument. Why was it his obligation to notice? She'd been proselytizing for years before his arrival. She didn't need a keeper.

He didn't want to be her keeper. With his arms filled with the soft, voluptuous heat of a woman's body, he wanted to be her lover.

He'd given her pleasure. He'd shown her the explosions of light that came with sexual release. The triumph was his. No other man would claim to be her first. That meant he would claim her virginity, too. In Tallis's mind, it was a given. They would be lovers in all ways. Holding that firmly in mind had been the difference between tasting her feminine sweetness and burying his prick within her willing body. They'd been too tired. Too edgy. And he hadn't trusted himself to be gentle. He wanted their first time to live up to the adventures they'd already shared, but he didn't want to scare her. Dragon damn, he didn't want to hurt her.

He wanted to make her gasp his name.

Just the thought aroused him. Eyes open. Hands tightening. Cock ready.

As a youth, so serious and proud of his intellect, he'd wanted to be Sath or Indranan—Dragon Kings whose minds ruled the day. He was beginning to see what a blessing his fury could be. There was no one stalking around the corner to take it from him, manipulate it, keep him from sleeping out of fear it would be used against him.

So, enough of that. He was a Pendray. He harbored a nasty beast down deep where most men stored ugly things. Fantasies about inflicting pain. Fantasies about rape and murder and theft and running away, because cowardice was just as ugly, just as worthy of concealing. Those uncivil fantasies glimmered like a distant mirage—moments where the mind took a backseat to very old instinct.

He opened his eyes fully. The sun had dipped toward the western horizon. Maybe three hours of daylight left. He stared. He didn't blink. He felt a part of himself open to that dare, man against nature against beast. At his best moments, he was all three.

The beastly little bastard inside him wanted what it always did. Food. Fighting. Fucking. The order didn't matter.

What did *Tallis* want?

I want to go home.

"Do you want to think about something else instead?" Kavya spoke directly against his throat.

"I thought you were sleeping."

"No."

"Lying here being bored?"

"Just resting."

"Wait, think of something else," he said. "What did you mean by that?"

Her gaze fixed on his. Wide. Unblinking. Did she see a fool? A killer? A lunatic?

What Tallis wanted, apparently, was for her to see someone else entirely, because he wanted her to see him as a good man. With his hand moving up and down her arm, then slipping lower to caress the span of her ribs, he wasn't a good man at all. The beast's dark thoughts spilled into his rational consciousness, twining sex and violence and tenderness with the image of Kavya—her splendor while nude and aroused. To see that would be a blessing unlike any he'd known because, unlike his visions of the Sun, Kavya would be real.

"Don't worry. I wasn't poking around in your mind. But like I said before, sometimes you feel things so strongly. Just now, you thought something sad and shocking. That's all I know. So . . . I'm hoping it had nothing to do with waking here with me."

Tallis exhaled. She phrased it in such a way as to leave the door open. He could explain, or he could move on. He wasn't ready to explain. The raw impulse of wanting to return to Scotland wasn't new, but he hadn't felt its visceral punch so strongly before.

"Nothing at all. What about you? If you didn't sleep, how did you occupy your time?"

She stretched. Was she purposefully pressing her high, firm breasts against his side? "I've been remembering what you did to me. I don't want to wait until we get to a hotel. You need what I had. It would work some of the tension out of your body. You're strung so tightly."

"If I said I feel stiff, I'd have to admit to the shame of making an unbearably bad pun."

She was beautiful when she frowned. Not serious. Not scolding, even. Just more inquisitive than usual. "Pun?"

"I'm stiff, Kavya. My prick. I woke up with you lying curled into me and I got ideas. Very quickly."

"About us, no matter the sadness I felt."

"Forget that. I've been honest about my desires from the moment I knew them myself. What I gave you was a prelude. You're curious about me and even more curious about sex." He tapped his temple. "I've got no psychic weapons up here to mess with your mind."

"I know. I want to reciprocate. Here."

Tallis grinned as if she'd made another teasing jest, but her expression revealed that same frowning inquisitiveness. "Wait," he said. "You're serious."

"I am."

Speaking bluntly, he wanted to test her resolve. "With your mouth or your hand?"

She inhaled, eyes so wide that he could see a ring of white around her amber irises. "My hand. Easier for you to guide me."

He couldn't help a groan, which banished her hesitancy and made her smile. It also made her bold. She fumbled with the button and zipper of his cargo pants until she'd made room enough to slip her fingers inside. "Fuck," he said roughly.

"That's the idea."

"You have *no* idea."

With her free hand, she guided his beneath the waistband of his briefs. He made a fist around hers. The pressure, the heat—Tallis arched his neck, greedy for air. How long had it been? He couldn't remember. And he knew that no matter how much time passed, he'd never forget Kavya's tentative pace becoming more assured.

She clutched him tighter. Her fingers were caught between his and the swelling ache of his hard-on. But Tallis was the one caught. He couldn't focus. It was either close his eyes to savor the pleasure ripping up from the base of his spine, or watch Kavya. Watch her eyes as they darted from his face to where she'd bared his cock. Watch her parted lips as she began to softly pant. Watch as she learned the rhythm of his desire.

She propped on one elbow. Although awkward, she managed to yank open his shirt. Her awed sigh made Tallis feel powerful, that his body aroused this mind-blowing woman.

Smiling with age-old female trickery, she began to experiment. She pushed his fist away, changed the rhythm, teasing him, increasing the pressure, gripping his swollen head, pumping his long shaft.

"The old-fashioned way, Tallis," she said, her voice breathy. "You can't give me your thoughts. Give me your words."

"You think I can speak now, *lonayíp* woman?"

"Yes."

His head was spinning in circles that kept time with her strokes. "Don't let up."

"You made me feel amazing. Is this as good?"

"If you felt half of this, I did bloody well."

She licked the fevered skin of his upper pectorals, then blew across the damp trail. "Beautiful."

"I'm not."

"Yes, you are. There. Like that—arching against me, your hips off the ground." Kavya sounded overwhelmed. "I've never seen anything so powerful. I've never *felt* so powerful."

"*Faster.*" He was thrusting up to meet every downward clench of her tight fist. So close, burning, he moved to enclose her hand in his once again.

"No," she said sharply. "Mine."

Leaning down, she found where his neck met his shoulder and sucked, licked, scraped her teeth across his heated flesh. It was her teeth, and the appreciative moan she hummed against his taut muscles—primal.

Urgent. Earthy and strong. The combination sent him rocketing over the edge.

He cried out a hard curse and snapped rigid. The sky closed to black along with his eyelids. He didn't see colors or stars; he only *felt*. Kavya pumped twice more before he came, streaking his abdomen with the hot proof of his release.

"Oh! *Oh my*." The first was shock. The second was satisfaction. "That was . . ."

"Bloody fantastic," Tallis scratched out. He tried to swallow but couldn't. He needed water. He needed a steady breath. *Later*. "Are you sure you haven't done this before?"

"Never." She licked up to his earlobe, then caught his lips in a kiss that balanced between sweet and savage. "But I liked it."

"Not more than I did."

A blush—her blushes were always a surprise—turned the apples of her cheeks golden pink. "That was all right?"

"Very all right." He pulled her close for another kiss, this one sweet enough to make him think, if only for a moment, that they were the forever sort of people. That wasn't the case and never would be.

After a cursory cleanup, he forced a smile. "We'll definitely need another bath," he said blithely. "Not that I'm complaining."

"And there you go again." Her eyes were hazy and distant, when she met his gaze at all. "Tallis gone. The Heretic returned."

He stood sharply, which meant shoving her off and away. Not his favorite chore. He set about reassembling his armaments and looked down at Kavya, who'd brought her knees to her chest. Obviously she wasn't in the mood to explain herself, and he wasn't in the mood to listen. The orgasm that had held back his worries wasn't strong enough to keep them at bay forever.

Still sitting, Kavya aligned her knuckles in that odd, fastidious way.

He couldn't resist. Not again. "Why do you do that?"

Her brown eyes were lightened by the sun, which made them look more like caramel. She narrowed them, but beneath her outward aggression was a different timbre—as if she'd been caught doing something wrong. "What are you talking about?"

Tallis nodded toward her knotted hands. "Your fingers interwoven, clasped so exactly."

"I do nothing of the kind."

"Keep lying about inconsequential things and we won't be allies much longer, let alone lovers."

"I should only lie about the consequential things?"

He offered a rueful shake of his head. "I can spot the big lies. The little lies, though—they chip cracks in mortar and wear away stones. As powerful as the elements. So . . . your call."

"You act like this is some sort of test," she said.

"Why shouldn't it be? If I'm going to make a plan with anyone . . ." He shrugged. "Then it's all about trust."

Kavya looked down at her interwoven fingers. "How did you know?" she asked softly.

"Just my eyes and a really strong desire to know who the hell you are." He touched beneath her chin and urged her face up, up, until she couldn't look away. "I had a dream version of you, and a version of you intended for the rest of your followers, and then . . . here you are. Forgive my curiosity."

"They're—" Kavya had to stop, swallow, start again. "They're the mountains. My knuckles. They're the mountains and valleys of the Northern faction, where I was raised. I've never liked their chaos. The randomness. Too many hiding places and secrets and places where the sun came over the ridge at different times, different intensities. Nothing could be counted on."

"Your homeland."

She nodded. "My mother showed me how to line up my fingers and the knobs of my knuckles *just* so."

"Like that?" Tallis knelt and traced the even bumps. "Perfectly aligned?"

"Yes."

"Order out of chaos?"

She unclasped her fingers and shook feeling back into her numb hands. "But not anymore."

"Because I caught on? That's not fair. I've been surrounded by shadows and mirrors for longer than I care to remember. I find *one* solid, reliable truth and a woman willing to open up and explain what it means— and what? Should I apologize? I won't, Kavya."

Standing, she grabbed his pack and adjusted her stance. Not exactly order out of chaos, but with the strong foundation of the mountains. "We'll reach the nearest village in a half hour or so. Then you'll need to steal a *moped*, not a car. You'll learn why when we get into Jaipur. We should reach the Old City before dark. Perfect place to hide. Plenty of time to plan."

Kavya kept her steps evenly paced although she was

crumbling on the inside. Everything she'd known was shattered or frozen or covered in blood. Pashkah would find her, eventually, no matter where she bedded down for the night. The tension in her spine promised as much. Tallis had her back. He was a living, unpredictable cyclone—the same entity, but always changing speed, direction, force.

He caught up and walked beside her in silence, as if they hadn't shared the most intimate acts of her life. Her feet ached and started to bleed, but she said nothing. The physiology of the Dragon Kings meant she would heal quickly once they took shelter for the night, but that didn't mean it hurt any less in the moment. The agony built until she was burned by hot coals with every step.

"I need to stop," she said abruptly.

He eyed her as if she were a tree that deigned to speak. "Are we far off?"

"No."

"Then we keep walking."

"I'm stopping." She sat as abruptly as she'd spoken. Immediately she pulled one foot cross-legged into her lap. Blood covered her fingers.

"What in the Dragon?" Tallis squatted and balanced on the balls of his feet. "Why didn't you say something?"

"You're the one in tune with the physical world. Or maybe that ebbs for a while after you come."

"So mouthy now that you know what you're talking about." He stared back along their trail. The tight defensiveness in his expression fell away. "Fuck."

Kavya followed his line of sight. Smears of blood marked their progress. "Do you have any water left in the bottles?"

"Yeah. Give me one foot."

"Why?" She pulled her stinging foot more closely against her body. "Just give me the water."

"No." He proved his will by pulling her leg across his lap. His strength was always such a glorious surprise. In this case, however, it was also infuriating when he tended her feet as if she were a child with a scraped knee.

"Fine," she said tartly. "Start working on that plan."

"You still want to unify your people."

"Of course. Pashkah killed my allies. Now I look like a victim, a traitor, or a cohort. I need to restore that faith and work to fix the chasm between the factions."

"Say that again," he said, his blue-eyed glare made indigo by the shadows cast by the sun at his back.

"To fix the chasm? What of it?"

He drizzled water on her feet until the worst of the grit and blood washed onto the ground. Then he removed one of his seaxes and cut the wool lining from his jacket. Efficiently, he tied the wool in a field dressing that offered both absorption and padding. A layer of sliced leather followed, to give the sole more protection. Head bent, he concentrated on his task. His hands were respectful, if that was possible, but Kavya couldn't help responding to the sensitive way his skin slipped along hers as he held her calf, her ankle. She wanted him to push farther up her legs and keep touching, to put his mouth on her again—or, more daring, to take what they both wanted. They both wanted Tallis to claim her virginity.

Kavya was tired of his erratic behavior, which seemed to include pampering her. She'd never been one to indulge her own needs. "You're still being guided by forces I can't understand," she said. "I've been nothing but frank from the start. Start talking, or we part once we reach Jaipur."

"We part when I say so."

"I know these cities. I know their alleys. If I want to disappear, I will. You'll never see me again."

He offered a surprising nod. "Fine."

"Fine that we'll part or fine, you'll talk?"

He tied off the second leather dressing, his expression grim. "The vision I've dreamed about . . ."

"The one you thought was me?"

"She planned to see the Five Clans unified. That was her phrase: the Chasm isn't fixed. Every action I've taken was in deference to her larger vision. In a way, I was one of your people. A true believer."

"What changed?"

"Anyone can lose faith. The particulars are just that. Particulars." He rubbed a hand over his face, then around his grit-smeared neck. He was more than a man; he was an explorer from another century. "The issue is what to do now. If I help you, I'm helping whoever's been infecting my dreams. I won't risk that. I'm no longer in her service. Once I figure out who or what she is, I'll leave you to your mountain to climb, and get my life back."

"Your *life*? Circling the world again? Wearing the word *heretic* around your neck like a weight? That's a death sentence, like Nakul up in the valley. You might as well ask me to wipe your mind and have done with it."

"What I do with my life is my choice."

"Great plan so far, Tallis." She grabbed the water

bottle and took a hefty swig. That didn't help swallow the fear that had balled in her throat. After wiping her mouth, she eyed him. "Why protest her goal of unification but support mine regarding the Indranan? Or are you just tagging along for the sex?"

Dust had filled the tiny lines at the corners of his eyes, and had cast an unnatural hue across his skin. "No," he said darkly. "It's because you've never commanded me to kill."

⟡ CHAPTER ⟡
TWENTY

An hour after Tallis stole a moped, they arrived in the Old City of Jaipur.

Kavya had passed through Jaipur on occasion, always on her way to another place to regroup. Holding on to Tallis around his waist, she took the time to do what she'd never been able to. She soaked up the flavor of the famed Pink City. Clean, square-cut sandstone was the architectural theme, but that austerity was made romantic by pink paint on every possible surface. She'd never seen such a seamless blend of modern and ancient India. Neither era suffered. The union was unusual and beautiful, in ways that brought unexpected tears to her eyes. She was just tired. On so many levels. Being pressed against Tallis's broad back for the duration of their trip hadn't been relaxing. She'd spent that time poised between wanting to melt into his comfort and holding herself at a distance after the chilly end to their hours in the cornfield.

Tallis parked among a cluster of no fewer than a hundred other mopeds. They were within walking distance of the Johari Bazar. He craned his neck, circling, a frown creasing his dusty brows. "Why pink?"

At least the bitterness was gone from his voice. The longer they were in each other's company, the more he seemed willing to admit that she was not the woman haunting his dreams. Perhaps he'd spent those miles on the moped reliving her intimate initiation, not cataloging the rifts between them.

"Some believe it is a color of welcome, and that a raja doused the whole city before welcoming the Prince of Wales." She smiled and leaned closer, as if revealing a conspiracy. "Some think it was simply the cheapest, most prevalent color he could find."

Tallis smiled, too. "It's just so very . . . *pink*."

"Don't let the whimsy fool you. There are forts and fortifications everywhere."

"Are they pink, too?"

Feeling lighter—a welcome return to the rapture he'd offered as a gift—she tucked her fingers into the folds of his shirt. "Some of them. But beautiful things can still be dangerous."

"Don't I know it. You know what else I know?"

Kavya shook her head.

"I'm sleeping in a bed tonight. Period."

"Alone?"

He grasped her lower back and brought their hips together. "Of course not."

"You think you're in charge," she said, her heart speeding. "Here. Kiss my fingertips."

Tallis did without hesitation, just a brush of warm skin across each tip. Then he stared into her eyes until she was too hot, too tight, too much in need of him. *Again*.

"So bossy," he said quietly.

She pulled away but kept hold of his hand. "The bazaar is this way."

They had more to trade than Kavya had realized. Tallis kept his seaxes, but he was able to exchange the high-quality, decorated leather scabbards for a plainer pair. That and the last of Kavya's jewelry—her belly-button ring—ensured they could shop for food and clothing without worry.

Tallis frowned and shook his head while adjusting the straps of his new scabbards. They didn't cross over his back but hung off a simple leather belt. "I just thought it a shame that you had to trade your ring."

Her blood slowed. She became honey, all sticky, rich sweetness and the unlimited energy that came with it. "It's just another piece of jewelry."

But she knew differently, as his gaze intensified. His pupils were small and sharp under the sunlight, which only accentuated the dark blue magnetism of his irises. "Show me your stomach."

Kavya shivered, but she didn't protest. She wanted him to see her body, preferably after they'd had the chance to freshen up.

Only seconds passed before Tallis helped unwind the center swath of her sari. His hands were insistent—not educated in the intricate wrapping of her people's garments, but determined. Folds parted. Layers opened. He probably wasn't above ripping the cloth if he couldn't find a polite way inside, and he could do the same to her untested body. She looked skyward, eyes closed, and swallowed. His fingers found her skin. She laced her hands over the backs of his as he rubbed his thumb around her navel.

He bowed his head, watching where he touched. Enraptured. She knew, because she was, too. "I liked kissing you here," he said. "While you were adorned."

Kavya caressed up his arms. All that strength and a leashed anticipation was hers. She tunneled her fingertips into his silver-tipped hair. "Me on my own isn't good enough for you, Pendray?"

"*Bathatéi.*"

"That's better." She cupped his jaw, then his cheeks. She missed touching him that way. She missed being able to feel the twitch of thoughts when they fluttered beneath her palms. "If we're going to share a bed, we're doing so with you feeling absolutely blessed to lie next to me. Jewelry or not."

He offered a chagrined smile that made his expression into the perfect personification of Tallis: cynically good-humored, a little baffled by the world, yet willing to learn more about the mysteries he hadn't yet solved. For all his wandering and anger, he still seemed genuinely curious about life and accepting of new adventures. He didn't like the unknown—who did?—yet he sought new experiences with an intensity that suggested he'd be bored with anything less.

"And you, goddess? What will you feel lying next to me?"

She couldn't breathe, not when he stood to his full, impressive height and stared at her with predatory intensity. She wasn't his enemy, but she did feel like his prey. "I'll be scared."

"You don't show it often. Being scared."

"And I won't tonight either. That doesn't mean it won't be true."

Kavya readjusted her sari. She was speaking the most suggestive, honestly sexual words she'd ever uttered to the man who would take what she'd given no man. The urge to be beautiful for him was becoming an imperative, like eating and breathing.

And why not? Sex was just as elemental.

She took a deep breath. "Hand over the money."

"You think I can't haggle?"

"You don't know how to haggle here, in possibly eight languages. And there are Dragon Kings."

"Indranan?"

"Of course."

"Why haven't we been jumped and beheaded?"

"The ones in hiding don't want to be found. They live in a metropolis for a reason. Make their living. Stay clear of their siblings. Live to see the next day. Some might be lucky enough to live happily in a pod." She threaded her arm through his. "Think of it this way. Have you ever been in a bar when you could feel the tension? Where under the surface, a brawl was waiting to touch off?"

"Better to ignore it. Keep drinking and talking."

"That's what it feels like here. Indranan keeping their heads down. If you feel that little tickle of awareness, Northern or Southern, you ignore it and move on."

I'm coming for you, sister.

The words were a memory, not an immediate threat. But he *was* on his way. He wouldn't stop. That constant awareness made Kavya more reckless with Tallis than she might have otherwise behaved. Events had moved between them at four times the normal speed, all because she dreaded the next day, the next hour. As long as Pashkah lived, she would carry that fear—and she would try to stay with Tallis.

And after . . . ? If she was lucky enough and prepared enough and strong enough to take Pashkah down, would she and Tallis part ways?

Why wouldn't they?

The next stall sold clothing, which gave Kavya a much-needed means of avoiding thorny topics. "This one," she said bluntly to the stall owner. The sari was plain cotton, dyed blue, with few embellishments. It bore a striking similarity to the maroon one Tallis had stolen. She still wore it, but it had suffered the rigors of the day. Even a simple change of clothes would make her feel like a new woman.

"And this one." Tallis held up his choice.

She froze.

No. Not that one.

She wanted to tell him the truth, but it was too terrifying. What he'd chosen was the style of garment a woman wore when she was ready to commit fratricide. When she was ready to claim the other half of her Dragon-given gift. How could she explain the significance of an outfit that blended seamlessly with the market stall's other vibrant wares?

I can't buy that, Tallis, she'd have to say. *It would set the future in stone. I would be obligated to kill Pashkah. I would take his mind into mine. I would go really, truly mad—beyond logic or redemption.*

I would lose you.

Instead she forced a harsh laugh and turned back to her simpler choice. "That's practically a costume. Better suited for belly dancers."

"So? You already know I've thought about your belly. If you aren't going to wear jewelry there, the least you can do is give me an unobstructed view."

"You and everyone else."

He slunk closer, his shoulders curved around hers—the slightest intimidation, as if he could cage her with just his stance. Maybe it was true, because she didn't move.

"What's the matter, goddess? Afraid of showing off who you really are?" He stroked her cheek with his knuckles.

Kavya worked to hide a shiver that had nothing to do with Tallis's touch.

Who I really am.

"And to think I couldn't read you at all," he said, smiling. "Now it's like rereading a book. You want it, too."

Kavya eyed the outfit, chilled by the double meaning to his words. The two-piece sari had a bodice of amethyst silk that shimmered in the waning sun, with an underlayer of deep purple velvet. The skirt would hang low on her hips, where two bronze medallions adorned with more flowing purple and layers of brocade in shades of gold, orange, and red. The scarf was of the same graceful amethyst, with the barest fringe of gold trim. The colors should've been garish together. Tallis couldn't imagine how those colors and that cut of fabric called to her in primitive ways.

"Haggle away," he said in the common tongue of the Dragon Kings. "But we're getting this, too."

He stood near enough that she could see the tick of his pulse along his neck and at his temple. He had a wild gleam in his eye. The gleam spoke of something deeper than haggling and the marketplace. Perhaps some part of his gift? The berserker side? She couldn't tell, because he was also simply . . . Tallis. A man. A Dragon King.

Yes—a living god.

They didn't need telepathy after spending days reading each other's every movement, watching for clues, depending on each other. That was as frightening as the ornamental bronze medallions she stroked with her thumb.

"Yes," she said quietly "We're getting this, too."

He moved behind her and curled warm, broad palms on her shoulders. "You'll be beautiful wearing this, Kavya. I'll be proud to stand by your side when you do."

They finished shopping, during which Kavya had concluded the long-winded process of haggling for every item. She and the vendors spoke so quickly in some local tongue, maybe Hindi. Tallis hadn't been able to keep up. That she came away with a nod and a small smile told him of her satisfaction with an exchange. That he'd walked away from each encounter with a few extras tucked in his pack—old habits died hard.

The process was repeated at a few stalls containing foodstuffs and hand-milled soaps. They even found him a relatively new leather jacket, this one lightweight yet durable. He might actually feel like a man again, rather than a wild animal that had crawled down from the mountains. Those weren't his mountains, and the animal was firmly set on its target. He would have Kavya alone.

In *that* hotel.

"We're out of money," she said. "We can't afford to stay there."

"We can't afford to, but we're staying."

He took her hand and practically dragged her to the back of the building. An ancient fire escape was an obvious choice for breaking in, but he eyed the metal. It was rusted and pitted with holes at the hinges. Either it wouldn't hold them, or it would make hell's own noise as he pulled down the bottom set of steps. Yet as a man who'd spent twenty years without a home, he wasn't out of options. He liked to think he never was, but he glanced back at Kavya and knew better. She was another wild mountain creature, blazing with fire and an unknowable darkness that had overtaken her in the market.

She was alive with a vitality he wanted to suck into his bones. His bones felt old.

A thought that felt ancient jumped to the forefront of his mind. He'd fallen in love with the vision in his dream. How could he not? Whoever had been invading his mind for the last twenty years knew triggers to elicit that response. Kavya was different. She was stubborn and sometimes too naive for her own good, just as she was brilliant and so optimistic that he couldn't help but be drawn to her. She was a genuine person, with all of the complexities of a sentient being. Her perseverance was a magnet, drawing him closer, becoming the true north he'd thought altered beyond rediscovery. Apparently he was standing in a city called Jaipur, somewhere in India, but he didn't feel lost.

Reconciling his difference in feeling between his dreams of the Sun and Kavya . . . it was a useless exercise. One had been uncomplicated and fake, while what he was beginning to feel for Kavya was very complicated.

"This way," he said gruffly, shoving aside thought in favor of action. It was always better that way.

She was obviously reluctant, but took a deep breath and followed. Only her eyes shot sparks of warning.

Tallis searched the base of the building until he found a service door. It was partially hidden, probably intentionally, behind a large round metal canister of rubbish and abandoned junk. It was as rusted as the fire escape. The monsoon season must wreak havoc on everything.

"In we go," he said.

"You and what crowbar?" Her expression was dubious, with a hint of the quality he kept mocking her about—a goddess reluctant to stoop. Considering what they'd endured over the last few days, he was happy to see her disdain alive in force. She still maintained a touch of stuck-up arrogance that said she was in charge. That she wasn't at all times didn't matter. The attitude suited her a lot better than making choices based on fear.

He couldn't afford her panic. Not only did he need her to help out with his visions, he wanted more. More than sex. More than he could picture, let alone name.

"Do you think this is my first time sneaking in? Have a little faith."

"Said the heretic to the goddess."

Grinning, he knelt by the small service door and dug away the refuse and dirt that suggested the little entry was practically forgotten. "Hand me the pack."

Although she remained obviously dubious—which was beginning to irk Tallis—she tossed him the roughed-up knapsack. It was in sorry need of a wash. From it he withdrew a small metal case that contained tiny tools. The lock on the door was rusted, almost impossible to open, but he managed after twenty minutes of patient prodding. He'd never encountered a lock he couldn't pick, nor a hotel he couldn't shimmy into for a solid night's rest. In bigger places, he found it useful to walk in at midday, make his way to the employees' areas, and begin working. No one looked twice. A pilfered key or security card meant open access to any of the rooms he found empty after dark, when few additional guests would check in.

This place was large enough to remain anonymous, but with probably twenty rooms. They would be noticed if they weren't careful. The advantage was less technologically advanced security.

Such as an unattended service door.

He shoved his foot against the door when it wouldn't budge by hand. A massive creak and the scattering of some internal debris gave him pause. He waited a moment. Then he was inside, feet first, stomach toward the inner wall. He lowered himself using the strength of his arms and the toes of his boots. Kavya threw down the pack without the need for prompting, before repeating his backward entrance. Only, she wasn't as strong.

Tallis wedged his fingers in the fold between her thigh and the curve of her ass. "Let go. Push away from the wall."

Kavya paused a few seconds. "Right."

Using her hands and the momentum of her fall, she propelled backward. Tallis caught her with his arms under her knees and across her upper back. "That wasn't so hard."

She shook her head. "You have a funny sense of perspective on things like that."

"It must be funny." He set her gently down, but she winced when her soles touched the pitted concrete floor. "Because you're smiling."

"Are all Pendray a little touched in the head?"

Tallis shrugged. "It's been a little while since I've been back. Who knows what twenty years will do to a people. Probably not as much as I fear. Besides, none of us are as bat-shit as your people."

Rather than take offense, Kavya chuckled quietly. "Can't really argue there. Where to?"

They poked around the underground storage until they found a hose and utility sink. "This will have to do."

"Oh no. Not again."

"We can't be too picky. If we go upstairs looking like vagabonds, they'll throw us out on the street. Trust me."

"You've looked like a vagabond before, Tallis? Don't disillusion me."

"You don't know—"

Another huffing laugh revealed her sarcasm, which made him feel a fool for getting his back up so easily, and equally impressed that she'd accumulated a quick knack for his quiet humor.

She pointed to a plain door on the far side of the tight, moldy basement. Some writing adorned it. "The laundry," she said with a note of triumph.

They were inside with the door shut and locked within seconds. Again, Tallis felt an off sense of having reluctantly met his match and satisfaction at having done so. He'd been on his own so long.

The laundry was barely functional, but at least its utility sink offered warm water. He began to strip.

"What, no tease this time?" Kavya was watching him, her pale brown eyes avaricious.

"You think I have the energy to try seducing you again, goddess?"

"No energy?" She made a noise as if contemplating the situation. "You seemed rather . . . vigorous in the cornfield."

Leaving him stunned and likely marked for life, Tallis watched as Kavya unwound the maroon cloth of her sari and unfastened the bodice, all without ceremony.

She stood naked before him.

After what he'd dreamed and what he'd already discovered of her flesh, he was revealed as a fool for thinking he knew what to expect. Not even close. Unnerving visions and real life had never diverged so sharply.

She was thin with fine, long bones. Breasts that would fill his hands with bountiful flesh to spare were perfectly formed. Her nipples beaded beneath his riveted gaze. The muscles of her stomach were lightly defined, as were the curves of her legs. Walking had made her into a woman of refined grace and strength, but with softly rounded shoulders and flaring hips that made him eager to learn more about the texture of her coppery skin. His mouth watered when his attention alit on the small thatch of dark hair at the apex of her thighs.

On top of his desire was layered his greater impulse, his true imperative: he would make her first time one she never regretted. Kavya of Indranan would know what it was to be revered not as a goddess, but as the most beautiful woman he'd ever seen.

→ CHAPTER ←
TWENTY-ONE

Kavya had never stood naked before a man until that moment, when Tallis of Pendray consumed her with eyes darkened by hunger. He might consume her with his mouth and claim her with his body, but his eyes promised it would never be enough.

Promised?

Threatened?

She didn't care.

On the inside she was trembling with anticipation and a touch of fear, but she stood before him calm and still and proud. She had borrowed too many images from other minds to doubt that she aroused men. That she aroused and had even satisfied *this* man gave her confidence. She felt hot to the touch, although her skin was pebbled with goose bumps in that small, enclosed laundry room.

"I want to kiss you," he said, his voice rough and primal.

Her body was on instant alert—not in preparation for a fight, or to muster the strength of calm to inspire her followers—but because she knew the next few moments would change her forever. "Not until I wash."

She flipped on the tap and, because there was no plug for the drain, she shoved her maroon sari to the bottom. Hot water soon filled the sink. He leaned heavily against the wall beside the sink, soaking in her every movement. She retrieved the bar of soap from their possessions and lathered it beneath the streaming faucet. The scent of sandalwood filled her nostrils and set off her imagination. She wondered how the notes of that fragrance would change when layered with the musk of Tallis's clean skin.

The process of washing was simple yet luxurious. She lathered and rinsed, then bent over the filled sink to wash her hair. Tallis kept his hands tucked behind his lower back. His expression was turning. Changing. *He* was turning. There was little left of the thinking man she had come to know. The beast inside him was taking over—with sex in mind, not violence, although, the two seemed inexorably linked among the Pendray.

She should have been afraid, but her nerves and her fears disappeared with the last of the soap from her long, clean hair. In the field, beneath his mouth, she'd felt like a goddess, but not the one he used as a tease. She'd been both powerful and helpless. Tallis looked that way now.

She squeezed out the excess water, then snatched a towel from a stack of clean laundry on a wire shelf. The luxury continued, not because the towels were soft, but because she emerged from that enveloping cloth as a new woman.

Tallis took a deep breath. He yanked his gaze away from her naked body. The speed with which he washed made her smile, even as his nudity sparked gorgeous flames in her blood. He leaned over the sink. Kavya had the most exquisite view of his arched back, the strong ladder of his ribs, the taut clench of his buttocks, and the muscles that trailed from his thighs to his calves. His legs were sleeked with hair that darkened when he scrubbed with the wet washcloth. He remained turned away from her. Rather than the teasing way he'd washed his groin in the room above the high valley pub, he rubbed the cloth quickly between his legs as if it were just another few inches of skin.

Kavya was glad for it. She wanted the heart-deep, lung-deep shock of seeing him turn around, presenting her with an offering.

He would be hard. Yearning. For her.

Sandalwood and steam made her dizzy, as did anticipation. She wanted and craved and needed in ways she'd never thought possible.

He stopped washing. Water dripped from the ends of his hair, along the column of his neck and down the dip and ridges of his back. His spine was a single row of mountains, perfectly straight. Kavya liked that.

Moving slowly, she retrieved another towel from the shelf, then stepped to within inches of his tight, hunched body. His knuckles were white where he gripped the edge of the sink. Kavya started with his hair, gently tousling the dark mass until it was dry enough for the silvery tips to shine again. She caught the drips that trailed down his neck, back, ass—which is when he flinched. Not his whole body. Just those tight twin globes, powerfully shaped.

No, she thought. Not a flinch.

More like a thrust.

She couldn't resist touching. As if to check the progress of her work, she smoothed a flat palm from his hairline to the span between the divots at the base of his spine. His ass, however, deserved more attention. She laid the towel over her shoulder and pressed her hands against his flanks. With her thumbs she caressed curving slopes of erotic muscle. Tallis hissed, then groaned. She glanced at his knuckles. Either he'd bust bone through skin, or he'd crush the edge of the porcelain sink into powder.

She kissed the back of his left hand before changing sides and kissing his right. So near, he pried his fingers loose and pushed damp strands of hair back from her face. She risked a glance up. His eyes were squeezed shut. He was touching her without looking at her, as if touch would be enough—or as if he were a man on the verge of losing himself to dangerous impulses.

She waited for that.

Had she ever entertained fantasies of how she would lose her virginity, she might have imagined tenderness. Care and comfort and soft touches. Her nightmares shoved violence into the picture, where *giving* herself was not an option. She would be taken— just another street girl assaulted or dragged into the underground sex trade. Just another Indranan woman valued as breeding stock and as fuel for continued warfare.

Nothing included this level of eroticism, where a sense of gorgeous control was woven with the knowledge that Tallis could steal that control at any moment.

Would he?

Would he hold back?

She didn't know what she wanted more. If he took her, she wouldn't have to make the decision.

But no, deep inside she knew that if she didn't tell him otherwise, he would stand there naked and motionless, with hands ready to do damage to a sink rather than to her. They might don their clothes and pretend the incident had never happened.

Kavya returned to drying him. She pushed the towel around his sides to dry his stomach and chest. She smoothed the terry cloth around the tense caps of his shoulders, then down defined ridges of triceps, biceps, and stone-hard forearms. Only when she'd tended to everything else did she venture to the place that would end her silent, overt flirtation and take the moment past the point of no return. She traced his flanks once again, around, slowly, until she rubbed the towel between his inner thighs and up along his hard shaft.

Tallis groaned a curse.

He turned so quickly that Kavya stumbled away. She hit the wall at her back. A surge of air jumped from her lungs. Part of that was from surprise and the impact of her body against cinder block. Part of it because Tallis was tall, vital, intimidating, so very *male*. The light in his eyes was viciously blue, as if the color could burn down the whole city. Instead it burned into her and melted what little remained of her hesitation. His cock jutted up and toward his navel at an angle that suggested the upward thrust of what would be his initial penetration—and every tight thrust that would follow.

Kavya still couldn't breathe. She was wet between her legs. So hot. Her skin was shrinking. Tension made her ready to burst free of that confinement.

Again she was drawn to the sight of his erection, which was even more intimidating than when he'd lain prostrate in the field. His body was worth admiring and worshiping with everything she had—her hands, her lips, and the clench of her untested sex.

"We'll dress and find a room," he growled.

The berserker was in him, not controlling him but certainly fueling him with urges that touched her primitive core. The Indranan were not primitive people—at least they didn't like to think so. Mind above body, no matter their thousands of years of violence. At that moment Kavya knew without doubt that such pride and pretense was a lie. She was as deeply primitive as Tallis. She wanted to rise to that challenge, that dare, that shocking desire.

"No." The word was a tight squeak, but she continued with assurance. "No getting dressed. And no room. I want you. Here. There's nothing to stop us now. Show me, Tallis. Show me what I've never had."

Tallis took the naked, brazen temptation of a woman in his arms before his next breath. He could have played the gentleman. He could have tried to talk her out of making such a decision in a rash, hurried way.

He could have, had he been a different man.

She lived half a life, and that life could end tomorrow. That she hadn't experienced the most transcendent experience of body to body seemed an insult to the Dragon.

With arms wrapped around her low back, Tallis held her flush and tight. He kissed her, diving deep, relishing her moan that walked a delicate line between surprise, pleasure, and protest. The protest dropped away as she drew her hands up to clench his hair. She was divinity—soft of skin, firm of flesh, eager of spirit. She didn't back away when he deepened their kiss. The angle of his head allowed him to push farther with his tongue. His teeth scraped her lower lip. Kavya repeated the motion. Her dainty teeth abraded thin, wet skin, shocking him with physical pleasure. More shocking was how he responded to making her wild.

This would be no soft initiation. Whatever softness he possessed, he'd given that to her with his mouth, there beneath a blinding blue sky. She made her harder passions known with every pinch of her fingernails against his scalp, and the way she hooked her heel behind his calf. The rock of her pelvis against his shot white sparks through his blood.

He palmed both of her shoulders and pushed her back. Kavya struggled once, again, but he had her upper body pinned. Rather than question him or try to melt him with a pleading look, she scowled. Her expression was that of a child whose present had been snatched away. He grinned. He would not be her present, but her tool.

"If I ask for patience," he said roughly, "it's important. Look in my eyes. Tell me what this pause is costing me."

She sucked her lips inward, then licked them, as if she needed to take more of him into her mouth now that she'd been deprived of the source. "You're half wild."

"Yes."

"If we'd been preparing to fight and you held your seaxes, you'd be murderous."

"Yes."

"Instead . . . the beast wants to use that power with me."

"*Yes.*"

"I'm happy you're not trying to talk sense into me. But why stop?"

"The door."

He pushed away and tossed towels onto the floor. Tallis wedged the wire shelf under the door's handle. The precaution wouldn't hold if someone was determined to get inside, but it would give Tallis enough time to arm himself.

Kavya stood where he'd pressed her against the wall. The sight of her made his mouth go dry. Yes, she was stunning, but the hunger in her amber eyes revealed how much she wanted this moment. Softness and tender caresses would wait for another time, if they had another chance at all. The quick lift and fall of her chest, which hefted and lowered her breasts in an erotic rhythm, was almost as exciting as her nudity.

I'm not going to stop.

"Good," she whispered.

Tallis closed the scant distance between them and brought his mouth down to her neck. "Don't do that again."

"I can't help it if you're screaming."

"Don't do it again," he simply repeated. "Stay with me."

She nodded. "Right here, Tallis."

She was clean and warm, delicious and intoxicating. He let his mind slip down to where he savored the elemental. The raw. The crazed. She responded with restless hands that skated over his chest, around his ribs, and down to his ass. As she had when she'd used the towel, she laid her palms flat. Only now, she grasped handfuls of muscle. He replied with a thrust. His cock rubbed between their lower bodies, nestled against the firm muscles and soft skin of her abdomen. Kavya gave him a long, mind-numbing exhalation.

He repeated the thrust every time she squeezed her fingers. His power was hers—for the moment.

Her breathing was sharp and uneven when he returned to kissing her lips. Taking those puffing exhales into his mouth was more proof of her excitement. Every hair and every pore and every deep clutch of her fingertips wrote erotic poems.

He sucked her tongue between his lips and bit the fleshy middle. The urge to use more force would've been enough to crush the bones of lesser men, but Tallis was still in charge of his inner frenzy. He only wanted to give her a sample of the aggression he withheld. Kavya slipped her taut hands up his back. She held on to his shoulders, bracing her weight against his, and accepted his testing assault. Only when he released her tongue and licked it, soothing, did he pull away to see her reaction.

Her eyes revealed every color of fire. "Again."

Tallis recaptured her mouth. She forced her tongue between his lips, between his teeth. A dare. He clasped harder, holding the bite as if he'd sunk his teeth into the sensitive skin at her nape. The thought of claiming her in the Pendray way shook his control. That manner of claiming symbolized permanence among his clan.

He didn't lose control. He didn't bite deeper. But he realized that an imagination was a bad thing when he was already so overwhelmed. To picture him bowed over her body, both of them on all fours, was an invitation to ruin her first time by default—not because he would hurt her, but because he'd be some untried lad who came before sinking home.

He released her tongue, then traveled lower. She seemed to like his hair, because she threaded her fingers into the thickest locks at his crown. Her touch didn't guide him, but as when he'd licked and sucked her pussy, she offered tiny flinches as signposts. She liked slick tonguing kisses on the undersides of her breasts, and she liked a hint of teeth across the tips of each nipple. She liked the way he breathed against her damp skin, and how he slid his caress down each gracefully strong thigh.

He knew, because she was one of the most articulate lovers he'd ever taken. She spoke with the unconscious language of her body. A week and a ream of paper wouldn't have been enough to transcribe what he learned from dipping his tongue in her navel. She offered praise and encouragement with goose bumps, panting breaths, and restless hands across his upper body. Everywhere she touched, she trailed flame.

Kavya's skin. Tallis's skin.

They still had names. They were still contained in separate bodies.

Time to change that.

He knelt on the ground with one knee on the hard concrete and one accidentally padded by a strewn towel. Only once did he glance up. Kavya had lowered her chin and was staring at him with more of that unspoken fire. She smiled. "I like this part," she said, the words full of husky teasing.

Tallis tasted and teased her honeyed sex. Every lick dragged him closer to the moment when he would need to be inside her. Somehow. *Anyhow*. He could become addicted to her as easily as he'd become a supplicant to his dreams.

But no.

He stood abruptly and kissed her again, sharing the taste of her by plunging deeply, giving no quarter. This was no dream. He was with Kavya. She moaned. The sound reverberated down his throat and his chest, until that humming excitement ratcheted his arousal. This was real because it was imperfect. A laundry room? The basement of a hotel he'd broken in to? Imperfect, yet just what he needed when the perfection of Kavya's responses raised his suspicions that she was too good to be true. Too much like his dreams.

Her slender hand grasped his cock.

"*Bathatëi!*" He snatched her wrist and pinned it against the cinder block. "Don't do that again."

She held his gaze, flames watching flames, and smiled. "I have before."

The shock of her other hand was just as powerful. Only this time, Tallis didn't pull her away. "Fine," he ground out, closing his fist around hers. "If you want to play, play."

Her rhythm was more assured this time. Long strokes down. Long pulls up. Tallis pressed harder so that their hands became overlapping vises to torture his engorged flesh. He'd taught her the rhythm he liked, the speed he liked, but he hungered for the closeness of his closed fist around hers as they pumped.

"You're big. Did I forget to mention that?"

Grinning felt out of place, but then again—no, she

was smiling and he wanted to as well. "I am. And you did forget."

"You're practically monosyllabic. Although I'm impressed I can talk at all." She wiggled the wrist he'd pinned against the wall, silently asking permission to be freed. He complied. Cupping his cheek, still gripping and caressing his cock, she gazed up at him with an expression of wonder layered over with frustration. "I didn't think I would, but I wish I could read your mind right now."

"I'm glad you can't." He grunted on a particularly fast trio of strokes.

"I wouldn't like what I found?"

"No. Just . . . pointless. Thinking. Feeling. Inseparable right now. Tell me I'm wrong."

Kavya closed her eyes and let her head fall back against the wall. The hand holding his cheek slid down, down, until she found the meat of his upper arm. She smiled softly, contentedly, although her body still hummed with want and pent-up energy.

"You're not wrong," she said. "Thinking, feeling. All the same. When I think about your size, my body aches. Thinking, feeling . . ."

"Come here. Up."

He cupped the back of her head to drag her to face level. Her eyes were hazy, yet sharp with curiosity. He would've loved to fuck her against the wall, just *taking*, which would scrape the living hell out of her back. The demon in him wanted that overload of sensation.

Tallis released her hand and forced her to release his shaft. "Hold on. Your arms around my neck." She complied, and he lifted her off the ground. The crooks of her knees locked over the inside bend of his elbows. He gripped her ass, then braced himself with his back to the wall.

"This is your first time, Kavya." He shook his head. "I can't trust myself."

"Tell me," she whispered.

Tallis closed his eyes. "Against the wall. Or down on the ground."

"You'd lose control."

"Yes."

She purred in the back of her throat, with a cat's smile to match. "Someday, maybe. But for now?"

"You're going to fuck *me."*

→ CHAPTER ←
TWENTY-TWO

His words jolted through Kavya with as much force as every physical torment he layered over her body. He wasn't kissing now—not anywhere—although the memory of his mouth between her legs released another rush of wet, hot readiness. He was enormous. She was ready for him.

He held remarkably still, considering how closely they were perched on the edge of falling. It felt like falling, into an abyss of sensation that would fill her mouth, flood her lungs, and drown her. She sucked deeper until those sensations became air and untold boldness. She leaned forward and licked from the notch at the base of his throat to his thin lower lip.

"Again," he rasped.

Because he'd complied with her equally blunt demand—when he'd bit her tongue, just shy of pain—Kavya returned the favor. That was the best part of sex so far. Returning favors.

He was sandalwood-scented, as she'd imagined, but retained a slight hint of salt and musk. The scent and taste of Tallis. Although the notch was smooth, his skin turned rougher, pebbly and scratchy with stubble as she dragged her tongue up his throat, over his chin, and back to the utterly sleek welcome of his kiss.

"Put my cock between your legs." He swallowed tightly. "I'm holding you. But I can't be the one who starts this. But once we start . . ."

"You'll set the pace?"

A ragged grin turned up one side of his mouth. "Yes, I will."

Kavya reached a hand between their bodies and grasped his thick, hard shaft. She'd loved the rush of power that came with stroking him. Now . . . now her body would do the same. Perhaps her youthful fears of being forced had made the act seem so one-sided. There was only penetration and being penetrated. But Tallis would be just as helpless as she, sucked into her warmth and pulled by the need for more and more pressure. She saw it so clearly now.

There was penetration, and there was being consumed.

They were *devouring* each other.

She rubbed a drop of slick fluid around his throbbing head. He hissed. He shifted his grip. "Do it, Kavya."

"I could tease you all night," she said against the hollow behind his ear. She licked there, then applied a test of teeth to his lobe. His reply was a thrust and a squeeze. She loved that call-and-response.

"No teasing." His voice was suddenly brittle. She heard bitterness and emotional pain. "Kavya . . ."

"You're right. No teasing. That's not what I want. I've been curious since those first moments in your tent. I've been hungry since you stripped for me. I've been half-mad since you tasted me in the sunlight. It's been long enough. More than that, it's been more than enough since meeting you."

With a shift of her pelvis, she angled so that the head of his cock nudged between her slick lips. She took a breath. Looked him in the eyes. Smiled.

She kissed him when he slid home.

Pain bolted through what had been perfect pleasure, leaving aftershocks of surprise and a gasp that he swallowed with a deeper kiss.

"So full," she gasped again, barely able to connect words. "So . . . Tallis, oh, Dragon *damn*."

"Big." He thrust up, deep. She'd thought once was spectacular enough. "Right now you can't believe it's possible. How I'm filling you." Dipping his head, he licked the tops of her breasts. "You're greedy to learn how much more you can take."

With her temple pressed down against his, she laughed. "*Now* you can talk."

"Only one of us at a time." He caught her gaze. The animal—his great gift—was staring out from Tallis's deep blue eyes. "But we've started now, Kavya."

"Yes. I don't know what I need. You do. Please."

A feral smile replaced his crooked tease. "Hold tight around my neck. I won't let you fall."

He started by drawing back from her, until his ass must've touched the wall. The entire time, he held her hips with his big, widespread hands. His surging return shook her thoughts into scattered puzzle pieces. Kavya threw her chin toward the ceiling and shuddered. He withdrew and returned. Withdrew . . . and slammed back. Each time, the feeling came as a surprise—being stretched and filled, as if she'd always been missing this questing pulse.

She tightened the insides of her knees against his arms and began to work her hips in a matching rhythm. They parted. Their eyes caught. They joined. The intimacy was breathtaking. This was feeling. *Feeling*. She'd never been closer to another living soul, in ways that had nothing to do with thought and little to do with the flesh. The flesh was the inspiration for something far deeper.

Her heart fluttered in her chest, out of time with the rest of her body. She shoved aside confusing emotional reactions in favor of ones that made sense. Tallis had bared his teeth. Each thrust freed another glimpse of the raging violence he kept leashed *for her*. A growl followed. His eyes were hazy and intense and burning and lost.

Kavya used his body. She hadn't known that was possible either, but it was so simple. She trusted his strength and his solid hold. When the pressure of pleasure began to build—almost baffling, in that it could be so much more intense—she pinched the caps of his shoulders. He took her aggression and fed it back. He drove into her with such speed and force. Sweat shimmered over his gold-flushed flesh and dampened his chest hair. She bowed her head and licked. Tallis lifted his hand, holding her mouth against his skin. He bucked up, up, up as she dropped her hips to meet him.

With her face held firmly against his chest, and her legs spread, and the whole of her stability—her satisfaction—dependent on Tallis, she finally gave up on thought. She was being penetrated *and* consumed. There was nothing of hers that he didn't master. Taking. Giving, until Kavya held nothing back. The beautiful pleasure became the pounding of drums. Bright. Sharp.

Loud. She cried out against his chest, then bit into firm muscle.

And burst apart.

She shook and gasped as distilled pleasure bathed her nerve endings. Sugar and wine and rain. Behind her lids was only white upon white.

Tallis grounded her.

Until it was his turn.

He slapped both hands back on her ass and immobilized her pelvis. She hadn't realized how much freedom he'd given her to move. This was for him. He *took*. Head lifted, Kavya watched him hurtle toward release. She could sympathize now, envy now, appreciate now—how the tendons on his neck were tight cables and how his bared teeth gave him the appearance of a man in pain rather than on the cusp of pleasure.

"Kavya," he breathed—a whispered growl. "You're real."

She crossed her arms behind his neck and pulled their upper bodies close. She was coming again, slower this time, but with a stronger power, diffuse, slamming her from all sides. Finding one of those tight tendons, she bit his neck as the shocks and aftershocks, ripples and undertow sucked her down again. In a beautiful fog, she realized what he needed.

"I'm real, Tallis. I'm Kavya of Indranan. You've just made your goddess into a woman."

He growled, tensed, drove deep one last time, until his breath became her name in a shuddering chant.

Tallis slowly eased free and lowered Kavya to the ground. Her knees buckled as she took her own weight.

He was exhausted, his mind blown, his body sated, but he pulled her to his chest in a protective, solid hold. The wall at his back was steady, just as he was steady for her. They stood that way, naked and vulnerable. He traced the length of her drying hair. She made a contented sound and nuzzled deeper. Her cheek pressed into the hollow between his pectorals. She'd be able to hear his heart, which was only beginning to return to a normal pace.

She shivered.

The room was cold, but only with that delicate shake of her shoulders did Tallis realize it. He stooped to grab one of the towels and threaded it around her back. She hugged into it, then returned to his embrace.

"Thank you," she whispered against his skin.

He was humbled. He was definitely speechless. Few events in his life had affected him with such power. To have pleased her while being given the gift of her trust was miraculous. This wasn't something he could smile about while walking away.

Especially when she shifted her weight and winced.

He glanced down. "Oh, fuck. Your feet."

Blood smeared the concrete where she'd rested the weight of one foot.

"It's not as bad as it looks. You know it'll be healed by morning."

Tallis was unmoved by protest. "Come here."

"Another go? So soon? I guess I never thought to wonder if Dragon King men possessed yet another gift—one human men would envy."

Returning her arch smile, Tallis scooped her into his arms. "And here I'd thought I was just a special case."

"You are a special case," she said, swirling her fingertips through his chest hair.

"Now you're just being a flirt." But her words were enough to still his heart—before sending it speeding to double time. "Sit here. I've got your back."

"That's the sexiest thing a man can say to me."

He nuzzled the hollow beneath her jaw. "I've got better. You just caught me out in a laundry room."

"Took you by surprise, did I?"

"Very much so."

"Good. I wanted to."

Tallis turned on the warm water, still supporting her so that she perched on the edge of the deep utility sink with her feet dangling inside. "Why was that important?"

"I was at a disadvantage. You'd given me a preview, but I didn't know what to expect. I'm not used to going into a situation where I can't get a read on it. I liked that you didn't know what was going to happen either."

"With you, Kavya, I never know what's going to happen."

She turned to kiss his shoulder. "I'll take that as a compliment."

Because he was again at a loss for words, Tallis set about tending her injured soles. "Lean forward and grip the faucet. Hold your balance while I grab more towels."

She did so, naked and glowing with clean skin, vibrant energy, and the sexual authority of a woman who'd been thoroughly satisfied, and who apparently knew what it was to level a man with her creativity and responsiveness. Tallis had been leveled. She peeked sideways through her draped hair, watching him as he gathered a trio of towels. Her smile was soft and private, yet invited him to return.

He draped the towels all over her. "As much as I'd want warm water for you, it has to be cold."

"To help stop the bleeding. Yes."

Taking each calf in hand, with his chest pressed against her graceful back, Tallis realized that no matter how satisfied he'd been by their first encounter—that was the catch. He wanted to think of it as their first, not their only. The first of many. Because her calves were beautifully sculpted with soft muscle and elegant bones. Her feet were dainty. Her ribs were narrow but told him that her breathing was picking up speed again. Those details were innumerable.

He'd never learn them all in the span of a few days. That realization stabbed regret behind his sternum and choked off his next breath.

A quick fuck against a laundry room wall wasn't enough. He was a greedy ass for wanting more than what had just blown reality onto another plane, but there it was. He wouldn't be satisfied with one taste of this woman. His deeper, animalistic soul wouldn't be either. There was tenderness to be had, and there was blood-stirring aggression—the kind he hadn't been able to indulge for her first time.

Kavya hissed when the cold water sluiced over her feet. "Oh, Dragon be. That's just mean."

"At least it's not the mountains?"

"I'll never be warm when thinking about that day. Not ever."

She began to shiver in earnest. Tallis held her closer, sharing his warmth. He rubbed her upper arms and the tops of her thighs. A gentle moan worked out of her throat.

"I guess that's not so terrible," she said.

"But we don't need you frozen either." He used one of the towels to pat dry her soles. The terry cloth came away tinged with watery pink. "Not perfect, but better."

He hoisted her from the sink and sat her on the pile of white he'd tossed down from the wire shelf. She still huddled into one towel, but it didn't cover beautiful glimpses of her body. Copper skin poked out everywhere. The backs of her hands, the slope of her throat, the tops of her knees. He shook his head and focused on his task. He couldn't get them up to a room without looking the part of a guest.

The hotel room was the goal. He wanted her there, in bed, in his arms.

Then they'd talk about Scotland. He had a plan, finally. She needed to know why he was contemplating the unthinkable.

Going home.

Tallis pulled on his new clothes.

"That's hardly fair," she said with a smile.

"You're the invalid. Get better, then you can make the rules. I'm not playing nurse while kneeling naked."

"You just don't want me to see you when you're not so Dragon-damned impressive."

He wiggled his eyebrows above a smirking smile. "Doesn't matter. You know what's waiting for you when you want it."

"I want it."

She didn't look away or blush like a girl, nor did laughter tickle behind her words. It was a blunt, assured statement that unmoored him again. Tallis knew how things ought to have been. This wasn't it.

Only, he couldn't find it in himself to wish for anything else. Just him. Kavya. A cold cement floor. And a magnet-strong attraction between them that neither could deny.

"Did I hurt you?"

"Not any more than I wanted." She trailed her fingertip up down his forearm. "It was . . . There aren't words."

With his gaze riveted to hers, he said evenly, "You'll have it. Me. My prick. At your beck and call." He paused, but realized he had one more promise to make—for him, a man who didn't make promises. "And I'll have your back."

She stilled her petting caress on a soft, "Oh."

Tallis had to look away. She infected him with a complete loss of perspective. He'd experienced that same feeling before, when under the spell of his dream version of the Sun, and swore he'd never again fall for that spinning, twirling sense of losing his way.

Being with Kavya was being lost and found.

He used the point of his seax to shred pieces of a towel, then fashioned them into neat bandages that looked a little like socks. Not the most traditional of Indian garments to be worn with a sari, but he only needed to fake their way upstairs. Carefully, he smoothed her new slippers over the wrapped cloth. He helped her stand and retrieved the simple blue sari from their collection of new purchases.

One look at the yards of fabric and he simply handed it over. "Can't help you there."

"Oh, but you help getting it off just fine."

She pleated and twisted intricate folds until she was swathed in blue. The color didn't bring out her eyes so much as create an undeniable contrast. The purest sunrise blue against amber-brown mountains. With a few deft moves, she braided her hair and tied it off with a piece of the ruined maroon sari. Up and around, she curled it into a dark, lustrous crown, then wrapped the last swatch of blue cloth over her head, around her throat, and down one shoulder.

Tallis stared, blinking only when she asked, "Respectable enough?"

"Just enough."

While packing their things and setting the laundry room to rights, he shivered. Only once, but it penetrated into his marrow and every cell. The basement cold wasn't to blame, but the realization that with regard to Kavya of Indranan, he was in very deep trouble.

⋆ CHAPTER ⋆
TWENTY-THREE

Tallis escorted Kavya up the rear steps and toward the check-in desk. A young clerk sat on a narrow stool reading a celebrity tabloid. Through the use of her gift and an extra bump, bump of her hips, Kavya seduced the clerk within moments.

"Key to the top floor." Her voice was the essence of sweet innocence.

His reaction was as predictable as phases of the moon: the clerk nodded and retrieved the key. His eyes were unfocused, his jaw a little slack.

Kavya placed a finger on her lips. "Shhh. Don't tell."

Only when they were up the stairs and out of sight did Tallis level her with a questioning glare. "And if he does tell?"

She shook her head and wouldn't meet his eyes. "He won't remember us in a few moments. We'll be nothing more substantial than a story he read in that paper."

"Why didn't you tell me you could do that in the first place?"

"You seemed so heroic in trying to find a back way in."

"You're teasing me. What's the real reason?"

"I told you," she said with quiet sobriety. "I don't use

it for personal gain. Two times now, both for a roof over our heads. It feels as wrong as prostitution."

He gripped her shoulders until they stood face to face. "Then I won't ask you to do it again. Promise."

"You can do that?"

"I've made more promises in the last hour than I have in a decade."

After a quiet intake of air, her eyes wide, Kavya keyed the lock. Tallis was equally taken aback by his words, but that didn't make them less true. He followed her into a long room with narrow walls and a low ceiling. The bed would accommodate two people, and the sink had faucets. There was a mirror and a small padded chair, the upholstery of which was worn but serviceable. In all, he was pleased with his choice of hotel.

"How many guests?" he asked.

"Nine people in the building," she said, her concentration plain. He liked the reassurance of being able to recognize when she used her gift. "That will probably change come evening."

Tallis shut the door, caught her by the waist, and pressed her against the white-painted wood. Her sensual mouth was within inches of his. "You *will* sleep tonight, even if I have to stay awake until dawn with both seaxes in hand. We have a long way to go. And you'll need it. I have plans for us."

"Plans? Do tell."

"Later. Right now we have better things to do."

Tallis kissed her with a degree of feeling he'd never experienced. There was passion, the mating of mouths and the struggle to taste, feel, explore even more. There was tenderness, so that his gift didn't overpower his higher-level thinking. He wanted to make love to Kavya with both halves of his nature.

Always in the past, that balance had been a struggle to maintain. He'd stay too cloistered in the logic of a thinking man, or he'd leave rationality behind in favor of easy, beastly impulses. Only upon emerging from one of his rages did he feel anything other than bloodlust—or in this case, the lust between a woman and a man. He compared himself to a junkie who lived for the high, when nothing else mattered, but who suffered the regret of again having given in.

This was no struggle. Two halves blended in harmony, kissing Kavya.

He braced his palms flat against the door, on either side of her head. She had the freedom to touch him. He refrained. For now. Her touch was enough, as she skimmed her hands beneath the layers of his shirt and new coat. She was the most intriguing mix of eager and tentative, as if even now, after her wild initiation, she remained unsure of what to do next and how to get what she wanted. He was tempted to show her more, but not yet. How would she go about tackling the puzzle of her sexual inexperience?

This was . . . novel. Sweet. Intriguing.

Kavya pushed her tongue into his mouth, then made a frustrated noise. She pulled away, met his gaze. "I liked your teeth."

"Then ask for them."

"No. Bite my tongue."

"So bossy," he said quietly, smirking. "Fine. I'll oblige."

Taking her head in his hands, Tallis held her steady

while he plundered her mouth, tasting. *Savoring*. She was hot enough to singe him to cinders. She pushed her tongue forward again. An offering. He nipped at the tip, scraped along the sides, then bit the meaty center. Her body stilled, as did the restless caresses under his shirt. Tallis's heart thudded. They didn't move. Together, they melted into the moment as he sank his teeth more deeply. How much could she take? Was there pleasure in her pain? The thought surged blood into his cock and made his lungs burn.

He moaned. She replied with a squeak of a gasp.

What seemed like an eternity later, bound in that dangerous test of wills, she scraped her nails down his spine before digging them into his sides. Tallis released his bite, then plunged again. They sucked each other into a vortex of passion that jacked up eight notches with a single act. Although he still kissed her deeply, he kept from touching her by drawing on an unknown source of control. This was her show to direct.

Kavya was not a woman to disappoint.

She broke their kiss to look down and unzip his jacket in one clean sweep of metal. She pushed his hands away from the wall even as she continued to undress him. The jacket hit the floor. After quickly unbuttoning the neck of his henley, she pulled it over his head. His plain cotton undershirt followed.

He stood before her, naked from the waist up. Her breathing matched his—as if she was ready for another fuck against the wall, her cravings that intense.

She only looked at him, overwhelming him with a keen amber gleam. Nothing in Tallis's life had felt so charged with potential. The next hour could take one of a thousand directions. For now, that direction was hers to dictate, although his mindless brutality was slowly amassing. His best intentions wouldn't last.

She smoothed a fingertip along his left collarbone, then down between his pecs. "This is your fault."

"What is?"

"It was a dare when you stripped for me, but it's part of us now. You on display. Don't move. I just want to touch and look."

Tallis tipped his head to the ceiling and swallowed. He nodded.

"You see," she continued, "my senses have never been as important as knowing people's thoughts. That was my best defense. That was the best way I could assess if a person was a threat. This . . . this is my senses trying to keep up. A steep learning curve compared to you."

Her gaze scorched him everywhere. Her hands followed. She teased down the trail of his chest hair to where it edged around his navel and arrowed toward the waistband of his cargos. The next slide of her hands was both palms up his ribs. She took her time, then grabbed both pecs and squeezed. Just once. She moved on to his shoulders and down the length of his arms. That was delicate, almost tickling. She clasped his hands briefly.

Her mouth took the place of her hungry gaze and questing fingertips. She placed openmouthed kisses on his biceps and tugged the far side of his neck so she could burn another against the cap of his shoulder. "So tall," she said against damp skin. "I like that."

Tallis shuddered. He was being seduced. He knew

it and liked it and feared it at the same time. This was eerily reminiscent of some of his dreams, when the Sun would dominate him.

"What is it?" Kavya had stopped kissing him. She was looking at him with obvious concern.

"In my dreams of . . . of who I thought was you . . ." He shook his head, surprised by the suffocating embarrassment that crept up from his chest. Kavya's hand kept him in the here and now. Perhaps she felt the flushing heat of his idiocy. "I was seduced, like you're doing now. Only, she was more practiced. She was never unsure of herself, or unsure of what I wanted. She would edge me to such a frenzy. I . . . Dragon damn it, Kavya, I gave in to her demands but she never followed through. I spent two decades perched a half step away from satisfaction. It wasn't a life, just a string of betrayals and waning faith. I should've realized . . ."

"You were manipulated by a force beyond your control. After so many years, how could you have known your own thoughts from the ones she gave you?" The press of the sari against his skin was cool, slightly rough. Grounding. "I've known those doubts. After each Mask. After living among too many people, too many minds for so long—there were times when I couldn't sort through the basics of my own wants and needs."

"How do you manage?"

"Indranan are taught from a young age how to keep thoughts in boxes. Mine go in one box, separated and memorized—the better to make sure they're mine. Impressions from other people and old Masks have boxes of their own, like quarantined contagions. Sometimes they seep through. I get confused. I have to sort through the glimpses, remember who I am. Tallis, look at me." They locked eyes, locked souls. "Whatever evil invaded your mind used sex as a weapon. That's not me. No matter what happens between us, that will *never* be me."

"Another promise so soon?" He masked his dizziness with a quip, then a quick kiss to the bridge of her nose. "Dangerous."

"We've already been playing dangerously." She nestled her mouth against his upper arm, talking directly against his skin. "I've made myself vulnerable. The Indranan are reserved for a reason: self-preservation. Before arriving here, I doubt you've met many on your travels."

"I haven't, actually. Those I've met have been crossbred, or in service of the cartels. The latter weren't the kind I'd want to sit down with for a long chat. Twice-cursed, all of them."

"See? You might not understand the full extent, but I've done what few of my people ever dare."

He took her hand and led her to the bed. They sat side by side, fingers linked. "Tell me?"

"It's all about senses, as I've said. When I'm with you, like this, or when we're fighting and plotting—focused on each other, from those first moments in the camp . . . I'm me."

With his free hand he unwrapped the blue linen that concealed her hair. "What does that feel like?"

"Terrifying."

"Should we stop?"

"No." Her eyes were slick with a sheen of moisture. Tallis wanted to shut his own eyes, to shut off the source of the ache that made his pulse pick up an odd rhythm. "I want this, because it's the freest I've been in my life."

"Terrifying," he repeated. "That feels just about right. I've been half convinced everything I do is still based on another person's dictates. That hasn't been the case for these last few days, even when you're bossing me around."

"I don't *boss*. I delegate." Kavya took a deep breath. "But if what I'm doing is too much like your dreams, what now? I can't avoid being what she imitated."

His mind made up, Tallis turned their bodies so that they faced each other on the bed. He unbound her hair. No matter how difficult it was to wrap a sari around a woman's body, unwrapping one was like opening a gift. He released the linen pleats and tucks until the fabric pooled at her waist. A matching blue bodice, which resembled an elaborately decorated yet concealing bra with wide straps, covered her breasts.

"It's like you said." His voice was rough, but he was surprisingly in control. Again . . . he had that sense of having been able to do with Kavya what he'd never done before: join his two natures in common purpose. "Our senses. Talk to me. Touch me. Let me hear you with my ears and feel you with my skin. I want to keep tasting you until I've memorized it beyond anyone's ability to fake. Ground me in what she couldn't know. Be the free woman you described. Be Kavya. Be my real woman."

His words were too much like an endearment for Kavya to bear. There was nothing to be gained from this man other than the physical: safety and gratification. Yet she couldn't help a new, unfamiliar affinity adding weight to her soul while lifting her shoulders—as if he'd used that same physical prowess to alleviate unseen burdens.

"You know I'm real," she said matter-of-factly. "You know the difference now."

A glimmer of his usual humor returned. "Then by all means." He stretched back on the bed, hands pillowed behind his head. "Continue."

Kavya didn't know where to start. At the start of each new encounter, she repeated the same phrase. *I don't know where to start.* That was the glory of leading with instinct rather than thought. She simply reached out for the buttons of his fly.

He was already firming beneath her hands as she loosened the fabric. The bulge of his erection shaped his briefs, tempting her to reveal him to her greedy eyes and curious touch. But it was too soon. She had bared so much of his beautiful body. Time to return the favor. She stood and unwrapped the rest of her sari's overlapping layers, not to tease him but to keep it from tangling as she crawled atop him. Wearing only her undergarments, she forged a path of discovery from the waistband of his briefs to his throat, using only her mouth. Then her fingernails. She licked and kissed and scratched, absorbing as many details as she could. Salt. Silk. Musk. Sleek hair and firm—Dragon damn, such firm muscles.

He watched her perusal with little remaining of his dark suspicion. Instead he smirked with a knowing expression. He knew that she wanted him, so she shot the same knowing expression right back. Had she been able to talk to his thoughts, she would've told him, *You can't wait to be inside me again.*

She stopped mid-lick along a ridge of muscle bisecting his abdomen. Why wish for what she couldn't do? She couldn't communicate with him that way, and he'd specifically asked for speech. Her voice. Something he could hear with his ears and know was real.

She swallowed thickly. "You can't wait to be inside me again."

Tallis flinched. *"Yes."*

He grabbed her head with both hands. The flare of fire in his deep topaz blue eyes turned nuclear. "And since we're in the mood to try new things, take off the rest of my clothes."

Tipping her head, Kavya frowned. "You're in charge now?"

"New territory to explore."

She held his gaze a little longer—an abject dare. "Lift your hips."

Within a minute, she'd dropped the cargos and his briefs to the floor, revealing his impressive body to the late afternoon sunlight that slanted through the room's small window. Slats of wood over the window lit stripes across his stomach and down his legs. His thick cock lay heavily on his low abdomen, with the head reaching for his navel. That massive organ had filled her. She didn't know exactly how, because the physical dimensions didn't make logical sense. But she remembered the fullness, the completeness of having taken that length deep inside. She wanted that as much as he did.

"Come here with that curious mouth." His voice was dark and low again, but without the worrying suspicion. He was entirely aroused, which reflected so plainly in his tense ligaments, his stiff limbs, and the heavy power of his ravenous stare. "I want your lips here."

Kavya looked on in shock as he took his prick in hand and smoothed the head with his palm. The rhythm was just as she remembered, how he'd loved to grip her fist in his, setting a pace that should've been painful. She knew better now. It was glorious.

She'd accepted his dares and challenges from the beginning. No way would she stop now, especially when he was right—new territory.

She straddled his naked body, with her knees bracketing his calves.

"Hold your hair out of the way," he said. "I want to watch."

A shudder of desire shook up her spine and out across her shoulders. With deliberate care, she twined her hair and handed it to him as she leaned into place. "You hold it. I'll be busy."

The first touch of her tongue was the most pure. The most shocking. He jerked. She flinched back. His salty spice lingered in her mouth. She bent down for another taste. He was hotter there than anywhere else on his body. In fact, the only heat that matched the throbbing head of his cock was the sweet ache between her legs. They matched in that fiery impatience.

She did everything by instinct. Tongue swirling. Mouth sucking. Lips moving up and down his steel-hard length with a light mimic of the rhythm she'd already learned to be his preference. Tallis tightened his hand in her hair and added his encouragement with whispered curses, endearments, and raunchy commands.

"Just . . . Shit, just like that. Ah, Kavya. Yes. Yes, suck me."

Kavya become bolder as her awkwardness melted

away. There was no time for awkwardness when presented with such an unexpected thrill. She took him in hand and matched the pulse of her mouth to the pulse of her strokes.

"See?" His taunting word was said with a smile and a gasp. "I'm back inside you."

As if to punish him for being insolent, she tucked her teeth behind her lips and nipped at his sensitive head. He moaned, thrust, twisted her hair.

"Again?" she asked innocently.

"Yes. Again and again."

She indulged him because he wanted it and, more powerfully, because it pleased her. She was ready to straddle higher up his body and sink onto that magnificent length, but she lingered. The deliberate prolonging of pleasure was the most beautiful torture. Not teasing. Not promising something she wouldn't deliver. This would make fusing their bodies even more powerful. She was still a novice, but that much she knew.

A drop of fluid slicked across her tongue. She tested the potent essence with closed eyes. Her breasts grew heavy and full, aching, needing the urgency of his hands. Her thighs trembled.

"Enough," he said with a growl.

An honest, soul-rending *growl*.

Kavya's world spun when she found herself on her back with the ceiling above her. Then Tallis's face. He was half-crazed. How had he hidden that so well, with his body nearly motionless during her exploration? However he'd managed, he held nothing back now.

"You." That one word was a sharp burst from her

lungs. "*You*, Tallis. Talk to me. I don't care what you say, but I need to know you're in there."

His jaw bunched. His nostrils flared. His blue eyes were lost to the commanding authority of his gift. He still held her hair in a tight fist, whereas his other hand gripped her hip with equal ferocity. He'd paused at the most provocative moment, with his cock poised to enter her with one unrelenting thrust.

"Hold on," he gritted out. "This is going to get rough."

→ CHAPTER ←
TWENTY-FOUR

Tallis let himself go. He let himself become what they both wanted, wild yet contained. His goal was not to hurt Kavya of Indranan, but to pleasure her in a way that satisfied his deepest, most brutal instincts. The gift that gave him power as a warrior gave him prowess as a lover.

With a precise stroke, he angled into her body and buried his cock until their abdomens pressed flush. He groaned in the ecstatic relief of having his urges appeased. Her wide-eyed surprise fueled a second groan. She was a wild creature beneath layers of restraint. *Why isn't she mine?* He couldn't catch his logic long enough to remember the reasons.

Kavya clenched the muscles of his ass and whispered, "Perfect, my gorgeous beast."

He tucked his head beside hers on the pillow, where he could kiss and suckle her neck as he set their pace. He used long, plunging thrusts that seemed almost languorous. Only the force he put behind each return to her slick channel said he wasn't being kind—not to either of them. She was a freshly tested woman, whose body wasn't used to such treatment. He was a man holding on to civility by threads as thin as a spider's silk.

She would come first. That wasn't up for debate. He needed to hold on a little longer. Read her cues. Listen to her gasps. Feel when the clench of her deep muscles signaled his turn for bliss.

Bowing lower, he palmed one of her breasts and shaped it toward his mouth. He caught the nipple in his mouth, swirled his tongue, grazed it gently as she'd done when going down on him. Kavya arched into his erotic touch and tunneled her fingers into his hair, as she seemed wont to do when sensation took her words and sense.

No, she had one word left. One word that meant her thinking mind was offering her body wholeheartedly. "More," she rasped. "More, more, more."

Tallis intended to ask what she meant. Which more? But that wasn't the result. With her chant in his ears, he bared his teeth and scraped them across her nipple. She arched toward him. More of that. Yes. She revealed herself more than perhaps she knew, craving pain and pleasure intertwined.

Dragon damn, he wanted to claim her.

How?

How much more?

There were steps he could take. The traditional ways of the Pendray—ways that would bind them forever. He . . .

Can't stop.

"Don't want you to stop," she whispered.

"Witch."

Withdrawing from her sleek heat was nearly impossible. Kavya clawed his ass and back, trying to keep him close, which made it even more difficult. Only his goal made the brief absence bearable.

He shoved her down so roughly that the bedsprings creaked and the headboard smacked against the outer wall. "Over," was all he managed to say.

When Kavya didn't comply fast enough—so new to this, so untested—he shoved his arms beneath her lower back and flipped her onto her stomach. She squealed and fought. Tallis grinned tightly against the rush of power that came from being able to grab her wrists and keep her from slipping free. "Going somewhere?"

With his free hand, he lifted her pelvis to create the perfect angle for his return. He pulsed inside her, looming over her, his back an arch around her squirming body.

"Because this," he gasped against her nape, "this is where I want you. Where else would you go?"

"Nowhere." The word was more breath than sound. That was new. That was welcome. Kavya wasn't perfect, and neither was her seduction. She was artless. The studied calm of her cultured voice slipped away in favor of animalistic sounds that matched his inner tumult, stoking them to greater heights, bathed them in hotter fires. "Nowhere but here. What do I do?"

He made the mistake of letting go of her wrists. She caught his hand in one of hers and bit the fleshy pad at the base of his thumb. Tallis thrust harder, but she kept her primal hold on two inches of his flesh. He liked it, too, that blend of possessive pain and the utter pleasure of knowing he'd taken her down this road toward sexual madness.

"Keep that," he said. "Yours. Show me what you do with things that are yours. How you own them."

She tightened her jaw. Tallis felt as if she'd break skin

with her sharp little teeth, but he knew what his skin could take. He could take anything she wanted to give. She let up and licked, sucked, started again.

He dragged her up to all fours. Only briefly did he remove his hand from the vicinity of her mouth, so that he could hook that arm under her body. He supported her torso, with his forearm between her breasts—and put his hand back where she needed him. She kissed his palm, his fingertips, and the twin crescents of teeth marks she'd embedded in the lower stretch of his thumb.

She was the most unexpected woman. Erotic. Needy. Fearless.

With a last pull toward restraint, Tallis pushed her hair away and nuzzled his mouth at the base of her hairline. "I want to bite you here," he said against her skin. "How much could you take?"

"Anything you can give."

His mind was splitting in two: good sense on one side, greed on the other. If he sank his teeth into her flesh, *right there* . . .

He'd claim her. By Pendray tradition she would be his, and she wouldn't even know it.

Tallis groaned, tossing her hair so that it covered that temptation. He returned to mating their bodies in a fierce dance. No more foreplay, even if that foreplay had involved some of the roughest sex he'd ever indulged. At that moment, he'd tear her open and live inside her skin, burrow into her bones, swim in her veins along with the blood that powered her heart.

He gasped in relief and surprise when she thrust her hips back to meet his, twice, three times, and thrashed her head. Chin toward the ceiling, she cried out her release. Every ligament and joint tightened. She was frozen in the grasp of the orgasm that washed over her and through her and up into Tallis.

It was the permission he'd waited for.

Pulling her up to a kneeling position, he crossed both arms around her torso. Big hands. Full breasts. Tight hold. He was all body and force of motion. One hand crept up to her throat and held her chin to the ceiling in a mimic of how she'd arched when she came. Tallis pressed his lips against her throat and took, took, took. The brilliant colors that danced behind his eyes were almost distracting, until there was nothing left but a blaze of red so strong that it rivaled the burst of his orgasm. Sensation shot from his balls and the base of his shaft, until nothing was spared—no nerve centers, no hidden places. He was blasted open by pleasure as potent as moonshine and as pure as his rage.

Only he wasn't a Pendray in the midst of a berserker rage.

He was a devastated man.

Kavya didn't sleep, and neither did Tallis. They lay together in the near-darkness of twilight, as the city's electric rainbows played over their bed. The room was cold. Wrapped with Tallis beneath the covers, Kavya idly caressed the varied textures of his skin. Smooth shoulders. Rough cheeks. Silky hair down the length of his chest, the hair changing texture around his sex. She touched him because they both needed her to, just as she needed to be touched. Connection.

The frustration of being unable to read his thoughts had given way to fascination. So many other ways to communicate. Some were inept by comparison to the streamlined sharing of knowledge between one mind and another, but she was known as the Sun. Her speeches were all delivered orally. She'd long since learned the value of intonation and hesitation and cadence.

Now she was communicating with Tallis in a way that was so intimate that she reminded herself to breathe. She was pressed flush against him from the calves on up, with her head pillowed by the hollow below his shoulder. She was fatigued and felt utterly pampered. What a strange thing to find in the arms of a Pendray.

"Are you sore?"

It was the first he'd spoken since having finished what had been . . . astonishing. Kavya hadn't known that ferocity lived within her. What the Sun gave her followers was an insipid, limp thing compared to how she and Tallis had become as mighty as lava hitting cold ocean water—gusts of steam and fire that wouldn't die.

"I think I will be," she said quietly. The darkness made for a reliable confidant. She could talk to him without too much latent embarrassment. She didn't *feel* embarrassed, but her throat closed and her face heated on a wash of memories. Talking to him within night's shadows was nearly as private as being able to speak into his mind. She kissed the outer curve of his chest muscle. "We didn't hold much back. Unless . . . Did you?"

He chuckled softly. The amusement rumbled in a low hum that infused her bones. "Hold much back?"

"Yes. Was that a leisurely stroll for you?"

"I wouldn't say a stroll, no." Tallis tightened his arm around her shoulders and kissed the top of her head. "But yes. I did."

Kavya searched her memories for any sense of hesitation. Only one came to mind. "You wanted to bite the back of my neck. I even dared you."

He took a deep breath. "That would've been more than sex, Kavya. For a Pendray, anyway. Had we done that after the blessing of my family, we'd be married."

A shot of adrenaline threatened to burst her skin with that single word. Married?

To this man?

To *any* man?

No, not just anyone. Tallis was unique in that.

"How . . . ?" She needed to swallow. "How do you mean?"

"My clan's tradition."

His voice sounded trapped between affection and resignation. It was the tone people used when speaking about family, religion, and cultural differences. Sometimes there was no denying that even the most treasured customs could appear ridiculous. Kavya had felt it—that urge to apologize for aspects of Indranan life that flummoxed outsiders.

"The man and woman are blessed by an elder," he said. "That person could be anyone of standing in a community, even a senior member of a household. A trusted guarantor acknowledges the union on behalf of the clan." His fingers climbed her spine and settled at the base of her skull. Her nape tingled. "After that, the deed is consummated. There's no ceremony. No structure. Nothing witnessed by anyone else."

"Just sex?"

"I know you didn't have experience, but did that feel like 'just sex' to you?"

Kavya shook her head. He continued to stroke the back of her neck, which had suddenly taken on more significance. He seemed to catch himself doing so, but he didn't stop. He pulled back loose strands to bare her skin completely.

"No, not casual. It was . . . intense. Concentrated? A thousand things distilled into one moment."

"Which moment?"

His chest had stilled. He wasn't breathing, awaiting her answer. She didn't know what he wanted to hear, or whether knowing would change what she said.

Truth or lie. Both held separate dangers.

The truth was all that mattered.

"When you could've bit my nape," she whispered.

A shudder worked up his long body, with its elegant bones and lithe, taut muscles. "It would've been . . . uneven. I can't explain it any more eloquently. For you it would've been just another part of the experience. For me . . ."

Kavya pushed onto her elbow and found an angle where the lights from the slatted window shone across his face. Just his mouth. She would've liked to see his eyes, but his lips were so expressive. Everything about him was expressive. Were all the Pendray this way? So open? Not so constantly guarded? She envied them, if that was true.

She cupped his cheek, feeling for truth. "It would've been the act of joining without the meaning. That significance must be woven through every fiber of your ancient soul." She softly kissed his mouth. "You stopped to protect yourself, didn't you?"

"Yes. A life ritual with nothing behind it. I couldn't

do that. I would've thought I had more claim to you than I do."

Kavya shivered. Again she was overcome by the idea of being bound to Tallis. Married? How could she even think the word if she didn't love . . .

Oh, by the Dragon.

I do love him.

The back of her neck practically burned with the passion and possession he'd kept from them both.

Her entire life, all she'd wanted was the right to make her own choices. She didn't want to be another Indranan woman caught in the net of vicious traditions and deadly cycles. With Tallis, however, she almost wished he had taken that choice from her. Then she could love him, have him, keep him, without the staggering fear of picturing their future. One on the run? Constantly? They'd break into hotels and fly airplanes through snowstorms—not because they wanted to, but because external forces toyed with their lives.

She wouldn't accept him on those terms. She wouldn't let him accept *her* on those terms.

Kavya loved Tallis of Pendray. As with so many instances, she was glad he had no access to her thoughts. She needed to bury that realization so deeply that even she couldn't bring it into the light and admire its bright prism of colors and hope. Keeping her heart intact depended on it.

He turned his face so that his mouth nestled in her palm, pulling her free of her trembling reverie. "How do the Indranan marry? No one would ever tell me."

Ah, the Indranan way. That would help keep her fancies in check. She wanted nothing to do with love and a forever partner if it meant doing so by the dictates of her clan.

"Kavya?" He kissed her fingertips.

"The Indranan are bound with their minds. They . . . open themselves. All their thoughts. They throw open the doors and cupboards and boxes—everything that holds a piece of a secret. It can take days. Imagine how much of your life resides in your mind. All that makes you Tallis. And all that makes me Kavya." She hunched her shoulders to wiggle deeper under the covers. "I've never been able to fathom that."

"Revealing every detail? No, I can't even imagine." He laughed a little. "But look what we did here. You were a virgin. You offered me that rare gift, and I managed to believe I could make it worth your while."

"You worried about disappointing me?"

"And hurting you, yes."

Stated so bluntly, Kavya realized just how easily he could've taken advantage of her willingness. Knowing his strength, his size, his passions—now she understood the care he'd taken to keep her safe. Another man might not have been so vigilant, while still being generous in giving her exactly what her body had demanded: a frenzy of release.

"You made me wild, Tallis. *That* was a gift."

"It was in you the whole time. But it was fun to see you let loose with me."

"I felt like a different woman." After a deep breath, she kissed him again and closed her eyes. Darkness. Safe to say whatever she needed to say. "The woman in your mind. Did she ever bring out that impulse in you? To bite her?"

He sat up, leaving her cold. "No."

"And she never offered it as temptation?"

"No."

Each refutation was stark. His skin became a field of goose bumps beneath her hands.

"Then she might not have known the ritual," she said. "Is it well known? You had no luck learning the Indranan way."

"I can't imagine many Pendray bragging about our customs, not among the Five Clans. We're already considered little better than dogs. All those werewolf stories through the years. Rabid canines. Wouldn't the other clans love to learn how close to home those stories hit? We fuck like animals."

Her chest was tight. Breathing had become some magical skill possessed by other people. "So you said."

"And we marry like animals. Biting and scratching. If a couple doesn't emerge the next morning wearing each other's war wounds, people start to talk."

"No passion?"

"No trust." He turned on the bed and caught her face in his hands. The gentleness he was capable of demonstrating was all the more potent when contrasted with his hurricane potential. "How deep to bite. How long. How much pain to inflict and take. I suppose it's the physical flip side to what you Indranan do. Lay everything bare and see if a union withstands the process."

He kissed her, licked her bottom lip, delved inside to stroke his tongue over hers. She exhaled through her nose and sank more deeply into his attentions.

Only when he pulled back did she find the presence

of mind to bring reality back into their room. "But that wasn't us. Not here tonight. This was . . . Thank you, Tallis."

"You thanked me in the laundry."

"I meant it then, too."

With a lopsided grin, he ran his hands through his hair. The motion lifted his arms, stretched his chest, bared the undeniable masculinity of his underarms. "Anytime, goddess. I've never been thanked for something so easy to give."

"Easy? I don't believe that."

They held each other's gaze in darkness shredded into strips by rainbow beams of light. "You probably shouldn't, no. But the issue remains: What now? Morning will come and, as much as I hate to admit it, we can't stay here for weeks and continue exploring each other until we're half crazed."

"Among the Pendray—does that crazed feeling wear off?"

"Let me ask you one in return. Among the Indranan—do the doors close again, barring off secrets?"

"No," Kavya said carefully. "Minds open. For the rest of their lives."

Tallis stood with a shrug. "There's your answer."

She shivered with the loss of his heat, and the implied knowledge that what had taken place between them would be how Pendray men and women . . . *made love*. Vicious and needy and daring. The prospect was exciting but intimidating. She had been a wild woman for a night. That didn't mean she could be that person forever.

Forever. With Tallis.

She cleared her throat. "So what was this grand plan of yours? The one you said could wait for later?"

"We'll need warmer clothes for you. And another moped if ours isn't there in the morning. The airport's some ways south?"

"About twenty minutes by the main roads. Why? You have someplace in mind?"

"I do."

Kavya frowned. "Out with it, Tallis. I don't want to play guessing games about something so important."

"No matter what we decide about my dreams or your clan, Pashkah will come for you again. Isn't that so?"

A shudder replaced the giddy, almost girlish joy she'd experienced with Tallis's attention—and the hot-cold terrifying joy of realizing that she'd fallen in love with him.

But no. Pashkah. Always intruding. *Always*.

"Yes, he'll always come for me."

"Then you're right. We'll face him, but on our terms."

"There can be no 'our terms' when we're here. Even now, among six million people, his personal army could be fanning out through the streets and alleys. We may have accidentally picked a place that will take some time to find. But he has the Dragon-forged sword he stole from my parents, and he *won't stop*." She threw up her hands. "In that, I'm out of luck. I've never been part of a pod to share a sword with people who'd protect me."

He turned and looked down at her, suddenly so calm and ethereally beautiful. "I have a Dragon-forged sword."

Kavya's heart leapt, only to be stilled by doubt and lit by a flicker of fury. "Don't joke, Tallis. Not about that."

"Especially not about that."

"So tell me, where have you been hiding it?"

His grin was slow and sultry, like a cherry-red sun taking its time to rise in the east. "I think it's time you visit Scotland."

"No."

"Yes. At my family estate."

"But . . . you haven't been back in twenty years. You're the Heretic." She joined him in standing and wrapped her arms around his trim waist. "A straight answer, now. What will it cost you to return there?"

He exhaled heavily. "All these years, I thought that if I truly wanted to, I could go back. Defend my actions. Stand trial, if I needed to. Face execution. Whatever the punishment, I'd at least be able to say good-bye to my family. At least I'd be home."

"Staying away means never having to know for certain."

"That's right." He retrieved one of his seaxes, then held it nearer to the window. A shaft of light made the steel gleam. He pressed her fingers against a circle in the hilt. "Do you feel where the metal's raised? It's a concealed gold inlay that can be removed in emergencies, like how pirates of old wore gold earrings to cover the cost of their burial. It hasn't been an emergency until now. We have the means to get to Scotland. If you want that sword . . . If you . . ." He shrugged.

Kavya curled against his side on the bed and stared at the gleaming metal, at how right it looked when Tallis held it with such assurance. "If I what?"

"If you want my protection. That's the only reason I'd be willing to return to a place that may never again be home."

Yes, she loved him. And yes, he had a plan. She could see it burning out of him as if his golden skin had been lit by a thousand candles. But she needed to hear an answer to the question she could barely form. "Why for me?"

Tallis didn't say anything. He only kissed her temple and settled his hand around the back of her neck, with his thumb gently caressing her nape.

❖ CHAPTER ❖
TWENTY-FIVE

Tallis emerged from the taxi and looked out over the barren waste of a long, long valley. There was no end to it, just gray-green grass that faded into the fog-shrouded place where the land met the sea.

"It's breathtaking," Kavya said at his side, her words hushed. "I've never seen anything like it."

He didn't want her to like his home. He didn't want her to get any closer to him than she'd already become. Emerging from the wildness of the Pir Panjal was nothing compared to the bureaucratic and financial nightmare of flying into Edinburgh. Normally Tallis took the slow route. Borders weren't borders when they were simply a set of coordinates on a map that no one took notice of in an official capacity.

To fly? By commercial airline? That was completely different. Governments and companies. Security checks and the process of thoroughly exhausting Kavya as she threaded them through human physical and legal barricades. He'd promised that she'd never have to use mind control for selfish reasons—to have that feeling of prostituting herself. But she'd insisted. It was the fastest way to continue their escape from India. His seaxes would still be in Turkey if she hadn't intervened. They would've been detained overnight in Hamburg without her ability to fuzz tiny details into nothing.

Much like the fog erased the details of a valley he used to know so well.

They had been together almost exclusively for more than three weeks. They'd been lovers for two of those three. And that was *not* the mental path to travel if he wanted to put distance between them. His defenses were so depleted. She could own him with a few choice words.

He had a few choice words of his own.

Stay away from bloody Scotland.

Keep running.

Leave Kavya.

He never did.

Because nothing mattered a Dragon damn when he sank into her soft, eager body. Whether she realized the influence she had over him was another matter. She was willing every time. She initiated many of their encounters, and when she hadn't, she rose to the challenge of meeting him at the edge of passion and violence. A trio of fresh scratch marks across his shoulder had yet to heal.

And, unexpectedly, as soon as they'd landed in Edinburgh, she had become . . . lighter.

"You're smiling again," he said.

"Is that a bad thing?"

Tallis shoved his hands into the deep pockets of his leather jacket. "No. Just wondered why. You don't seem as wary."

Her grin deepened. "If you'd spent most of your life waiting for an intruder to thrust into your mind and play, or for a mad sibling to track you down, wouldn't it be a relief to be here?" She lifted her chin and aimed her tiger-eyed gaze down the valley. "There isn't another Indranan for at least six hundred kilometers."

"You can tell?"

"A little. It's just a guess." Her brows furrowed. "The Townsends, I think."

"In London. Yes, I know of them. They control anything to do with the lives of Dragon Kings in southern England. I spent a lot of time in England before it became too rife with cartel types looking for Cage warriors." He joined Kavya in looking over the misty, gray-green swoop of land. "Tell me, if you'd been raised here, would fighting in a Cage hold any appeal?"

"Maybe. If I could be guaranteed a child. But that's the problem. If I bore children, I'd turn into my mother. Every day we drew nearer to twelve, the more haggard and frantic she became. Mood swings. Terrible rants and screaming fits."

Tallis turned in time to see her swallow and push a tear back from her eye. She was smiling more often, which made seeing her cry even more unsettling. He didn't want to see her cry any more than he wanted to wield a sword on her behalf. None of what he did for Kavya was in obvious service to his own goals: to find out who had poisoned his dreams, and keep that individual from success.

Reality didn't alter, however. He'd returned to Scotland because of Kavya.

He pulled her into his arms. His chin fit just atop her head. "Can you explain it to me?"

"Remember what I said about how Indranan marry,"

she said, her voice muffled by the folds of his jacket. "She and my father were linked. He had to make a choice: go mad right along with her, or sever the connection and try to prevent violence between Pashkah, Baile, and me."

"What did he choose?"

"To break their link of twenty-six years. She was insane within days. Not that it did my father much good either. He just . . . stopped being. Once Baile was dead, Pashkah put his sword to other uses. The blood of more than one family member colors its blade." She shuddered. "I'd already fled. I hated Pashkah. I hated the Indranan way. But I was glad my parents were out of their misery. In all ways that matter, they died as soon as they'd severed."

Tallis regretted that their conversation had taken her from carefree smiles to the darkest possible memories. He should've left it alone. On some sick, self-flagellating level, he'd wanted to know if he was the inspiration for her new, relaxed humor. No, she'd been smiling because Scotland was an escape from lunatics, freak snowstorms, and slum alleyways.

She was weeping because of his questions.

Leave it alone.

Leave her alone?

Impossible. He didn't want her to cry. He held her tighter and smelled jasmine as her hair tickled his mouth and nose. Their lives had been woven together, probably since the beginning of his dreams. Yet the woman he held was not the source of the visions he now considered nightmares—visions he hadn't experienced since that last dream by the Beas River.

That . . . entity had been gone. For weeks.

Had Kavya driven her away? Or had that been Tallis's choice, thrusting her out of his subconscious when he'd learned the difference?

"Here, look." Tallis gently disengaged and urged her to turn back toward the valley. He stood behind her and crossed his arms around her upper body. She leaned her head back against his chest, which pierced new perforations in the armor of isolation he'd worn for years. He'd wake up one morning and realize she'd disintegrated the leather and metal and hard, stubborn memories. He didn't know if his heart sped out of alarm or anticipation.

"Down there," he said, pointing toward the end of the valley. "Can you see where the land meets the sea?" He took her hands in his and held them so that her knuckles were perfectly aligned mountain peaks.

She took a deep breath. "No, I can't. The fog has it. Don't tell me you can."

"Not at all." He breathed the mist-laden air. The scent of being home—that was a stronger memory than he'd imagined, whisking him back to the moment when he'd become the Heretic. He concentrated on his story, distracting them both from so much that was wrong. "The place where the land meets the sea is sometimes crisp, defined. On clear days, it's almost too bright to look at—that beauty. Days like this, however, are considered sacred. The place where the land and sea blend into one is like the end of a rainbow. Neither is stronger than the other. You can't see it or touch it or even describe it. But it's there."

"Sacred."

"And in that mist is a boulder formation that resembles the ancient humans' fertility goddess, only she bears hallmarks of the Dragon. She's our interpretation. I know other clans believe the Dragon male, but not us. The boulder is called the Mother. She's the heart and soul of the Pendray, and what was once my center." He inhaled another breath of home. "But were we ever satisfied with the center? Of course not. Pendray have been racing toward misty, unreachable places for longer than history. It's taken us across the water, made us people of hills and waves. Both. Always both."

"The beast and the man. Both."

Tallis closed his eyes, knowing he had to let her go or he'd pledge himself to more than her safety.

"We have some walking to do if we want to reach the estate by nightfall." He shouldered his pack—a new duffel they'd bought in Istanbul, along with clothes more suited to English tourists. Kavya even wore jeans, a loose-fitting cowl-neck sweater, hiking boots, and a red wool coat that reached mid-calf. Zippered pockets on either side of the duffel held his seaxes.

Kavya followed. She was quiet, as was he, perhaps knowing they'd each said too much. They'd been saying too much for weeks.

Afternoon bled into twilight. He'd almost hoped he wouldn't remember the way. That would mean "home" was purged from his mind and his heart, and he could leave when the time came. Instead he was a carrier pigeon on a cross-country flight toward the place of his birth. Many Dragon Kings had abandoned the stately castles that had once been their domain. Yet Tallis's family was proud, holding on to old traditions to the very end.

No surprise.

"There," he said—the first word he'd spoken in hours. He and Kavya didn't share thoughts, but they'd become very good at sharing silences. "Do you see it?"

He pointed to a far hill where shadow rested atop shadow. Even the air there was darker than its environs.

Castle Clannarah, the local humans had named it. Tallis only knew it as home.

Kavya's gasp came before he felt the presence of another being. Tallis swiveled on his heel and found her held at knifepoint by a beautiful woman whose face had been worn weary by the years.

"Hello, Rill." His heart beat without any regard for how calm he needed to remain. "It's been a long time."

"Tallis?" Kavya's eyes widened as the knife against her throat pressed deeper.

"Don't worry," he said, stepping closer, never breaking eye contact with the older woman. "My sister won't hurt you."

Kavya held perfectly still. On the inside, she wondered if Tallis realized the irony. He was trying to save her from the very tactic he'd used against her in the valley encampment. She'd wind up with another couple knife cuts on her neck.

What welcome should she have expected when returning to the land where Tallis had become the Heretic? Apparently his family was as dangerous as hers. Somewhere deep and unexplored, she'd hoped for better for him.

"Rill." As if placating a wolf caught in a trap, Tallis's

voice was calm and low. "I need you to let her go. Look at me. Tell me I'm not your brother."

"My brother's dead."

The woman was nearly as tall as Tallis. She'd wrenched Kavya's arm behind her back at a painful angle. She was incredibly strong. Maybe that was a trait of Pendray women. Kavya was only just learning how little she knew of the Five Clans other than rumor and stereotype. Uniting the Indranan was a noble aim and she intended to see it through. But what of the Dragon Kings as a whole? Their race was dying. How could they discern the cause if they didn't even know basic truths about each other?

No matter the deception, and no matter Tallis's justifiable outrage, what if he really had been in service of a higher power? To unite the Dragon Kings. To solve the mystery of their slow extinction. There was no higher calling, although she knew how much his sacrifices had cost Tallis.

"I'm not dead." He held his hands out, devoid of weapons or fists. "Rill, you know I could prove it. Will you promise to let her go if I do?"

Although her hold didn't soften, the woman's posture changed in ways Kavya couldn't articulate. Using her telepathy, Kavya felt a mental shift—and was gratified that her gift was not barred to every Pendray. The woman had come to the decision that violence could wait, but the minutiae of her physical cues were beyond Kavya's grasp. She only knew Tallis to that degree. His posture said he was somewhat wary yet confident. His gaze was half amazement, half sorrow.

Twenty years. A homecoming after twenty years. Kavya's heart was breaking for him.

"Prove it, then." A thick brogue colored the woman's voice with the lilting rhythm and soft vowels of the Highlands.

"When I was seven, you saved me from certain annihilation. I'd been so angry with you and Opheena that I hurled a bucket of compost at you both. It was revolting. Every table scrap for three days splattered across the kitchen's rear wall." He chuckled at himself—this from the man who'd been practically nonverbal upon their first meeting. He'd lived a step outside of the world back then. Now . . .

His story turned wistful in a way Kavya had yet to hear from him. "It was sunny out. Midmorning. Mrs. Garrett had finished the morning's breakfast cleanup. I remember feeling a moment's satisfaction as you and Feena stood there, covered in scraps. Your expressions were stunned, then livid and ready to do murder. But you decided on the worst punishment imaginable. You said you'd leave it for Father to decide. Feena agreed, practically gleeful."

The woman, Rill, had definitely softened. Even the knife blade was not too threatening in its press against Kavya's flesh. She wondered if she could have overpowered the woman now. Doubtful, with so much strength at the Pendray's disposal.

Not that it mattered. She remained still. Her trust in Tallis's abilities and her eagerness to hear the conclusion of his story trumped all.

"I ran to my room," he said. "I knew I was doomed to stable chores for the rest of eternity. No more lessons with my fencing master. I'd only just started, but my training would end with punishment for an ignoble mistake."

"Only . . ." Rill stopped herself.

"Only when Father came home from his rounds, I didn't hear a thing. No rumble of his big voice through the castle walls. Hours passed. *Hours.* It was nearly sundown when I dared creep out of my room. You and Feena were watching a movie, both of you clean and dressed as if nothing had happened. You gave me this . . . look. And when I peeked into the kitchen, it was spotless. Every scrap gone, and every smear cleaned. I was seven. I never asked why you'd done it—just took it as a gift and grabbed a hunk of cheese and bread before running back to my room." He stepped forward, then another step. "After all these years . . . Rill, why did you do it?"

Rill shoved Kavya away and stood toe-to-toe with Tallis. Her expression of wariness and hope made Kavya's chest burn. The woman wanted to believe.

Despite the noticeable age difference, they looked so much alike. The same tall, lean frame. The same dark hair with silver, although Rill's reached mid-back. Silver flecks lined the tips of each strand, as if the thick mass was decorated with a hem of lace.

"We'd teased you mercilessly," she said quietly. Kavya worked to understand her brogue, which was thick with emotion. "You were so eager to please and impress. Every opportunity. That made it easy to make fun of you. The equivalent of a teacher's pet, I suppose, and all the jealous classmates. You'd finished your chores early, while Feena and I had stayed late in bed, reading fashion magazines. I still remember the fury on your face, just before you hurled your best shot. Our little berserker. We were in the bathroom, cleaning that rot off us, when Feena broke down. She couldn't let you take the blame for what we'd prompted. We were downstairs cleaning within a half hour." A slight smile tipped the woman's thin lips, almost an exact copy of Tallis's smile when he was in a sarcastic mood. "Letting you squirm for most of the day, dwelling on what would've been your punishment . . . that was satisfying."

"I bet it was."

He opened his arms. Rill fell into them with a little cry, then said his name over and over. Tallis held on, arms wrapped tight, with his face tucked in her hair. He whispered Pendray words that Kavya wasn't meant to understand. She would've been embarrassed to know what secret words of affection they shared.

The sight of two siblings holding each other in pure relief and happiness was more than she could take. A stab of envy left her breathless. It was a fairy tale no Indranan would ever believe. She turned away and tightened the sash of her red wool coat. The damp chill of the Highlands wasn't as biting as the frozen Pir Panjal, but she shivered anyway.

Glancing over her shoulder, seeing Tallis still holding on to his sister for dear life, she knew it wasn't just the misty weather that had made her shiver.

I want to be her.

Except that wasn't true. She was Tallis's lover. She only wanted to be held by him with that much abandon, with her love returned by the man she'd come to adore. The mental box she'd used to lock away her feelings for Tallis suddenly burst open. She would never be able to close it again.

"So who is this mysterious fey girl?" Rill asked. "A tiny thing."

"Just watch out for the claws." Tallis's eyes sparkled with amusement, never looking away from Kavya. "She's to be our guest. We were just on our way up to Clannarah."

"I'm afraid accommodations won't be to your expectations."

"What do you mean?"

For the first time, Rill didn't appear so imposing. More like furtive. "Twenty years is a long time to be gone, brother. Things have changed. For the worse, I'm sorry to say."

Tallis's posture seized. "Because of me." His expression assumed a hard edge, with his mouth pinched tight and his brow a series of unrelenting lines. Kavya didn't think that severity was meant for anyone but himself.

"Yes," Rill said quietly. "Because of you."

"Then put that knife to my throat instead. What's happened? This isn't kitchen scraps against a wall."

"Come up to Clannarah. Some rooms remain decent. It'll be dark soon. Remember how fast it can slink up on a body?"

Tallis nodded, his eyes focused deep within. Long memories? Regret? Worry? Nothing remained of the hopefulness he'd revealed when telling his story.

"But first, I need a name for this young woman."

"I'm Kavya of Indranan," she said, extending her hand.

Rill looked ruefully at her right hand, where she still gripped her dagger. She switched the weapon to her left. Even in that feature she was built like Tallis, with long fingers and rough knuckles. She was a scrapper. A fighter. Another berserker. It was hard to imagine of the older woman, who appeared haggard in ways that Dragon Kings rarely revealed. Gorgeous blue eyes were surrounded by tense lines and cupped underneath by heavy shadows.

"Sorry about twisting your arm," Rill said. "We don't get many visitors, and none are friendly. To say this is a surprise would be an unforgivable understatement."

"But you're happy to see him?"

A flash of unreadable emotion crossed Rill's features. Then it was gone, replaced by a friendly but neutral smile. "Of course I am."

→ CHAPTER ←
TWENTY-SIX

Tallis thought he was prepared for what he would see at Clannarah. Not the case. Not by a long shot.

What had once been a stately, centuries-old castle was pitted and crumbling, as if hewn of coral, not Old Red Sandstone from the Highlands. Modern amenities that had brought it into the last century—paved driveways, satellite dishes, and external lighting—were in woeful disrepair. Only one external light remained, over the portcullis they never raised. That dim beacon was unable to hold the dark at bay. Night haunted the place with demon memories of what had once been his home.

He stood slack-jawed and heartsick when they were within two hundred yards of the looming three-story castle. Old ramparts were crooked, rotting teeth. The portcullis offered a malicious grin. The grounds were sickly and abandoned. Where once splendorous grass had grown in blinding shades of green, the land was now infested with weeds and what appeared to be the creeping menace of mint vine. The topiary shrubs had reshaped themselves into warped, melted versions of the wolves and bears they'd once been. It was as if acid had rained down on the castle, stripping its skin and grandeur before leaving it to the elements—which, in the Highlands, were not much kinder.

Kavya stood beside him. She took his hand and said nothing.

"Let's go, then," he said roughly. "I'm cold."

He trudged up the cracked asphalt, with every step heavier than the last. *He'd* done this.

Rill led the way around the back to where the servants used to enter. He assumed no servants remained. He wouldn't have thought anyone still resided in the crippled old relic, but his sister did. It was shameful. Tallis's stomach was a tight ball. He held Kavya's hand like the lifeline it was.

He watched Rill fiddle with the rusted lock. If her key didn't work, Tallis would need to resort to using his lock pick kit to break into his childhood home.

"Is it just you?"

She made a noise of satisfaction when the lock clicked open. "No. We're all still here, plus one new. Honnas claimed a wife."

Tallis shook his head to clear the booming dissonance between his ears, but that wasn't going anywhere—not when he was choked by regrets that tasted of bile.

Just past a mudroom was the kitchen where he'd thrown compost scraps at his sisters. It was a shell of a kitchen now. Every cabinet and surface remained intact, but had aged with twenty years of hard use. His siblings seemed to have made the best of the situation, with what looked to be refinished wood and new hardware on the cabinets. The stove was old, and perhaps it didn't work because a microwave sat atop the burners. A rattling sound came from the fridge. The faucet dripped one, two, three patterns into a sink scarred with rust from the untreated, mineral-rich water.

"This can't be happening," he whispered to himself.

But of course it was. What had he expected? A shiny paradise, when he'd abandoned his family to the aftermath of his crime?

"Through here," Rill said.

She guided them through more dilapidated rooms. What was left of the grand furniture had been covered in sheets, as the servants of generations past would have draped before the family decamped to London during the harsh Highland winters.

Tallis and his family were creatures of the modern world. They'd never left according to the seasons. Radiators and electricity were boons his ancestors couldn't have imagined. The ghostly, white-draped furniture only added to his sense of having traveled back in time, to a place beyond his memories. A place in time where everyone who'd lived in this place of heritage and pride was long dead. The castle was a tomb.

They emerged into the main parlor, which had been remade decades earlier into a regular living room. It could've been part of any large house. Couches and recliners. Coffee tables and a television that looked ready for a pop culture museum.

"Feena?" Rill called. "Where are you, girl?"

"You call me *girl* one more time and I'll claw your hair out, you old crone."

Rill was the eldest, with Feena only two years younger. Best friends and worst enemies for more than seventy years. Because the natural lifespan of Dragon Kings was nearly two hundred years, they should've been in the prime of early middle age. Instead they appeared as careworn as human women of the same years. Where was their vitality? They should've been radiant, with little more visible hardship than Kavya wore on her lovely face.

A damning mantra had taken up in Tallis's head and wouldn't stop. *I did this*.

Kavya leaned near. "I won't argue the point, but I want you to stop thinking that. Please? Until we know the facts, at least?"

"Only if you stop prodding."

"If you stop shouting," she said with a pacifying smile.

Rill smirked at her sister's barb, then tipped her head toward Tallis. "Come on, then. We have visitors, you mouthy thing. Find some manners."

Only then did Feena turn. Her eyes widened to comical proportions. Her lips parted on a strangled sound of surprise. "No. You can't be . . . Tallis?"

She didn't wait for a reply before attacking him with a giant hug to match Rill's. She cried, smacked his back, asked a thousand questions he couldn't begin to answer. He only held on, taking in as much of the moment as possible. His sister in his arms. It was a dream come true set in the middle of a nightmare.

In the meantime, Rill must have rounded up the rest of the castle's residents, because the living room filled with people. He wouldn't have thought anyone lived in the shadowy mausoleum on a hill, but he was getting a lot of things wrong of late.

He wiped his face with his hands and found his touchstone. Kavya stood to one side wearing her unfamiliar clothing, knuckles in alignment, eyes darting across the chaotic assembly. But then he was standing before his older brother, Honnas. They embraced with fierce affection and hearty backslaps. Another brother, Serre, kept his distance, but Tallis was too overcome to reach out to his youngest, obviously bitter sibling.

One of their number was lost forever, but what remained of his family stood in the same room.

Unbelievable.

Honnas brought forward a petite redheaded Pendray he introduced as his wife. Tallis missed her name in the flurry of conversation. His four siblings and one sister-in-law inhabited a run-down castle—with no children to liven the dreary rooms and halls.

Kavya moved to stand beside him, composed in the way that said she was holding on to her calm by practiced means—for him. He couldn't imagine what she was thinking.

Thinking . . .

Could she read his siblings' minds? That would help him understand something of the strange barrier between him and Kavya. Was it just him, just his family, or an inability to read any Pendray?

"This is Kavya," he said with a roughened voice. The lump in his throat wasn't going anywhere. "She's Northern Indranan, and we've come a long way to get here. I had to use the inlay from one of my seaxes to make the journey."

That would speak volumes to his family. No one sold their inlays unless the situation was desperate. He had been that desperate.

"Why have you come back?" Serre asked. Ten years

Tallis's junior, he was the only one of the siblings to appear more wary than welcoming. His gift had only just been revealed when Tallis accepted his exile.

Accepted my exile.

What a farce. He'd run, pure and simple. He'd done murder for a higher purpose, but he'd run from the blood he was responsible for having spilled on a church altar.

"I'm here because of Kavya. She's an Indranan triplet, and her brother has already killed her sister. He's after Kavya now, and there's no telling what creature he'd become if he takes her life, too. I've come back to retrieve our family's Dragon-forged sword and make sure that doesn't happen."

Murmurs of obvious distress slunk across the room, led by Serre's harsh voice. Tallis sat on the nearest chair. The muscles in his legs were stiff, as if he'd run the entire way from Jaipur. Kavya stood beside him like a protective sentinel, rather than the woman he was professing to protect. It was all backwards.

"And you bring her here?" Serre glared. His back was straight and his eyes full of violence. "Haven't you done enough damage?"

"Serre," came Rill's authoritative tone. "We've heard rumor and what we know to be outright falsehoods. Twenty years is a long time to weather other people's opinions of a loved one and not be tainted by that negativity. But you'll behave with civility toward your brother. Presenting his side is his right. It's what we owe one of our own. Besides, you know how things have changed."

Tallis looked up. The chandelier had been stripped

of its antique crystal teardrops. Had they dismantled it? For money?

"I can see how things have changed," he said with lead in his chest. "I've made life for you unbearable."

"No, brother." Feena smiled warmly. "You've changed it for the better."

Kavya stood by Tallis as he and his siblings shared stories. So many stories. She'd known the Scottish and Norse reputation for storytelling but now realized how much of the tradition must've come down from the Pendray. This clan had lorded over hearty people who trudged through rough, ragged lives without regret or apology. There was no caste system as in India. There was no elevated sense of self-importance as in continental Europe, where the Tigony had done so much to make Greek and Roman civilization the envy of all history.

Tallis told their tale first, because his brothers and sisters had insisted. They weren't saying a word until Tallis related the journey that had led him and Kavya to Scotland. She was impressed all over again by the strange events that meant she was standing in the parlor of a decrepit hilltop castle. She also noticed what he left out: them. The "us" of their travels was limited to their run-in with Pashkah, their travails, their weeks-long struggle to reach the Edinburgh Airport. They'd become lovers along the way, but that wasn't a subplot. Not even a hint.

That didn't stop curious sets of blue eyes from skirting between her and Tallis. Rill had seen them holding hands, and maybe Opheena had, too.

As Tallis added details about Pashkah's intentions and madness, Kavya prepared herself for the worst. These Pendray would kick her out. They would kick Tallis out.

What then?

She was exhausted, and so very tired of living in fear. The smiles Tallis had pointed out upon their arrival in Edinburgh had been a temporary respite. She was still a hunted woman. Tallis would not stop searching for the person who'd directed his life for so long, warping him into the man she knew. He'd fought back, retaining a certain sense of honor among his cynicism and fatalistic approach to life, but he'd lost something, too. She knew it. He'd lost his innocence and his faith. What did he believe in now? What would remain of him if his need for revenge was ever slaked?

Each question took on more and more importance when filtered through her deep, abiding affection. She loved him. But she wasn't foolish enough to believe he'd want to stay with her. Tallis of Pendray would keep on moving. He was only in his ancestral home because her life had become entangled with his goals. He would leave his family and certainly leave her once he solved the mysteries of his mind.

He would walk away. Would she watch him go, or would she beg?

She blinked back tears that must have been exacerbated by fatigue. She wanted to lie down. Only, Tallis's siblings hadn't explained the changes that had taken place since his departure. She needed to know, too. She needed to know the aftermath, so she could better understand how to comfort him. He was already taking so much blame on himself. She saw it in every mournful glance he stole when looking around the living room.

Comfort him?

She may as well have been a little girl with fairy-tale wishes. Families like this were not for the her kind and never would be. Kavya gave up on envying that happiness.

"He'll come for you," said Tallis's older brother, Honnas. "Won't he?"

Kavya met his eyes. The man loved his wife's hands, their grace and slender perfection. He regretted never having been able to conceive a son, who would've had a stubborn chin and a stubborn nature. He was afraid of lightning—the sky was being ripped in two—but he'd never told a soul.

She could read all of their minds. One at a time. Same as always.

Just not Tallis's.

"Yes," she said after a deep breath. "He won't stop. We were born with our gift split into thirds. When it comes to the powers given to us by the Dragon, I'm the weakest in this room. A third of an Indranan. He wants to be whole. He won't stop until that happens, just like he won't stop until he stokes the embers of civil war back into an inferno."

"To what end?"

"I don't know." She glanced at Tallis, knowing his theory on the matter—his dream specter and its foul wishes. "It's possible he wants to end the civil war by bringing all Indranan out of hiding. They'd wage open war on their siblings, from all corners of our territory. Our population would be halved, but everyone who remained would be a twice-cursed telepath. Powerful. Influential. Driven slowly mad by two minds shoved into one."

"That would be . . ." Feena trailed off. She shook her head. "They . . . you . . . No, *your* people would become a threat to the balance between the Five Clans. How could any of us trust the Council's decisions if telepaths were able to control their thoughts, even the thoughts of the Giva?"

"He's the Usurper," said Serre sharply. "Our people didn't help choose him, and neither did Clan Garnis. He's the leader of the Five Clans by choice of only three—the Sath, the Indranan, and his own Tigony. That's not a true leader."

Honnas sat forward on his chair. His wife, so tiny compared to Tallis's sisters, had short auburn hair that showed off her pixie ears. She was always annoyed when her husband snored, but she loved nothing more than to submit to his bites on her nape. She'd done so only moments before Tallis's return. That meant she would still be able to feel the sting deep inside her skin.

Kavya shivered and tightened her thighs. That was the problem with being among people whose emotions were so unguarded. She was subject to all the good, bad, shameful, proud, petty, and erotic. Only now did she have the experience to truly understand the latter.

"Serre," Honnas said, with a warning in his voice. "It's not the Giva's fault the Pendray were so divided that we didn't send our own kind to the Chasm to hear the Dragon's choice. We were nearly as divided as the Indranan. It's amazing we didn't shatter into a hundred little factions, and scatter to the four winds like the Garnis, lost forever."

"Now it's different." Feena seemed the most eager of the bunch. She appeared older than her years, and the silver tips of her hair weren't as brilliant, but she carried herself with the regal bearing of a queen and the artlessness of a child. She loved lilacs and chocolate chips straight from the bag. "The Pendray are stronger than ever. That priest . . ." She shuddered. "Dragon be, what he'd been doing to our people. Creating division. Stoking petty disagreements. Abusing those who sought to give him their trust—unspeakable things."

Tallis frowned. "What did he want?"

"The best we can tell," Feena continued, "is money. His home was full to the rafters with priceless artifacts from Pendray families. He created arguments, then helped smooth them over. Grateful people gave him gifts. Then he became more prominent. Pendray didn't rely on themselves or even basic civility, but on his guidance. That's when the real fractures began—those who believed he was some sort of prophet, and those who saw him as a charlatan." She smiled with the whole of her face. "Tallis, you did an amazing thing by exposing him in death."

"No, I cleaved his head from his body and I ran." He craned his neck to indicate what appeared to be one of the only inhabitable rooms in the castle. "I left you all to this."

"And that was a hard time for us." Rill's smile was beatific, as if forgiving Tallis of every failing he'd ever heaped on himself. Kavya could only hope he took that offer of forgiveness. "Afterward, an investigation revealed that the priest was corrupt."

Kavya chose that moment to join Tallis on the narrow

settee where he held himself as rigidly as a fence post buried in frozen ground. She didn't care if his siblings knew what . . . *emotion* had developed between them. He needed her, and she needed to hold his hand when he did.

"Then why do you still live this way?" he asked.

"Because the findings were kept secret." Serre's bitterness was unmistakable. Kavya flinched back from his mind, which was filled with hurt and a sense of having watched a treasured idol laid low. "The Leadership thought it better to unite everyone around their hatred of you, and it worked."

"Serre, it's been worth the sacrifice," Rill said. "We could've revealed what we know, but then Tallis's exile would've been for nothing."

Serre kept his head ducked low and to one side. He nodded, then met Tallis's gaze head-on. Kavya was surprised to find that a sheen of moisture brightened the young man's blue eyes—eyes so much like his brother's, the one he'd thought lost forever. His anger made sense now. It wasn't the sacrifices of wealth or standing, but that Tallis's deed had meant Serre grew up having thought two siblings were lost forever.

"It's been too long, Tallis," he said roughly.

Tallis made Kavya proud. First he kissed the back of her hand, proclaiming their affection to all of his siblings. Then when he stood. He walked to where Serre sat, back tense and shoulders hunched. Extending his hand, Tallis waited with equal tension—waiting for Serre to welcome him home, too. And maybe to forgive him.

The younger man's tentative handshake turned

fierce as soon as their palms met. Tallis pulled him up and into a ferocious masculine embrace. They were potent in strength, and equally potent in their shared affection. "Yes, brother. It's been too long. And I'll never be gone that long again."

Kavya swallowed back tears, as the rest nodded their approval. By chance she caught Rill's eye.

"It's our right and privilege to do what we can for the Pendray," the woman said. "Everything we do is to protect our clan, and particularly our family." Rill wasn't so unabashed in her acceptance of Kavya as she had been with Tallis, but she offered a small, promising smile. "No matter who makes the threat."

⇴ CHAPTER ⇴
TWENTY-SEVEN

Tallis turned on the single bedside table lamp in the room Rill had made up for him. The kiss he'd bestowed on Kavya's hand put to rest any need to make up a separate room for her. Not that they had done much to hide their connection in any other way. The very nature of his return to Clannarah was linked with her—with his growing affection for her.

Deeper than affection. He didn't dare go near what he feared were his true feelings.

He sloughed his pack and duffel on the floor, then removed his seaxes and slid them under the bed within easy reach. Exhausted to his bones, he didn't realize he was undressing until Kavya began to assist him. She stood behind him while she eased his button-down shirt from his shoulders, petting his skin as she did. She kissed between his shoulder blades. Kissed his biceps. Kissed around until she faced him, touching moist lips to a dozen places across his chest. He inhaled deeply.

"Oh, I like that," she said. "Do that again."

Tallis couldn't help but grin. "Do I impress you, goddess?"

"Yes. Now don't keep fishing for compliments. Just do as I bid."

"Bossy, bossy," he said as a chant against her skin. "I'm my own man and I make my own decisions."

She angled a secret, mysterious smile upward. Her eyes were hidden by thick lashes. "Then make your decision. Are you going to please me by showing off your gorgeous chest, or are you going to leave me disappointed and your masculine beauty unexploited?"

"I'm going to use that choice against you one day."

"I'll look forward to it. My response will likely be dependent on yours right now."

With an effervescent feeling of relief—at least he could count on Kavya to make him feel better—he sucked in a lungful of air, as if pulling all the troubles of the world into his chest. She kissed him once, right over his heart, before whispering, "Now let it go, Tallis."

He did. One long, gusting exhalation. It felt marvelous.

He wrapped her in his embrace. Their kisses were more familiar now, but that opened new avenues of intimacy. He knew more of what she liked, the depth, the speed, the leashed violence. She tasted of the mead Rill had brought out during the evening-long discussion. Kavya had sipped hers, her eyes all over the scene of family and uneasy welcomes home. Old tales. New revelations.

And forgiveness—that most unexpected wonder.

Kavya had been beside him the entire time.

Yes, he counted on her to make him feel better. When had that happened? And when had that assumption deepened, that it wasn't just his physical comfort she attended?

Did it matter anymore? The timing, the circumstances, even the future . . . He wanted Kavya for the rest of his life. The realization should've stolen the strength from his knees, but he'd never felt more powerful.

"You're a strange, remarkable woman, Kavya," he whispered against her temple.

"I like remarkable. Strange, not so much."

"Strange that you're here with me."

"We've already established that I find you inescapably handsome, especially your body."

"Ah," he said, beginning to undress her. "So it's just my body. I understand how it is."

She took hold of his wrists. "I don't think I want to joke about this anymore."

Tallis moved to finish the decadent task of revealing Kavya's body. Although not as exotic as her sari, her sweater and jeans fell away to reveal sexy matching bra and panties, all decked in lace and satin.

He pulled her toward the bed, where he removed the last of his clothes, save his briefs. She joined him, wearing her beautiful new undergarments. "At least we have a place to bed down," he said.

"They'll let us do more than stay." She curled beside him under the quilts. Sleek and lithe, she drew up her knee so that it rested against his navel. Her slender thigh hugged his side, and her calf trailed between his legs. "In fact, they'll do everything they can to help."

"How do you know that?"

She reached up and tapped his temple. "They don't have whatever it is you have. I can read each and every one of them."

Tallis flinched. "You can," he said evenly, not a question.

"You don't trust me to respect their privacy?"

"I . . ." He sighed. "I don't know. It's not an issue we've come up against before. Boundaries weren't our primary concern in getting here."

"But with your family, it's different."

"Exactly."

"I told you about the boxes in our minds. I have a new one now. Tallis's family. They're secrets I don't want, and ones I won't share with anyone, not even you."

"What do you mean about not wanting the secrets?"

She shifted so that she lay flat atop him. She crossed her hands on his chest and rested her chin there. "Your people are so . . . Just *open*. Like your expressions. Down there, I was bombarded by imagery and thoughts. Their minds tell stories as quickly as their mouths. It was all I could do to focus on you, keeping their enthusiasm for life from overwhelming me. Nothing was held back. I've never felt its like."

Tallis pushed hair back from her face, so that he could admire her beauty and study amber eyes clouded by swirling thoughts. "Not exactly the Indranan way, is it?"

"Not at all." She looked away, then set her mouth at an angle that suggested she'd made a decision. "I tried not to, but I envy you."

"Me?"

"Why not? In this sad old castle are five family members who'd kneel before a chopping block if it meant taking your place. The way Serre hugged you—"

Her voice cracked. She tucked her face against his chest, between her hands. A sob shook her body. She swallowed it down as quickly as it came.

"I've been waiting for that hug for twenty years," he said, "never knowing if it would happen. The trouble with loving anyone is that when they're no longer in your life, it's harder to bear the absence. It isn't just a hole—a vacant thing. It's a burning sore."

"Here?" She kissed the skin above his heart once again.

"Yes."

Their gazes caught. Tallis could have seduced her at that moment, with his cock growing impatient beneath the slight weight of her body. But something held him back. As Kavya had said, this was no longer something to joke about. Nor was it something to avoid by relying on easy pleasures that conspired in their own way to reveal, even create, deeper feelings.

Her eyes darkened and her mouth softened. She licked her lower lip, which was what Tallis desperately wanted to do.

She stopped him with five words. "Why did you stop believing?"

"Believing . . . ?"

"The visions in your dreams. No matter who put those thoughts in your head, it was for the benefit of the Pendray, I can definitely relate to how you sacrificed yourself for the good of your clan."

"My family, too," he said. "And they weren't given a choice."

"Considering the weapons used against your subconscious, I don't think you were either."

"I'd love to take the easy way out and go with that. I just don't think I can."

Kavya sat up and unhooked her bra. It fell away, taking Tallis's breath with it. "So, the rest of it. When did it change? When did it become revenge against . . . well, against a semblance of me?"

Tallis stared at her, absorbed her, adored her with every shift of his eyes. She was a vision made flesh. "When that semblance of you knelt above me, much as you're doing now, and told me to help abduct my niece."

Mouth open, Kavya shook her head softly. "I . . ."

"Her name is Nynn of Tigony. She's the Giva's cousin and my niece. I had one more brother, Vallen. He married the Giva's aunt, who became despised by her clan. Bearing a child by a Pendray? From what I understand, Nynn was only accepted because of Malnefoley's influence. He is the Giva. Who of his clan would contradict him to his face?"

"You said *had* one more brother."

Tallis tried to calm his heartbeat, but that wasn't happening anytime soon. He'd be lucky if he slept before dawn, no matter his exhaustion. "Vallen was killed sometime after Nynn's birth. Our best guess is that some angered Tigony did the deed. Nynn crippled her mother by accident, with the first manifestation of her gift. Malnefoley swung the sword to end the woman's misery."

"Such a powerful gift? By the Dragon, that must have been terrifying."

"Nynn is . . . special. Crossbred. She was banished because of those exceptional powers. She married a human and bore a son."

"So the rumors are true? That's her?"

"Yes. Jack is the first natural-born Dragon King in decades. My brother Serre must've been among the last born to our generation, as conception became harder and harder to achieve."

His chest ached. More of that void, when loved ones were far away. Serre was far away in spirit, and Tallis had no idea where Nynn and her Cage warrior, Leto, had disappeared to. He'd only just found his niece again, before leaving, before being able to apologize.

"The last vision I believed came to me the night she commanded me to help the Aster cartel find Nynn. Just for questioning, she'd said. Everyone was curious about her son. I balked at first, with more strength than I'd ever used to resist. She seduced me. No, it was cruder than that. Remember the story I told you at the inn, when she'd straddled me but refused to join our bodies? She'd never taken me so far, only to leave me begging. It was . . . Dragon damn, Kavya, it was like being raped in my mind."

"*Lonayíp* witch."

Kavya crossed her arms over her bare breasts and turned so that her hair created a curtain separating her expression from Tallis's gaze.

"Kavya, I didn't know the difference before, but I bloody well do now." He took her hands and placed them flat against his chest. "That . . . *thing* drove me to madness, making me promises for months. One last assignment. One more deed in her honor. Then she would disappear while riding an incarnation of the Dragon—one I've never seen. Some mix of all Five Clans' interpretations."

Kavya frowned. Her eyes glittered with unshed tears. "She even invoked the Dragon? That's unholy."

Tallis arched his chin toward the ceiling and blew out a ragged breath. "Yes. The same pattern each time. That's how she was able to brainwash me and keep me servile for two decades. Or maybe I wanted to believe it was her fault. Because I led members of the Aster cartel to my niece's house. Nynn and her son were kidnapped by force, and her human husband was murdered. It took me a year to find out where she was being held, and a little longer than that to convince the Giva to help me free her."

"But it was too late, wasn't it? For your niece . . . the damage had already been done. By you."

Tallis flinched beneath her.

"Yes," he said without looking away. Either he was the most insensitive man on the planet, or he'd spent countless, endless nights learning how to find peace with his mistakes. She knew he wasn't the former, and the latter was still a work in progress. "The damage had been done. To Nynn, personally. I felt the need to atone for her loss, to save her and her son. But in that year, she became one of the most powerful Dragon Kings I've ever met. Part Pendray, part Tigony. She wields lightning with a berserker's intensity. She'd fallen in love again, too. Leto was a Cage warrior—part Garnis, part Indranan."

"Garnis and Indranan? How?"

"Dr. Aster had fulfilled his promise to Leto's father, who won some ridiculous number of Cage bouts and annual Grievances to earn conception. Three children, including Leto. Only, his mother and father were both Garnis, and Leto's powers were clearly a mixture. He and Nynn are out there now, trying to find out why he's half Indranan, and to learn the secret of Dr. Aster's methods."

He seemed to blink away the past, while Kavya held on to the present by an unraveling thread. "It could be as easy as . . . crossbreeding?"

"I don't think anyone would call it easy." Tallis shook his head against the pillow, tangling the silver-tipped hair she adored. "Just that it makes some sense. Rifts have split your people. Centuries of raids have been to gather breed stock from other tribes of Indranan, yes? Like Pashkah was gathering there in the valley?"

"Yes. Three thousand years ago, it was easier on all our populations. We reproduced without worry. Except the Indranan split according to geography. Some in the Himalayas, believing themselves closer to the Dragon, and some down by the seas—even sailing to Australia. We remained one clan, but births dropped off over a few centuries. During the original severance, six hundred men died. Can you imagine the extravagance of that much waste? These days it would likely level half the Dragon Kings on the planet. They died in battles to protect their women. Raiding parties. Mass rapes. The selfish gene—is that what the humans call it?"

"Perhaps. The Indranan method of mass abductions isn't the way to go, but there might be merit in the thinking. We've become so fractured." Tallis held her hands and kissed her knuckles, the backs of her hands, up her forearms, until he pulled her down for a kiss on the mouth. "What did we truly know about one another's people before spending this time together?"

"Rumors and misconceptions, or missing knowledge

no one bothered to fill in." She touched the back of her neck. "Bonding rituals, for example."

Tallis lay back, with his hands behind his head. She loved that pose. So utterly, confidently masculine. The muscles of his torso stretched in long lines, while those of his arms bunched in strong, potent relief. That his prick was a hot rod beneath her bottom only added to the sudden flush of her need.

"You keep coming back to that subject, Kavya. Makes me wonder what you have on your mind."

"I'd show it to you if I could."

"Old-fashioned way and you know it. And no jokes, remember?"

Rather than answer, she stripped her underwear and his, then returned to her straddling position. It was a simple thing to lift her hips, position his shaft, and sink onto it with one long, moaning, melting move.

Tallis hissed. "*Bathatéi*."

"What?"

"You sinking down on me. No pleading or bargains or nauseating anger. You're what I never knew I truly needed. It's a miracle, Kavya."

"No," she said, rocking her pelvis. "It's just *real*."

He arched off the mattress, pushing deep. Kavya set their pace. Although Tallis massaged and toyed with her breasts, wearing an equally stunned, bemused look, she used his chest to more purpose: for balance as she lifted and lowered at the command of instinct. She would come quickly this way. The angle suited her body. The speed of it was a complete surprise. Another four or five quick bursts of her hips against his and she cried out, arching into his tight hands.

"Dragon damn." Tallis gathered her close. He whispered near her ear, lips tucked in her hair. "Do you know what you do to me?"

"Tell me," she said, dazed and gasping.

He was still achingly hard within her. She would only need another few rolls of her hips to come again. She moved. Tallis cursed. He smacked his hands against her ass and held on with a fierce grip as she writhed, using him, grinding down, over, around his cock. The second orgasm blacked out her mind and snapped through her body with even more potency. Something was building in her, and she didn't know . . . didn't know . . .

"Tell me." She licked the sweat from his neck. "Tell me what I do to you."

"You make me want to push you off me right now."

"What?" Kavya tried to sit up and see his expression, but he held tighter. His hips picked up speed and revealed his selfish intent.

"Give me the word," he said on a grunting thrust. "I'd push you off me, stalk down the hall to find my family, and ask them to acknowledge our union." He grasped the back of her neck. With two fingers he pinched the scruff. "Then I'd slam the door behind me, toss you down, and fuck you how we both want. I'd claim you. My teeth here. For good this time. I wouldn't let go until we both came. Until you'd screamed out your pain and pleasure, and I'd given you everything I can give. We'd be joined forever." He was thrusting in earnest now, urging Kavya toward another release. "That's what you do to me, Kavya of Indranan. That's where you take my mind and how you tempt my body and how you erase what's left of my sanity."

"Does it feel insane?" She groaned, then sucked hard where his neck joined his torso. That curve was meant for mouths, lips, teeth. She sucked until she was certain a bruise would appear come morning. "It feels hectic and selfish, but does it feel insane?"

"No," he said on a sharp gasp. "It feels primal. I want to mark what's mine. You're mine, Kavya."

"Then do it. Tell them to acknowledge us. I want your teeth on my nape and your cock inside me."

"Off."

Kavya could hardly believe the words she'd thrown down—a dare as powerful as his. He was telling her to get off. She'd been on the verge of a third orgasm, but she forced her protesting body to comply.

But he didn't leave. He sat up, cross-legged, with his slick erection jutting between his legs. Kavya wanted to lean over and slip her lips around his hard length. She'd taste herself and Tallis, mingled, joining. A moan built in her throat.

"The last time I agreed to anything so life-changing, I was mesmerized by the promise of sex." He ran shaking fingers through shimmering hair. "I won't make that mistake again. Breathe, Kavya. You're glowing like a candle. Calm down and look me in the eyes. If you believe what you just said, tell me again."

Kavya looked down at her hands, which were already aligned into perfect hills and valleys. She dug deep beneath the layers of emotions and thoughts, old lives and new, Masks, memories that weren't hers, fears, desires. She kept digging until she found a shining kernel of something innocent, young, and beautiful.

The effort it took to lift her head and take his stare

head-on was tremendous. To accept the weight of his expectations was another challenge. But saying the words was not difficult at all. They reflected what she wanted, for herself and Tallis. "I want to be joined with you."

"Why?" he said roughly. "Tell me why, and by the Dragon, Kavya, make me believe you."

As if drawn to the need to touch fire or swim rough waters or, yes, stroke a wild animal, she took his hand. "I've never been with another man, and I never will be again. I've never been in love before, and I never will be again. Tallis, the only man I'll ever love is you."

⋆ CHAPTER ⋆
TWENTY-EIGHT

In the three minutes between donning his cargos and striding down the corridor to Rill's room, Tallis could've changed his mind. He could have changed his mind had he had a sensible mind left to change.

He should have been panicked. Echoes of the last decision he'd made while under the power of a woman with Kavya's dear, familiar face . . .

He pulled up short.

His whole body rebelled, shaking with anger. That vision had never been Kavya. There in the darkness of the corridor, he closed his eyes for even more privacy. Glimpses of the woman from his dreams were fading. He was left only impressions. Pure sensuality. She'd had perfect eyes, a perfectly formed mouth, and a low, throaty, syrup-sweet voice that had acted as a snake charmer's whistle.

Kavya had eyes nearly too wide for her face. They threw off any chance at symmetry, and lent her a child-like look that belied the wisdom in those amber depths. Her mouth was lush, with full lips shaped in a pout that her demeanor never fostered. She had strong cheek-bones and an even stronger jaw, which balanced the hints of innocence. The body he'd touched, worshiped, and initiated wasn't all rounded curves and soft flesh. She was resilient. She was muscle underneath silken skin and a woman's lustrous shape. Sexy but tough—so much tougher than he'd given her credit for.

Kavya was flesh and blood and real.

He pounded on Rill's door. Although he'd reined in his arousal, he couldn't help the speed of his respiration or the impatience with which he knocked again.

Rill opened it wearing a wrapped-tight robe and a surly, sleepy expression. "Unless the castle is on fire, go away."

"Will you acknowledge us? Me and Kavya?"

With a pair of blinks, Rill became fully alert. She smiled and pinched him on the arm. "I'd assumed you had been already. An Indranan, though? I guess stranger things have happened." She sobered briefly. "Just . . . don't you dare get yourself killed. It's eerie, Tallis. You've returned like Vallen did, in the company of a stunning woman from another clan. Then he was killed. This brother of hers is likely to pursue you both to the edge of the Chasm itself. Have you wandered so long that you're resigned to such a harsh fate?"

"Yes, I've been on the run," he said quietly, full of emotion he hadn't meant to express. Kavya was right when she'd said his people were not the kind to hide their feelings, especially among family. It was the heart of their gift. "Is this where I belong? Am I a part of this clan? Am I an ally to our Giva, or a villain for my deeds? Ask me any of those questions and I couldn't answer."

Rill nodded. Her eyes softened, and for a moment, she appeared less careworn. "You were dubbed the Heretic when you left. Prove them wrong. What do you believe in, Tallis?"

"Kavya's goodness."

"And if this isn't home, where might it be?"

Tallis swallowed. He was growing more calm with each question, although his heart still beat with the rhythm of a man running a flat-out sprint. "With her."

"Then who are you?"

"*Hers.*"

"You'd better tell her all of that after your claiming." Rill made a shooing motion. "You're acknowledged, brother of mine. Don't stand here wasting any more time."

After a brief kiss to his sister's cool cheek, he returned to the guest bedroom. He wanted to sprint, so that the motion of his body matched the eager, hopeful throb of his heart. That hope tunneled down deeper, until he felt it quivering in every cell. That certainty. His faith was Kavya. His home was with Kavya.

She hadn't moved from her place on the bed. Looking up from intertwined fingers, she showed him eyes as full of hope as was his chest. He crossed the room in three strides and stopped at the side of the bed.

"What did she say?" Kavya asked, more uncertain than he would've expected. "Your family's opinion about this means a lot to me."

"Why?"

"Because they mean a lot to you."

He fisted his hands. Patience? Calm? Did he have any left? She was naked and kneeling on the mattress. The part of him that was deeper than Tallis of Pendray wanted to be set free. He swallowed, then blew out a tight breath. "Rill acknowledged us."

For a flaring second, Kavya beamed. Only when he stripped his cargos once again did her unspoken happiness transform into outright hunger.

"I could lie on my stomach," she said with a dark taunt. "Lie there passively."

"You could."

"I could get into position on all fours. Make it easy on you."

Tallis's head was going to explode. "You could."

"But we don't want that."

He inhaled, feeling the flare of his nostrils. He pictured a bull taking a breath before its bloodlust charge.

She pushed up onto her knees on the mattress. Leaning forward no more than a few inches, she dipped her tongue in the hollow at the base of his throat. "You want me to fight, Tallis. I've never been a fighter, but I am with you."

"For me."

"And for myself. I've survived so much, but I never gave myself credit. I don't know why." She lifted her arms in a provocative pose before flipping long, lustrous hair back over her shoulders. Her tight nipples mocked his self-control. "That ends now. I give myself credit for keeping up with you."

"You're asking for it. Something holy and dangerous and—" He gritted his teeth. He was seeing Kavya and he was seeing red.

She took his fists in her palms, then kissed the back of each. "Do you love me, Tallis? Not the animal want. Not some need for revenge. *Love*. If this is for all time, I need to know."

He closed his eyes against a flush of dizziness. Forcing words into the air was as difficult as sawing off a limb. He was slipping away, becoming his other self, but he held on for his woman.

"Yes," he said with utter certainty.

"Then do your worst. Your *best*. I know you won't do a thing to me that I don't want." She touched her lips to each fist once again, then lifted her eyes like a suppliant, not a goddess. That she might be both for him was just as arousing as the idea that he could be man and beast. For her. "So I won't lie here, Tallis. Toss me down, like you threatened. Show me what it is to be claimed by a Pendray."

Tallis grabbed a fistful of her thick, dark hair and twisted. She cried out. Her head jerked back until he'd turned her upper body, her throat arched toward the ceiling. The crown of her head pressed against his chest. He placed the sweetest, softest kiss on her forehead.

Then he threw her down against the mattress. She kicked the covers, scrambling toward the headboard, but Tallis caught her ankle and hauled her down the bed. He yanked her hips up. The woman who'd been so calm and artificial on that distant altar was spitting mad, with a violent passion that flowed between them like fire meeting barrel after barrel of gasoline.

Kneeling behind her, Tallis flashed back to the last time he'd held her in this position, with his hands taut at her hips. He'd been so tempted. Bite her. Claim her.

This was different.

This is forever.

"Yes," she whispered. "Please, Tallis."

On some level he'd been waiting for those words.

He'd wanted her permission and her desire—proof in one word.

He aligned his hips with hers and drove deep. They moved together with the trust of two people deeply committed and thrown over to the abandonment of that commitment. Kavya still fought, with gasps and foul words that stoked him hotter, higher. She reared back to meet him with the same force of his thrusts. Sweat slicked the coppery skin of her back. She looked over her shoulder. Amber eyes glowed fiercely. She was a woman in the midst of a fight for the rest of her life. In so many ways, that was true. Those eyes flared wide. Her body tightened as her breath ratcheted toward release.

Tallis wanted them to go over together. United.

Hips suddenly, achingly still, he bent low. "I'm claiming you, Kavya," he rasped against her nape.

He sank his teeth into her and tightened his arms around her body, holding them both steady with the strength of his abs and thighs. She cried out. Reflex made her shake. She grabbed his nearest hand and bit down as well, slaking her frustration and perhaps the last need to resist. Tallis gloried in that poised moment of shared danger and beauty. They were bound together in pain, in the giving and receiving of it, with the anticipation of pleasure on the horizon. They moved together in a dance few else would understand. Fierce. Beautiful. Filled with the trust he wouldn't give another woman.

For the rest of his life.

Sensation gathered in his balls and intensified as he resumed his relentless rhythm. He bit as hard as he dared, which at that moment was as hard as he could. Kavya's moan sank into the pad of his thumb just before she released him from her fearsome teeth. She arched, shuddered, and screamed. Her clenching sheath welcomed his cock one last time as he drove home. Tallis spent his passion and staked his claim with a furious, mindless growl against the back of her neck.

Kavya lay sprawled on her stomach, with Tallis layered over her. She should have felt crushed, abused, exhausted. Instead she smiled against the pillow and took her first calm breath since they'd taken off their clothes for bed.

She'd never been an impetuous woman. She'd grown up knowing that caution meant invisibility, and invisibility meant safety. There, on that night, she'd made one of the most impetuous choices of her life.

She'd never felt safer.

Perhaps that was because a very satisfied berserker with muscles to spare and who possessed not one but two vicious Norse seaxes pinned her so deliciously to their marital bed. Tallis made her remember what it was to be strong. If she could fight and win against such a man, in a contest of bodies, hearts and wills, then she could take on all comers.

She elbowed upward, connecting with his ribs. "A little air, please."

Rather than roll away, Tallis shoved his arms beneath her body, hugging her while holding her fast against the mattress. He kissed her nape, licked, suckled the sore skin. She shivered, knowing with bone-deep certainty that in the future, he would only need to touch her there—and she'd be ready for him. Such a sensitive place. So much primitive symbolism.

"You were right," he said, the words rumbling from his chest into her back. "You kept pace. Fuck for fuck."

She elbowed him again as he laughed. "I wasn't that crude."

"You acted like it."

He used those sure arms to roll them both over. She tucked against his side and sighed. Did all brides feel this way on their wedding night?

Looking up at Tallis's sharp jaw and the untamed mass of his sweat-damp hair, she had her answer. No. No other bride had felt this way, because they hadn't been with her man.

Her husband?

Yes, that felt right. In her heart. Forget the human trappings of ceremonies. This was the Pendray way. They were married.

A tiny, almost silent voice in a tucked-away corner of her heart wanted the Indranan way, too. She didn't need to know everything in his mind, but she wanted a taste of how he processed thought, how he saw color, how he heard sound. A married Indranan couple would share those little intimacies. She would never know them about Tallis. No matter how exhilarating their commitment had been, part of her remained restless.

She loved him. She trusted him. But she didn't *know* him the way an Indranan wife would know her husband.

"I don't make idle promises," she said, working to push those misgivings aside.

"I'm learning that."

Stroking his stomach, she kissed his throat just below his stubbled jaw. "I love you."

"I've said that before," he said carefully, "but not to you."

She elbowed up so she could look at him face to face. Her breasts pooled across his upper chest. Soft to hard. Heart to heart. "To her? Whoever she is?"

"Like a kid professing his love for an actress." He waved one hand haplessly toward their entwined bodies. "How was I supposed to know?"

"Know . . ." Kavya tilted her head. That heart to heart was hammering now, tense and breathless—just shy of scared. "Know what?"

His blue eyes had never been clearer or more earnest. "What love is supposed to feel like. It feels like us, Kavya. I love you."

Swallowing was impossible. So was knowing anything but the miracle of his words. She flung her arms around his head in history's most haphazard hug. He rolled her again, both of them laughing and whispering words Kavya had never thought she'd hear. Love, commitment, the rightness of being together and the unconventional choice they'd made.

"But I'm not going to rest until you're safe," Tallis said. "There's too much of me wrapped up in you. We won't make choices born of fear. And I need to know who infected my brain all these years. I love you, but we're not there yet. I can't . . . settle. Do you feel that in me?"

Balancing her elbows on either side of his throat, she placed her palms flat against his cheeks. She'd done that from the first. It remained the surest way of reading him. "I can't say I feel it so much as know it. You're an honorable man, beneath all you've done. What you've done was in service of a higher, noble goal, no matter her slithering techniques."

"Maybe. But then I think of the other people I've harmed, not just my niece. The other Dragon Kings I've killed. Some ends have been worth the means. Others . . . I don't know whose ends they benefited. The greater good, or the person behind the voices and dreams?" The jaw muscles bunched beneath her palms. "I can't live like that."

"*That's* what I know. Things are different now that you know the truth. I don't sense it like a telepath might, skirting over thoughts or digging deeper in search of the truth. I don't need that with you. You're *good*. And within you is a beast that knows right from wrong. Between the both of you, you'll set this to rights."

He placed his hands over hers and squeezed her fingers. "My Kavya."

"Yes." She kissed him full on the mouth, giving him the emotion bubbling and fizzing through her body, infusing her heart with such clarity. "Yours."

She lay against him, with her head cradled in that special spot where his shoulder hollowed in its sloping reach for his chest. Closing her eyes was . . . easy. With Tallis, she could sleep. It was another beautiful gift that she'd never thought possible for her. She was once-blessed. Never cursed. Together they would find a way to solve both of their problems and make a future with each other.

The last thing she heard in the quiet mist before sleep was the low, gentle rumble of Tallis's soft snores—

an audible reminder that she was exactly where she needed to be, where lassitude was welcome rather than something to be warded off at all cost.

Boneless.

Melting.

Dreaming.

Screaming.

She bolted upright and screamed again. The seaxes. She needed them. Run. Where was she? *Fight.*

Strong arms clasped her upper arms. "Kavya, stop. Stop!"

The voice was deep and dear, but she couldn't obey. She twisted and kicked. She saw only black, then red, then a familiar face dripping with blood.

"Chandrani!"

→ CHAPTER ←
TWENTY-NINE

Tallis's blood seized, frozen like a river during an Arctic winter.

Chandrani?

"She should've been back with her family," he said. "You made sure of it. That's what brought Pashkah down on us in Bhuntar."

"I did." Kavya's voice was stripped. She vibrated beneath his hands, ready to hit him or run—either seemed likely. "But . . . I saw her beaten. She was stripped almost bare. Black Guardsmen had her."

"Where? Back in the Panjal?"

For the first time since screaming them both to wakefulness, Kavya calmed somewhat. She turned. Her beautiful face was haunted by shadows, with sunken cheeks. Her focus was divided between Castle Clannarah and a distant place. She blinked, looked down at where he gripped her arms. "Tallis?"

"Yes, I'm here."

"Where she is . . . I don't know. But there was no snow. There was a—" She shook her head. "There was a tall . . . rock? It was covered in gray moss. I smelled salt."

"We need more than that, goddess. Think hard. Go deeper. I know you can." He pushed the hair back from her temples and held her head in his hands, cradling the place where she stored so many amazing gifts, the least of which was that bestowed by the Dragon. "*Remember.*"

"It was a dream. They go. It's not real."

Tallis made a frustrated noise. "They're not real—most times. But they leave clues. Images and real things that follow you to waking. Follow those clues. The boulder, moss, and salt."

She angled her neck so that her crown pressed against his chest. He continued to smooth her long, passion-tangled hair until she shuddered, then sucked in a fast breath.

"Sacred," she whispered. "Sacred place. The land and sea. The . . . the Mother."

"The Mother? You can't be sure."

"Tallis, it's breathtaking. The blend of woman and the Dragon." She stared up at him, her certainty increasing with each blink. "Yes. She's here."

Powered by an instant flush of adrenaline, Tallis jumped clear of the bed and began to suit himself in sturdy clothes and his leather jacket. It would serve as waterproof outerwear. His seaxes were the last. He strapped them around his waist using the cheap scabbards they'd used for trade.

"If they're here in Scotland, Pashkah will be with them, too," Kavya said. "I won't let you face him alone."

"What?" Tallis spun as he snapped out the word. "You'd rather go? I can kill the bastard and be done with it. He won't ever threaten you again. What could you do but make yourself vulnerable for him to do his worst? I won't let that happen."

"You could just as easily be killed. Make me a widow on the same day we married? I'm going with you to see this through. He's my brother and I despise what he's done to my life. I'll be there to see him fall so I can sleep—finally, Dragon be—finally sleep." She was out of bed now, dressing with the same efficiency. "And Chandrani, I'm not leaving her to be used and butchered. I *will not*."

Tallis was a mass of anger and confusion, especially when he realized that she'd donned the ceremonial garment he'd leveraged her into buying in the Johari Bazar. "Forget it," he said with a crude curse. "You'll freeze to death before we get there."

"This isn't an idle choice, and it's not for dancing girls or playing dress up. It's what Indranan women wear when they call out a sibling. The only time my clan doesn't wear white while in mourning is when we commit the murder ourselves."

"That's why you resisted."

"Yes. And why I ultimately gave in. I knew I'd need it someday." She lifted her chin. "I'm going, I'm wearing this, and you'll stop arguing with me if you want to help. Tallis, please. Show me where that madman has Chandrani. Bring me your family's Dragon-forged sword. I'm done running, hiding, hoping. I want my people back, and I want a life—a life with me and you, where I'll never fear anything but the day when the Dragon takes you from me."

Tallis stood there for a trio of heartbeats, but in that time, he took in an incomprehensible amount of detail.

She'd braided her hair, although streamers curled out from the hasty plait. The midriff-baring outfit took on ominous beauty now that he knew its purpose. Her breasts were crisscrossed by the heavier purple fabric, and covered with flowing layers that would catch the wind off the North Sea. The purple and orange skirt was muted by the single nightstand lamp, but the bronze medallions gleamed, catching light at every angle.

"The medallions. What do they say?"

"By the gift of the Dragon, I earn my Self."

His chest was heavy, burning, too tight for breath. He would slaughter Pashkah without thought—no matter who'd been responsible for his dreams. It didn't matter at that moment, when Kavya meant to take on her brother. "If you want that sword, you let me wield it."

"It's my responsibility!"

"To take his insanity into yourself? *No.* If you believed in what we shared last night, you'll let me do this. Killing him will be my pleasure, and doing so won't drive me mad. Tell me the same could be said if you did the deed."

Her hands were clasped so hard that her knuckles were uneven and bone white. "Hold the sword. Take his head. But you're not leaving me here." She lifted her head and revealed eyes as blatantly vengeful and powerful as he'd ever seen. In that moment, he would have sworn he was standing before a Pendray woman on the verge of letting loose the full strength of her fury.

"My family is coming with us. No way are we walking into some nest of Guardsmen with three swords and your skirt flapping in the wind." He touched her chin, kissed the bridge of her nose. "You'll distract me that way, my Kavya."

But then it was all business. He stormed through the castle, banging on every door. He didn't know which were occupied, so he made a hell of a racket.

"Wake the dead," he called, using a centuries-old call to arms. "Gather the ancients. Pull sword from scabbard and bathe blades in red. Trouble has come to one of our own."

Kavya was his wife now. She had joined his clan by blood and love. If his family cared for him at all—no, if they maintained years of honor that extended beyond their affection or bitterness—they'd close ranks, too. There was little the Pendray did better.

Within fifteen minutes, his groggy siblings had assembled. Dawn's palest light gave extra contrast to the shadows in that rummage sale of a kitchen, but his family stood ready for war. Modern clothes were layered with armor, from chain mail to modern Kevlar. Rill stepped forward and extended her hand toward Kavya. "For you."

Kavya took the metal collar. Although he hid his shiver, Tallis was reminded of the collars Cage warriors were forced to wear during their captivity. The damping properties nullified their gifts until the collars were deactivated for bouts. It had been a relief to rival few in his life when he'd seen Nynn and her lover freed of those shackles. No Dragon King should ever be restrained, made human in abilities if not in biology.

"It's to protect you," Rill said. "Dragon-forged swords can cleave most metal with a single stroke. Not this. You get one chance. After that, his blade will slice through the collar and your neck."

"Why have we never heard of these?" Kavya asked. "They would be nearly as prized as the swords."

"Every clan has secrets." Smiling, Rill's voice held a malicious edge of pride. "It's made from the smelted remains of Dragon-forged swords mixed with lesser metals. We've made do with what more powerful armies left behind."

Tallis could practically see protests forming on Kavya's tongue. She'd find some stubborn reason to put the collar on someone else, keep a different person from harm. On some level she must realize the importance of her own safety—how vital it was that she not be part of creating a thrice-cursed murderer—but her naive optimism was still so strong.

Tallis made the decision for her. He snatched the collar from her hands and tossed her loose braid out of the way. After a swift kiss on her nape where his teeth marks were bright and sensual, he snapped the lock. Her elegant throat was concealed by the shine of un-earthly metal, which bore a resemblance to the pale glow of a Dragon-forged sword.

He kissed her on the temple and gave her bare arms a squeeze. "Consider it a wedding present from my family."

"And this, big brother," said Serre, "is our present to you."

With both hands on the hilt and the tip point toward the floor, Serre held the family's millennia-old Dragon-forged sword like the tribute of a peasant to his liege.

Tallis took the weapon and tested its weight. Power unlike any in the universe surged through into his skin, his bones, his cells. The Dragon lived in him when he held that amazing weapon—the *real* Dragon, not a vision co-opted by a nighttime demon. Their Creator would spin in fury right alongside Tallis's berserker, which was more than ready to protect its woman.

"Is all forgiven then, Serre?"

"We're still family." His little brother offered a lopsided smile that made Tallis's heart pinch. It was like looking in a mirror and seeing a younger, less jaded version of himself. "And family is a benediction for all manner of sins. Unless you're Indranan," he said tightly, glancing at Kavya.

"Then it means a death sentence." Her words should've been listless and resigned, but edgy violence pulsed from Kavya. She was ready. Tallis was proud, and relieved that she would have no regrets. "And I'm not dying today."

So that was the color of his eyes.

Kavya knew it was an absurd realization, just as she knew she should be frozen through and through as Tallis had warned. Yet the fire in her belly kept her warm, and the sight of the North Sea crashing onto the craggy rocks of the northern Scottish coast filled her with peace. She would never know the deep secrets buried in her husband's soul. Now, however, she knew that his eyes matched the waters of this sacred place. She'd been right. They were the color of an ocean she'd never seen. Frothy, white-topped waves reminded her of the silver flecks adorning each strand of his wind-tossed hair.

The family followed her and Tallis as they climbed the jutting shores and followed a path to the west. An hour passed. Then two. She kept her attention focused on Tallis, lest she telepathically give away her approach. Pashkah's pet monkeys would obviously be able to sense an oncoming party of Pendray, all dressed to the hilt in armor and mean intentions, but perhaps her presence could be hidden until the last moment.

So she banked the temptation to reach out to Chandrani. To see if her friend still drew breath would be the equivalent of a scream in Pashkah's ear.

She watched Tallis as he walked with unrelenting strides, each the same distance and intensity no matter the terrain. She had to hop and pick her way across craggy shoals just to keep up. His family was equally fleet of foot as they protected her back. This was their territory, just as the Pir Panjal had been hers.

When Tallis stopped and held up a hand, Kavya's lungs seized. Didn't work. For a panicked span of seconds, her mind was trapped in a vessel that wouldn't move, *couldn't* move.

Then it was gone. She was clad in either the last garment she would ever wear, or the last garment she would ever wear with family yet in the world. That responsibility and grim reality renewed her strength. She was growing more powerful with each passing moment, as if the overnight gift of Tallis's fight and strength had seeped from his gracefully muscled body into hers.

"Beyond this rise," he said. "It should be the boulder you saw. I need you to climb up. Stay low. Signal me if I've got it right."

Kavya nodded and moved to go.

Tallis took her hand. Rather than kiss it or bid her good luck—sentimental things a husband might offer his wife—he unsheathed one of his seaxes and pressed it into her palm. They shared a tight smile. That was more fitting. Equal sentiment, but with deadly purpose.

"I'm beginning to like how you Pendray think," she said.

The climb up the rise was arduous. She wasn't cold, but her knees felt the sharp pinch of rock. A fingernail sheared away. Her stomach closed into a tighter ball until her guts were made of stone. She was calcifying, becoming part of that sacred place. It wouldn't have been a bad place to spend eternity, with a view of the ocean the color of Tallis's eyes. Only, she wanted the real thing even more. She wanted his eyes every day, gazing down on her when she awoke, burning her with their intensity when they made love. On some evening yet to be, she'd position a mirror in front of their faces when he took her from behind. She wanted to see the sharp blue glow of his eyes when he bit her nape.

A shudder worked across her shoulders. She clasped the hilt of his seax with even more assurance. Pendray territory. A Pendray weapon. A Pendray husband. She was ready to crawl out of her skin with the need to do violence.

His family. She was drawing from his family. Not their gift, as the Sath did—known derisively as Thieves, temporarily stealing the powers of other Dragon Kings. No, Pendray had unlimited stores of confidence in battle. They were disrespected as a backward clan, but they knew how to fight. Hand to hand, weapon against weapon—nothing and no one equaled them in sheer ferocity. She relished its beat in her blood.

At the top of the rise, she lay low across the ridge, belly to rock. As Tallis had described, the distant boulder was shaped like an ancient Neanderthal goddess, all rounds hips and curvy stomach and heavy, ripe breasts. Yet touches of the Dragon were everywhere, in the lick of a serpentine tongue, the potential carnage of hooked claws, and the slanted eyes that would protect or threaten, depending on who looked upon that mystical formation.

It was the rock formation from her dream.

The Mother of Clan Pendray. Their symbol of the Dragon.

Down in its shadow waited the villains she sought. The eight Guardsmen surrounded Chandrani. Pashkah paced in a wide circle around the ensemble. He'd reach the twelve-o'clock position and turn back the other way. Clockwise. Counterclockwise. She'd forgotten that particular quirk of his, a similar means of sorting thoughts and maintaining calm that Kavya used when clasping her hands. His brown hair was covered by a heavy brocade headscarf, the tail of which whipped in the salty sea wind.

He wore purple and orange and winking medallions that promised he intended her death just as much as she needed his.

Without looking away, she signaled the others to join her. Tallis was by her side in a matter of seconds. The pulse of his fury had tickled her back and arced down her thighs, even while he waited at the base of the rise. When he lay on his stomach beside her, he was like a wood stove left unattended, burning, pulsing, until it flamed with heat enough to melt the metal trying to contain the fire.

She grabbed the hair at the back of his neck. It had

been shorter there when they'd first met, but weeks of travel meant she could find a passable grip. "I need you, Tallis. Tell me you're in there." She yanked his hair again, then shot him a wicked smile. "I'm not Pendray, so I'm not playing by all of your clan's rules. Forget a one-way claiming. I'm biting your nape one day. This will be mine. Do you hear me?"

A growl pushed out of his throat, his chest, his soul. "You think that'll calm my fury, goddess?" he asked, rasping, as if invisible hands pressed on his larynx.

"No, but you're replying with more than single words. I need you, Tallis. Thinking as well as culling. You've seen what he can do and what pain he can inflict. Your family has no idea." She kissed the back of his neck, before smoothing his wild hair into place. "Tell me who you are and why you're here."

"Protect my family, rescue Chandrani, keep my wife safe, and rid the world of a Dragon-damned piece of shit."

"Tall order."

"Big sword." He matched her tight smile before adjusting his grip on the weapon that hummed with as much power as he did. His eyes glowed mean and vital. "Now let's go."

❧ CHAPTER ❧
THIRTY

Tallis's surge down the crest toward the foot of the Mother followed a pattern woven into the fabric of his people's memories. The high ground. Swooping in like raging locusts intent on feasting. How dare they invade our homes? Threaten our women? Disturb this sacred place?

The only way a Pendray knew how to cleanse sacred places was to wash them clean with the blood of strangers. Enemies.

He accessed his gift more quickly and with more certainty of purpose than he'd ever been able. Halfway down the slope, he was no longer Tallis. He was a Pendray warrior, content in the knowledge that his family roared behind him with equal rage.

The Guardsmen were fast. Tallis gave them that much. The Indranan weren't known for being great physical warriors, but this lot was well trained in swordplay and had the advantage of telepathy. Tallis was already too far gone for their wizardry to reach him. What felt like mental bullets pinged off his thoughts. He'd wrapped Kevlar through the folds of his brain. The closer he got, the more quickly those bullets fired. He kept running, until he was a man without legs; he was a roiling storm cloud of anger so intense that his mind was wiped of all but two words.

Kill Pashkah.

Honnas was by Tallis's side when they charged the nest of men dressed head to foot in black Indranan armor. Swords lifted, the Guardsmen *seemed* ready. The pitiful nature of their defense said they definitely were not. When Serre joined his brothers in the fray, he did so as a monster contained within the body of a young man in his prime.

Blood surged through Tallis's body. Consumed him. Overwhelmed higher function. He was only turn, thrust, duck, spin, hack. They had taken on greater armies. They had taken on men with greater courage. And they had fought for the safety of their families. No opponent suffered more when stoking that enormity of purpose.

"They barely know how to wield a sword," Honnas said on a laugh.

By Pendray standards, Tallis's older brother was right. The Guardsmen had grace, yes, but their determination to see an attack through to its bloody conclusion was lacking. Had they relied on telepathy so much during their raid of Kavya's followers? Did these men have any real substance when it came to physical fighting?

With a low swing of his seax, he struck a Guardsman's foot from his leg. The man crumpled. His bravery was admirable in that he tried to keep fighting from his kneeling, crippled position. Tallis raised the Dragon-forged sword as a threat. The Guardsman's face melted into white, streaking fear as he dropped his weapon and rolled onto his back, bare hands lifted in surrender.

Might as well be dead.

Perhaps something of Tallis's higher thoughts remained, because he experienced a flash of pity. Any Pendray would have branded the man a coward. But what did this Indranan have worth fighting for? Without children to nurture and protect, very few Dragon Kings knew what sacrifice meant anymore.

Tallis knew. He'd seen Nynn and Leto rip open the world trying to find the people they loved, and to find each other. He was that lover now. He would die before he let anything happen to Kavya.

Then die.

Pashkah's psychic strike lanced down Tallis's vertebrae. His spine was a lightning rod that conducted pain through his entire body. He dropped to the rocky, sea-damp earth. His skull bounced off a mossy patch mere inches from a rugged upthrust of rock. Agony registered on all levels. Physically, his head throbbed as if it had been cleaved like a fresh melon. Mentally, he was a sizzle of fried nerve endings and thoughts mashed into a sickly soup. All of the layers that made him Tallis blended until they were screaming ghosts. Every victim. Every time he'd ever shed blood or taken a life. A lava flow of memories rolled over him.

He crawled to his knees. Around him the battle still raged. His sisters were fierce. Honnas's wife, Olla, was particularly adept at a Pendray woman's greatest strength: screams that had inspired tales of banshees. They fought as if their own loved ones were the potential victims, not Indranan strangers.

Another stab of anguish was beyond Tallis's ability to describe. His consciousness fled down, down, using his berserker as a shield. The animal could not be harmed. He scanned the scene with the quickness of a predator that had momentarily lost its evening meal. He gained sharpness to his eyes and sensitivity to his hearing. Pure instinct.

Pashkah.

The man stood a hundred yards away, in the shadow of the Mother. He was dressed in colors Tallis recognized on some higher level, but his animal side jumped in the way of those analytical thoughts. All the beast knew was that those colors meant death. Death for Kavya.

Pashkah held a sword that gleamed gold in the fresh rays of dawn. Dragon-forged. They would finally meet each other as equals in armaments.

Tallis jumped to his feet and ran. His boots gripped with sure traction, even on the slippery coastal rocks. A Guardsman put himself between Tallis and his enemy, which made that Guardsman another enemy—one simpler to dispatch. Tallis lifted the Dragon-forged sword without thought. And sliced.

The Guardsman's head spun away from the lifeless body that collapsed sideways in a sickly arc.

The animal was satisfied, although Pashkah was still his target. The rest were mosquitoes to be swatted away.

Pashkah was laughing, and he was attacking again. The warmth in Tallis's brain turned to hot steam, then burst into an inferno so hot and deadly that he crumpled. And he understood a new, terrible truth: Pashkah could kill his family with a single sweep of his crazy mind. If they emerged from their fury long enough to become thinking creatures again, they would be paralyzed from the inside out.

Pushing up to his knees—forcing his body to cooperate—Tallis staggered toward Kavya's brother. Pashkah's amber eyes glowed with manic energy and a nauseating twist of madness. At his feet was Chandrani, hog-tied and gagged and bloody. Her armor had been stabbed, leaving red-stained holes. None of the wounds would be fatal. That hadn't been the purpose.

"I couldn't find Kavya," Pashkah said with a snake's smile, "I needed a compass."

The man's features were a mystery. He shimmered and altered with every few syllables. He was fragments sewn together in an ever-morphing skin. Nothing genuine remained except that he was shorter and thinner than Tallis. "Kick a beloved puppy. Listen for where the puppy screamed. Keep traveling in that direction. Until . . . here? A wasteland."

"My home."

"Keep thinking, Reaper. I'll make you suffer for it."

Tallis stabbed his seax into the ground and attacked. Dragon-forged energy snapped with sparks when their swords collided. In strength alone, Tallis had the advantage. He hacked and thrust, welcoming the return of every fighting, spitting impulse to guide his weapon. Pashkah staggered until his back hit the boulder, then he retaliated with his mental prowess—just enough to slip inside Tallis's mind and wrench. Pain was a wash of red paint.

Pashkah grunted, then spun away. The quick maneuver gave him a few seconds to recover, but Tallis pressed the advantage.

"She took so long to find," Pashkah said, adjusting his grip on his sword's hilt. "Maybe that had something to do with the Reaper animal she'd taken as her lover.

You're quite the beast. Have you made her into a dog, too? Rolling in the grass and howling to the moon?"

Had he been able to shut out spoken words, Tallis would have done so. *Just fight.* He parried, braced with a low squat, and thrust up toward Pashkah's sternum. The man barely jumped away in time.

"I'd never hoped anything for Kavya. That she sank so low as to crawl into your bed—that was a gift I'd never expected. To know she'd been so debased before I saw her again. Just precious."

He stabbed the sword into a swath of earth softened in the shadow of the boulder. From behind them both, Chandrani screamed. Kavya's scream followed, as if her heart were being torn from her chest—or her brain from her skull.

"Do you think I want you dead, Reaper?" Pashkah held his hands wide, inviting attack. "I couldn't care less. You're that mosquito you pictured. You've done so much killing. Your life is dripping with blood. Now listen to those women scream, your beloved Sun—your Kavya— and I'll tell you exactly who you've been killing for."

Tallis's hesitation was enough—that moment that wasn't a moment, when his decades-old need to know won out over every other consideration.

To be free of it, at last? To *know*?

Two Guardsmen stripped his Dragon-forged sword and felled him with three sharp blows.

Kavya saw Tallis fall. Slow motion. Nightmares.

She screamed her husband's name.

Her barely imagined future lay in an unconscious heap.

Across a battlefield where berserkers clashed with Guardsmen, she met Pashkah's eyes. He looked as if he hadn't slept in as many months, years, decades as her.

As if without fear—although she feared the next few seconds more than any in her life—she walked through the melee. She wasn't there. She was only with Pashkah. This was the duel they'd postponed for most of their lives.

"Let them go," she said with spoken words.

His eyes widened, apparently taken by surprise. When the first manifestation of their gifts had been more amazing than fearful, they hadn't used tongues, mouths, or lips to vocalize thoughts. They'd been so close. Baile, too. It was a cruel joke for the Dragon to play, bonding siblings so closely, only to have those siblings turn on one another.

"This ends here, Pashkah. I'm not running. I'm not hiding. I'm returning to the Indranan to repair the damage you've done."

"With this disgusting Reaper?" He kicked Tallis in the stomach, who was slowly rousing but pinned to the ground by four Guardsmen.

"He's going to kill you," Kavya said. "Not even the Dragon could change that now."

Pashkah strode forward, his Dragon-forged sword in hand. Kavya backed up a step, then another.

She was defenseless.

Around them, the fray had eased. Everyone knew why they were there. The Guardsmen and Tallis's family were foot soldiers as the generals squared off.

"You always thought you were above the rest of us." Pashkah's face contorted in a blend of expressions. "You thought you could erase thousands of years of suspicion and hatred. It can't be done. She said the same thing, and she forced my hand."

"She? What are you talking about?"

"Baile! Don't you remember what we promised? We'd never succumb to what the others did. We were stronger than that. Kavya, you remember how we vowed."

"And then you killed our sister! What sort of vow is that?"

"One I couldn't keep when she attacked me with Father's sword."

Kavya staggered back a step. "No. That's not how it happened. You betrayed our trust and you killed her."

"I did kill her, yes." His single nod reminded her more of her lost brother than anything ever had. His voice wasn't the same, nor his looks nor his demeanor. Kavya caught images of unfamiliar men and women, but mostly she saw Baile. Their sister. Her so-distant features flickered over his. But Pashkah had used that particular nod when absorbing new information or admitting a wrong. "It was her life or mine, not because I meant to betray anyone. Who was the strongest of us, Kavya?"

She swallowed. The cold was getting to her now, although the sea winds had nothing to do with it. Old memories realigned. She adjusted her grip on the hilt of Tallis's seax, if only to urge blood back into her pinched, numb fingers. "She was."

"And who was the strongest of us, physically?"

"You."

Pashkah shone through his own eyes. He was taking

control of . . . something. Even the appearances of his shape-shifting features had slowed, calmed, resumed their usual configuration. He'd always been so handsome. Now Kavya saw that he'd have matured into a magnificent man. "And who of us was the least threat?"

"Me. My gift was weaker. I was weaker."

"We were all wrong on that score." He twirled the hilt of the sword their father had kept safe. Their pod had been so peaceful. He and Mother had assembled another three couples. The sword had been insurance, in case adult brothers or sisters came with murder in mind. It hadn't been intended for one child to use against another. Members of the pod had worked tirelessly to teach the siblings tolerance and peace—that they were better than the greed of their gift.

"That's right," Pashkah said. Kavya had been with Tallis for so long that she'd forgotten how invasive that could feel. "Tolerance and peace. You learned that lesson better than any of us. Baile smiled along. She hid from us even then. Tell me in truth that you knew our sister. Knew her heart, her fears, her deepest thoughts. Tell me whatever it is you think you know and I'll tell you it was a lie. She wanted both of us dead, and she started with me. I never saw it coming, and you wouldn't have either. She wanted a stronger body to keep pace with her mind." He smashed his left fist against his skull and roared in pain that didn't seem physical. "Then we'd come for you."

"This is long past, Pashkah. It's *too* long past. Fight her now. Let Chandrani and my husband go. We can walk away. Or . . ." Her voice broke, thick with emotion. She didn't like seeing him this way—as her brother. As the brother she'd loved long ago. "Or, Dragon be, you can help me. Our people need us."

A telltale sneer reshaped his face. Baile again. Even his voice took on her inflections and cadence. "Always so good. It's not going to happen, Kavya. You're going to die today, so I can stop chasing you and begin the culling that needs to take place."

Kavya raised the seax, although she knew it would be destroyed if they clashed weapons. She growled. Only then did she glance at Tallis where he remained pinned. The dawn bathed his face with a pink light that added more vitality than he possessed. Blood dripped from his temple, and his eyes were unfocused. She knew that look. Constantly bombarded by psychic pain.

And yet . . . She looked again.

Her berserker was in there. And he was waiting.

"He's a mindless Reaper." Pashkah grinned. "But he knows the truth. She's been feeding it to him for years."

Kavya stilled. "She?"

"Our sister dearest."

"Baile?" Kavya lunged on pure instinct. The seax stabbed deep into the joint that powered Pashkah's right shoulder. He cried out and clutched the wound. "Baile has been in Tallis's dreams?"

"Using your face," came the singsong taunt of madness. They were blended into one now, brother and sister, both of them tying Kavya's gut in a sick spin of knots. "And using your body and the sweet innocence of your ideals of peace. Funny thing to find those same ideals in a Pendray. We searched the world. He was the one who seemed happy to see us. Happy to do our *honorable* bidding. But we couldn't have you two figuring that out, could we?" Pashkah's mouth formed a smile that eerily echoed their dead sister's. "So we blocked your thoughts. No sharing secret weapons. Only these crude pieces of metal."

"Pashkah," she pleaded. "I know you're in there. Fight her. Help me end this!"

"Oh, I plan to." He stepped forward.

Kavya knew to stand her ground. She saw it and heard it in every aspect of her brother's body, face, warped mind.

He doesn't want me dead.

"You're right on that score," he said. "And neither does Baile. You see, I'm through fighting her. Help you end this? There's no other way than to end my life."

She swallowed a flash flood of grief. "Then give Tallis the sword. He can end your misery."

"I would." Pashkah lifted his fists, one of which swished the sword through the air. The other tugged his hair with so much force that he could have stripped his scalp clean off. "But she doesn't want to die. Our dear departed Baile. She wants you to do the dirty work, Kavya dear. The three of us together as one. All those followers ready to do your bidding again. Your pretty face. Your endless optimism."

The horror of that scenario made Kavya want to vomit and scream, but her skin held her body together. She trusted that it would until the Dragon took her back to the Chasm for eternity. "I would have to kill you, Pashkah." She shook her head, correcting herself. "I'd have to kill both of you. But I won't be a vessel for your insanity. I won't do it."

"Yes, you will. Or your new husband loses his head."

⁂ CHAPTER ⁂
THIRTY-ONE

Tallis watched the unfolding scene as if he were a much younger man, experiencing his first dream vision. The colors were all wrong. The sounds in his ears and the taste in his mouth—they were distorted. He could hear sugar and taste velocity. It was all wrong.

Because, head bowed, Pashkah was kneeling in front of Kavya.

His neck was exposed. And a Black Guardsman had forced Pashkah's Dragon-forged sword into her hands.

The surreal situation didn't stop there. His kinsmen had laid down their weapons. They stood entranced, but he knew the Pendray didn't do so by choice. They were victims of the Guardsmen's telepathic process. Even Tallis could sense it. They formed a ring like Stonehenge made out of bloodied, armored, panting Dragon Kings, all of whom had been stopped mid-motion. Weapons littered the ground. Even Rill, with her indomitable spirit and forgiving heart, didn't seem . . . awake. He wanted a touch of Kavya's powers.

Wake up!

The only change was when another Guardsman

stood over Tallis with his own sword poised for a cutting blow.

Kavya darted her eyes between Pashkah's exposed neck and Tallis's eyes.

More than anything, he wanted to talk to Kavya's mind. He wouldn't tell her to wake up, because he'd never seen her more alert. Every emotion a woman could wear across such beautiful, dear features was there to see. Her outrage and fear, her heartsick mourning and her love. He wouldn't tell her to wake up; he'd show her what was in his heart, especially how he'd changed himself for the better, freeing himself, reclaiming his free will and his hope for a better future. Maybe then she'd have the courage to do what needed to be done.

But he had no telepathy. He'd only ever had words—when he was lucky and the berserker gave him leave to speak. Kavya's love had taught him how to bring both halves together. Oh, he was raging and he was speaking. Pashkah didn't stand a chance

"Don't do it, goddess. Don't you dare. Dragon damn you if you do."

"No! I can't let them kill you!" She swallowed, tightening her hands on the hilt of that deadly weapon. "I'm stronger than them. I'd use their powers to make people trust me again. Make them see how good peace will be."

"Yes," Pashkah said, his voice slinky and soft. "What's right. Make them see."

"*Make* them?" Tallis's voice, by contrast, was a bellow. Rage clawed out from his throat. He lay on the ground, stomach pressed flat. Fury built beneath his skin, pressing his bones against the solid, unforgiving coastal rock like a volcano about to burst. "Kavya, you've made yourself ill when you've needed to use your powers selfishly. That clerk in the hotel. The customs agent in Istanbul. Afterward I held your hair back as you threw up."

"Enough!" Pashkah sounded like a demon.

Tallis wasn't close to being finished. "One-third, Kavya. Remember? The rest has been your conviction and conscience. Peace is not yours to *make*. They want it bathed in blood, not earned through trust."

"Shut him up!"

Obeying his master, the Black Guardsman drove the pommel of the Dragon-forged sword into the base of Tallis's neck. A human would've been crippled. Paralyzed forever. Tallis only boiled. That was where Kavya had promised to kiss him.

He locked eyes with his wife. They held each other's hearts for a second—one second of the lifetime they had yet to share.

She smiled.

"Shut him up?" Kavya backed away from her insane brother. "No, my berserker is just getting started."

Tallis roared. He threw off pairs of binding hands as if he'd been held down by toddlers. After spinning onto his back, he kicked up toward the looming Guardsman's shin. His boot connected sideways against the man's tibia, breaking the limb in two. A compound fracture. Tallis wanted to do more damage, but he didn't need to. The man crumpled onto his ass, bellowing and clutching his ruined leg.

Kavya whirled on the man holding her in place, ready for the kill, and kicked him in the chest. She grabbed the seax Tallis had given her, stabbing the long blade through the Guardsman's shoulder. He was pinned to the ground. His screams ended when Kavya decapitated him with the Dragon-forged sword. She yanked the seax free and wiped the blood against her skirts.

The flurry of surprise shocked the Pendray to life. Guardsmen did their best to get up to speed.

Tallis snatched up his family's Dragon-forged sword along with his other seax. It was a hard test of his control to keep from knocking heads off the men who'd nearly allowed Pashkah to get his way. To kill Tallis's family. To force Kavya into unending madness.

Kavya!

The hand-to-hand battle had resumed its bloody fury, but he caught sight of her across the wind-strewn clearing. She was an avenging angel. Her colorful skirts whipped around her legs. She held two swords, as he did, and was wearing the red proof of her victory. She sprinted forward to where Chandrani remained captive.

Tallis didn't like it. Something wasn't right.

Because Pashkah was nowhere to be seen.

"No!" he shouted.

His spring was fast, exceptionally fast in the midst of his rage, but it wasn't fast enough. Pashkah snatched a hand out from the ground where he'd fallen. He grabbed Kavya's ankle and twisted. She spun in a half rotation before landing hard on her back. Her head bounced off a broad, flat rock. More blood, this time from the woman Tallis loved.

Pashkah struggled to wrest the sword from her hand. Her grip was surprisingly unforgiving. She snarled and fought—a genuine warrior now, with rage to compensate for a lack of skill. She used her left hand to stab upward with the seax. Pashkah was forced to relinquish his fight for the Dragon-forged sword. Instead he defended himself with the only shield he had—the bare palm of his right hand. The seax cut through skin, bone, and tendon with such strength that the blade slammed into his collarbone. Kavya abandoned that weapon, scrambling away, unable to catch her balance and stand.

A scream of rage shot through the clearing. Rocks rumbled. Loose gravel and even a few smaller boulders toppled down from the Mother. It was Pashkah. A rage born of madness and a gift that literally shook the world.

Kavya matched his scream, but she didn't do so to destroy. She cried out in pain. The sword dropped from her hand as she buckled. She clutched her skull. Her whole body shook, twitching, kicking out in all directions.

More screams, as the Guardsmen again turned their telepathy on Tallis's family—with the intent to cripple. Tallis bounded over bodies and past pairs of growling Pendray who fought on, despite what must be agony daring them to give in.

Tallis knew they wouldn't.

Another boulder shook loose from the Mother, right above Chandrani's bound, helpless body. Tallis was nearest her. By instinct he grabbed the large woman and hauled hard under her arms. The huge sandstone rock crashed down where her chest would've been. A crushing blow. The kind a Dragon King would never recover from.

He pushed the hilt of his seax into Chandrani's hand. She'd fight free.

He turned to find Pashkah straddling Kavya. The point of the Indranan's Dragon-forged sword was aimed directly at the hollow at the base of her throat. "Is this collar some Pendray bauble? How long will it withstand just how angry you've made me?"

"Don't do this," she whispered.

Pashkah shook his head. "Even now you can't use the gift you were given. Are you afraid of talking to me on my turf? Because that's what this mind is, Kavya. *Mine*. Just as yours will be."

"What happened to wanting my body instead of yours?"

"Doesn't matter now. She'll control us both, no matter the physical form." Pashkah's rigid hold on the sword slipped. A resigned sadness infused his voice—that of a regular man. A man who was so very tired. "Kavya, sister, you have no idea . . ."

"And she never will." Tallis swung with all his might. The sideways arc of his blade parted Pashkah's head from his body in a bloody gush.

In the next instant, Tallis heard Kavya's voice in his mind for the first time.

Thank you, my love.

Kavya stared up at Tallis. They were both grim creatures, as if they'd spent the last two hours butchering cows.

His eyes were wide, his mouth slack. Smiling a little crooked.

"What was that?" he asked.

"I said, 'Thank you, my love.'"

"No, you didn't say it."

Frowning, Kavya tested gently, so gently, all the while watching Tallis for clues. *I love you.*

"I love you, too."

With a joyful cry, she heaved herself off the ground

and into his arms. They collided in body as they had in life. Unexpected souls brought together, *bound* together.

"You can hear me now?" She used a swatch of fabric from her ceremonial sari to wipe blood from his mouth. He returned the favor, although the attempt was makeshift at best. "You heard what I said to you?"

"Yes." He hesitated, hiding it behind the act of tucking her wickedly ruined hair behind her ears. "And you? Can you . . . Can you read my mind?"

She hesitated, too. After a quick, hard kiss, she said, "Now isn't the time."

She grabbed her family's Dragon-forged sword and strode toward where Serre still clashed with one of the Guardsmen. "Stop. Now."

Both men seemed startled by her authoritative tone. Their eyes went wide—Serre's bright blue, and the Indranan's dark brown.

"The fight is over. Pashkah is dead." Turning her words on the Guardsman, she pointed the sword toward his neck. "If you want to continue breathing, consider returning to your family in the Punjab. Take the rest with you. When I see you next—and I will—you'll be happily married in a peaceful pod, or we'll conclude this moment in a much messier fashion."

The man dropped his sword and held up his hands. Serre lunged, but Tallis was there to stop him. "Peace, brother. Believe it or not, there is a time for it. No matter what he's done, he's laid down arms. This is for the Indranan to decide now."

"Pashkah was not the Indranan," Kavya called to the other Guardsmen. "Neither am I. We have a long way to go before we learn who we are as a clan. But this . . ."

She gestured to those who lay dead and mangled. "This isn't it. We're better than this. We'll fix this chasm and become stronger for it."

The Chasm isn't fixed.

She whirled on Tallis. She'd heard those words as clearly as if he'd shouted them across the clearing.

"What did you just . . . ?"

"The Chasm isn't fixed." He shook his head. "I thought she was gone. Your . . . Dragon-damned sister."

"That wasn't Baile's voice," Kavya said. "That's been part of you forever, not from some outside place."

Anger shook out from Tallis's limbs. He sheathed his weapons and grabbed Kavya's upper arms. His dear, dark blue eyes were clouded by confusion and fury. "I wanted this done. That I saved you, too—I had no idea. It was the revenge I didn't know I'd find here. But I wanted the past to stay in the past, without pieces left to echo through me forever."

"I've heard it, too," came a soft voice.

Kavya found Olla, Honnas's wife, standing beside them. She was as battle-tousled as anyone else in the clearing, despite her fey, ethereal appearance. Fey and beautiful. Her banshee screams must've been effective, because she was unscathed after having fought with a Guardsman twice her size.

"I've heard it, too. The Chasm isn't fixed. It's not just you. What that . . ." Olla glanced toward Pashkah's fallen, headless body. "Whatever that *person* did to you, Tallis, had nothing to do with those words. As familiar as my name, ever since childhood."

"As familiar as your name," Tallis said, his voice oddly relieved. "Yes. Exactly that."

"Do you dream of the Dragon? I dream he's coming back to us." She shook her head and smiled, appearing embarrassed. "But what's in a dream?"

Tallis frowned deeply. "Too much. Sometimes far too much."

My love?

Kavya reached up to remove his hands from her upper arms, to hold them in hers. "So Pashkah—or, Dragon help me, Baile—was responsible for the block the entire time. Keeping you off-balance. Extending your belief in her and your determination to exact her commands."

"All the while fostering the idea that you were the one to blame," he said. "Otherwise I wouldn't have acted as I had that afternoon in the valley. I wouldn't have done a lot of things."

Needing his warmth, his body, Kavya wrapped herself in Tallis's vital embrace. He fed her heart with his strength. "They never wanted to kill me at all. They wanted to use me. She would've sacrificed him as just another body to get what she wanted."

"Your influence," Tallis said against her temple. "She would've poisoned it, changing you, maybe even convincing the Indranan to unite through a civil war of mass murder."

Rill sheathed her weapon and slapped Tallis on the back. "No longer. Not by this lunatic's hand, anyway."

Chandrani joined them. She had a limp and cuts up and down her forearms, some so deep they'd scar. Her face was a mass of bruises.

Kavya hugged her dear friend. "I'm so sorry. So sorry. Please, forgive me."

"Nothing to forgive," Chandrani said with her assurance that sank into Kavya's soul. "I owed you a debt. Long ago."

"I never asked you to repay it, but I'm forever grateful that you did. Thank you, my friend."

Chandrani grinned. "Maybe now I'll get to go home."

"Unless . . ." Kavya looked from Chandrani to her husband. "Unless you want to come back with me. Our people need a lot of reassuring, and new hope. I'd like to think I won't be alone in that."

Shaking hands with Tallis, who nodded respectfully, Chandrani said, "I'll go back with you, Kavya, but not because you'll be alone. I'll do it for the same reason I always have. I believe in what you stand for. Never more so than now."

"But first, back to the castle?" Honnas called. He was already halfway across the clearing, hands cupped around his mouth and his wife at his side. "I stink and would dearly like breakfast."

"You go on," Tallis replied with a strong voice. "We'll be right along. Chandrani, you, too. My sisters will tend your wounds."

Kavya watched her tall, imposing friend walk with the Pendray as if they'd been comrades all her life. That idea warmed her heart and gave her another shot of hope. Maybe this could be done. Maybe she could start again.

So much depended on Tallis.

"India again, eh?"

She blinked. He held her hands between them, their knuckles lined up like the mountains where she'd grown into a woman. "But you've only just returned to Scotland. What about your family?"

"I didn't mean right away. A month's sleep and a lot of lovemaking have an appeal not even you can deny, goddess. And I'd like to make my peace here. Repair Clannarah. Stand before the Leadership of the Pendray to clear my name. No loose ends before we go." He kissed the backs of her hands. "Then the real work begins. The Indranan deserve peace, and . . . the Chasm isn't fixed. It's bigger than me. What Olla said is a relief beyond description."

"You really want to come with me?"

"We committed last night." He offered a crooked smile. "Unless you're bored of me already."

"Bored? That word will never make sense when applied to you."

He kissed her lips. Kavya tasted blood, but it didn't matter. They were both alive. She would never need to look over her shoulder again.

But she did need something.

"Tallis, the Indranan way . . ." She swallowed. "Of bonding."

He looked away briefly. "I know. You gave yourself over to my desires, completely and passionately. I—I'll submit to the Indranan way, if you ask it of me. Because I love you."

Kavya gently held his cheeks beneath her palms. The old means of reading him. She could've slipped inside his mind and taken what she wanted, but that had never been them. "You have secrets you never want brought to light. Manipulated by my sister. Driven to murder and exile. That's done and gone. I know all I need to know about you. Right here. Right at this moment."

"What if I insist?" He knelt before the Mother—that

place so sacred to the Pendray—and touched the back of his neck. "You promised me a kiss. Give it to me, and I'll show you something beautiful."

Legs shaking, she knelt and draped her body across his broad back. He pulled her arms down over his shoulder and held her hands.

"Kavya," he said softly. "Make me yours."

With surprising greed, she bared her teeth against his nape and nipped, scraped, bit. Nothing so harsh as what Tallis had claimed, but the significance of it shuddered into her soul. All the while, in the deep center of her mind, she gloried in the images he shared. The sea through his eyes. The salt-laden air as he smelled it. The feel of her touch and how it warmed his coldest, darkest corners. Then he revealed glimpses of Kavya from his perspective. Eyes, lower lip, breast, teasing smile, toes, and then back to her eyes.

In doing so, he did more than share impressions. He proved his trust that she would never take more than he offered. It was just the show of faith Kavya had longed for.

They were Pendray and Indranan, well and truly bonded.

"I've traveled this world, aching to be home again," he said, aligning their knuckles over his heart. "I thought it was Castle Clannarah. My family. Or after my revenge, I'd find a place of my own. But I got it all wrong."

"Where is home, Tallis?" She nipped and kissed again, where his silver-tipped hair met the silky skin at the top of his neck.

"Where else would it be, my Kavya? It's with you. Wherever we go, you are my home."

Continue reading
for an exclusive excerpt from

HUNTED
WARRIOR

The Dragon Kings
Book Three

by

LINDSEY PIPER

Coming from Pocket Books in 2014

✦ CHAPTER ✦
ONE

She was called the Pet, but she didn't think of herself as a creature in need of protection, care, or condescension. She'd left that life behind. Neither was she a captive, as she picked her away through the ruins of a crumbling rock labyrinth on the island of Crete. How she'd come to be there was a story she didn't dare contemplate for fear of madness. There was no rhyme, no reason, no guide other than the future she saw in bits and patches.

The sun was fierce and gorgeously freeing on the back of her neck. She was a Dragon King, and Dragon Kings loved fire. Most wouldn't admit how much the cold sank under their skin and sapped their sense of godlike invincibility. Maybe that was for the best. Too many of the would-be gods romancing the planet believed themselves immortal, no matter the press of extinction. They didn't realize that all empires ended, even those blessed with access to what humans would consider the supernatural.

Turning to stare into the blinding white-yellow glare, she didn't bother to shade her eyes. Her second sight—the gift from the Dragon that gave her the ability to see the future—was always with her, no matter its unpredictability. A man sought her. A violent man who hid his violence behind titles and lineage.

Time was slippery like moss on a riverbank or slime on the carcass of a dead fish. Time was viscous on her fingertips. Time was running out.

With no further hesitation, she continued her cautious journey through the abandoned ruins of ancient kings. The walls had been reduced by countless rains and droughts, days and nights, until all that remained were bleached waist-high spikes and jagged edges. The stubborn ground was strewn with pieces of the crumbled labyrinth. There was nothing to grab should she fall—not without impaling her hand. Dragon Kings healed rapidly, but some damage was too much for even their extraordinary physiology to repair.

Archaeologists had dubbed the site of little historic worth, with its condition so degenerated that they could gather scant new information about the Minoans of long-ago Crete. How wrong. How blinded by the hubris of a society that believed itself the most advanced of its animal counterparts. Any thought as to the Dragon Kings' existence was disregarded. Fairy tales of Valkyries and Olympians and messiahs. The woman called the Pet knew differently. All the myths were true. What was once would be again.

And the Chasm wasn't fixed.

The Dragon Kings were dying. Why her predictions of the future had led her to Crete as a means of stopping that slow extinction was beyond her. She had to trust. She'd always needed to trust, when little in her life stood as examples of why that must be so. Maybe her real gift from the Great Dragon wasn't the ability to see the future, but to have faith in what she couldn't explain.

The labyrinth was waist-high, yes, but it was still a tangle of dead ends, wrong turns, and twenty-foot-deep pits that barred any attempt to pass. When she realized she'd made a mistake, she couldn't simply climb over the wall and continue on. Her hands would be shredded. So, as with all mazes, she doubled back and kept the details firmly in mind. The conventional wisdom was that if one picked a direction and stuck with it—all left turns, always, no matter what—the heart of the geometric puzzle would be revealed.

Those occasional pits were too deep to escape. And time . . . Yes, time was slippery.

She needed to hurry, because the man was coming for her. Yet she couldn't even describe what she sought.

A gift for Cadmin. That's all she knew. She drew on powers as both soothsayer and true believer to remind herself of her journey's importance. Cadmin, the closest she'd ever known to having a baby of her own, although the fetal child had developed in another woman's womb—that of Cadmin's true mother.

"It took some time to find you," came a voice at her back. "But you couldn't expect that I'd give up trying."

The Pet turned and met the steady glare of Malnefoley of Tigony, the Honorable Giva. With that title, he should've been the unquestioned leader of their people. With the derisive nickname of the Usurper, however, his leadership was a listing ship, barely righting itself in time to escape the swallowing swell of a wave.

"I escaped," she said. "I didn't attempt to hide."

"I'm taking you back to Greece." He flicked dark

blue eyes across the irregular half walls. Although he couldn't climb across three lanes to apprehend her physically, he had a gift far more crippling and violent than hers. Electricity was his plaything.

"I don't want to go back to Greece." She rolled up one sleeve of her thin purple blouse, which contrasted with her militaristic cargo pants and heavy boots. She was a lover of contrast. In revealing bare skin, she also revealed five parallel incisions across her left biceps that had healed to papery scars. "There's work to be done. For all five clans."

"You were Dr. Aster's companion for countless years. You commit blasphemy when speaking of the five clans."

"*Was* his companion. Now I'm not. These are the reminders I gave myself as proof of my freedom and my loyalty to our kind."

The intensity of Malnefoley's expression increased a hundredfold when he narrowed his eyes. His lips tightened. He looked like an emperor whose displeasure would result in countless deaths. Did others see him as she did? Were they so awed or angry that they missed the signs?

"You'll forgive me if I don't believe a brainwashed servant."

"I didn't serve him."

You wouldn't understand. No one would.

In some warped way, her relationship with Dr. Heath Aster, heir to the human Aster cartel, was that of a torture victim coming to love her torturer. He had hurt her. He'd also left her in isolation for months at a time. She'd been twelve years old. After a while she'd craved his attention, no matter how painful, because being alone was far more devastating. Love was a strange emotion to feel for the man her logical mind knew was her abuser, her dismantler, her maker.

"You simply aided in the perpetuation of his crimes," the Giva said.

"Your mind won't be changed by anything I say."

Without looking at him again, she resumed her slow, careful push through the ruins, searching, not knowing what her eyes needed to find.

"You can't walk away from me." His voice was louder now, more commanding.

"I can if you don't know the way to follow."

The hair on the backs of her arms and neck lifted—such susceptible little pores, frightened by the smallest wash of fear. The Giva, however, was no slight threat. On a par with the Pendray berserkers with regard to the violence of their gifts, the Tigony were like turbine engines. They pulled bits of electricity out of the air, down to the barest hint of static, then whirled and intensified them into storms worthy of the mighty Zeus throwing lightning bolts. The Pet briefly wondered if Malnefoley was descended from the Tigony man who must've inspired those timeless Greek myths.

"You'll come back with me," he said, his voice darkly ominous. "Now."

She turned a corner, then another, looking back only briefly.

He was the revered, hated, distrusted, *undeniable* Malnefoley of Tigony.

He should've looked ridiculous wearing Armani in the midst of an abandoned archaeological site, yet, tall and imposing, his body was built for the well-tailored suit. Electricity snapped from his fingers and arced like a heavenly rainbow across his well-bred features. The sun was merciless, but it cast shadows as it dipped toward the west. The Giva had banished the shadows. He was completely illuminated. Blue eyes were bluer. Cheekbones were more dramatic. Blond hair was transformed into filaments of gold.

He was a powerful man and bore that power as if it were featherlight.

Surrounded by the proof of his clan's magnificence, he adopted a grim, humorless smile. "Don't make me repeat myself. And don't give me reason to lose my temper."

"You won't hurt me. I spent enough months detained in the Tigony fortress to know that. You're too convinced of my worth—the information you seek."

Her heartbeat was a metronome that kept time using a sledgehammer, pounding a frightened tempo in her chest. She had survived so much. She would survive the Giva in all his tempestuous conceit. But the process of surviving was wearisome. *Rest* was a word from another language.

Cadmin was waiting for her, perhaps, maybe, somewhere. The Pet could only pick her way through the rubble and wait for the worst to happen, let it pass through her, and move on. That had been her life. That would always be her life. The Tigony absorbed electricity and magnified it exponentially. *She* absorbed sadness and pain, then reduced it down and down and down until she could breathe.

The bolt of electricity, when it came, stole her vision, obliterated her ability to hear, and seemed to peel back layer after layer of skin. In the moment between strike and agony, she was glad she couldn't see her half-bared arms, for fear of finding exposed bone rather than whole, sound flesh.

But the agony would not be denied. Her heart's metronome stopped its clicking smash. She blinked three times and fell to the rough, rocky ground.

Malnefoley was used to restraint, no matter the generalized bitterness that simmered deep in his bones. He was a politician. He was the head of the Council that served and oversaw the governments of the Five Clans.

He was not a man used to giving in to the urge to solve disputes with force rather than words. That weakness had been abandoned to a younger, impetuous version of himself.

Dr. Aster's Pet, however, was an exception.

Five days ago, she'd escaped from the stronghold of Clan Tigony high in the mountains of Greece. He didn't know how. None of his guards—loyal and tested—knew how. It was as if she'd transformed into air, swished through ventilation shafts, and caught the first breeze south to Crete. And she'd told the truth. A woman who feared getting caught would've made a better point of hiding. She must've known he would come for her. For Mal, finding her had been simple. Ask about an unusual, plain-speaking, coltish young woman with wild raven-black hair, and the answers were quick and sure.

He wasn't through with her. She had served Dr. Aster as his devoted companion—so devoted that no one referred to her as anything other than the Pet. She must know the madman's secrets, including how he had been able to solve the riddle of Dragon King conception. One so connected to the highest echelon of the Aster cartel was invaluable, and Mal wouldn't see her gone.

So he'd used his gift. Unlike members of Clan Pendray with their berserker furies, the Tigony were a refined people. Mal knew his gift's potential down to the slightest variable. To deliver his electric punch, he'd taken into account an estimation of the Pet's weight, her physical condition, and even the ambient temperature. The result was a strike strong enough to knock her out for no more than two minutes, without lasting damage.

Then he breathed. He put his fleeting, petulant anger away. For two decades, he'd been the Honorable Giva, even in times when behaving like a calm, neutral leader had felt like a full-body straightjacket. That meant rational thought, smooth negotiation, and measured discussion—the training he'd received from his parents, the heads of the Tigony royal house. For years, he'd kept his powers close like a gambler holding a straight flush. The result of pairing anger and the true extent of his gift was destruction. Unchecked destruction.

The village of Bakkhos remained a scar in a distant Grecian valley. Because of him.

The Pet was too canny for Mal's peace of mind. He needed her back in the Tigony stronghold. And he needed her to start talking.

That meant finding her.

She'd dropped to the ground following the force of the blast. She'd disappeared behind the rugged half walls of the ruins. Why here? What scheme was she enacting? Something on behalf of the Asters?

That didn't ring right in his mind. Had she wanted

to remain with the insane doctor, she would've escaped with the man when Mal had helped liberate his niece from the Asters' laboratories in the Canadian tundra. Instead, the Pet had stayed behind. She'd surrendered to Mal without protest, which stood as the full extent of her cooperation. Every moment since had been a study in silence and frustration—silence from her and frustration strong enough eat away at Mal's patience.

He didn't have time to find her by navigating the labyrinth. After removing his suit coat, he wadded it into a ball. The expensive fabric served as protection as he climbed a jagged half wall. Navigating one at a time, he hoisted himself up using the coat as padding for his hands and knees. The ancient, crumbling rock was flaked and chipped like shale honed to razors.

He had just topped the last wall when a jerk behind his knees sent him sprawling onto the unforgiving ground. The Pet. She'd been pressed flat against the wall, waiting for him.

His head connected with a boulder the size of a large melon.

"*Bathatéi*," he shouted, using the worst curse in the shared language of the Dragon Kings.

The sun overhead stole his vision, which meant he jerked his head to the side by instinct alone. Metal scraped against rock and shot sparks against his cheek. Those sparks might not have been visible to the naked eye, but he reveled in their minute flashes of power.

Only, he didn't have time to collect his thoughts, his gift, and those tiny bursts of electrical ammunition. The Pet landed another blow in the form of brass knuckles against his breastbone. Thudding pain shot out from the center of his chest and infected the rest of his body with paralyzing quivers. She landed two more strikes, one against his temple and, as he rolled—again by instinct, away from his attacker—one to the base of his spine. He couldn't see, and he couldn't move.

She landed atop him, squatting. Her boots were heavy. They fortified her slight weight. Beneath his dress shirt, the skin of his back was stretched by the industrial treads of their soles.

The Pet grabbed a fistful of hair and yanked his head off the ground. "You're bleeding."

"That would be your fault."

"The rock's fault. I take credit for making you fall." She shoved his head back down, then smeared her palm across the back of his shirt. He caught the distinctly coppery smell of blood.

His blood.

Anger wasn't a strong enough word for the fire gathering in his hands. That's where his gift started, and where it found its full manifestation. His palms felt as if beetles and maggots wiggled across his skin. The only way to make that feeling go away was to let the electricity build and burn—then hurl it away.

He flipped over. She didn't lose her balance, but needed to jump away. She was agile, petite, and canny. The way she'd recovered from his initial blast was impressive. She stood in a loose fighting stance. Only, now she held a switchblade.

"You don't experience pain," he said, standing and squaring off against her.

"I experience pain. You'd rather think that I don't."

He called on deep muscle memory to fight her

hand to hand. Another concentrated, precise strike took time to build, but his power was already prepped and ready to burst. At that moment he could've blown up a mountain, but he didn't want to lobotomize her. Martial training was the only alternative.

He swept his leg to try to catch behind her calves, but she jumped straight up like a leaping frog—then landed with the ease of a cat. That cat attacked again, twirling to one side and stabbing him twice in the shoulder. Her control of the blade was faster than he would've thought possible, which meant she was a deadly combatant. Only after that thought registered did the sharp, burning spike of her assault make his nerves scream. He grunted.

Mal snatched out and caught her trailing wrist. He yanked her against his body, spun, and used that momentum to slam her against one of the half walls. She caught her balance with both hands gripping the razor-sharp shale. Her scream was as wild as it was anguished. She dropped the switchblade. Mal tried to pin her, but the attempt wasn't fast enough, wasn't sure enough. When was the last time he'd used his body to fight? His muscles were unfamiliar weapons, but they were weapons he relished rediscovering.

She twirled and launched off the wall, throwing that propelled power into a punch. Brass knuckles connected with his jaw.

He reeled. His lip was split.

They squared off again, circling each other like two starving wolves whose only option was cannibalism.

"I'm walking away now," she said simply.

"I can't let you do that."

"Then we keep fighting until one of us is a cripple. How long until you lose your temper and do too much damage?"

Mal breathed heavily through his nose. He would've rather been dangling over a volcano than have his options so limited. Let her walk away or risk debilitating her. She might as well have been carrying a bag of butterflies that would be crushed by too much force or would fly away forever if he let her escape.

"Why are you here?" he asked. "You didn't bother to cover your tracks. You could've bribed any bus driver or boat captain who helped you escape the mainland."

"I have nothing to use as a bribe."

"Women always do."

Her eyes became slits, her expression murderous. "I've had enough of that life."

Mal chose to put that eerie comment aside. "Why are you here?"

"I'm looking for something."

"For what?"

"I don't know."

"Don't play games with me," he said. "Nothing good will come from testing me. Because you're right. I might lose my temper. I might destroy the only link I have to the Aster cartel and the answer to Dragon King conception."

"A tempest in a suit. Does the Council know who sits at the head of their table?"

"Probably not." He stepped forward. "Do you think I need you in particular? You're convenient. You're valuable. Yet other Dragon Kings are connected with the cartels. I'll find them, one by one, just like I found you, until I get the answers our people need."

She tsked as if patronizing a child or a simpleton. "Altruism propels you, I'm sure."

"What do you mean?"

Standing at her full height for the first time, which wasn't very tall at all, she smirked. She packed so much disdain into the single lift of a midnight brow. "Our people? No. In your heart, Honorable Giva, you only want to win. At any price."

Love with BITE...
Bestselling Paranormal Romance from Pocket Books!

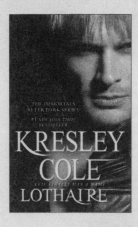

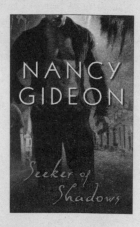